DIVISIBLE MAN™
THE THIRD LIE

by

Howard Seaborne

Copyright © 2018 by Howard Seaborne

DIVISIBLE MAN is a registered trademark of Trans World Data LLC

This is a work of fiction. Names, characters, places, and incidents are the product of the author's imagination or are used fictitiously, and any resemblance to actual persons, living or dead, businesses, companies, events, or locales is entirely coincidental.

ALSO BY HOWARD SEABORNE

DIVISIBLE MAN
A Novel – September 2017
DIVISIBLE MAN: THE SIXTH PAWN
A Novel – June 2018
DIVISIBLE MAN: THE SECOND GHOST
A Novel – September 2018
ANGEL FLIGHT
A Story – September 2018
DIVISIBLE MAN: THE SEVENTH STAR
A Novel – June 2019
ENGINE OUT
A Story – September 2019
WHEN IT MATTERS
A Story – October 2019
A SNOWBALL'S CHANCE
A Story – November 2019
DIVISIBLE MAN: TEN MAN CREW
A Novel – November 2019
DIVISIBLE MAN: THE THIRD LIE
A Novel – May 2020
DIVISIBLE MAN: THREE NINES FINE
A Novel – November 2020
DIVISIBLE MAN: EIGHT BALL
A Novel – September 2021
SHORT FLIGHTS
A Story Collection – Coming 2022
DIVISIBLE MAN: NINE LIVES LOST
A Novel – Coming 2022

PRAISE FOR HOWARD SEABORNE

"This book is a strong start to a series...Well-written and engaging, with memorable characters and an intriguing hero."
—*Kirkus Reviews*
DIVISIBLE MAN [DM1]

"Seaborne's crisp prose, playful dialogue, and mastery of technical details of flight distinguish the story...this is a striking and original start to a series, buoyed by fresh and vivid depictions of extra-human powers and a clutch of memorably drawn characters..."
—*BookLife*
DIVISIBLE MAN [DM1]

"Even more than flight, (Will's relationship with Andy)—and that crack prose—powers this thriller to a satisfying climax that sets up more to come."
—*BookLife*
DIVISIBLE MAN [DM1]

"Seaborne, a former flight instructor and charter pilot, once again gives readers a crisply written thriller. Self-powered flight is a potent fantasy, and Seaborne explores its joys and difficulties engagingly. Will's narrative voice is amusing, intelligent and humane; he draws readers in with his wit, appreciation for his wife, and his flight-drunk joy...Even more entertaining than its predecessor—a great read."
—*Kirkus Reviews*
DIVISIBLE MAN: THE SIXTH PAWN [DM2]

"Seaborne, a former flight instructor and pilot, delivers a solid, well-written tale that taps into the near-universal dream of personal flight. Will's narrative voice is engaging and crisp, clearly explaining technical matters while never losing sight of humane, emotional concerns. The environments he describes...feel absolutely real. Another intelligent and exciting superpowered thriller."
—*Kirkus Reviews*
DIVISIBLE MAN: THE SECOND GHOST [DM3]

"As in this series' three previous books, Seaborne...proves he's a natural born storyteller, serving up an exciting, well-written thriller. He makes even minor moments in the story memorable with his sharp, evocative prose... Will's smart, humane and humorous narrative voice is appealing, as is his sincere appreciation for Andy—not just for her considerable beauty, but also for her dedication and intelligence...Seaborne does a fine job making side characters and locales believable. It's deeply gratifying to see Will deliver righteous justice to some very bad people. An intensely satisfying thriller—another winner from Seaborne."
—*Kirkus Reviews*
DIVISIBLE MAN: THE SECOND GHOST [DM4]

"Seaborne...continues his winning streak in this series, offering another page-turner. By having Will's knowledge of and control over his powers continue to expand while the questions over how he should best deploy his abilities grow, Seaborne keeps the concept fresh and readers guessing... Will's enemies are becoming aware of him and perhaps developing techniques to detect him, which makes the question of how he can protect himself while doing the most good a thorny one. The conspiracy is highly dramatic yet not implausible given today's political events, and the action sequences are excitingly cinematic...Another compelling and hugely fun adventure that delivers a thrill ride."
—*Kirkus Reviews*
DIVISIBLE MAN: TEN MAN CREW [DM5]

"Seaborne shows himself to be a reliably splendid storyteller in this latest outing. The plot is intricate and could have been confusing in lesser hands, but the author manages it well, keeping readers oriented amid unexpected developments...His crisp writing about complex scenes and concepts is another strong suit...The fantasy of self-powered flight remains absolutely compelling...As a former charter pilot, Seaborne conveys Will's delight not only in 'the other thing,' but also in airplanes and the world of flight—an engaging subculture that he ably brings to life for the reader. Will is heroic and daring, as one would expect, but he's also funny, compassionate, and affectionate... A gripping, timely, and twisty thriller."
—*Kirkus Reviews*
DIVISIBLE MAN: THE THIRD LIE [DM6]

"Seaborne is never less than a spellbinding storyteller, keeping his complicated but clearly explicated plot moving smoothly from one nail-

biting scenario to another. As the tale goes along, seemingly disparate plot lines begin to satisfyingly connect in ways that will keep readers guessing until the explosive (in more ways than one) action-movie denouement. The author's grasp of global politics gives depth to the book's thriller elements, which are nicely balanced by thoughtful characterizations. Even minor characters come across in three dimensions, and Will himself is an endearing narrator. He's lovestruck by his gorgeous, intelligent, and strong-willed wife; has his heart and social conscience in the right place; and is boyishly thrilled by the other thing. A solid series entry that is, as usual, exciting, intricately plotted, and thoroughly entertaining."
—*Kirkus Reviews*
DIVISIBLE MAN: THREE NINES FINE [DM7]

Any reader of this series knows that they're in good hands with Seaborne, who's a natural storyteller. His descriptions and dialogue are crisp, and his characters deftly sketched...The book keeps readers tied into its complex and exciting thriller plot with lucid and graceful exposition, laying out clues with cleverness and subtlety...Also, although Will's abilities are powerful, they have reasonable limitations, and the protagonist is always a relatable character with plenty of humanity and humor...Another riveting, taut, and timely adventure with engaging characters and a great premise."
— *Kirkus Reviews*
DIVISIBLE MAN: EIGHT BALL [DM8]

THE SERIES

While each DIVISIBLE MAN ™ novel tells its own tale, many elements carry forward and the novels are best enjoyed in sequence. The short story "Angel Flight" is a bridge between the third and fourth novels and is included with the third novel, DIVISIBLE MAN - THE SECOND GHOST.

DIVISIBLE MAN ™ is available in print, digital and audio.

For a Cast of Characters, visit **HowardSeaborne.com**

For advance notice of new releases and exclusive material available only to Email Members, join the DIVISIBLE MAN ™ Email List at

HowardSeaborne.com.

Sign up today and get a FREE DOWNLOAD.

ACKNOWLEDGMENTS

This is the Divisible Man's sixth mission. The flight crew deserves a medal at this point. Stephen Parolini is always first up the boarding ladder and leads the mission with impeccable editing. Test pilot, Rich "Maddog" Sorensen logs the pre-mission test flight, bless him. The ground crew at Trans World Data—David, Carol, Claire, April and Rebecca—work miracles to keep the ship flying while the G-2 Section, Kristie and Steve, stare for hours at reconnaissance photos so I can concentrate on flying. No preflight inspection is complete without a great crew chief, Roberta "Eagle Eye" Schlei, whose amazing copyediting spots the gremlins lurking in every paragraph.

And thank you, Robin—call sign "Polly Pureheart"—for being the perfect copilot.

*For all who didn't make it.
And for those who tried to save them.*

"Lie to me once, you're on my shit list.
"Lie to me twice, we're done.
"Lie to me a third time, I'm coming for you."

—Earl Jackson

PART I

1

"Stop." My wife pressed her hand against my bare chest where a moment ago she had been idly tracing three capital letters with the tip of her index finger.

"What?"

"You can't start a story like that." She rolled to face me. "That's the original cliché."

"Whoa, whoa! You asked me how it went. I'm telling you how it went." I picked up her hand. "Go back to doing what you were doing."

"What…this?" She traced the three letters slowly, starting at my navel and ending just above my diaphragm.

"Yes," I said. "That. Now let me tell my story."

Gold-flecked green eyes warned me of undisclosed mischief. She dropped her cheek to my shoulder. Her hair spread on my skin and I drew in the intoxicating scent she uses to enslave me.

"Fine," she said. "You may begin again."

"Okay. It was a—" her hand slipped down to my ribs, then up into my armpit, where I am ridiculously ticklish "—about an hour and fifteen minutes after civil twilight and radar showed widespread convective activity across most of lower Michigan and Ohio. In other words… it was dark. It was stormy. It was night. I don't know how else to put it."

Her hand slid back to my chest. Reprieve.

2

I scanned the engine instruments. Oil pressure looked good, but the right engine oil temperature wiggled on the high side. I tabbed through several screens on the Insight engine monitor and stopped at the display for individual cylinder head temperatures.

Gotcha.

I checked our position on the moving map. Nine thousand-plus feet below, the northwest shoreline of Lake Erie slid behind me. I touched the audio panel to join my headset to the in-cabin intercom.

I glanced back.

Sandy Stone and Arun Dewar faced each other across a small foldout table. They traded Education Foundation papers back and forth under a cone of warm light from the cabin overhead. Sandy pushed aside a tired lock of blonde hair and glanced toward the cockpit. Catching her eye, I tapped my headset. She untangled hers from the seat's armrest and slipped it on. Arun followed suit.

I said, "We've got a problem."

Arun's dark eyes grew wide. "What kind of problem?"

His reaction tempted me to reply with *It looks like the right wing is loose* but it's bad form to screw with sensitive passengers.

"I've got a cylinder running hot." Arun opened his mouth to panic. Sandy raised a calming hand. "I'd like to land in Detroit and have it looked at."

"Will there be anyone to work on it at this hour?"

"No. I know a shop on the field at Willow Run that will give us priority in the morning. If it's minor, we could be on our way by noon. If not, Arun can get us a flight out of Detroit Metro. Either way, it's an overnight stop."

It had been a long day, our third on the road. The Pennsylvania trip followed closely on the heels of two trips last week and one the week before. With the start of the school year nearing, Sandy seemed determined to cram in as many Education Foundation trips as she could before returning to teaching kindergarten.

"Whatever you think is best, Will," Sandy said.

"Arun, do your logistics magic. I recall a nice Holiday Inn close to the Willow Run airport."

"On it." He reached for his phone.

I returned to the flight controls and flicked off the autopilot. My fingertip hovered over the push-to-talk switch on the control yoke, waiting for an opening on the busy ATC frequency. The sector controller had his hands full helping flights work their way around the weather. He wasn't going to appreciate my request.

THE CYLINDER HEAD in question suffered a sticky valve. A sharp Willow Run mechanic named Nolan knew it before he had the cowling off the next morning. He said he could take care of it but needed a few days. I called Doc, the resident Airframe & Powerplant mechanic at Essex County Air Service, for a second opinion. I hoped he would put together a parts-and-tools kit and get Earl Jackson, our boss, to run him across the big lake for a ramp repair. Instead, Doc asked to speak directly with Nolan. The two gearheads agreed that Nolan was better equipped for the job. I broke the news to Sandy. Arun pulled out his phone and booked three seats on an 8:20 p.m. Delta flight that had us arriving in Milwaukee at 8:27, accounting for the time change.

I don't like flying commercial. Flying a Piper Navajo cabin-class twin for Sandy Stone's Education Foundation means I can deliver Sandy from the stairs of the airplane to the door of a waiting car at any of ten thousand general aviation airports. Commercial flying, laden with the cattle-drive process of check-in, security and reporting to the gate for boarding, takes far longer. In the hours required to make a commercial flight from Detroit to Milwaukee (only forty minutes of which consist of actual flying) I could have flown us over and back again and still met Andy for dinner.

After threading our way through the eye of the TSA needle at Detroit's Wayne County Airport, the airport tram and people-mover combination carried us to our gate with relative efficiency. I began to think the process wouldn't be as painful as I anticipated.

I was wrong.

"Is that...?" Arun pointed at the wall of windows near the gate.

"Some serious weather," I finished his thought.

Bruised and boiling clouds loomed in the western sky. Lightning crawled between giant cumulus buildups and stabbed the earth. An angry line of aerial violence blotted out the setting sun.

We found seats in the waiting area. The terminal grew darker. Anxious passengers swiped device screens. Arun pulled out his iPad and studied ugly blotches of radar imaging.

"There's a tornado watch in effect," he reported, his voice high and tight. Born and raised in Britain, Arun didn't have much experience with Midwestern tornados. I was less concerned with a twister than the fact that the jetway for our gate had no airplane attached.

"*Watch*," I said, "means conditions *might* produce a funnel cloud, but it does not mean an actual tornado has been spotted."

Arun buried his nose in his screen, looking for better news.

The gate agent picked up her microphone.

"Ladies and gentlemen as you can see, we have a bit of weather approaching. We've just been informed that air traffic control is holding arrivals until these conditions pass. It means that the aircraft taking Flight 1931 to Milwaukee has not landed yet and will be late reaching our gate. When it arrives, we will unload and service the aircraft quickly and try to get you on your way. We appreciate your patience."

"Aw, fuck that shit!" A loud voice behind me turned heads. "*What the fuck!* Let's get this show on the road!"

Someone laughed. The loudmouth had an audience.

I twisted in my seat.

They were a party of three. Two men and a woman. Loudmouth stood at the center of their small cluster. I guessed his age to be in the mid- to late-twenties. He easily topped six-feet-six and showed off a heavily muscled physique with a tight silver t-shirt that advertised a fitness club. He wore crewcut hair bleached bright white with three horizontal black stripes on each temple. Thick gold chains hung around his neck. Gold bands adorned one wrist and a heavy, multi-dialed watch —the kind of watch people think pilots use, which we don't—weighed down the other.

The young woman on his arm wore bright pink tights that left nothing anatomical to the imagination. On top, she bundled a pair of abundant breasts into what looked like a yellow elastic bandage. She covered a minimum of it with a tiny leather jacket decorated with dozens of silver studs. Her scarlet hair and heavy makeup spoke as loudly as her boyfriend.

The third star in this constellation wore long hair in a man bun and squeezed himself into a "tiny suit"—a jacket three sizes too small over trousers tapered to a snug fit at the calf. Under the glossy suit jacket he wore a black t-shirt weighed down by gold chains, although not quite the mining haul the trio leader draped across his chest.

Loudmouth carried on.

"C'mon! Get us some pilots with balls and let's bounce! I'll fly the motherfucker!" The girl tugged on his bulging arm.

"Derek, buy me another drink!"

Derek gave it a beat. Then he turned to a heavyset man who had been trying hard not to pay attention from a nearby seat.

"Dude watch my stuff," Derek commanded. He pointed at the man and then at three bags laying in the aisle. "I'm holding you responsible! Anybody fucks with my stuff it's on you."

The hapless man stared at Derek's thigh-sized arms.

Derek and his troop set off for the bar on the other side of the next gate.

I thought about reporting the unattended bags. Airport police destroy first and ask questions second. The policy struck me as perfect justice for an ass of this magnitude. I decided instead to watch the other storm—the one dumping sheets of rain on the runways. Lightning speared the earth while thunder cracked. The absence of delay between flash and boom betrayed the proximity of the strike.

I checked on Arun. He was staring at the trio strutting toward the bar. He wore an alert expression, the sort one might adopt when encountering a snake. Arun is a small, bookish young man. I wondered if hard experience had outfitted him with a visceral wariness of bullies.

It took another two hours for the weather to clear, for our plane to reach the gate, and for the aircraft to be unloaded, serviced and made ready for boarding. No imagination was required to see that most, if not all, of the Milwaukee-bound passengers were on the last leg of a long day of travel. Listlessness and too much carry-on luggage weighed people down. Only a few passengers, universally under the age of six, exhibited anything resembling energy by the time we lined up to board.

Before stepping into the jetway, I glanced back at the cluster of carry-on bags orphaned between two now-empty rows of gate seats. I crossed my fingers that Derek and his pals were too busy chumming with Jack Daniels to notice that the flight had been called.

Thanks to last-minute booking, our boarding passes took us to uncomfortable seats in the rear of the plane. Arun and Sandy squeezed into the window and middle seats on the right side of the aisle. I slid into a left-side aisle seat one row back. A woman in her sixties or seventies nestled politely beside Sandy, who tossed me a relieved glance.

Sandy Stone is a remarkably attractive young woman who has confided in me that her greatest fear when flying is sitting beside a man attempting to generate enough conversation to justify a marriage proposal by the end of the flight. She, like everyone else on this flight, simply wanted to go home.

My watch said we would land in Milwaukee after eleven. It would take several hours after that to reach Essex.

A loud voice erupted from the forward section of the plane.

"Move it or lose it!"

I looked up. Derek and his dominoes lined up in the aisle. Derek towered over everybody. He bobbed and danced impatiently to a beat in his own head. A family ahead of him hurried to settle themselves. His shuffling steps were unsteady. His eyes, bleary.

"Let's go people," he said. "Let's light the fuse on this rocket!"

His girlfriend giggled and jiggled. Her heavily lidded eyes scanned the men she passed, daring them to gaze at her chest. The third wheel in the group shuffled along wearing mirrored sunglasses and a stone face, wobbling slightly, as if the still earthbound plane navigated light turbulence.

Derek compared his boarding pass to the seat numbers. "Ariel, baby, *what did you do?* You got us sitting in fucking Siberia!"

"It was all they had, honey!"

The trio worked their way past me trailing a cloud of cologne and whiskey. They found their assigned seats two rows aft of mine. The new issue became the packed overhead bin.

"What is all this shit!" Derek jerked open one plastic door after another. He tried shoving bags sideways to make room. "Fuck!"

"Sir, your bag will fit under the seat." A flight attendant ventured into the fray. "If you would please take your seats now."

"*If you would please take your seats now,*" Derek mimicked. "Bitch, where'm I gonna put my feet?"

The flight attendant, whose day had probably started four cities ago, chose not to engage.

After aggressive jostling and maneuvering, the carry-on bags were stowed under the seats. Third Wheel took the window. Ariel took the center seat and immediately flipped the armrest up to snuggle against her man. Derek dropped in the aisle seat with one leg in the aisle.

The show might have been over if we had pushed back from the gate.

Instead a voice from the flight deck told us that although the heavy weather had passed, ground control remained backed up.

"Folks," the captain said with a marked lack of enthusiasm, "we are now holding for clearance to push back."

The storm may have moved on, but the effects of diverted and delayed traffic, compounded by the late hour, stacked up against us.

We waited.

"Fucking plane is overloaded," Derek announced. Someone shushed him. It might have been Ariel. He paid no attention. "I saw this shit online. They overload the plane and it messes up the gravity. Puts all the controls out of balance."

Idiot, I thought.

"This one plane, they put too much baggage in the back. It took off and the front end went up and then it did a big old nosedive right into the runway. Splat!" Heads turned to issue reproachful looks. I gave the effort small odds. Subtlety is lost on those who wear loafers without socks. "Every freakin' person on board died," Derek continued. "They couldn't tell which body parts belonged to which passenger. Fucking goo."

"Sir," a woman said quietly, "please. There are children here."

"That's what happens, lady. They overload these planes and they just fall outta the sky!" Inexplicably, Ariel giggled, which made Derek laugh.

"Hey!" A man's voice this time. "Can you keep it down, pal?"

"Pal? Are we pals? Cuz' I don't remember having any pals with such an ugly-ass face."

"Just keep it down."

"Or what?"

The man did not reply.

"Fucking pilots don't know shit and that's why people get turned to jelly in these things, *pal.*"

I unsnapped my seatbelt. Sandy shot me a warning glance, but it was too late. I took to my feet and stepped into the aisle. At the back of the plane, a flight attendant caught sight of my move and started forward. I didn't wait for her. I turned and hurried up the aisle to the forward cabin. The lead flight attendant, preparing for the safety briefing, saw me coming.

"Sir, you need to—"

I pulled my wallet from my jeans pocket and flipped it open. I held it up and gestured for the woman to step up into the space behind the cockpit door, which had already been closed. The wallet move—hinting at law enforcement—threw her. She stepped back.

"I'm a pilot." I held up the plastic flap that showed my FAA license.

It wasn't what she expected. She rebounded quickly. "Sir, you really—"

"Listen," I said softly. "You've got a problem passenger in row forty-three. He's drunk and he's running his mouth and frankly, he's upsetting the other passengers. He's also looking for a fight."

Her gaze shot to the back of the plane and landed on Derek. I hadn't told her anything she didn't already know.

"Here's the thing," I said. "Federal Aviation Regulation ninety-one point seventeen states that 'Except in an emergency, no pilot of a civil aircraft may allow a person who appears to be intoxicated to be carried on that aircraft.' Now, I don't want to cause you trouble, but it's going to get ugly back there. I for one don't want to be cooped up in this pressurized tube with him when it does. That man and his companions are clearly drunk. He is menacing and scaring the passengers around him."

She sent a resigned look in Derek's direction.

"Listen, I don't want to be an ass about it. But you've now been made aware. If things go bad—and I sincerely believe they will—this crew will be operating in violation of FAR ninety-one seventeen."

She looked at me like I was the bigger asshole. I didn't blame her.

"No one wants that. May I make a suggestion?"

THE FLIGHT ATTENDANT handled it beautifully. A few moments after I returned to my seat, she strolled back, leaned down, and spoke softly into Derek's ear.

"Yeah, baby! That's what I'm talking about! Grab your shit, sweetcakes. We're movin' on up!"

The flight attendant backed away. Derek stood up a little too quickly and lost his equilibrium. He leaned into the row across the aisle. His hand went wandering. A woman shrieked. "Whoa, lady!" he muttered. "Don't get your panties wet. You ain't got anything special up there anyway."

Ariel threw the woman a superior look and pushed her boyfriend forward. The forward attendant met them in the aisle. "We just need a few minutes to clear the seats and restock with fresh pillows and blankets. Please follow me." She dished out a big smile. "Can I offer you a complimentary beverage?"

Derek ordered a whiskey sour and weaved his way forward, pinballing off the seatbacks as he went. At the front of the plane, the smiling lead flight attendant said, "We'll just have you wait on the jetway while we prepare your seats in First Class." She ushered all three through the still-open door onto the jetway.

I leaned over and tried to see out the nearest side window. The view wasn't great, but through slit windows on the jetway I caught sight of law enforcement uniforms. Almost immediately, the attendants closed the forward door, a chime sounded, and a tired-sounding voice welcomed us aboard for what the crew hoped would be a short, smooth flight to Milwaukee.

A cheer rippled through the cabin.

"What did you tell them?" Arun asked.

He hurried to keep pace beside me, anxious to learn a new secret. Except for the stream of passengers exiting our flight, the Milwaukee terminal lay empty. The shops wore metal grates for the night. A maintenance worker pushed a vacuum across a sea of carpet.

"I told them to offer the asshole a first-class accommodation. They did. First Class courtesy of the Wayne County Sheriff."

We followed the subdued flow of passengers to the escalator that descended to the baggage claim. Arun grinned.

"I've never seen that before! Brilliant!" Something about the episode charmed him.

"It's against federal law for a pilot to operate an aircraft carrying someone who appears to be intoxicated."

Sandy laughed. "That's got to be one of the least enforced laws on the books!"

I hopped the escalator and shrugged. "Maybe. Flight crews don't like confrontation. They *really* don't like to remove a passenger. It's bad for business, especially with everyone carrying video cameras. Most often, if they can just get a plane in the air, it quiets people down. That guy was not going to settle down. The crew got lucky, getting him off the plane."

Approaching the bottom of the escalator I spotted a familiar face.

"Hey, Lyle! What are you doing here?"

Lyle Traegar works with my wife as a part-time patrol officer on the City of Essex Police Department. He served under her supervision when she still wore sergeant's stripes. I hadn't seen much of him since she moved up to detective, although I remembered him in uniform at Mike Mackiejewski's funeral.

Lyle stood with his overweight frame stuffed in a black suit, white shirt and black tie. The neatly printed sign in his meaty hands told me that if he was still working for the Essex PD it remained part-time.

"Hi, Will!" he grinned. "My other job." He wiggled the sign.

"You're a driver? Chauffeur, I should say."

"'Til I can get Chief Ceeves to hire me full time. Tell your wife to put in a word for me. How 'bout her making detective! That's something!"

"She never ceases to amaze me." I sidestepped his request that I nudge my wife on his behalf.

Arun tapped me on the shoulder. "I'll get a car." He bounded off toward a row of rental car desks with more energy than seemed possible at this late hour. I didn't like his odds. The desks looked deserted.

"You just come in from Detroit?" Lyle asked. "Flight 1931?"

"Yeah."

"That's the flight I'm waiting for. Jesus, you're like three hours late. I've been cooling my heels here forever. What happened?"

"Weather." I read the sign in his hands. "D. Santi? That wouldn't be a Derek Santi, would it?"

Lyle looked at me like I'd just done a magic trick. For a big man, he had a boyish veneer—the perpetual look of someone who didn't quite get the grown-up joke. I wondered if that might be the reason Chief Ceeves hadn't offered him a full-time position with the department. "You know him?"

"Nope. Wild guess. I'm afraid you may have a really long wait." I explained what happened. Lyle dropped the sign to his side and shook his head.

"Yeah, that sounds like the guy. He was an entitled ass on the phone. Demanded top shelf liquor in the car." Lyle cast a glance up the stairs. The last of the passengers from our flight had already descended and milled around the baggage carousel. "Crap. Yours is the last flight from Detroit tonight."

"Oh, he won't be flying tonight. Not commercial, at least."

"I guess I'm dead-heading back up to Essex."

"Want company?"

"Sure!"

I waved at Sandy. "We have a ride! In style, I might add. I'll go fetch Arun."

Three hours later, in bed, I finished explaining to my wife why a stretched limousine dropped me at our back door. She said nothing. Her hand lay motionless on my chest. Her breath came and went in a slow, steady cadence. I estimated she had fallen asleep around the time I got to the part about the cylinder head temperature.

3

The war council gathered around my counter-height kitchen table. A light evening breeze whispered through the open kitchen windows. Andy sat to my right. A slim blonde woman with a low tolerance for fools took the seat opposite Andy, which represented more than just a seating arrangement. Most of what Lillian—whose last name she refused to divulge—had to say landed in direct opposition to my wife. Lillian may have been a rocket scientist and mathematician with multiple doctorates, but Andy continued to refer to her as "The UFO Nut."

The fourth member of the council floated on Andy's laptop screen. Dr. Doug Stephenson joined us from his home office via Facetime. Andy propped the laptop on an empty Evermore shipping box.

Stephenson inadvertently introduced Lillian to our lives and my secret after she got wind of someone who had tripped over a piece of debris from my accident. The debris shared the characteristics of *the other thing*—a mystery unresolved.

Lillian, in what had become a pattern, dominated the floor.

"Evermore, North Carolina. Lewko built the town from scratch and named it after his company. Christ, I think he'll name his firstborn after the company. The state had a collective orgasm when the press reported the location as the new site for Evermore's corporate headquarters. Imagine their surprise when Lewko announced it was only a research facility and shipping hub. Things got testy between the bureaucrats and the billionaire because the state gave him a huge package of tax incentives. When the legislators suggested rolling back the tax package, Lewko threatened to drop the whole thing and the state caved. The corporate welfare check came to well over a billion. The state picked up the tab for the infrastructure while Lewko retained the deed to all the land. It's the same playbook Foxconn used here in Wisconsin. And may I say, you guys really got hosed on that one."

Andy ignored Lillian's political leaning. "How sure are you that he took the *thing* to North Carolina?"

"It's there."

"A little proof would be nice."

Lillian huffed. "Lewko dropped out of sight. Going to that kind of trouble means he's doing something important. Nothing, believe me, is more important to him than the piece of debris from Will's crash. I've got sources that put him in Evermore, so that's where the artifact is."

"What sources?" Andy demanded.

"Dark web sources."

"That doesn't prove anything."

"Dark web?" I asked. It always sounds like something from a comic book to my ear. "What? Do they follow the guy?"

Lillian looked at me like I was stupid. "They follow all those guys. Bezos. Zuckerberg. Brin and Page. Gates. Jobs, back in the day. They'd get stool samples if they could. It's all about trend, and no piece of intelligence is insignificant. Knowing where the major players nibble their *foie gras* is golden. It gets checked against other players—financiers, bankers, Senate committee chairmen. It signals conversations, coalitions, chemistry. Every discarded Dixie cup is a clue. Can you imagine the stock run if you had intel that Larry Ellison booked the same B&B as the CEO of Southern California Electric?"

Lillian says everything like she thinks you should know what it means. After tolerating a moment of blank stares, she blurted out, "Nuclear power! Oracle in bed with nuclear power!"

Stephenson patiently reeled her in. "Is there any intel on his team?"

Lillian shook her head, but she eyed the screen suspiciously. "Spill it Big Bear. What are you groping for?"

"Big Bear?" I looked at Stephenson. The neurologist may be in his seventies, but the man looks twenty years younger. Andy and I knew he and Lillian were casual sexual partners.

Stephenson hesitated. The video connection made it hard to tell who he was looking at. "Do we tell her, Will?"

I guessed it was me.

"Tell me what?" Lillian stiffened. She shot glances between Stephenson and me. "What?! Are you two holding out on me? That's not our deal!"

I wasn't aware we had a *deal*. Stephenson raised a hand to calm her.

Andy shifted uncomfortably on her chair. This was touchy for her. It had not gone over well when I confessed to her that Stephenson and I were testing one of the unexpected characteristics of *the other thing*. Andy wasn't against it. She also wasn't for it.

"Either we're all in or I'm out!" Lillian declared.

"Relax, Honeybee," Stephenson said.

I clamped my jaw against a grin.

"Will?" Stephenson asked.

Lillian fixed her laser-focused glare on me.

"Okay," I said slowly. "You know about the disappearing act. You know that when I vanish, gravity lets go, which is good and bad. You know that I lose my mass—"

"Inertia. That's different," Lillian corrected me.

"Inertia. Fine. I'm not subject to the laws of inertia and mass and gravity."

"We went over all this, Will. What are you holding out on me?"

"He wasn't holding out on you," Andy said tersely. "We've just been cautious about revealing too much. I'm sure you can appreciate that."

Lillian gave no sign of reading Andy's tone. "I don't solve equations in the dark. What haven't you told me?"

I swallowed. "It turns out I can take people along for the ride."

"Like the little girl in the fire. What's-her-name."

"Lane," Andy said sharply.

"At first, I thought I had to wrap them up. You know, like wrap my arms around them. But it seems like all I need is a good grip on someone. If I push hard—in my head—they vanish with me."

"And?"

"And…it has a side effect," I added. "Last Christmas, well it's kind of a long story, but I had an Angel Flight—a charity flight where we take—"

"I know what Angel Flight is, Will."

"Right. So, we had this little girl with leukemia, and we were trying to get her into Marshfield for treatment, and the weather was shit, and we couldn't make the landing. She was going downhill, so I did my thing—and I bailed out of the plane with her and dropped her off at the hospital."

"You bailed out?"

"No, not like that. I didn't abandon the airplane. Jesus! Pidge was flying the plane."

"Pidge. Who the hell is Pidge?"

I explained. Then added, "Pidge and the flight nurse stayed in the plane."

"Christ!" Lillian slapped her hand on the table. "Two people saw you?! Why don't you just take out an ad in the *New York Times*? What about Greg LeMore? Does he know? Because you told me not to tell him why we were looking for Lewko! He's going to think I'm a bumbling—"

"No. Greg doesn't know."

Lillian rolled her eyes.

"That's not the point here, Lillian," Andy said.

"No," I jumped in before something caught fire. "It's not. The point of this story is what came after. That kid, that little girl—"

"What about her?"

I shrugged. I didn't know how to put it.

"Lillian," Stephenson came to my rescue, "the child emerged from the effect in remission."

Three of us gave Lillian a moment to calculate. She turned to Stephenson.

"Partial?"

"Full."

"N.E.D.?"

"Appears to be."

"Cellular regeneration?"

"Regeneration. Cleansing. I don't know. I wasn't privy. She exhibited Polycythemia Vera, which metastasized into Leukemia, which—simply went away. Will climbed out of the aircraft with a dying child in his arms. He handed a child in full remission over to the staff at the hospital."

Lillian stared at the screen. I knew better than to think of her as speechless.

"I've done what I could to follow up," Stephenson continued. "I know her primary. He can't stop talking about her. It's been over six months. The child is healthy. Better than healthy."

Her gaze slowly shifted between me and Stephenson.

"Subsequent testing?"

He nodded.

"Blind?"

"Ish."

"Quantifiable results?"

"We don't have access. We think eighty-eight percent."

"How many subjects?"

"To date…twenty-nine."

I thought about a girl named Anastasia, who drew pictures of her own death. I thought about a little boy named Benny, who giggled when I took him flying. I thought about others I'd held in my arms in the dead of night. Frail. Light. Pale skin that seemed to glow in near darkness. I didn't think of them as *subjects*.

Numbers crunched behind Lillian's eyes.

"This is bad," she said slowly. "This is very bad. I need some air."

Lillian slid off her chair and stepped out of our kitchen without another word. We heard the screen door slam. Andy and I traded glances.

"Give her time," Stephenson suggested. "Call me later."

The screen winked out.

4

Andy pulled a pair of cold Coronas from the refrigerator and suggested we move to the front porch to catch the last of the evening light. I steeled myself for a serious and one-sided discussion about Lillian. There hadn't been an opportunity for conversation since the woman rolled her Prius into our yard unannounced that afternoon.

Two weeks had passed since Lillian sent me a text message claiming she and Greg LeMore knew where Spiro Lewko had taken the only known piece of debris from my midair collision. In that time, she made contact only twice. Both times, she offered no elaboration on her first message. Instead, she breathlessly asked if we were being watched, then abruptly ended the calls.

Andy led me to our front porch. The yard surrounding our rented farmhouse isn't large, but Lillian had disappeared—probably by taking a stroll down the old cow lane behind the barn. The lane leads to a woods and former pasture on the other side of the corn fields behind our house. Ample expanse for meditation.

I settled on my ratty old lounge chair. Andy slid onto the cushion facing me, nestling a knee against my thigh. She held up her cold beer.

"Us," I said, clinking mine against hers.

"Us." She sipped and I mirrored her move. She turned and studied the evening sky. "I called the rehab hospital in Omaha."

This was about Lee Donaldson, the injured FBI agent who had pulled Andy into his off-book investigation of the internet conspiracy theorist and all-around jackass Josiah James. Donaldson had sustained a bad head injury thanks to another jackass wielding a baseball bat.

I felt mild relief that we weren't going to argue over Lillian.

"Anything new?"

"No. Nothing since his last surgery." Agent Donaldson's head injury put him in a coma. Serious swelling prompted several surgeries.

"I'm sorry, kiddo," I said, taking her hand. She nodded and her eyes acquired a light glitter.

I never trusted Donaldson. But the blow he took had been meant for my wife. Things like that elevate a man.

"The FBI won't talk to me," Andy said. "I don't dare call his boss. That was made clear."

"But that's because—"

"Oh, I know what you're going to say. I made a deal."

"I wasn't—"

"And I get it. Rayburn is doing me a favor. He's keeping me out of it."

Special Agent in Charge Rayburn's investigation into a Russian oligarch's funding of an internet conspiracy theorist's media empire ignited a national firestorm. I shared the FBI agent's desire to keep my wife out of it.

"I get that," Andy said. "But he's putting a wall up around Lee, too."

"He's also putting Lee up as the agent who broke the story. He doesn't want you muddying that."

"That's crap. Rayburn is protecting Rayburn's claim to fame."

"Dee, the FBI—and law enforcement in general—has taken a lot of shit from the administration about Russia. Yes, Rayburn is an opportunist, but his ambition aligns with setting the record straight. I'm okay if it also protects you."

"Rayburn is making sure Rayburn gets the credit," she muttered.

"Doesn't matter. Lee's in good hands."

She looked out through the screen at a pastel blue sky. Dreamy pink cumulus slowly fragmented as the sun headed for the horizon, taking its atmospheric energy with it.

"I want to see him," she said distantly. She turned quickly back to me and took my hand. "You know what I mean. Visit him."

"I know." Jealousy triggers easily with me, but I also know when it's unfounded and irritating to Andy. "Tom read you the riot act about taking any more time away from Essex." The chief of police had been pleased to see his protégé drawn into an FBI case—and in equal measure annoyed that once again the trail she followed took her away from her job.

"Tell me about it. I won't be asking for any vacation time for a while."

"On the other hand, I just happen to know a pilot who might be willing to make a quick run to Omaha."

Andy's face brightened. Something told me this was her plan all along. "Are you sure? What about Sandy?"

"Oh my God, Dee! That woman is constantly pushing me to take you someplace—preferably with palm trees. Why not Omaha?"

"Are you *really* sure?"

"Affirmative! It's only a couple hours. We'll do an overnight next time you have two days off."

She hesitated. "What about this thing with—you know. You can guess what *she* wants. She wants you to retrieve that thing."

"Maybe."

"What do you mean, 'maybe?' She's in an absolute panic that it's in Lewko's hands. It's one of the few things she and I agree on."

I wasn't sure I felt the same but didn't want to argue the point. Not yet.

"Doesn't mean we can't bop out to Omaha. When are you off again?"

"I'm on for the next eight straight. This weekend I'm covering for Jeff." She broke out a smile. "Your wife is lead detective."

I clinked my beer against hers. We drank a silent toast to her success. In mid-gulp I leaned sideways and squinted into the western sunset at a figure on our quiet country road. At first, I thought Lillian had found her way around the cornfield. Then I saw that the person approached on a bicycle.

5

Lane Franklin pumped the pedals. She swerved off the narrow blacktop, dove through the ditch, popped across our driveway and rolled wildly up to our porch. She dismounted the rolling bike on the run. It might have been mistaken for urgency, but it was just Lane being Lane. Her bright eyes competed with a brilliant smile. Her long black hair flew wildly in her wake.

"Hi, Mister Stewart! Hi Andy!" She hopped the porch steps and threw a hug around Andy.

Lane, the fifteen-year-old daughter of Essex County Air Service's real boss, Rosemary II, often strikes me as an optical illusion. She is her mother's daughter, a beauty in the making, capable at times of looking like a woman well beyond her adolescent years. Then in a flash, the awkward knees and elbows of a growing girl emerge. The two images conflict, jumping back and forth like the start and end of time lapse photography.

"Hey, Lane," I greeted her as she doled out a hug for me, though I did not rise. "Who are you going to fly for?"

"Anybody I want, given the pilot shortage. When do we start?"

She meant flying lessons. A delicate subject. I had every confidence Lane would begin soon. The trick would be convincing her mother. That was a bridge under construction and had been for most of the past year—one that was not ready for traffic. Her single-parent mother harbored fears of aviation diverting an academically exceptional girl from more serious studies. Rosemary II also worried about the looming cost of college and more than once had labeled flying lessons a frivolous financial drain. Andy and I still had not settled on a means of telling Rosemary II that her daughter's education, at college and in the air, had a leg up on funding, thanks to a sack of cash I'd stolen over a year ago from a drug dealer.

"Patience, young pilot. What brings you to Casa Stewart today?"

"Oh, just out and about. Thought I'd swing by to say Hi. I didn't know you had company." She glanced at the Prius in the yard. "I should go."

"No," Andy said. "Our guest is wandering the fields. Meditating. Or contacting the mothership. You're not interrupting anything."

I caught a glint of relief in Lane's eyes, and with it a nervous glance at Andy. "Well...um..."

Andy picked up the hint.

"Some girl talk?" She took Lane by the arm. Lane nodded. Andy turned to me. "Don't you have little propeller thingies to play with in the garage?"

I grabbed my Corona and stood. "I do. By the way, Lane, check it out. Basic Linear Aerial System for Transport, Electric Rechargeable."

"BLASTER! That's awesome!" Lane bounced on the balls of her feet.

"Do not encourage him." Andy kissed me on the cheek. "You. Scoot!"

Lane smiled, proud of Andy's big-sister attention. The growing girl image flashed.

"It *is* awesome," I muttered on my way off the porch.

I STOPPED in the mud room at the rear of the house and snagged two BLASTER units from the cabinet, feeling renewed admiration for their new name. I stuffed a propeller and one power unit—roughly the size and shape of a compact flashlight—in my back pocket. I snapped a prop onto the second power unit. A flick of the slide control produced a strong spin of the prop.

At the top of the back steps, I stopped. The sun touched the horizon and the perfect evening air held its breath. Every leaf in the yard hung motionless. The string of thunderstorms that interrupted the Pennsylvania return trip had been generous. Fresh-washed air shimmered with a crystalline quality. Lush leaves competed to show off supernatural hues of green.

Perfect flying conditions.

I filled my lungs with the rich, clear air and took a two-step leap off the top of the back stoop.

Fwooomp!

I vanished. A cool sensation enveloped my skin. Gravity relinquished its grip and the leap sent me gliding across the backyard grass toward our small free-standing garage. Had I launched with a purpose in mind, I would have aimed the power unit—which vanished with me—up and over the black asphalt shingles. Instead, I pulsed the BLASTER briefly. The spinning prop pulled me left. I aimed for the tractor path that began where the driveway ended. The path curved around the old red barn.

I know without testing the theory that air resistance will eventually bring me to a stop. But it takes a while. I let myself glide in silence about ten feet above the tractor lane. The barn flowed past. Cornfields spread out before me as I inched higher.

Flight! The sensation flooded my senses like a drug, fed by the magical shift of perspective as I rose.

I hit the power unit again and adjusted my path over the old cow lane that goes straight north from the back of the barn. The lane bisects the cornfields but is too narrow for the industrial-strength harvesters our landlord uses. He doesn't care what happens to it. I keep it mowed. Some evenings Andy and I walk the lane to the woods and a small creek on the far side of the cornfields, usually before the mosquitos claim the night for their bloodlust.

I cruised twenty feet up, imagining the lazy twice-daily march of the milk cows that were once raised on this farm. Perhaps the owner strolled behind them, nudging the herd to the barn. Perhaps he dispatched his children who would have prodded slow movers with sticks—when they weren't slapping the cow pies with the same sticks.

I cruised to the end of the lane, which opened into a wooded area that once doubled as a pasture. Pastoral woods are only that because livestock munches away the undergrowth. With the cows long gone, the land beneath this stand of old hardwood trees had gone wild, choked with buckthorn.

I zigzagged between tree trunks, loosely following the main path toward a small creek that snaked through the property.

Lillian sat on a fat log—all that remained of a tree that had gone over ages before I rented the property, taking its fan of roots with it to create a vaguely oriental sculpture. She faced the creek. Water moved beneath her feet with more haste than usual, thanks to the recent rains.

I wasn't sure whether to reappear and stroll up, giving her fair warning—or sneak up and startle her. I compromised.

"This is a nice spot," I said.

"Except for the mosquitos." She slapped her arm.

She turned around to say something more, then stopped when she failed to see me. The gimmick didn't throw her for more than a second.

"Cute."

"I figured you should see how it works." I moved the slide on the power unit and swung off the path above the tall grass. I performed a circle maneuver with Lillian as the apex. Her hearing didn't fail her. She turned her head and followed the low hum.

"Is that your propulsion system?"

"I call it a BLASTER."

"Good God, Stewart, are you twelve?"

"Pretty much."

I completed the circuit. She stopped following me and went back to watching the water burble past her feet. I maneuvered toward her, lifted my feet over the log and aimed for a position beside her. I meant to drop onto the log when I reappeared, but it took some adjusting and maneuvering and the trick was spoiled. When I finally reappeared—

Fwooomp!

—I dropped a little farther than I expected and almost bounced off the log. Lillian threw out a hand and grabbed my arm to steady me.

"Yeah, it's not as easy as it seems," I admitted.

She laughed. I hadn't seen that before. She nurtures the image of a serious, often paranoid woman with an intellectual chip on her shoulder.

Lillian's mirth faded quickly.

"I was wrong. In Florida. I was wrong to tell you to run. You were right to go after those morons in Wichita. If you had been a day earlier, you would have been in time."

"…could'a…would'a…should'a.."

"Will, you have to get that thing away from Spiro Lewko. And this time it will be nothing like breaking in on some pizza-eating, beer-guzzling gamers. This time there will be serious risk."

"Oh, I think I'm pretty hard to catch." I plucked a strip of loose bark from the log and tossed it in the creek. It sailed downstream.

"That attitude will get you killed," she snapped. "Tell me something."

"Sure."

"Bashar al-Assad."

"Syrian dictator."

"The man is a mass murderer and a tyrant. Do you agree?"

"It's well documented."

"Then, why don't you fly into his palace and assassinate him? You might save the next village he plans to gas."

I've had this discussion with Pidge.

"Aside from certain moral issues, there are practical problems. I don't speak Syrian. Arabic? I don't even know what language is spoken in Damascus."

"What difference does that make?"

"Really? What building is he in? What room is he in? What's his schedule? What did one guard just say to the other guard? How do I unlock the door to his chambers? How do I even get in the country?" I held up the power unit. "This thing is nice for hopping around Essex County, but it's only got about half an hour's power and it makes noise."

She listened somberly. I waited for her to score my response.

"That's good. You see the minutia. The logic. The limits. That's something in your favor. People who make plans like low-budget movie plots are idiots."

"Not to mention that what you're proposing is murder. My wife has issues with that."

"No doubt. What about you?"

I sidestepped. "What does this have to do with Lewko?"

"Evermore. Lewko's home-built town. His research facilities are more private than The Pentagon and he deploys better security. Full techie overkill. Getting within fifty miles of the place without having your picture taken and fed into his servers is almost impossible. Except maybe for you. But that means you won't be able to take anyone with you—not anyone normal. And you're going to need help. Unlike said movie plot, we have no real idea what he uses to lock the doors. Or which door has the artifact behind it."

I tossed another slice of bark into the water.

"What?" she asked.

"It's just…okay, I'm—"

"If you say 'thinking outside the box' I will slap you. I fucking hate that expression."

"Fair enough. But who says we have to go *get* this thing?" Storm clouds formed across her brow. "No, hear me out. It's a piece of something that knocked me and my airplane out of the sky. It can't be seen, and it isn't affected by gravity. Your guess is probably the same as mine. What happened to me *came* from that thing, or whatever it was connected to, because I think we're both pretty sure this chunk broke off of something bigger. Good so far?"

"Your point?"

"What if we don't go get it? You said it yourself, Lewko has a cutting-edge research facility. He's working on next-generation phones, self-driving cars, brain implants, God-knows-what else. Didn't you say he's got his own space program? Why not let him play with it? He might forego the government's tendency to militarize a find like this. Why not let him spend his billions figuring out what that thing is? I certainly don't have the resources or the knowledge to tackle the question. Why don't I just go there and introduce myself and work with the guy? I know those clowns in Wichita didn't give me up to him, but he's not stupid. He's going to figure out my involvement at some point." Lillian opened her mouth to set me straight, but I interrupted her. "Furthermore, let's consider the scenario that says the object I hit was military—that it belongs to the government. If that's true, they're only going to want it back. Isn't it better to have civilian researchers work on it?"

"Low percentage—that it's military," she said. I thought I knew what she considered high percentage. This is what prompts my wife to refer to her as a "UFO Nut."

"Point is, it's not like we can give it over to the government. They're either going to lock it—and probably me—away somewhere to study it, or they already know what it is, and they'll lock it and me away just for tripping over it in the first place. They'll put us both in a box in that warehouse with the Lost Ark."

"Well, you're right about one thing. We have three prominent choices here. Government research, which is a non-starter. Private research by an amoral billionaire, which likely results in terrible abuse of whatever this thing is. Or you get it back and bury it somewhere here on this farm and never speak of it again."

"Well, that's bleak. I'm not sure there isn't a fourth option."

She pulled a piece of bark from the log and tossed it.

"You're getting it in your head that it can be used to save little children with Leukemia."

"What if it does? I can't do that alone. That's highly impractical. But maybe something about that piece of debris can be harvested to do something genuinely good. Not by me. Tinkering with it in my garage would be stupid. But a guy like Spiro Lewko? Someone who has the resources and the cash to do serious research...?"

"You'd have to reveal yourself to him."

"And steer him in the right direction."

"No good deed goes unpunished, Will," she said. "Ever hear of the Sackler family?"

I lifted my shoulders. I had no idea.

"Pharmaceutical. Came up with a revolutionary pain killer. An opioid. OxyContin...you may have heard of it. Highly effective. But it wasn't enough to render it unto the medical community to relieve pain and suffering. They schemed to plow that stuff into anyone with a back twitch, real or imagined. They made billions and tore a hole in the soul of this country."

I knew what she meant. I'd seen it first-hand. Lane Franklin nearly paid the ultimate price as collateral damage.

"Will, suppose that thing *is* capable of curing cancer? Have you considered what would happen if control of the technology or magic or whatever it is comes down to one man? One corrupt billionaire?"

"That's the way it is now. One man. Who goes to bed every night thinking he shouldn't be resting—he should be out visiting another hospital. What if Lewko's resources can find a way to make it distributable? Instead of me sneaking in and out of random hospitals, praying I don't wake the wrong patient."

"Don't act on hope, Will."

"Why not?"

"Because hope kills. Read history. Hope is going to take you away from all this—" She waved her hands at the quiet country scene. "—and lock you up in some lab to be dissected. I've been clear about this from the start, Will. It might be the one and only thing your cop wife and I agree on. You've got to get that piece of debris back! Then bury it. Or better yet, shoot it out into space. Just pick it up and throw it as hard as you can toward the sun. If it has the properties you say it does, that should be enough."

"And sacrifice what it could mean to science? To a possible cure for cancer?"

She fell silent, but her silence failed to mask that she never stopped calculating. Her gaze settled on a vague middle distance, seemingly on nothing, yet seeing clearly, looking down dozens of possible paths, factoring variables into equations that engineered scores, perhaps hundreds of possible outcomes. To no one, certainly not me, she shook her head slightly from side to side as each outcome revealed itself.

Purple dusk settled around us, turning the trees to black silhouettes against the fading glow in the sky.

Lillian said nothing for several long minutes.

When she finally spoke, she said, "My sister died of Leukemia. When she was fourteen. Her name was Eileen."

I waited.

When she added nothing, I said, "I'm sorry."

Without looking at me, Lillian said, "Now you know the price of my convictions."

6

Lillian and I walked back from the creek. I offered to give her a ride, but she waved me off like I'd suggested a neck tattoo. Dusk lingered until we strolled through the yard to the house. Photosensitive yard lights lit up the grass, casting diamonds on the lawn as dew formed.

Andy's car was gone. It's not unusual for Lane to bike out for some big sister time with Andy. When the chatter runs late, Lane texts her mother for permission to stay longer on a promise that Andy will load her bike in the trunk of the car and drive her home. I was surprised they had departed already. I expected to find them huddled on the porch, conspiring against me.

We have guest bedrooms, but no guest beds. I set up the pullout sofa in the living room and warned Lillian that the mattress was once used by the Spanish Inquisition. When I went for clean sheets from the linen closet, she stopped me. She made a quick trip to her car and returned with a backpack and a rolled-up sleeping bag. I offered a pillow, but she claimed to have everything she needed.

While she unrolled her sleeping bag, I checked my phone.

A text message from Nolan the Mechanic at Willow Run airport reported the Foundation Navajo as airworthy. I logged into the Flight Schedule for Essex County Air Service. The gods smiled on me. Pidge had a morning deadhead to Lansing. I sent a text to her that said I'd be taking a jump seat and would need a drop-off at Willow Run. Before I could thumb my way to a new screen, she fired back a response.

Then you can fucking preflight. Have my coffee ready. ;)

"You know, I used to be chief pilot..." I muttered through a half smile.

"Beg pardon?" Lillian asked.

"Oh," I waved my hand, "just talking to the phone. I now have a butt-crack-of-dawn departure. Andy and I have a rule that I don't use *the other thing* in the house without letting her know or wearing a bell. These old floors creak, so you may hear me sneaking out in the morning."

"Creaking floors I can ignore. The idea of you floating around the room would keep me up all night. I appreciate the protocol. Does this mean I won't see you tomorrow? We have unfinished business."

"You'll see me. I should be home by lunchtime." The phone in my hand vibrated and another message appeared. "Um, looks like Andy got called in to the office. She says she'll be late tonight and not to wait up. I'll let her know I set you up here in the living room."

"Emergency?"

"Probably just small-town cop business," I said. "Happens all the time."

"Your wife is not a small-town cop. You should know that by now."

7

It doesn't matter what time I set on the alarm; I wake up ten minutes before it goes off. Rolling over to hit the switch, I discovered that Andy hadn't come home. Her side of the bed remained untouched. I lifted my phone off the nightstand. If offered nothing new since Andy's warning that she would be late. I knew better than to call, so I tapped out a text telling her about the trip to pick up the Navajo.

I dressed quickly and tip-toed through the house. I was about to pat myself on the back for not disturbing Lillian when my eyes adjusted to the dark and revealed that the sofa bed lay empty. I checked the driveway. No Prius.

Lillian had gone.

PIDGE WASN'T KIDDING about making me pull the plane from the hangar and perform the preflight. She showed up ten minutes before the scheduled departure time, strolling across the ramp with her flight bag in one hand and a McDonald's coffee in the other.

"I love having an FO to do the grunt work," she declared, climbing into the cabin and taking the pilot's seat.

Pidge ran through the pre-takeoff rituals and had us in the air quickly. We climbed east to meet the dawn over Lake Michigan. Except for sharing the airwaves with the disembodied voice of air traffic control, we had the cockpit to ourselves. We didn't speak until after Green Bay Departure handed us off to Chicago Center.

"The captain with that Challenger told me to call him for a right seat job."

Pidge said it quietly. Voices over a good intercom system are intimate, transmitted directly into your head via noise-cancelling earphones.

"The one with the blown nose tire?" The visiting jet had blown a tire on landing. I theorized that the captain came in hot and rolled long and had taken the turn to the taxiway too fast. The captain claimed it was foreign object debris. Either way, the jet sat idle on the ramp while Earl Jackson oversaw repairs. "Could be a good gig," I offered.

"Captain makes six figures. He says. They're based in Newark. Regular runs up and down the east coast. Out west. Sometimes South America."

"Jet time."

"Uh-huh."

We fell silent.

At twenty-three, Cassidy Evelyn Page—or Pidge, as she had been nicknamed shortly after she began taking flying lessons at Essex County Airport—holds every rating except rotorcraft and seaplane. She's logged more than enough hours to sign on with any regional air carrier. She's the best pilot I've ever known, and I include myself in the competition. Twice, she's used an unwieldy cabin class airplane like a surgical tool to save my life. She's what chief pilots dream of finding in a stack of job applicants.

I had always known that she would eventually move on.

I glanced at her—a petite blonde girl-woman sitting on an extra cushion with the seat pulled all the way forward so that her feet could reach the pedals. She'd been my student and it filled me with pride to see her knock off one rating after another. But the student had long ago surpassed the master.

I wanted to ask if she planned to apply, then realized I didn't want to hear the answer. Which made no sense. I, more than anyone, wanted to see Pidge ascend the ranks of professional pilots.

She had similar wishes for me. Pidge is one of a handful of people who know that I can vanish at will. On more than a few occasions, she has harangued me to use the unexplained ability to do something meaningful—although from her it always has a comic book ring to it. Superspy. Crime fighter. She wants to see me do more.

"You should go for it," I said, confronting my reluctance head-on. "They'd be idiots not to take you."

"It would sure as hell beat having Earl up my ass all the time."

You'd miss him most of all, I thought. I wanted to talk about something else. "Hey, how are things with you and Arun?"

"Screw you, Stewart," she laughed a little too abruptly. I sensed relief in the change of topic. "I'm not telling you about my love life!"

"Jesus, Pidge, you used to tell me the size of a guy's—"

"That was my sex life, dummy! Not my love life!"

I mock-gawked at her. "Did you guys trade the 'L' word? Oh my god!"

"Shut up! No! We haven't!"

"Seriously, have you guys even traded spit yet?"

"Fuck you."

I kept the grin on my face for a few nautical miles, just to harass her. She didn't bring up the question of a career move again.

PIDGE DROPPED me off at the FBO at Willow Run. I think if she'd had the choice, she would have done a low pass and literally dropped me. She let the engines run while I jumped out. She started to roll before I had time to close the airstair. I had to jog a few yards to get it latched. When she turned, I saw her laughing.

Willow Run airport once housed a Ford-built factory nearly a mile long that, at its peak during World War II, produced one B-24 Liberator bomber every 58 minutes. Henry Ford built the factory from bare ground after the war began. It teetered on the brink of failure, then gained momentum to become an enduring symbol of America's wartime role as the Arsenal of Democracy. I sometimes wonder what it might have been like in its heyday. The sound of countless rivet guns hammering. The shriek of air drills. The rumble of the assembly line pushing silver aircraft forward day and night. Thousands of workers toiling in heat and cold under relentless pressure. I wondered if they felt a lifelong pang of loss after the war ended and production shut down. A loss of comradeship. A loss of cohesion with a nation on a mission. The factory never found a meaningful purpose afterward. Today, only a single section remains standing, though still imposing.

As Pidge taxied away, I strolled past a handful of executive jets and into the FBO annex attached to the original factory building turned hangar. Several years ago, on my first trip into Willow Run, I'd been curious. A willing FBO manager showed me around the huge hangar. A General Motors president kept his personal L-39 fighter jet in the hangar. The manager told me another section of the building once contained the shattered remains of a Northwest Airlines MD-80 that crashed on takeoff from Detroit Metro

Airport. He said the parts and pieces were kept in limbo for a couple decades until the last of the lawsuits were settled, then they simply disappeared.

I remember looking at the bare concrete floor and wondering what it must have been like. Since then, after my own accident—after seeing my own aircraft in pieces—I harbored no desire to enter the vast hangar again.

"Nolan around?" I asked the woman behind the counter.

She looked up at me with a narrow face and a wide smile. "Are you Will?"

"All day."

She rose and pulled a work order from a slotted plastic divider. After shuffling and separating papers, she pushed a sheet toward me. I gave it a glance and handed her the Foundation credit card. She took both and headed for an interior office.

The FBO lounge was empty. A flatscreen TV mounted in the far corner caught my eye. I turned around and leaned on the counter. Onscreen, a reporter stood in front of a low, modern-looking brick building that could have been a twin to the Essex Police Department building where Andy works. I idly wondered if the same architect had designed both before I woke up to the caption on the screen that said, "NFL Hall of Famer Arrested in Essex, WI."

"Here's your card." The woman's voice came from behind me. "Just sign here." She put the receipt slip on the counter where it curled up under a pen.

"Can you turn that up?" I pointed at the screen.

"Ach! I can never find the darn remote." She rummaged around the desktop as I stared at the screen.

No question. The CNN reporter performed her on-the-scene remote from the sidewalk in front of the Essex PD building. Behind tinted glass over the reporter's left shoulder, my wife maintained her busy but orderly cubicle—and maybe stood watching me as I watched her.

"Found it!"

Too late. The reporter mouthed a few words, then set her face in a "Back to you, Bob" expression. The scene changed.

The FBO clerk behind me held her arm out and jabbed the buttons on the remote. Nothing happened. She rose on her toes and extended her arm farther as if an extra inch would do the trick.

"Any idea what that's about?" I asked. I pointed at the screen again.

"That? That's been going on for a couple days. Horrible. Can you imagine? Why isn't this working?" She examined the remote.

"A couple days?"

"It's all anyone is talking about."

I glanced back at the screen. The frame behind an anchorwoman showed a telephoto shot of a farm. Half a dozen emergency vehicles, lights strobing, sat in the driveway and on the road. I tried to place the location but couldn't. The screen caption had changed.

FARM FAMILY BRUTALLY MURDERED

"In Wisconsin?"

"That? No that's up north. Near Pellston."

I squinted at her in confusion. "And they arrested an NFL player?"

"What? No. I don't think so. I don't think they've caught anyone yet." She shook her head at me, then glanced at the TV and the light went on. "Oh, you're talking about a different one. I'm talking about this story." She pointed the remote at the screen again and jabbed it forward while she tried the volume button again without success. She shrugged and gestured at the TV. "This one is the one that's on non-stop. Just horrible. Parents and kids killed, and they're saying that whoever did it cut up the—"

"Sorry," I interrupted her. I had no doubt it was horrible, but I didn't need to hear the details. "I meant the story before that."

She looked at me blankly.

"Never mind."

I hurried out of the FBO. Outside, I found a spot shaded from the early August sunshine and pulled out my phone. Nothing from Andy.

She stays busy when she's on duty. And if a television crew had camped outside the City of Essex police headquarters streaming a national story to CNN, busy would be an understatement.

Before closing the phone, I touched a screen icon for CNN headlines. Half a dozen news links appeared. At the top:

MICHIGAN MURDERS SHOCK AUTHORITIES

I scrolled down. The Essex arrest story apparently hadn't transitioned from Breaking News to online content. I tried Google, looking for something about Essex and a football player, but I am neither adept at internet spying nor patient enough to succeed. A useless list of links to sports sites appeared.

I tucked my phone in my pocket and headed for the freshly repaired airplane. Sitting on the ramp, it looked as if it had had enough of the earth and needed to fly.

Me, too.

An hour after breaking the wheels free of Willow Run, I closed the Foundation hangar door back at Essex County Airport. The Navajo's engines ticked against silence as they cooled. My phone rang.

"Is Lillian gone?" Andy spoke in a low near-whisper. I heard voices around her.

"She was when I left this morning."

"Did she come back?"

"I'm not home yet. What's going on? Can you talk?"

"Not now. It's a mess. I'll be home for dinner."

My wife trusts me to know when to hang up.

"Okay. 'Bye."

"'Bye."

8

I may be clumsy around a search engine, but I knew someone who wasn't.
"Arun, buddy." I leaned into his office. "Got a minute?"
"Will, I was about to come and tell you: I just got off the phone with Ms. Stone. Minnesota is confirmed for Wednesday." Arun cannot call Sandy by her first name. He also knows better than to email trip itineraries to me.
Sandy is really squeezing the schedule.
"Can you run a search on the computer for me?"
"Of course, but may I ask you something first?" He gestured at one of his occasional chairs. I hesitated. I wondered if this involved his crush on Pidge. I visualized myself flying out the door fast enough to leave behind cartoon contrails and a ricochet sound effect. My fears heightened when he swallowed and nervously twined his fingers.
"What's up?"
"The other night…um, what would have happened to us if the engine had stopped?"
"Huh?"
"You know…when you said we had a problem. If the engine stopped, what would happen? Would we…crash?"
The impulse to make a joke bubbled up. I bit my tongue.
"Oh, hell no. Arun, where's this coming from?" I took the seat.
"I didn't really know when I took this job how much I would be flying in a little airplane." I hate it when people refer to general aviation aircraft as *little*. He read my slightly stiffened posture. "I mean to say light aircraft. I

did some research. The safety record for piston-engine twins is not very good. I thought two engines would be better, but so many times when one engine stops the airplane crashes."

I leaned forward. "First off, I'm glad you decided to talk to me about this. Arun, if you ever have any concerns about flying, tell me, okay? Second, your research is not off the mark."

My admission surprised him.

"The record for piston twin aircraft is not stellar. But there are factors to consider when you look at the statistics. Yes, we fly a piston twin. Yes, they have a poor, or let me say poor-er, safety record, but the way we operate, it's safer. For example, I wouldn't fly a single-engine airplane across any of the Great Lakes."

"Why?"

"Simple. The chance of an engine failure is miniscule, *but*—! *If* such a thing does happen, and they do, and you're over the lake in a single engine airplane, you're going to wind up in the lake. And you will die. Period. Even in the middle of August when the water is as warm as it ever gets you will die of exposure. A life jacket only keeps the dead body afloat."

"We fly across the lake all the time!"

"Yes. In a twin. If we're forced to shut down an engine, we have a means of making it to land."

Relief dawned on his face but slipped away quickly. "Then I don't understand the statistics for twin-engine airplanes. Why do they crash if one engine is running?"

I chose my words carefully. "A twin offers a margin of safety, but performance on one engine isn't guaranteed. Weight, density altitude, height above terrain and pilot proficiency all come into play. Fully loaded on a hot day, we might not be able to maintain altitude with one engine."

"We would crash?"

"No. We would gradually descend to an emergency landing."

"Then I don't understand the statistics."

"Because there's one more thing involved. Let's say we lose an engine. And let's say we can't hold altitude, but I do something stupid. I keep pulling on the yoke to make the airplane stay up. Pitching up bleeds off airspeed."

The blank look on his face told me to start with basics.

"Look, if you go out in the hangar and turn the controls all the way to the right, will the airplane turn in the hangar?"

"No."

"Why not?"

He thought about it. "Because there isn't enough wind to make the controls work."

"Airspeed. Exactly. You need air flowing over the control surfaces to make the controls work and make the airplane do what you want it to do. And how do you get airspeed?"

He tipped his head to signal that I was talking to him like a child.

"The engines."

"Yes. But, what about a glider? Doesn't have an engine."

"It's gliding."

"Exactly. We either use engines or altitude to create airspeed. Either way, speed is life."

"But if we lose one engine, do we lose our airspeed?"

"Not necessarily. Besides, that's not the issue you're asking about. Picture the average piston twin." I held up my hand to make an airplane in the air. "You have an engine on this side, and an engine on this side. Both use power to pull the airplane through the air. Hundreds of horsepower on each side. But if you take away one engine, what happens?"

"Less power? Less airspeed?"

"Less power, but not necessarily less airspeed. Remember, I can push the nose down to gain airspeed. But what else? What's no longer symmetrical?"

He looked at my hand, picturing the airplane.

"Power is not symmetrical. You have power on one side, but not the other."

"Correct! I have loads of power out there on the left wing trying to pull the airplane around." I rolled my hand to the right. "To counter that asymmetrical thrust, I input left rudder—the thing on the vertical part of the tail."

"I know what a rudder is."

"At cruise speed, I don't need full rudder deflection. Why?"

"Lots of air flowing across the control surface."

I gave him a respectful nod. "Talk that way around Pi—er, Cassidy—and she'll swoon."

He might have blushed.

"But the slower I go the more rudder is needed. Is that variable infinite?"

"No!" he said brightly. "Eventually you will be applying the maximum deflection of the rudder. You run out!"

"And what happens when I run out of rudder, but the good engine continues to give us full power?"

"The airplane turns!"

"Violently. And right there is where your piston twin safety record goes bad. Pilots who have lost an engine for whatever reason who then allow their speed to decay to the point where the thrust from the good engine overpowers the controls and torque-rolls the airplane. And if it happens at low altitude, where there's no room to recover..."

His eyes went wide.

"Arun, you're one of the smartest people I know. Let's say you're the pilot, and you're holding left rudder, but your speed is decaying. You're headed into this kind of torque-roll-stall situation." I demonstrated with my hand. "What's the simple, idiot-proof way of avoiding it?"

"You lower the nose to gain airspeed. Trade altitude for airspeed, which assures you of control."

"But what if you're too low? What if you just took off?"

He stared blankly.

"C'mon man!" I said. "How do you get rid of asymmetrical power that's threatening to flip the airplane?"

He grimaced. "You...turn off the good engine?"

I pointed. "Bingo! Reduce the power on the good engine."

"But now you're going to crash!"

"Probably. But *you maintain control.* Period. If that means maintaining control so that you can glide to a landing on a runway, great. If it means maintaining control so that you steer the airplane between two buildings or through a highway overpass or into an open field, great."

"I don't like the sound of that."

"The other night...let's say I had to shut down the right engine. I can tell you without doing the math that at our weight I could have easily maintained a safe altitude *and* a safe airspeed, and therefore maintained control. We were at ten thousand feet. We had plenty of altitude. Even if we were unable to maintain altitude at a safe speed, we could have sacrificed two or three hundred feet per minute for a long time without any issue. And the lower we went, the denser the air. Eventually, we would no longer need to descend to maintain airspeed."

"Then it is the airspeed that matters."

"The critical airspeed is called *Vmc.*"

"Vee em cee?"

"Minimum controllable airspeed. The number gets hammered into a pilot's head when flying a twin. But even more important than that is *Vyse.* Best rate of climb speed, single engine. We can actually climb on one engine at *Vyse.* Or at least minimize the descent. If I ever lose an engine in a twin, you won't see me go below *Vyse.*"

"Then why are there accidents?"

I heaved the sigh shared by all pilots who read NTSB reports. "Somebody should have pulled the throttle on the good engine—and that's incredibly hard to do—in order to crash straight ahead rather than have the airplane flip out of control."

He sat thinking. It worried me.

"Arun, having two engines is safer than having one. Plus, you have one hot-shit pilot up front who's never going to let it get to the point of losing control. You're in good hands. Ask Cassidy."

He blew out a cleansing breath. "It's good to know the mechanics, I suppose."

"Sit up front with me sometime and I'll demonstrate."

His hands flew up between us. "Oh, no! Theory suits me. I do not need a demonstration."

We both laughed. His felt forced.

I pointed at his silver laptop—the only item on an otherwise spotless desk. "I saw something on the news at an FBO in Michigan this morning. Something about a football player being arrested here in Essex last night. Can you run a search for me?"

"Oh, my God! Oh, my God, Will! You haven't heard about that?"

"Just a blip on a muted television."

"Here," he said. He waved for me to step behind him and limbered up his fingers. "It's a major news story. I am certain Andrea is on this case!"

He clicked and scrolled and jumped pages. When I first started flying, I struggled with motion sickness. I worked hard to overcome it, but if I'm forced to watch someone rolling and scrolling a computer screen my eyeballs start to spin. I glanced away until he said, "Here it is!"

ALL PRO STAR RUNNING BACK ARRESTED

The story came from the online pages of *The Milwaukee Journal Sentinel.*

"May I?" I reached for the laptop and turned the screen, mainly to keep Arun's fingers away from the touchpad.

I scrolled through the story at my own pace. When I finished, I rotated the keyboard back to Arun. He looked up at me with an eager expression. I headed for his office door.

"Where are we going?"

"What?"

"In Minnesota...where in Minnesota?" I didn't want to talk about what I had just read. Not until I got the real story from Andy. I also needed to untwist the knot in my gut that came with wondering if Lane Franklin's need to talk to Andy had anything to do with a sexual assault arrest.

"Oh," Arun replied. "Brainerd."

9

Andy had suggested we meet at Los Lobos—the restaurant attached to the *other* bowling alley in Essex.

The server arrived to take drink requests. I ordered for both of us, but Andy quickly turned down a Corona. "I might have to go back."

"Jesus, Dee! You haven't slept!"

She shrugged. Unchecked, Andy would work until she dropped. I detected a hint of omission in her averted eyes.

"Tom booted you out, didn't he? I bet he told you not to show your face until morning."

A protest formed on her lips, but I cut it off.

"Two," I said, holding up fingers to make sure the server understood. He ducked away quickly.

Andy pushed her fingers into the smooth tight sheen of her tied-back hair, then lifted her arms and worked her ponytail free. She shook her hair onto her shoulders and rubbed her eyes.

I win.

The server came back carrying two bottles with lime wedges jammed in the necks. They know us at Los Lobos. They probably pulled the bottles from the cooler the minute we walked in.

We touched glass to glass.

"Us," she said.

"Us."

Andy took a sip, then looked around. Being early on a Monday, we had the dining room to ourselves.

"Usual disclaimer?"

"Usual disclaimer."

She settled in her seat, dipped another chip in salsa and took a bite. Her eyes met mine. In stark contrast to her tired affect, her eyes were alight.

"You already know we arrested Clayton Johns last night. This morning, technically."

"I saw it on CNN while I was in Detroit. Jesus, Dee!"

She made a sour face. "Those TV trucks jammed up the whole street at the station. They've been there since dawn. I'd like to know how they found out so fast."

"Five-time pro-bowler. League MVP at least once that I know of. I'm surprised you didn't have reporters from ESPN."

"They might have been there," Andy said, dipping another chip. "We've got stations from Green Bay, Milwaukee and Madison. And they're feeding national outlets. CNN. Fox News. How much do you know?"

She munched the chip and dipped another while I talked.

"When I got back, Arun looked up the online story from *The Journal*. I only know what they reported."

"First things first. Did Lane showing up last night have anything to do with this?"

"Ah. You got that. I couldn't leave you a note with any details last night."

"Tell me she's not involved."

"She's not. Not directly. She might have to be interviewed for background, but she's in the clear."

Andy's reassurance didn't feel reassuring.

The server returned to ask for our order. I went with the three-taco plate I always choose. Andy asked for a shrimp quesadilla. She waited until he cleared the room and then lowered her voice.

"Lane needed to talk last night. I thought it might be about her mom. All teenaged girls go to war with their mothers and they've been butting heads for a while. But that wasn't it. Lane started right in about Sarah."

"Lewis?" Lane's friend Sarah figured prominently in a case Andy worked last winter. I remembered how the girl's brush with suicide came to our attention during another Los Lobos dinner. "Is she okay?"

"Sarah? She's okay, although when a kid who goes as close to the edge as she did, you worry. The path to self-destruction has been broken in."

"How do Lane and Sarah connect to a retired NFL running back?"

"This gets a little teen-twisted, but here goes. Lane said Sarah was feeling the gravitational pull—yeah, I know, that's how Lane put it—of some of the older girls on the pompon squad that Sarah joined. Juniors and seniors. Sarah told Lane those girls were partying at some rich kid's house on The Lakes. Some upperclassman. Parents away on weekends—the usual John Hughes screenplay. Lane said Sarah was trying to get invited, but after school let out Sarah's parents sent her away to camp for a few weeks, which diffused the issue."

It felt like taking the long way around, but Andy likes to stand up all the dominoes before she flicks the first one over.

"When Sarah came home last week, the story changed. The *in* for these parties wasn't the girls on the pompon squad, it was through another girl, Stella Boardman."

Andy lifted her eyes at me. Like I should know the girl. I shrugged.

"Boardman? Will, you've heard the name. They live in Horizon Homes. Their house was a regular stop when I was on uniform patrol. The Battling Boardmans?"

I had no idea but nodded with great authority. Andy has often talked about the Horizon Homes subdivision in the southeast corner of Essex, a low-quality 1960s development that attracted frequent visits from the police.

"The apple and the tree, I'm afraid. The parents are a piece of work; the girl has been on our radar for a while. She's had half a dozen run-ins. It seems she's the conduit to these parties, and she's the one that reached out to Sarah."

"Why? Doesn't sound like they're crowd compatible."

"They're not. But, remember I said the story changed? Turns out the house at the lakes isn't where some junior or senior boy lives. Lane told me last night that the parties are hosted by older guys—men—who like to mix with younger girls. The Boardman girl has the in. She invited Sarah, only it wasn't Sarah she wanted. It was Lane."

"Lane?" My skin crawled.

"The Boardman girl sold it to Sarah as way better than immature Essex High boys. She told Sarah these guys are sophisticated, hot and experienced. Ready to party. She told Sarah getting an invitation is a great way to…lose *it*…with someone who knows what they're doing."

"It?"

"*It*, Will. You know! At some point a girl has to think about things like that."

"Are you saying Lane—?"

"No! Yes. I mean, no, Lane is nowhere near ready for anything like that, but yes, she's thought about it and we've talked about it and she's got her head on straight."

Of course, she does…I hope…

"Lane said that Sarah said that Stella said that lots of girls are going up to this lake place. There's a pool, a hot tub, and a chance to, as Sarah put it to Lane, *do things* if the girl wants to."

"And what if they don't want to? God!" I rubbed down the goose bumps rising on my arms. "Wait, you said that the Boardman kid wanted to go through Sarah to invite Lane. Why?"

"I'll get to that. Anyway, the Boardman girl didn't take the rejection well and got a little ugly about it. She told Sarah she would take Verna Sobol instead."

"Jesus Christ! Who's Verna Sobol?"

Andy tipped her head and raised her eyebrows at me. "Sobol? Her dad's a city maintenance supervisor. Cecil? You've met him, Will!"

Me and names and faces; I'm terrible, but I have an out. Andy knows and remembers everyone. I figure that knowing Andy covers me.

"They're one of the only other African American families in Essex. Verna is a year younger than Lane."

"Younger? She's only fourteen?"

Andy nodded slowly. "And a bit of a wild child, according to Lane. Which is why Lane needed to see me last night."

"Are they friends? Lane and Verna?"

"Not particularly. Lane thinks it's funny that everyone thinks they're supposed to be, like they're some sort of color combination. But no, not really. There's the age difference. A year at that age is a big difference. And they move in different circles. But last night Sarah told Lane that Stella told Sarah that she was taking Verna instead."

"Say that three times, fast."

"I guess it was meant to stick it to Sarah and Lane for turning her down."

"Given the older man component, I'm going to guess you called Cecil."

"I did call Cecil. But Verna's older brother answered. Cecil and Diane went away for the weekend. I called Cecil's cell, but it went to voice mail. While I was on the phone with the brother, I asked for Verna. He said she was staying overnight with a friend."

"Ding! Ding! Ding! Alarm!" I lifted my beer and took a healthy drink, calculating the distance to empty, the timing of the delivery of our meals, and the prospects of ordering a second. Andy's stood largely untouched.

"Exactly. Suddenly I have a situation. Lane didn't know where on The Lakes this animal house is, but she thought Sarah might. I decided it would be best to have that discussion in person. Sarah trusts me—and it would be harder for Sarah to withhold something to my face. I packed up Lane and we drove over to the Lewis place. I got lucky. Sarah's mom was at choir practice and her dad was at the Planning Commission meeting."

"Oh, right. That." Robert Lewis, Sarah's father, had tried to recruit Andy to a citizens group fighting state highway expansion in the northeast corner of the county. Andy, citing the fact that the city signs her paychecks, declined.

"Sarah was home alone, so it was just us girls. Sarah didn't know the address, but she knew it was on Leander Lake, at the north end, and that the house has an infinity pool."

"A what?"

"One of those swimming pools where it looks like there's no edge. I immediately knew the property. I've been there."

"Is that the place with the crazy sculptress?"

Andy nodded and sipped her Corona.

"The one whose husband threw all her iron statues into the lake? And then she threw him in?"

"The same. I responded to six calls up there before they divorced and moved away."

"To be replaced by a retired NFL player with a taste for young—"

"Don't say it! Yes. And I hate to put it in these terms because it has undertones I don't subscribe to, but it made sense that Stella Boardman was recruiting two pretty young African American girls in Essex to party with an African American sports figure."

I left that alone, knowing how hard Andy works to walk a colorless line in her job.

"More to the point, I suddenly had knowledge of a minor child who might be in jeopardy. I made a bee line to drop off Lane and called the station to see who had Eastside Patrol last night. Guess who?"

I had no idea, but I could tell Andy wasn't pleased. I came up with Sims, because he's the smallest officer in the department. I pictured Sims up against a muscle-bound ex-NFL player.

"Sims is on paternity leave. It was Traeger. Your chauffer-buddy. He's not the brightest bulb."

"But a nice guy."

"Not my first choice, Will, when I'm about to knock on the door of a very wealthy, very well-known individual and ask if he's committing statutory rape. The guy probably has lawyers live streaming. I called County and asked them to have a deputy meet us there."

Andy leaned forward, signaling an uptick in the story's intensity. She checked the small room for the tenth time to assure herself that all the other tables remained empty.

"You're not going to believe what happened next." I misread the cue and started to guess, but she cut me off. "I stopped around the curve, you know, where Sunset Circle swings across the top of the lake? I waited for Traeger. He pulls up behind me but leaves his headlights on and then sits in his car waiting for *me* to get out. Seriously, Will. I get why the chief is holding back on him. Anyway, I go back to his car and get him to turn off his damned lights, although my night vision is now shot. He's on the radio with Mae at dispatch. Guess what?"

"Um…"

"There's a noise complaint. Somebody's partying with loud music at the Johns place. So, I told Traeger to follow me in. That property is huge, Will. I think the original owner wanted to build a hotel there.

"Anyway, we got to the front door and there's no answer. I told Traeger to keep trying the bell. I went around the side of the building and down to the deck with the pool. By now I can hear the music, only it's not coming from the house. There's nobody in the house that I can see. Nobody in the pool or hot tub. And while I'm poking around the deck, I almost had a heart attack because Lyle came around the corner with his hand on his weapon. I told him if I see him do that again his arm will wind up in a cast. I mean—I like the guy, but not behind me in the dark!"

"It's a boat," I said. "The music was on a boat. Boy, that's a big no-no on Leander Lake after dark. Homeowners up there are absolutely rigid about that kind of shit."

Andy ignored me, which told me I was right.

"I grabbed Traeger's flashlight and went down to the boat dock. There was no moon last night, but I picked up a reflection from one of those big aluminum pontoons—way out on the water. There was no other boat at Johns' dock, so I sent Lyle to the next property over because they had one. He woke up the owners and got the keys to their speed boat and picked me up. He might be a little clumsy as a cop, but he sure can handle a boat.

"We found one of those big pontoon party boats about a quarter of the way down the lake, just sitting there. No lights. Motor off. Music blasting."

Dinner interrupted. After assuring the server we needed nothing further and waiting for him to return to the bar, Andy leaned over her plate and spoke just above a whisper.

"Johns was there. So was Verna Sobol. She was on one of the side cushions. Passed out. Nothing on." Andy tipped her head slightly, wordlessly filling in the rest.

"What about Johns?"

"We found him across the deck from her. On his ass on the floor, also passed out. And…"

"And?"

"And it was all hanging out. He didn't have a stitch on and…um, it was pretty obvious what happened."

I must have given her a blank stare. She spun her hand in a *you know what I'm talking about* gesture.

"Oh. You sure?"

I got The Look. She was sure.

"Lyle pulled alongside. I jumped on the boat and checked to make sure the girl had a pulse and was breathing. She smelled like a distillery. Her clothes were all over. Knotted up—you know, like pulled off in a hurry. I'll wait for the lab report, but if she wasn't roofied, I'll eat the report. The thing is, I think Johns accidently roofied himself."

"What?"

"There were bottles and glasses and a lot of liquor, and I think he slipped her something, but then must have drunk from the wrong glass because he was incoherent. Even after we rolled him over and cuffed him, he was barely conscious."

"Jesus! That could have been Lane!"

Andy leaned back. "I don't think she'd ever put herself in that position."

"The girl…did he…?"

Andy nodded. "No question. It was…on her. I recorded the scene with my phone. That's why I couldn't call you. I took a bunch of photos then had Traeger bag my phone. Traeger called in the cavalry and I have to say, he did a decent job of towing that boat back to the dock."

"Wow."

"No kidding! In pretty short order, we had everyone there. The chief. The sheriff. Westside Patrol. County. The night supervisor. EMTs. The works. Tom got right down in Johns' face and told him to stay put. Tom himself took swabs off the guy. He got pretty agitated, but the chief made a big impression."

"Can you do that? Swab a guy like that?"

"The guy was a walking crime scene, Will! Sure, his lawyers will try to have it all tossed, but this wasn't a search warrant situation. We found him that way. Plus, I had photos. *Close up photos.*"

"So many questions I don't want to ask. What about the girl? Verna?"

"As soon as the EMTs arrived, Tom put me in charge of her. As in, 'Don't let her out of your sight.' I spent the better part of the morning at the hospital. I would have preferred going back to the scene. DCI is lending their forensic team. The parents didn't show up until almost eleven. I guess they were over in the Dells and forgot to pack phone chargers."

I'd been working over my tacos while Andy talked. Her dinner sat nearly untouched. Now, for just a moment, she stared at her plate. She lost herself in deep thought.

"It sounds like this is a slam dunk," I said.

"Huh..."

I waited, but she didn't move.

"For Johns. Pretty hard to play the He Said She Said card. Or the 'I thought she was older' card."

Her eyes came up slowly, squinting, looking through me.

"Did Verna's parents consent to the rape kit?"

"What? Oh, yes. Yes, Johns is toast ..." She trailed off.

"What?"

"Okay, I know this comes a little after the fact. Maybe it's the alcohol talking..."

"Dee, you've had like two sips."

She leaned back in her chair and stared at me.

"Thinking back on it, now that I've had a chance to think, I remember something I kinda put aside at the time. When it was just me and Traeger. Before the whole circus arrived. A feeling..."

"Like?"

"Like I was being watched."

ANDY DIDN'T FINISH her beer. I did. After paying the bill, I proposed driving her home. One word to the owners and her car could stay in the Los Lobos lot overnight. I promised to get up with her at any hour and return her to it.

She refused.

"I'm going back." She pulled her keys from her bag.

"What? No! That's ridiculous! Don't make me call the chief."

"I need to find out who called in the noise complaint. We might have a witness."

She stepped close to me, slipped her arms around me and pressed her body against mine. Gold-flecked green eyes blinked at me beneath long dark lashes, sending a coded message I didn't understand but my body did.

"Dammit, woman," I muttered. She grinned.

"I won't be long."
She cut off my ironclad objection with a kiss.
I watched her drive away, thinking *What just happened?*

SOMETIME AFTER MIDNIGHT my wife slipped into our bed. Her breathing quickly eased into the smooth rhythm of unencumbered sleep, telling me that whatever had drawn her back to the station had been settled, at least for the night.

10

"Have fun!" I flipped Sandy and Arun a jaunty wave as they walked away from the airplane. Neither looked back. Their attention had already fixed on the small welcoming committee waiting inside the Brainerd Lakes Airport FBO. The anxious cluster looked like every other welcoming committee I'd seen since I began flying Sandy to these meetings. Expectant. On their best behavior. Hoping their plea to the Christine and Paulette Paulesky Education Foundation would yield a new science curriculum, or a chance to replace outdated computers, or hire new teachers to relieve overcrowded, underfunded classrooms.

It would, of course. No one got to the point of a physical visit without having been thoroughly vetted by Arun. And Sandy's heart did not have the capacity to say No. I liked to think that every time Sandy wrote a check, it gave Bargo Litton, the corrupt billionaire who funded the Foundation, albeit at gunpoint, a stab of pain in his dried up, black heart.

This trip promised a treat for me. Brainerd Lakes Regional Airport hosts the Wings Airport Café. I'd been to the café before. After Arun told me the destination, I skipped breakfast in anticipation of a divine airport meal.

My expectations were well met.

At the cashier's counter, I peeled off a generous tip, which earned me a sweet smile from the girl who made my change.

"You have a great day and a wonderful flight, now," she said.

"And you take the rest of the day off. Tell 'em I said it was okay."

She laughed. "I wish!"

I gave her a parting smile and then stopped. A small display on the counter caught my eye. A glass pickle jar held wrinkled singles and a layer of change. A hand-made card, lettered in a rainbow of colors read:

FOR ANGELINE.
HELP HER WIN HER FIGHT AGAINST LEUKEMIA.

A photo taped below the card showed a thin young woman standing on the stoop of a plain-looking home. Two small boys leaned against her legs and stared at the camera with expressions that said, *I AM smiling!*

Their mother wore a brave, cheerful face beneath a bright silk kerchief tightly wound around her head. Her smile beamed light and warmth, but the shallow depressions in her cheeks and the prominence of her facial bones told another story. Thin fingers clutched the two boys as if hoping the moment, like the photo it rendered, could last forever.

"How's she doing?" I pointed.

Sadness flashed in the girl's eyes.

"Angie? Oh, she's hanging in there! She's a fighter. Can you spare a little something for her? We're trying to help with some of her medical bills and maybe something to help take care of her two boys."

"I can," I said, pulling a few singles from my wallet, "but I wonder…do you think you could tell me how to get in touch with her or the family?"

"I don't think we can give out any personal information, but if you want to give me your name and a message, I can see that she gets it."

I shrugged. "It's just that—that plane out there—the one I flew in? It belongs to a charitable foundation. They help a lot of different people with a lot of different things. It's always a lengthy process, though. There's an application and it goes to a committee and blah blah blah—but I might be able to get the ball rolling faster. Does she have an advocate? Maybe a doctor or attorney overseeing things? I'm here for a couple hours and I'd be happy to talk to somebody."

"Millie!" the girl called over her shoulder. "Millie, can you come out here?"

A formidable block of woman with a tight hair bun and a generously stained apron joined the conversation. I noted a family resemblance with the counter girl.

"This fellow wants some information about Angie. He's…um…"

"I'm with a charitable foundation. I saw the card here. It looks like a tough situation."

"It is," the woman said, settling a judgmental gaze on me. "That gal's been through the mill. She went into remission last year, but this year it's not so good."

"It seems to me if anyone could use a little help, she could. I have a few hours to kill. I have some forms with me. I'd just leave them with you, but honestly, it could shave months off the process if I could meet her and get her to apply today. You have no idea."

Millie huffed a sad sigh. "Time is not that poor dear's friend." She took a long look at me. "You got a name?"

"I'm Will." I put out my hand. She wiped hers on the apron and we shook.

"Let me make a phone call, Will."

THE FBO DIDN'T HAVE a crew car, but they offered rentals. I pulled out a credit card. The young man behind the counter looked like he had better things to do.

"How long do you need it for?" he asked.

"About an hour."

"Tell you what. Just take it. If you keep the car, I get to keep your airplane." He slid a set of keys across the glass counter. "It's not worth the paperwork. Just put some gas in it when you're done. It's the red Camry in the second space from the end."

"Thanks!"

I ducked out of the office with my flight bag in hand and a slip of paper containing an address in my shirt pocket. Behind the rental's steering wheel, I took a moment to pull my iPad and map out the directions to the address I'd been given. Millie had spoken to someone who said they would meet me.

The drive took me into Brainerd, a town with broad streets and well-spaced older homes matching the plain construction of the home in the pickle jar photo. I found my way through town on Washington Avenue and turned left onto a placid, tree-lined 4th Avenue. The blue line on the iPad took me past an elementary school into a neighborhood of small, square cottages. Awnings from the 1950s hung over doors and windows. The yards were neat, the gardens simple.

The house number I hunted for stood in black wrought-iron relief on white siding. A severe-looking old man sat on the stoop. He wore a white t-shirt and cobalt blue work pants. He had thin strands of hair the color of iron swept back on a largely bald head and held in place with shiny grease. He watched me pull up and step out of the car.

"You Will?" he asked before I could close the door.

"I am. Are you Mister—" I glanced at the note "—Landry?"

"That's my daughter's married name." He didn't seem inclined to give his name and I didn't press. He looked at me with a mix of weariness and suspicion.

"I don't mean to interrupt anything."

"Nothing here to interrupt. Same old same old." He stood and took a step toward me. The step looked like it caused pain. "Millie said you needed something signed."

"Is your daughter here?"

"She's resting. I can sign whatever papers you have. I have her power of attorney."

"That won't be necessary. I just needed to verify some information. The address. Correct spellings. Is this where your daughter lives? Here with you?" I read the address and opened my iPad to take notes on the ForeFlight scratchpad.

"This is where she lives. With me." I caught the warning and made a note. "What kinda help are we talking about here?"

"We have several different programs. Assistance with medical costs. Assistance with living expenses. Help with the children's education. Help with treatment programs."

He drove a steady stare into me. I felt the kind of flutter that awakens when the edges of a lie begin to fray.

"She's done with treatment now."

"Is she doing better?" The look on his face made me wish I hadn't asked.

"No. She's just done with treatment. It was too much, too painful. She knows it won't do any good and it only runs up the bills—not that it matters anymore. Those bills won't be paid in either of our lifetimes. I 'spose you're gonna tell me that you don't shell out money for lost causes."

"No sir."

The awkward silence that fell between us softened his expression slightly.

"Well, then, if there's anything you can do, it will be appreciated."

"Sir, are you sure I can't see her? Just for a minute?"

He shook his head. "My daughter was a pretty girl. And proud. She—she doesn't like to be seen the way she is now. I tell her—" His voice hitched. His faded eyes glittered. "I tell her she'll always—"

He stopped. Gathered himself. Nodded twice.

"I think I have everything I need. Thank you for your time."

He turned and climbed the stoop, then disappeared inside.

Shit.

I parked the Camry around the corner and checked the homes lining the street. No gardeners. No one mowed their lawn. I tucked a power unit and prop into my shirt and waited for a car to pass. I took one more look around.

Don't fly angry.

I couldn't help it. I didn't like lying. I didn't like having to skulk around. I didn't like feeling helpless or bumping into the limits imposed on the help I could provide.

I didn't like being told by Lillian that I should take what I can do and bury it.

Fwooomp!

I vanished and popped the car door open. Clear of the door, I realized I couldn't swing it closed. Floating next to the car gave me no leverage. I checked the street again. Seeing no one, I reappeared long enough to slam and lock the door, then vanish again. I pulled out the power unit, added power and surged over the roof of the car and across a lawn. I angled right and cruised a few feet above the grass across two yards to the former Landry home.

My first move took me to the front door. It was a warm day, suitable for leaving a front door open with a screen door to welcome a fresh breeze.

No such luck. The closed door and locked knob forbid entry.

Plan B. Check the back door. After that, maybe the old Ring the Doorbell trick. I backed away and eased the power unit into a low growl that pulled me off the front stoop and over a short concrete driveway that ended at a slightly sagging garage. My path took me around the small rectangle of house.

I killed the power abruptly when I saw them. The old man sat in a white plastic lawn chair with a hardcover book on his lap and a mug of coffee on a matching white plastic lawn table.

Angeline Landry lay on a folding lawn chair. Despite the warmth, a patchwork quilt covered her legs. Another enveloped her shoulders. The chair had been angled to face the midmorning sun. She wore nothing on her head, which glowed like a pale mushroom.

I drifted. The yard lay silent, forcing me to slow myself with a bare minimum of power. Most of the small lawn passed beneath me before I halted short of a low fence at the back of the property. I turned around and eased back toward her.

She was pretty, despite the way disease had drained health and life from her skin. She had fine features, a movie starlet's nose, and large child-like eyes, which gazed at the blue sky. She wore the inverse of her father's bitterness and resignation, a veneer of peace and expectation.

She was also farther gone than children I'd seen at night in hospital rooms. And older. Well into her twenties, if I had to guess.

I had no idea if this would work—not that I ever had any assurances. Making matters worse, she had a witness within touching distance. I wondered if I could draw him away. Would he hear the doorbell if I rang it?

Why does this have to be so hard?

I aimed for her chair. The glide across the lawn took forever, hindered by a light breeze. When the old man looked up from his book, I cut the humming power completely.

He looked around. Lacking a satisfactory explanation for the sound, he returned his attention to his book.

I had just settled on simply grabbing the girl by her fragile-looking hands when she turned her head and spoke.

"Daddy?"

"Mmmm?"

"Would you bring me some water?"

Yes!

The old man stood up, marked his page with a bookmark, and limped toward the house without a word.

I was committed to a collision with Angeline. I had no choice. I goosed the power unit to stop. The prop buzzed and the old man turned. He looked around the yard. After a moment he huffed and resumed his trek. The back-door screen slammed behind him. I drifted closer.

Fwooomp!

I dropped to the grass within arm's reach of the young woman and jammed the power unit into the back pocket of my jeans.

She startled and jerked against the lawn chair.

"Hi!" I said, smiling as brightly as I could. I leaned over and grabbed her hands.

FWOOOMP! I pushed it hard and we both vanished. She pulled to free herself, but I held on, trying not to squeeze fine bones.

She gasped. A desperate sound grew in her throat, rising and eventually escaping as a thin, hitching moan. She pulled and twisted but her arms lacked strength.

How long? I wondered. I have no idea. Logic suggests that holding someone in the vanished state longer should be more effective. She struggled and kicked and that was not good. Her kicks sent us upward. Her quilt, which had vanished with us, fell away and snapped into view.

"Shhhhhhh!" I realized immediately how sinister that sounded.

She yanked her hands trying to free them, which had the effect of shooting us back and forth toward each other like swing dancers.

Eight inches and climbing.

Too much higher and I would have to come up with a way to get her back down again. I didn't want to let go of one hand to try and use the power unit, so I decided to end it. I released both hands and felt the electric snap that crosses my skin when I let something go.

She popped back into view about twelve inches above the thin plastic straps of the lawn chair. Wide-eyed and flailing, she dropped, hit the chair and tore through faded old straps, sagging comically so that her butt touched the grass below. She screamed.

The screen door slammed open. Her father staggered forward, sloshing water from a glass he had drawn. He stopped beside her and watched her kick at the quilts and fight the aluminum frame.

"What in Heaven's name did you do?"

I didn't stick around for her answer.

11

The police waited for us when we landed. I saw them from a thousand feet up as I eased the Navajo into the downwind leg of the traffic pattern. Three vehicles arrayed on the ramp in front of the Essex County Air Service hangar winked blue and red lights against long shadows and dusk. I said nothing to Sandy and Arun. She stared into a paperback. He shuffled papers and reports, as he often did until we rolled to a stop.

I greased the landing as if I had an audience—which I did. My mind raced through possible reasons for the reception.

Angeline described me to her father.

Angeline's father connected me to Millie. *That guy you sent here attacked Angeline.*

Millie remembered the airplane. *He said his name was Will.*

The kid at the FBO counter matched me up to the airplane. *Look up the N-number officer!*

Brainerd police called Essex PD. *We're looking for a Will Stewart...*

Shit! Shit! Shit!

I let the airplane roll out on Runway 31, saving the brakes and taking the last taxiway. All doubt disappeared. They waited for me. In addition to the three marked units, two unmarked units and Andy's car sat on the ramp. Men in uniform, men in suits and one strikingly attractive woman watched me hang a left and pull up in front of the Foundation hangar.

I wondered if it would be Andy putting on the handcuffs. *"Will Stewart, my darling idiot husband, you're under arrest for assault."*

My mouth went dry.

"Um, Will, do you have any idea what's going on?" Sandy asked from the cabin after I pulled the mixture controls and killed the engines.

"Your guess is as good as mine," I replied as innocently as possible. I ran through the shutdown checklist and then heaved myself out of the pilot's seat. I squeezed past Arun and Sandy and opened the airstair door. They followed me down the steps.

Andy led the way across the ramp. She looked grim. The chief, towering over her, walked two steps back. He led a troop of men wearing suits and the look of professional law enforcement. Andy's eyes met mine. I expected her to speak first, but she deferred to one of the crew-cut men in a suit.

"Sandra Stone?" he asked. "We need you to come with us."

Andy hurried forward to clasp Sandy's arm. "It's okay. They're with the FBI."

PART II

12

"Dee, what the hell?"
 I rode shotgun in her car. She drove in a tight line of police vehicles led by the chief's marked SUV. The chief ran with emergency lights but no siren. Sandy and Arun rode in the back of an unmarked car ahead of us with two members of the FBI and a plain-clothed officer from the state DCI office. The second unmarked unit tailgated Andy followed by two trailing Essex PD squad cars.

"I don't know if I have time to explain, Will. We have to get Sandy to the station and into protective custody."

"Is this about Johns?"

She issued a choppy laugh. "Amazingly, no. It's worse. Far worse."

She focused on driving. The gap between us and the car ahead was less than twenty feet, yet our speed approached fifty miles per hour. We blew through a red light on Main Street. A sheriff's squad had stopped traffic on the cross street.

"Is this about our trip today? About Brainerd?"

"What?"

"I might have done something up there you won't like."

"What?" I should have kept my mouth shut.

"I'll tell you all about it later. Jesus, Dee—the FBI? What is all this?"

The radio interrupted. Dispatch asked the Chief for his ETA to the station. He gave his answer in minutes and seconds.

"There's been a killing—multiple killings," Andy said.

"Here? In Essex?"

Andy slammed on the brakes, following suit for the car ahead. How the bumpers managed not to kiss, I couldn't guess. I braced against the dash.

"No," she said. The entire line accelerated again. "Did you see any news today?"

The question seemed odd to me. We don't watch much news. Andy has a low tolerance for stories that are wrong and journalists who speculate.

"Nothing."

"Hang on."

Andy wheeled sharply left in tight formation. The Essex Police Department building appeared ahead. The street had a carnival appearance. Brightly colored television remote trucks with satellite dishes lined the curb in front of the building. City of Essex barricades—moved aside for the motorcade—blocked the street at both ends.

Andy took another left, barely slowing, into the city maintenance garage driveway. Like a serpent, the line of cars shot past the maintenance building, following the asphalt to the back of the building, then past the city gas pumps and oil recycling station. The driveway joined the rear of the police building. Rolling onto the back lot, I felt the sharp pang that comes each time I see the spot where Officer Mike Mackiejewski chose to end his life.

The moment evaporated. The caravan broke formation. The chief rolled into his reserved spot at the back of the building. The unmarked unit carrying Arun and Sandy disappeared into the sally port. The marked units split off like a flight of fighters. Andy pulled up next to the chief.

The brake lights on the FBI's unmarked car glowed red until the big sally port door closed.

"Stay with me," Andy said.

She hustled to catch up to the chief who moves on long legs and often forgets that his stride makes him faster than everyone around him. I hurried after my wife. We entered the side door to the sally port.

"My office!" Tom Ceeves called out to anyone listening as he stomped past the unmarked car. Arun's face was ashen. Sandy looked at Andy for an explanation. Andy hurried to her side and took her arm.

"Come with me," she said with as much reassurance as she could muster. "You too, Will."

We assembled in the chief's office. Arun and Sandy took the two occasional chairs facing Tom's big desk. Two suits from the FBI and one from the state DCI, along with Andy and me, stood.

Tom dropped into his oversized chair. It groaned under his weight.

"Tom, what on earth is all this?" Sandy asked.

Tom leaned forward and planted his elbows on his desk. He rubbed his huge hands up and down his face for a moment.

"Sandy Stone, Arun Dewar, this is Special Agent Mike Janos and Special Agent Leon Weldt from the Federal Bureau of Investigation." He pointed. Janos had a runner's body and crew cut hair. Weldt, pushing sixty, hadn't seen the inside of gym recently, if ever. Physically they were night and day. "That's Captain Lonnie Podolsky from the state department of criminal investigation."

"Ms. Stone. Mr. Dewar." Podolsky nodded to each.

"This is my husband, Will Stewart," Andy added. "He works for Ms. Stone and the Education Foundation as their pilot."

"He can probably go," Janos said.

"I'd rather he stayed," Andy replied. "Tom?"

The chief nodded. His deep voice dominated the room. "Sandy, I'm gonna start this off by saying no one in this room believes that what is happening is because of you or the Foundation or the work you've been doing."

"We can't be sure of that," Janos interrupted.

"The fuck we can't," Tom said calmly.

"What's happening?" Sandy asked. Tom looked up at Janos. All eyes followed.

He had been leaning against a bookshelf. He drew himself erect.

"Ms. Stone, did you see a news item out of Michigan a few days ago. A family of five was killed. Did you see any of the reports on that?"

"I did!" Arun volunteered. "It was on all the channels!"

"Miss Stone?"

Sandy shook her head. "I don't watch the news. And I don't follow social media. Sorry."

"Not a bad policy," the chief grumbled.

Janos cleared his throat. "I'll fill in the blanks."

"Leave out the damn details, please," Tom warned.

It surprised me to see Janos nod. "Last week—the time of death is not certain—a family of five on a farm near Pellston, Michigan was killed. It appears to be the work of an outsider. The family—by the name of Pedrosky—was not found for several days. As the chief requested, I'll spare you the details. What wasn't reported was that authorities connected the crime to a similar crime two weeks ago in West Virginia. Another family—the McConnell family. A remote farm. The crime went undetected for several days."

"That's horrible."

"It is. No doubt about it. There's now been a third incident. Here. In Wisconsin, north of Baraboo. Six people—the Williston family. Found this morning. Another farm. Also connected."

"Connected, how?" I asked.

"We—and the whole world, I'm afraid—now have reason to believe that all three crimes were committed by the same person or persons."

"The whole world?" Sandy asked.

"That goddamn circus out in front," Tom growled.

"At each scene, a message was left proving to the authorities that these three crimes are connected. The latest included a promise that these killings will continue until a payment of ten thousand bitcoins is made." Janos paused and looked directly at Sandy. "By you."

"Not you personally," Tom corrected him. "By the foundation that you operate."

"Ten thousand?" Arun asked. "My God! That's over a hundred million dollars!"

"Which, if I'm not mistaken, equals the current resources of your foundation, is that correct?" Janos asked.

"Not quite, but why?" Arun asked. "Who are these people?"

"If we knew that, we'd have them hanging by the balls right now," Tom said.

"We don't know," Janos said. "We were hoping you could help us."

"I don't have any idea!" Sandy looked at Andy. "I honestly can't begin to guess."

"It's not exactly a secret that the Foundation has money," Andy offered. "Someone could be simply picking them out as a target."

"Or someone is pissed off about something," Podolsky said. "We need to see your records. Every transaction. Every application. Anybody that's been turned down. Anybody that's applied or even inquired. Top to bottom."

"Of course," Sandy agreed. "Arun and I will open all our books and records for you."

Janos folded his hands like an undertaker. "A copy of the most recent message was sent to the media. They have this story and are running it. Part of the message included pictures taken by the killers at each crime scene. The media has them as well. Most of the news organizations are reputable and have agreed to withhold the photos. A few aren't. Some of the pictures are out on the internet and spreading like wildfire. DOJ is working with the big search engines to kill them, but it's like playing Whack-A-Mole."

"I think I already know the answer to this, but how out of control is the media coverage?" I asked.

"I've never seen worse. Not OJ. Not Epstein. That's part of why you got the reception you did today. This broke a couple hours ago. We couldn't take the chance that someone else tracked your flight. We couldn't risk you being pummeled by the press and every nutball out there. Your life is about to become…difficult, Ms. Stone."

"Again," Sandy said softly. Andy stepped up and put her hand on Sandy's shoulder. Sandy clasped it tightly.

"You should also understand that every law enforcement agency in this country is making this a priority," Janos added. "This thing has hit three states. It has no borders."

"I can't believe this is happening," Sandy said thinly. "How many?"

"Excuse me?" Janos asked.

"How many people have been killed?"

"Sandy," Tom said, "you can't go there. This is extortion. Straight up. It could have been sent to Bank of America or Bill Gates or Amazon or anybody."

She said nothing.

"This is getting the full court press. The Bureau is one hundred percent on top of this. Every field office has cleared the deck. Dozens of agencies have joined in. ATF. DEA. The Marshals. You name it. NSA and CIA may not be legislated for this, but don't think they're unaware, and if they have anything to share, they will share it. We're not ruling out foreign bad actors."

"Is she in any danger?" I asked. Arun threw me a startled look.

"She's the one they want to write the check. It's unlikely they would target her. And by going public, the perpetrators know we're throwing a wall up around her."

"Why Bitcoin?" I wanted to know.

"That's easy," Arun answered. "It's untraceable. It's the currency of kidnappers and pirates. It's secret and transferrable."

"If the payment is made, will they stop?" Sandy asked.

"Why should they?" Janos answered. His matter-of-fact tone chilled me.

13

Even Andy admitted to awe over the scope of the response to what had been dubbed the Farm Family Murders. The FBI brought a dozen field agents to Essex. Another dozen descended on Baraboo and surrounding Sauk County. Combined with state troopers and county deputies, the law enforcement teams fanned out canvassing neighbors, residents and businesses. Teams interviewed transport companies that may have had commercial vehicles moving over the roads near the scene of the Williston family murder. Vast collections of home, business and highway video were gathered. Tip lines were established and manned. FBI servers accepted downloaded photos and video from the public. Thousands of images poured in.

The Wisconsin victims were a husband, wife, three children and a father-in-law from a farm family that owned and operated a significant dairy operation not far from the town famous for its circus museum.

"Why farms?" I asked as Andy drove us north on Sunset Circle Road when we finally left the station well after sunset. Our headlights swept back and forth across the curves in the road. I watched the ditches more than the road. A large deer population occupies the undeveloped tracts of the Lakes Region of Essex County. "This guy hates farming?"

"It might have something to do with farming. It might not."

"What does that mean?"

"Someone wants a payday. A kidnapper holds a victim for ransom. It's not out of animosity for the individual. It's about the payday."

"Still, why farms?"

"Something you taught me," she said. "When I'm upset but I go off about something unrelated. You tell me, 'The problem is not the problem.' This looks like a crime against farmers, or farm families. It may not be. It may be that they've selected a crime they can commit that is high profile yet low risk. They could commit a mass shooting, but that has low odds of escape or survival. They could try bombing public places, but that leaves evidence and requires material that is too easy to trace. Hitting family farms, what do you have?"

"Seclusion."

"Sound proofing."

"Minimal potential for witnesses."

"Utterly innocent victims."

"Patriotic Americans."

"Trust."

"Trust?" I asked.

"Sure. We know they traveled to the farm. The farms that have been hit are remote, but not in the sense of a remote cabin. They're out in the country. You can't take a bus or the subway. That means motor vehicle. A car. Truck. Something. A vehicle drives into the farmer's driveway and pulls up to the house. What kind of vehicle does that and doesn't raise alarm bells?"

"Just about anything. I worked on a farm."

"See? But you have parameters before and after the crime. Before, you need something that can arrive without making the farmer grab his shotgun. *After* you have a new set of rules thanks to video and potential witnesses. Whoever is doing this has to know that we'll pull every image we can find— satellite if we can get it—to see what was on the road the day of the crime, or in the farmer's driveway if we get lucky."

"A fake police car would do the trick."

"Yes, for the first part, but No for the second. A marked police car will be checked against patrol logs, duty assignments, motor pool logs, tracking databases. Suddenly you have something that stands out. And sooner or later it's going to show up on a camera. Which means we'll get a look at the driver. Try again."

I would have, but Andy braked suddenly as we rounded a curve and met the back end of a line of stopped vehicles.

"Tom set this up," Andy said.

At the head of the line a pair of county squad cars parked at an angle across the narrow road, staggered so that drivers had to snake their way through after clearing the checkpoint. One or two vehicles did Y-turns to return the way they came.

"How much of the county are they quarantining?"

"Just this side of Leander Lake," Andy replied. "Where Sandy lives."

"Oh, Lydia has got to love this."

Andy chuckled at the idea of her sister negotiating police roadblocks to get to and from her lakeside home. Lydia lived two mailboxes away from the Stone property. "Actually, she probably does. She has told me more than once she feels a little isolated living in that big house with just the girls, Melanie and the two babies." Melanie, the nanny, delivered a baby boy just two weeks after Lydia delivered her third daughter. I pitied the poor kid, swamped in estrogen. My nieces confirmed my worries, virtually ignoring their new baby sister in favor of the novelty of a male child.

We waited patiently, advancing one car length at a time until reaching the barrier. A deputy aimed his flashlight at Andy, who had her window down and her badge and ID ready. I could tell by the grin on his face she needed neither.

"Hey, Andy!" the moustache-wearing deputy strolled to the window. He pointed the flashlight beam at my face, then swept the back seat.

"Hi, Mark," Andy said. "Been out here long?"

"Got the scramble in the middle of dinner. Couple hours. We just had a carload of feds and Senator Stone's daughter come through. Is that where you're headed?"

"Affirmative. She gets a protection detail until this is sorted out."

"Goddamn grim business," he said. "But holy shit on that Johns arrest, Andy!"

"All in a day's."

"Who's this?" He pointed the beam at me again.

"I'm Mister Detective Andrea Stewart." I waved.

"My husband. I'm still running background on him, but I think he's okay to pass through."

"You're a lucky man, sir!" he said, stepping back from the car.

"That's what she tells me," I replied.

He waved us through.

14

"Senator Keller," Andy said crisply, extending a handshake. "It's very nice to see you again."

The woman who met us at the front door of Sandy Stone's steroidal cape cod home brushed past Andy's outstretched hand. Perfectly coiffed and decked out in a designer suit, State Senator Lorna Keller pulled Sandy into a hug. Keller had been chief of staff for Sandy's father when he served in the state legislature. She accepted an appointment to replace him after his murder. As his long-time chief of staff, she had been family to Sandy and a fixture in the Stone residence.

I wasn't surprised to see her in Sandy's foyer.

"Andrea! Mmmm!" she squeezed my wife. "I am honestly relieved that you're here to help take care of Sandra!"

I did not like Keller and never had. Not that she'd ever done anything to me or Andy or done anything wrong that I could put a finger on. She simply rubbed me the wrong way. The characteristics that chafed me probably made her a great chief of staff, and an even greater state senator. I thought her a little too fast to analyze a conversation and dismiss the parts that didn't advance her point of view or agenda. A little too glib. I don't know. Just not my type, but then she would probably say the same of me.

"And Will! Nice to see you!" I got the handshake.

"Nice to see you, Senator." Before the words cleared my lips, Keller whirled and hooked Andy by the arm.

"Come! Let's see to our girl!" They set off toward the oversized, overly modern kitchen. A state trooper on guard duty near the front door looked at me with a smirk. I ignored him and fell in behind the women.

Sandy sat on a stool at one of the granite countertops. She wrapped her fingers around a coffee mug, as if to keep them warm. She looked pale and tired. It had been a long day even before the mountain of shit hit the galactic fan.

Andy slipped Keller's grip and gave Sandy's shoulder a squeeze, then sat down beside her.

"Will, I'm sorry you were dragged up here," Sandy said. "You must be exhausted. Really, Andy, I'm fine. You two should go home."

"What about Arun?" I asked. "Did they let him go without a cavity search?"

"They did, but he insisted on staying with me. He's in the study." She reached across the counter and grabbed a bottle of single malt whiskey. She deftly opened it and poured a healthy slug into her mug. She held it up in offering. "It's from my dad's collection."

"Pass," Andy said.

I waved it off.

Keller pulled a mug from the cabinet and poured for herself. She sat down on the stool beside Sandy, opposite Andy.

"You shouldn't have stayed," Andy said softly to her friend. "You didn't need to hear all that."

Janos's extended briefing had been terse and without sensational details. I didn't know if he withheld the gruesome parts out of courtesy for Sandy or as a matter of investigative security. Still, what he'd given had been more than disturbing.

It was estimated that the killer or killers spent up to ten hours at the farm near Parkersburg, West Virginia. There were signs of torture. Signs that the killers felt at ease and in no hurry. A cheap hardware store paintbrush with the price tag still attached had been used to stroke a large Roman Numeral I in blood above the bodies, which were arranged in a family tableau.

The killers took even longer in Michigan. Another family of five. The youngest had been a toddler.

In Baraboo, it had been similar, but this time all six were found in the watery bottom of an unused concrete silo. A high-quality archery set used for hunting—also belonging to the victims—appeared to be the murder weapon.

From these details the FBI and others concluded that there were at least two, and possibly three perpetrators. They determined that the perpetrators had significant body strength, used clothing or plastic to guard against leaving hair or skin evidence, had a knowledge of weapons, and employed a high degree of sadism.

At each scene, Roman numerals painted in blood indicated the sequence of the crimes. A large pool of blood outside the silo in Baraboo suggested that one of the victims had been bled before being thrown in, providing paint for the cheap brush that stroked a "III" on the concrete.

At the third crime scene, the authorities found a phone. Photos had been taken at all three scenes—before, during and after the murders—and left on the phone. The phone was sealed in a Ziploc bag and taped to a rung on the interior ladder of the silo. Janos told all present that no effort had been made to alter metadata on any of the photos. The image dates aligned with the estimated time and date of each crime.

"These people are supremely confident," he told us. "They shot pictures during the crime the way we shoot them after the fact. Our photographers were hardly needed."

In the phone's text app, a message had been found.

ONCE A WEEK UNTIL 10000 BITCOIN IS PAID
BY THE PAULESKY FOUNDATION

A coded sequence followed. Janos explained that it provided instructions for sending the money.

"Then just follow the money!" Tom Ceeves pounded his fist on his desk to make the point.

"You can't. That's how Bitcoin works. It's impossible."

"It's not impossible! Somebody knows! Find the sumbitch who knows!"

Janos didn't bother explaining the nuances of cyber currency to Chief Ceeves because Arun interrupted.

"We don't have that much," he said. "The Foundation doesn't have that much money. Ten thousand bitcoins in today's market is $103,275,000.00. The Foundation gave out over 4 million this summer. Accounting for interest earned, we're at slightly less than 98 million. More than 5 million short if we—"

"Nobody's paying anything," Janos cut him off.

"What if they don't stop?" Sandy demanded. "What if paying *makes* them stop? What if paying saves one more family from being —butchered!"

"And what if it doesn't?" Andy said. "Most blackmailers and extortionists never stop once they've tapped the well. Sandy, our best chance to end this rests in the expertise of the FBI and the scores of law enforcement professionals who are bearing down on this case. Those killers are outnumbered a thousand to one."

I looked for a hint of acquiescence in Sandy's stressed face. I had seen none during the briefing in the Chief's office and found none in her kitchen now.

Sandy's phone vibrated on the counter. She reached for it. Keller scooped it up first.

"Sandra Stone's phone, this is Senator Keller speaking," she announced.

I heard a male voice but could not make out the words.

"What does *he* want here?" Keller demanded. She listened, then turned to Sandy. "Dewey Larmond. Did you send for him?"

Sandy nodded.

"Fine. Send him up."

THE MEETING REMAINED in the kitchen under dim, indirect lighting, preserving the intimate feel even after Dewey Larmond joined the group in a full suit and tie. Larmond moved in choppy bursts befitting his short stature and darting eyes. He had been suggested to Sandy as a financial advisor to the Foundation by Earl Jackson. Larmond and Arun clicked from the first, relieving Sandy of all concerns about the management and disposition of the funds in the Foundation's accounts. Weekly reports were issued, which Arun dissected and Sandy ignored. *Pro forma* questions were asked of Sandy, which she approved without discussion. I marveled at the trust placed in Larmond, which apparently paid off as he found ways for the Foundation's funds to grow almost as fast as Sandy gave them away.

Larmond entered the kitchen and planted a weathered briefcase on the island of granite. "Is there coffee? I was up until all hours at the Planning Commission last night. And the man from DOT never showed up." He shook his head and rolled his eyes, condemning government in general.

Keller, taking charge as hostess, poured from a pot on the counter. The coffee aroma tempted me, but I felt the call of my bed and didn't want to hit the mattress jittering.

Larmond sipped and issued a satisfied, "Ahhhhh…"

Sandy brought Larmond up to speed. If the explosive arrival of a national crime story in his client's lap shocked him, he hid it well—until Sandy got to the part about the money.

"They want the Foundation's entire fund? How do they even know about that?"

"It's been in the paper," Andy said.

"Twice," Sandy added. "When we funded the library expansion and again when we donated to the district's new computer initiative."

The accountant confined his disapproval to a frown.

"Mr. Larmond," Sandy said, "I want to know the practical ramifications of making the payment."

"There isn't enough," he said brusquely. "The accounts are short of what they're asking."

Arun nodded energetically.

"I'm aware. But do you remember our discussion from last May? About the north end property?"

"I do," Larmond said. "But the lease prohibits any sale of that property. And Miss Stone, I recall your comments about what that property meant to your father. You said he would never sell it. That you would never sell it."

"Circumstances have changed."

"Sandy, you're not thinking of paying, are you?" Andy asked.

"I don't know what I'm thinking. Except that if this happens again because I failed to act to stop it—" She gave a weak shrug. "How could I live with that?"

"This is not a discussion that should take place under such exigent circumstances, Miss Stone," Larmond gestured at the whiskey on the counter, "or late at night or under the influence."

"No," Sandy said, "but I need to know every possible option, Mr. Larmond."

He gave a long, slow rendition of the shrug-gesture all accountants use to say, *Yes, but you're wrong and now you're wasting my time by making me find a way to tell you.*

"Understood, understood. To the question you asked, I do recall our discussion from May—"

"What discussion?" Andy asked.

Larmond deferred to Sandy.

"There's a standing offer for a property my father owned at the north end of the lake. Several hundred acres of farmland on the north and east sides of Sunset Circle and a section of the waterfront. I have a buyer who has guaranteed ten million for all of it."

"A very motivated buyer," Larmond added. "He has upped the offer twice."

"This is not the time to be making decisions like that, Sandy," I said.

"What? I'm too emotional? You were there, Will. Don't tell me that what the FBI told us didn't stab you in the heart."

"If I may," Larmond interjected, "there are other issues. There is a significant standing lease in play for the waterfront portion, which accounts for at least a third of the value."

"Then we cut that portion out. There should still be enough."

"No. The buyer has been specific. All or nothing. I'm afraid the buyer would never agree to a segregated parcel—and certainly not to excluding the waterfront. The farmland and wooded acreage offer no access to the lake. And there's not enough income from the farmers renting those acres to provide a return on the investment."

"Who's the buyer and what do they want with all that?" I asked.

"The buyer is anonymous. Which is understandable. Some people fear that if their name gets bandied about, prices go up. Regardless, Miss Stone, you're bound by the lease in place for—I believe—three more years on the key parcel. You can't sell it."

Sandy twisted in her seat. She reached across the kitchen island to a portfolio sitting on the granite. From it, she extracted a sheaf of legal documents. She slid them across the smooth surface to Larmond.

"Yes, I can."

I glanced at Andy. Her attention darted between the paper and Larmond, who picked it up and read.

He took his time. At a passage marked with a Post-It note, Larmond peeled away the yellow tab and read every word.

He looked up at Sandy.

"This could be open to interpretation."

"I doubt it very much." Sandy turned to Andy. "I know it's an active investigation, but the news reported that Clayton Johns was arrested for providing alcohol to minors. I know you can't tell me the details, but is that all there is to the story? Or is there more?"

"Oh, lord," Andy blew out a long breath, "that man is in very deep trouble."

"Can he get out of it?" Sandy asked.

"No. Never."

"Then it's all right there, Mr. Larmond," Sandy said. "He has violated the terms of the lease. The property is mine to sell."

"Would you excuse us?" Andy spun on her stool, dropped to her feet and took my hand. "We'll be right back."

15

Andy closed the French door behind us. She glanced over her shoulder at the empty living room, then pulled me across a wide deck to the far edge overlooking a boathouse and dock. The evening's warm air whispered through the trees. Leander Lake glittered beneath a clear, star-dotted sky. I automatically looked to my right, to the north, at the Johns property that anchored the north end of the long lake.

A perfect spot for a hotel.

Andy gripped the wooden railing. "Give me a minute," she said. She pulled and pushed air through her lungs. She brought her hands up and held her face and pressed on her eyes After a moment, she dropped them and asked, "Do you think it's even possible?"

"Which part? And before you answer, in my experience, tired people are way too vulnerable to conspiracy theories after dark."

"You know how I feel about coincidence. How likely is it that the demand from these killers manages to just barely exceed Sandy's resources —unless she sells a property to an unknown buyer—and that property can't be sold unless the person who signed the lease violates some sort of morality clause—which he did *beyond a shadow of a doubt less than 24 hours ago!*"

"Uh-huh. But step back, Dee. Is that really a chain leading to a result, or a chain constructed from the result?"

"Evidence shaped to the crime? I don't know."

"It's highly unlikely that the feds will allow her to pay the ransom. They want to trap the bastards."

"Will, this isn't like dropping a gym bag full of Benjamins in a trash barrel at the park! There's no dye pack or tracking chip on a hundred million in bitcoins."

"Don't sell the FBI and their brethren at the NSA short. I'm sure they have the wherewithal to track bitcoins. They just don't want the world to know it."

"No. They don't. That's partly why they don't want her to pay."

Andy dug her elegant fingers deep into the auburn layers of her hair. She squeezed her eyes shut. I wanted to pull her close, but this was not an emotional moment. This was a police moment.

"We have another big problem," Andy said just above a whisper. "Not a Sandy problem. A Will and Andy problem."

"Which is?"

"How far do you think Bargo Litton would go to get his hundred million back?"

"No," I said. "No, no, no, no."

"Will—!"

"The guy's a shit, Dee, but murdering families? Children?" I realized the error as soon as I said it. "Er—more children? If he wanted his money back, he'd send an army of lawyers."

She shook her head slowly. "Not for this. Not after it was made public that he 'generously' donated the money. What? He's going to change his story and claim it was done at gunpoint? By Sandy? Because there's no way he knows it was you. That much I'll accept on faith."

"Unless Donaldson said something."

"He didn't. He even agreed it wasn't us. But what if this whole thing is Litton making a play for his money in a truly heinous way? We need to talk to him. *You* need to talk to him. Again. The way you did before."

"Jesus, Dee! This is *so* not you!" I remembered the gut-wrenching fear I felt that I'd lost her because of what I unilaterally did to Litton the first time.

She stepped back and her posture stiffened. "Really? What the hell did you expect? Finding you broken in a hospital bed is not me! Learning that you blasted Lane out of a burning building is not me! This *other thing* wasn't listed in the wedding vows, Will! I've had to learn to roll with it, and if you think that's been easy—!"

I started to speak but she shot a hand up between us.

"I don't even want to know what you did up in Brainerd!"

I had hoped she'd forgotten my mentioning it.

"Look, this isn't the time or place to discuss my feelings. I can only deal with the facts. Those facts point to someone wanting to bust the Foundation and Sandy. You and I are the only ones who know who belongs at the top of that suspect list. Someone with the resources to pay professionals to stage horrific serial killings—and don't tell me Litton doesn't have the black heart to sleep like a baby while doing it!"

She had me there. "Fine. But I can't just go have a chat with the guy. Nobody knows where he is."

Andy turned to face the lake. Even in the dark, I read the set of her jaw, the prominence of her lower lip and the steel in her posture.

"I know someone who does," she said.

16

"I need an airplane."

"You got an airplane," Earl Jackson shot back at me. "A goddamn good airplane."

"The feds have it locked down."

"Talk to your wife."

"I did. And she'll square it eventually. But I need to beat feet now."

Earl tipped his chair back. It screamed at him. He ignored the protest. "Just what manner of cluster fuck was that last night? Did you run a load of heroin in from Mexico?"

"Hell, no. How do you not know—?"

"I know all about it! Aside from being all over the news, I was here when they lit up the ramp last night. How's Sandy holding up?" Earl had been close to Sandy's father. "I'd call her, but I'm not good at that touchy-feely shit."

A good decision. Earl's sympathy bears a strong resemblance to rage.

"I'll pass the word." I sat down in the only other chair in his cramped office. Dave Peterson ushered a gaggle of passengers down the hall for departure on a charter. I pushed the door closed. "The thing is, I need to get to Omaha. Now. But I don't want Andy making a fuss—"

"Because you don't want the *federales* knowing where you're going."

"No," I lied. "Well, maybe a little."

"You're gonna have to thumb it. I got nuthin'. We're booked out. 'Cept for the Baron, but that's in the shop for a hunnerd-hour."

"Let me pull it."

Earl scowled. He let his chair groan for him.

"This is important. It's for Andy."

"Don't use your wife on me, son. If I pull the Baron out of the hunnerd-hour, it knocks the rest of the week out of whack."

I saw the problem. It wasn't Earl. It was Rosemary II. She handles the charter booking schedule like a street performer juggling burning chain saws. Earl fears no man or woman, but he has been known to tread lightly around Rosemary II.

"If I can clear it with Rosemary II, will you let me pull it?"

"It's your funeral. I ain't sending flowers."

I stood up.

"One more question. You know anything about anybody wanting to buy up land around Leander?"

Earl tipped his head back and rubbed a calloused hand on his leathery scalp. "Somebody's always throwing around money up there. Doing the McMansion shuffle. Tearing down one nice house to build a nicer house."

"Nah. Something bigger. A developer?"

He shrugged. "Why?"

"Something Andy asked me to ask you. If you hear anything, give her a call, would you?"

"Happy to."

"I'll have your airplane back here tonight."

He shot a sharp look my way, letting me know the lie didn't fly.

"Like I said, it's your funeral."

"Earl said I could pull the Baron out of the shop," I told Rosemary II. "I need it to go to Omaha. Everything that was on the schedule for the Foundation this week is cancelled, so you can have the Navajo." I said it casually and reached for the manifest board for the Beechcraft Baron.

Rosemary II slapped my hand away. "You are a terrible liar, Will Stewart!"

Lane Franklin's mother replaced the original Rosemary as the all-knowing, all-powerful goddess of the flight schedule at Essex County Air Service. "If you take the Baron out of the shop, it means I can't get it in until Friday. Do you have any idea what that will do to my schedule?" Her dark eyes searched me for an answer I did not dare provide.

The daily flights performed on demand by Earl Jackson's air charter service represented a tightly choreographed ballet of airplanes, pilots, passengers, destinations and weather. None of it moved without Rosemary II's keystrokes in the holy schedule book app on the office computer.

"That's why you can have the Navajo. It's all clear and it's all yours," I promised.

"Then why aren't you taking it? Or would that police car sitting over there in front of the hangar have something to do with it."

"Andy will take care of that. I would wait for her, but..." I held up my wristwatch.

"Oh, my lord, do not ever cheat on your lovely wife, Will. You will never get away with it." She pulled the manifest clip board and attached a set of keys. She handed it over but kept a grip on it when I tried to take it. "Please tell Sandra she is in my thoughts and prayers. I hope this helps."

"I will," I said. "And it might."

I LIKE THE BARON. Compared to the Navajo, it's light and nimble. It goes just as fast and rides like a Mercedes-Benz. After a verbal shelling from Doc in the hangar, I helped him put the cowlings back on and pulled the airplane from the shop. I towed it to the gas pumps and loaded it with all the fuel she would carry. The sky hung blazingly clear, so I finished the preflight and fired up without filing a flight plan. I launched into the blue as a VFR flight, but tuned Chicago Center during a high-speed climb to eight-thousand-five-hundred feet.

Level and locked on autopilot, I programmed a flight route into the Garmin navigation system while I listened to the center frequency. The sector was reasonably quiet, as is often the case in good weather. I waited for an opening and called for a pop-up IFR clearance to Omaha. They came through like champions.

A little over two hours later, I touched the wheels to Runway 30 at Millard Airport, a single runway strip northwest of greater Omaha. I rolled the airplane to the gas pump and shut down. Self-service fuel and a short taxi into a tie-down spot took another twenty minutes. My watch read 10:45 when the Uber picked me up in front of the FBO. My phone showed a missed call from Doug Stephenson.

I called him back.

"Have you heard from Lillian?" I asked.

"Nothing. Which isn't unusual."

"She left without a word."

"Also, not unusual. She's not very happy with you and Andrea, Will."

"No kidding."

"She feels that you do not share her sense of urgency in this matter with Spiro Lewko."

"She's not entirely wrong. I don't know if you've seen the headlines—Andy's been caught up in two major cases within 24 hours. It is almost impossible for her to break away right now."

"I saw. What about you?" I didn't answer right away. "She doesn't think you share her concerns."

"I don't share her ideas about that chunk of debris, if that's what she means. Or charging in after it. You don't think that's what she's doing, do you?"

"If I had to guess, yes. Would that surprise you?"

"Not in the least. Listen, I need to ask you a couple things unrelated to Lillian and Lewko."

"Shoot."

I told Stephenson about Brainerd, and about Angeline Landry. I asked if he would track down her treatment physician. Doug Stephenson is a world-class neurologist and his reputation opens doors. I told him to say that someone from the Foundation asked for his help and would cover his costs. I knew Stephenson's clinical interest would pique when I told him the woman suffered the most advanced case I'd seen, and that she was older by far than any of the children I had caused to vanish.

"On it."

"Next question," I said. "What can you tell me about brain injury?"

"How many days do you have? For the short course?"

"Cliff's Notes for a high-school graduate, please. The subject took a baseball bat to the head—"

"Where?"

"Nebraska."

"No. Where on the head? Frontal lobe? Parietal? Occipital?"

"Where you'd part your hair—near the top of the head."

"Right or left side?"

"Left."

"Did the victim lose consciousness?"

"In a coma for a couple weeks. He had swelling. Numerous surgeries."

"How much damage to the cranium?"

"I don't know. He took a solid hit."

"What's his state now?"

"I don't know. He's FBI. Part of that business Andy had in Nebraska and the whole Pemmick affair. They clamped a lid on him after it happened, and she hasn't been able to see him or talk to him or his caregivers."

"Classic Big Brother. I think I know who you're talking about. I saw the FBI Director on *Meet the Press*. He mentioned an agent cited for bravery."

"Yeah, well, I don't know if they're pinning it on his chest or on his pillow. But I need to talk to this guy, and I need to know what to expect."

"Don't expect much. Without first-hand examination, I can't tell you anything more than brochure bullet points. And make no mistake—every case is unique."

"I get it. Just the basics."

"He will have difficulty understanding language. Speaking. Verbal output. His logic may be impaired. He may not see simple connections—which is not good for someone in his line of work. He could suffer from depression. Anxiety. Perhaps memory loss related to the event…"

I hoped.

"…but he likely has kept firm memory of things he could previously do that he now can't—which contributes to depression and anxiety. He may have decreased control over the right side of his body. The left side of the brain controls the right side of the body. He might have to learn to walk again. Or learn to write, if he was right-handed. He will have difficulty performing basic functions. It's not a pretty picture. Ever."

"Jesus, doc. What's the physical damage—I mean—what exactly breaks up there?"

"Neural connections. Thought and functions of the brain work on electro-chemical pathways. They're not linear. That's why you can sometimes come to the solution of a problem by literally going the long way around. When a path is blocked or broken, the mind takes a detour. When a lot of paths are scrambled and broken, you get everything I just mentioned, and more. The poor fellow might recognize a color and know that he knows the name of the color but the link to the word 'red' is snapped and he gropes around a lot of other words instead. Rhubarb. Reed. Fire engine. Brain injury is bad business. There's a gooey organ in our heads capable of carving an angel out of a block of marble, of inventing flight—or even of doing something that makes you vanish, Will. When it's damaged, it's not like you can stitch it up."

"Right."

"You need to speak to this man? You need something from him?"

"I do."

"Well, go in with low expectations, Will. Very low."

Great.

17

Sacred Heart Rehabilitation Hospital occupied a plain red brick building on Dewey Avenue, not far from the broad campus of the University of Nebraska Medical Center. Special Agent Lee Donaldson had been airlifted for emergency treatment at the University Medical Center after Andy and I rushed him to a small hospital in Norfolk, Nebraska. Donaldson and Andy exposed an attempt by a Russian oligarch to expand Russia's influence on the American political process. Donaldson's work earned himself a fight for his life. Andy's reward was to be cut off from all contact with the case and the injured agent.

My wife doesn't give up easily. Despite the brick wall surrounding Donaldson's condition, Andy was able to get the name of the rehabilitation hospital caring for him.

I asked the Uber driver to let me out a block short of the destination. He made his pitch for a good review and then rolled on his way, leaving me on the tree-lined street. I adopted a steady pace on the sidewalk, the pace of a man on his way to an appointment. My flight bag remained in the airplane, but I wore my summer-weight Air Force flight jacket. The pockets contained three BLASTER units.

I decided not to try talking my way into the facility. The FBI probably didn't have someone on duty, but the staff would certainly be under orders to insulate Special Agent Donaldson from outsiders, press or otherwise.

Better to conduct my visit unseen.

Vanishing on an open street presents problems. I don't worry about casual observers; people will always doubt themselves when they see the impossible. But in an urban environment, I assume I'm on camera.

I turned down an alley between two red brick buildings—the one on my left, the hospital. The walls on either side lacked windows. A boxy white security camera hung on the hospital wall. The alley opened to a parking lot. More building-mounted cameras watched the parking lot. I dismissed the idea of ducking between parked cars.

At the back of the hospital building, a set of steps descended to a metal door below ground level. I looked. No camera.

I dropped down the steps. At the bottom I strolled toward the door, hand out to grasp the knob.

Fwooomp!

I vanished, kicked the concrete below my feet and rose. I pulled a power unit and prop from my pocket, snapped the prop in place, aimed the power unit upward and thumbed the slide.

The power unit growled, then hummed, then whined, pulling me up the brick face of the building. I angled my wrist to the right to veer away from the wall for a better look at my options.

The back of the building featured a loading dock, but I didn't want to have to start my search in some dark storage space.

I considered using a window. A few windows hung open to the summer air, and they had no screens. But the open windows I saw offered entry into rooms and offices which were more than likely occupied and may have closed doors.

I aimed the BLASTER straight up and shot past the roof lip of the four-story building.

The flat roof featured a greenhouse and a garden café. Brightly colored tables spread out in the greenhouse and on an adjoining deck decorated with plants in huge pots. A few staff members relaxed in the sunshine over cups of coffee. Patients, some in wheelchairs, some without, mingled with the staff or sat absorbing warm sunshine. One or two of the patients in wheelchairs leaned to one side or were propped in place by head restraints, their empty eyes fixed on nothing.

The greenhouse connected to a cube of brick structure that I took for a stairwell and elevator.

I spiraled into a flight path over the café deck and through the greenhouse. I had to weave slightly to avoid a woman in scrubs as she walked toward a table with a fresh coffee in hand. The scent tugged at me.

Beyond the greenhouse coffee shop, the elevator and a stairwell appeared as expected. I passed through a propped-open set of doors and floated to the stairwell railing. I looked down. Handrails angled back and forth all the way to the basement.

Perfect.

I pocketed the power unit and pulled myself over the railing, then carefully shoved myself downward in the space between descending flights.

The top floor revealed a hallway with doors on either side. Most stood open, exposing offices. I kept going.

The next floor greeted me as a vast open area bursting with primary colors and plush furniture. A row of pinball machines lined the far wall. A pool table and ping pong table filled spaces adjacent to a bank of windows. Potted plants lent green accents to orange, yellow, blue and brown padded furnishings. Bright paintings in chrome frames lined the walls. I had expected the hospital common area to be a sterile white room with drugged patients shuffling around or playing listless games of checkers.

"You watch too much television," I muttered to myself.

Patients used the space for reading, craft work, therapy sessions or in one corner what looked like a yoga class. Low music filled the space—a tune from a nineties grunge band. No wire on the windows. No Nurse Ratched. Patients wore street clothes. Staff members wore bright variations on scrubs.

I searched for Donaldson. Mid- to late-forties. Drill sergeant haircut (bandaged, I reminded myself). A solid man, physically, despite his injuries. I didn't hold out much hope. I expected to find him confined to a bed.

I pushed down the central spiral of the stairs to the next floor.

Donaldson stood in the hallway staring at me.

Just like that.

A thin bandage circumscribed his head. The wrap stretched across his forehead and above his ears like a headband. His hair had been shaved. Stitches peeked from the top of the headband, black hash marks against pale scalp. He wore a black polo shirt over khaki trousers. His trademarked outfit seemed incomplete without a shoulder holster and forty-caliber Beretta.

Donaldson stood in the center of the hallway, staring directly at me. As often happens when people look in my direction, I quickly and needlessly checked to make sure I could not be seen.

"That's good, now what?" The question came from a young man with medium brown skin and wild spiked black hair that reminded me of a jester's cap. He stood halfway down the hall wearing scrubs the color of a paint factory explosion.

"Fu...ck if I...know," Donaldson fought with the words. My heart sank.

"You had a plan. What was the plan?"

"Fu...cking...plan." Donaldson forced each syllable and squinted at me.

"We always have a plan!" the young man reminded him without a shred of impatience.

Donaldson dropped his gaze to the floor, searching for a clue.

"Fu...cking arrest...your ass." The words came hard, but the kid down the hall smiled cheerfully.

"Damn right! Come and arrest my ass, Mister FBI. But first you gotta execute the plan. We had a plan."

Donaldson snapped the fingers of his left hand. He took two steps forward and lifted his right arm as if it held a suitcase. He maneuvered his hand over the railing that I clutched. I smelled soap—he was that close. He dropped the hand on the metal railing.

"Tag."

"Good! Now come and fucking arrest my ass! Good job!"

In Donaldson's face, I caught the flicker of the hard-edged FBI agent who had dogged Andy into an investigation she never wanted. He turned abruptly and started down the hall toward his tormentor. He showed strength in his stride, but the pace was uneven. He had to concentrate to bring the right foot forward. I noticed his shirt hung a little loose. He'd lost weight.

The therapist walked to meet him. "Time for lunch. Are you dining in or out today?"

"Out." One word. Crisp. Delivered without effort.

"Cafeteria?"

"R...rrrr..." It wouldn't come.

"What does a dog say?" the kid snapped.

"Roof."

"See. It's there. You just gotta find it from a new angle. Who's the greatest baseball player?"

"Roof," Donaldson stopped at the elevator. "That joke...sits."

"Sucks."

"Sucks."

The kid waited and made Donaldson poke the elevator call button. He went for it with his left hand, but the kid grabbed his arm. Donaldson lifted his right arm and aimed his index finger at the button, hitting it awkwardly, like a drunk returning to his room at a convention hotel.

"Bullseye!"

I RETRACED my flight route back to the rooftop greenhouse and found a high corner of the framework. Donaldson and the kid appeared a moment later. Donaldson ordered a tuna salad sandwich and a coffee, black. The kid hung around chatting until his charge told him to fuck off. The kid grinned and slapped Donaldson on the back.

"Find your own way home, FBI," he said cheerfully and headed for the elevator.

Donaldson loaded his tray and carried it to a table out in the open. Coffee slopped onto the unsteady tray enroute.

A small group entered, crowded the counter and placed their order. Some wore scrubs. Some wore civilian clothes. I didn't know if the latter were office staff or visitors, but I gained confidence seeing more than a few people walking around in plain clothes.

I pulled myself out the greenhouse entrance to the elevator area. I veered left around the corner. After checking for cameras and finding none, I lowered myself until my toes touched the floor.

Fwooomp!

I settled onto my feet and walked back into the coffee shop.

Donaldson's tuna salad sandwich woke up my appetite. I ordered the same with cheese and a coffee. While I waited, I watched the FBI agent. He sat at the far end of the open café space with his back to me, his face angled into bright sunlight. Between sips of coffee and bites of sandwich, he leaned back on his chair to enjoy the warmth. He reminded me of Angeline Landry.

My order arrived. I collected it and walked to his table. Without asking, I slid the tray onto the table and dropped into the chair facing him.

He blinked once, then squinted.

"You're..." His mind grappled. His mouth waited, open. "...I know...you."

"You do."

"Andrea."

I wasn't thrilled that my wife's name came easily to his lips.

"Will. I'm Will."

"No shoot."

"Yeah," I agreed. "No shit."

"What are...you...dating..." He tensed. Frustrated. "...*doing*...?"

"Here? Having lunch. We need to talk."

He picked up his coffee and sipped, assessing me.

"It's good to see you. You're doing a hell of a lot better than I expected. I mean it. We were worried. Andy and me. She said to say Hi."

He put on a skeptical expression.

"Okay, I never trusted you and I think you're an ass for almost getting her killed, but—" I pointed at his head, at the bandage, "—you took that hit for her. I owe you for that. Do you remember it?"

"All of it." The answer surprised me. I needed a moment to think.

"Please," I gestured. "Eat. I'm starving." I took a bite. He followed suit. Except for the bandage, and without words to trip over, his sharp eyes and steady stare gave no hint of mental damage.

The sun warmed us. I slipped my jacket off. I finished the sandwich and settled back to enjoy the coffee.

He finished his sandwich and used his left hand to sip his coffee. His right hand lay on his hip, self-consciously relaxed.

"Tele…Confucius," he said to me, then he made a face knowing he had it wrong.

Damn.

"Telekinesis," I said.

"Bottles."

"Yeah." I studied his eyes and tried a lie concerning his memory of the fight that led to his injury. "That was a good trick."

"Bull…bull…" His grip on the coffee tightened and the liquid shivered.

"Shit."

He said nothing.

"Okay. That obviously wasn't Andy. That was me. Behind the bar, flinging those bottles at those guys."

The eyes didn't buy it. For a split second I felt grateful for his struggle with language or else I would have had an argument on my hands.

"It worked," I insisted. "Listen, I'm not supposed to be here. They won't let Andy see you, in case you were wondering. She wanted to, but your boss, Rayburn—"

"Prick."

"No argument from me. He's got a tight lid on you. The case you broke is huge. Are they telling you anything?"

"Fu…king mushroom…lawn."

"Mushroom farm. They're keeping you in the dark and feeding you shit." I smiled.

"I've seen…the…the cartoons…" he shook his head "…the…"

"News? You saw Pemmick?"

He gave an affirmative nod.

"Rayburn may be a prick, but he ran with your investigation and he is kicking butt. The Bureau is riding high again. DOJ has been forced to kiss some pretty righteous Bureau ass. Lots of people think you're a hero."

He shrugged it away, but I caught a glint of pride.

"That's not why I'm here." I leaned an elbow on the table. "I need your help. I need to know where I can find Bargo Litton."

He cocked his head and gave me the squinty eye again.

"Litton's reprising the Howard Hughes act, but if anybody knows where he is—or is likely to be—you do."

The squinty eye held. His head dipped twice.

"So?"

He shook his head.

Dammit.

"I'm not asking for me. I'm asking for Andy. Litton might be the one behind some hideous murders."

He shook his head again.

"Look, I know you're not ready for stand-up comedy, but don't give me this Clint Eastwood silent crap. I really need your help. Andy needs your help."

"I want a...deer."

"A deer?"

He rolled his eyes and struggled.

"A deal?" I asked.

His head dipped again.

"What kind of deal?"

"In."

I sat back and looked at him. He stared without flinching.

"That's not a good idea. I mean, you look good. I expected to find you drooling in a hospital bed. But you have a long way to go."

"I want...out of here."

"You're a big boy. If you want to leave, check yourself out."

"The Bureau...wants me in...prefab...pre—"

"Rehab. With good reason," I said. "Rehab is what you need. They're not wrong."

The head shake grew stronger. "They're putting me...on a—a place—a medicine—dammit! They're—!"

I didn't want to fill in the blank. The end of his career was written all over his face.

"Just tell me where I can find Litton. Then do whatever you want."

"My Bureau...ticket is...poked."

"Punched."

"I leave here...no office." He shrugged. "Sit in a...fucking...department..."

"Apartment."

"...with my thumb up my ass."

"Neural pathways," I said. I pointed at his bandage. "That swing for the fences fucked up your neural pathways. It's all there, but the circuits don't connect. You flick on the bathroom light switch and the garbage disposal fires up, right?"

He nodded. "It's a…birch."

"Bitch. But that's why you have to stay here. To get better. Are you on meds?"

He rolled his eyes.

"You want…Litton. I want in."

"What? No. No, you can't go with me. For lots of reasons."

He shrugged. "Okay." He sipped his coffee and put on a poker face.

"Are you kidding me?"

Nothing.

"This isn't some buddy cop movie. I'm not taking you with me! God dammit!"

"Soup yourself."

I opened my mouth to correct him, but the smug look on his face stopped me.

"You're being a prick. Which, by the way, is what I told Andy up front, just so you know."

He smiled as if I'd just paid him a compliment. I stood up and grabbed my jacket, but he didn't budge.

"You're just going to let me walk away?"

"Up to…you."

A few tables over, the small crowd that arrived ahead of me finished their lunch and bussed their trays. They slipped through the greenhouse and clustered at the elevator leaving Donaldson and me alone on the rooftop deck.

"God dammit!" I sat down. I still had coffee and didn't want to waste it. "Why?"

He shrugged. "Show them I can…do the thing…for pay."

"Work? No offense, but you'd have trouble solving a crossword."

"Soup yourself," he said again.

"Do you even know where Litton is?"

He folded his arms.

"God dammit!" I said. "Fine. I'll take you with me."

He shook his head again. "Not…enough."

"What do you mean, not enough? What else do you want?"

He pointed at me.

"You…telephone…" He waved a hand to erase that. "You…tell."

"Tell you what?"

"Tele...that shit you...bottled."

"Telekinesis? The bottles? In that crappy roadhouse? I told you. It was just a gimmick to distract those guys. A trick." It had been a desperation move in a bad situation. Donaldson saw me throw myself over the roadhouse bar. I thought I popped out of sight without being seen. Now I had doubts. "What did you see? What did you *think you saw?*"

"Everything."

We locked eyes and I decided I would never play poker with this man.

"I can't fucking believe you remember," I muttered.

He pointed at his head and winked. He took a long, slow sip of coffee and waited me out. I took a minute to think it through. Then another. The stone face didn't crack. He knew he had me.

Dammit.

I planted both elbows on the table and leaned toward him. I took a deep breath and said, "That's your price? For telling me where I can find Litton? I tell you some story?"

"No story. The truth."

Crap! Crap! Crap!

Voices argued in my head. Sandy. Stephenson. Lillian. Andy. Each with an opinion. Andy's carried weight.

I told Andy from the start I didn't trust Donaldson. I suspected him of knowing I breached Bargo Litton's security. Even after Andy maneuvered him into admitting he had no such suspicion I didn't trust him. But Andy did. Would she trust him now?

I thought about Sandy. If there was even the slightest chance that Litton engineered the killings of innocents in pursuit of his money...

"Listen," I said. "I'm gonna ask you something and you get one shot at this, okay? One shot. Marine Corps? Right? Before the FBI?"

"Semper fi." He reached for his right hand, guided it to his left sleeve and lifted the sleeve revealing the Globe and Anchor tattoo.

"You took an oath. To be a Marine. Will you take an oath on that oath?"

"Huh?"

"Will you swear something to me on your honor as a Marine? They say once a Marine, always a Marine. Will you swear to me on the oath you took as a Marine?"

The squinty eyes worked me over. He measured me. After deliberation he said, "Yes."

"And if we do this, you'll tell me where to find Litton."

"No."

"What?"

"Take you."
Double dammit.

"Shit," I said. I scanned the rooftop café. We sat alone. "Put your arm on the table." I pushed the trays aside and planted my left elbow as if to invite an arm-wrestling challenge. He matched my move. I clasped his hand. He generated a tight grip. We leaned closer. I drilled an unblinking stare into his eyes. "Swear to me, as a Marine, and on all you hold sacred, that you will *never, ever* tell another living soul what you are about to learn. On your last shred of honor, swear it!"

"I swear."

FWOOOMP!

The cool sensation snapped over me and I felt it extend through my hand onto him. He vanished. I dropped my right hand to the seat of the chair to hang on.

He tightened his grip reflexively but didn't try to pull free.

Silence. I thought for a moment his damaged speech capacity had failed him. Except for the sharp intake of his breath, I heard nothing but the sound of tires on the street below and a hushed breeze through trees that did not reach this rooftop height.

"I'm still here," I said. I squeezed. He squeezed.

Words came rapid-fire, unbroken, unhindered by shattered neural pathways.

"*I, Lee Kenneth Donaldson, do solemnly swear that I will support and defend the Constitution of the United States against all enemies, foreign and domestic; that I will bear true faith and allegiance to the same; that I take this obligation freely, without any mental reservation or purpose of evasion; and that I will faithfully discharge the duties of the office on which I am about to enter. So help me* GOD STEWART—WHAT THE FUCK?!"

"Man, you don't know the half of it."

18

F wooomp!
He dropped into view and onto his seat. He jerked free of my grip. His arm caught the corner of a tray and sent it sailing over the edge of the table.

He squeezed his face into a tight grimace and threw his hands up on both sides of his head as if to prevent it from bursting.

"GOD DAMMIT, IT'S COLD!" he grunted through locked teeth. "Fucking brain freeze!"

He leaned forward until his forehead touched the table. He moaned.

I felt panic rising. *What have I done to him?* I double-checked the empty café to see if anyone in medical garb was nearby to lend assistance. We sat alone.

"MOTHERFAAAA—!" he groaned. His head shot up and he sniffed like a hound on a scent. "What's burning? What's fucking burning? Is that me?!"

"Nothing's burning," I said, although I checked.

"You don't smell that?"

"I don't smell anything."

He sniffed furiously and held the sides of his head. "Christ! Christ almighty! What the fuck did you do to me?!"

"Um…I'm not entirely sure."

He squeezed his eyes shut and dropped his forehead to the table.

"Try to relax," I reached and clasped his shoulder. His muscles were stone. "I think what you're feeling is electrochemical overload."

Not that I had a clue.

He gritted his teeth, groaned and rapped his forehead on the table.

"Hey! Knock it off!" I snapped.

He stopped. His breathing became choppy and rapid. I worried he might hyperventilate. Slowly, he raised his head and leaned back. He released his hands and made fists. His knuckles went white, but after a moment the muscle lock dissipated.

"God dammit, Stewart! Talk to me! Speak. Verbalize. Converse. Descant. Enunciate. Expatiate—"

He stopped and stared at the space just beyond his mouth as if he saw the words spelled out in the air.

"Do you hear that? Do you hear me?"

"Yeah. You're a damned thesaurus," I said.

Bald wonder washed over his face. Then he sniffed again. "Is that coconut?"

Stephenson is going to have a cow.

Donaldson bolted to his feet.

"I need a drink!"

He turned, took a step and fell flat on his face.

19

Getting Donaldson out of the hospital properly would have required lengthy processing, medical examination and an equal measure of paperwork…if he cared. He didn't. After picking himself up off the rooftop deck, he tested his arms and legs and found he still didn't have complete control over his right hemisphere. He limped out of the café. I followed him to the elevator and then to a spartan private room on the second floor. He threw a few items in a gym bag and marched to an elevator that took us to the lobby and out the front door. No one stopped us.

"Where are you parked?"

"Uber." I pulled out my phone and read a text message from Andy.

How is he?

I had no idea how to answer. I ignored the text and lined up a ride.

"I'M NOT DRINKING," I told the bartender. He splashed Scotch in a tumbler for Donaldson as ordered. Donaldson downed it and pushed the glass forward for another.

We used the Uber to get to Barrett's Barleycorn Pub and Grill on Leavenworth, a short and disappointing two block ride for an Uber driver told to take us to the nearest watering hole. The Pub's lunch crowd had thinned. Donaldson went straight for the bar, but after downing his first he picked up the second drink and told the bartender we would take a table. He chose one in the corner and took the chair facing the door.

He cupped the drink between his palms and stared at me.

"Litton," I said.

"Yeah, yeah," he replied, not shifting his gaze.

A young woman broke his staring contest when she arrived with menus. Donaldson flipped his open. "The food in that place had no salt."

"You *do* know where he is, right?"

"Pretty sure."

I plucked the menu from his hands and slapped it down on the table. "Pretty sure?"

"It was you. Doing that—whatever the hell that thing is! That's how you got to Litton."

"This isn't an interrogation. From the sound of things, I did you a favor back there. You owe me. And you swore an oath!"

The waitress reappeared. Donaldson ordered french fries and a side of onion rings. He threw the scotch down his throat and handed her the glass. She strolled out of earshot, but he leaned forward and in a whisper.

"I'll let myself be gutted with a rusty butter knife before I break my oath, Stewart. I'll give you Litton if I can. But you can't sit there and tell me —*JESUS!*—do you hear me? An hour ago, I couldn't dig up the right word for taking a piss! My head feels like it's been flushed with a pitcher of margaritas. WHAT THE FUCK?!"

I held up a hand to calm him.

"Tell me how you did this!" he demanded.

"Well…" I gave him the shortest possible story of my accident and *the other thing*. With each word I took another step into a mine field. Andy wanted Litton, badly, but I wasn't entirely certain she would have paid this price for it.

"And Litton? In the desert?"

"I told you. I'm not admitting anything."

"Can I do it?"

"Do what?"

He tented his fingers, jerked them apart and spread them. *Poof!* "After what you did to me—can I do it, too?"

"Beats me. Try it." He might have, if I could have prevented a grin from slipping into the corners of my mouth.

"Asshole," he muttered. "Okay, it's crazy that you can freakin' disappear. Un-freaking-believable! But what's the deal with my head? You have no idea what I'm feeling! It's like you rinsed my brain with gasoline and pushed me through a wall of fog. The words were there—*always right there!* But I couldn't grab them. And sometimes when I did, as soon as I said it, I knew had it wrong. You can't imagine what that's like!"

"Like an itch you can't scratch?"

"Yeah! What the fuck?"

"Best guess, this *thing* affects the body at a cellular level. It must mess with neural connections. Or fix them. Maybe it's got a giant case of ADHD and can't stand to see a neuron out of line, so it fixes them. Like defragging a hard drive."

"Seriously, if you don't know, don't bullshit me."

"Haven't got a clue. I've got a friend, a neurologist, who is going to want to meet you and poke around your head if you're okay with that. Whatever happened to you, it's something new."

"Does he know about you?"

"Yeah."

"Who else knows?"

"Andy. A few others. You don't need to know."

"Fair enough. Did you know this would happen? That it would…*fix me?*"

"No. I only came for whatever you can give me on Litton."

I remembered what Stephenson told me—how a bad brain injury might prevent Donaldson from making connections. As he sat across from me salting his french fries and onion rings wheels turned behind his eyes.

"Andy, huh?" He jabbed a french fry in his mouth. "Litton. Parks. Seavers in Chicago. Brogan." He had no trouble making connections now.

"Those were Andy all the way."

"Your wife's a helluva cop, granted. But don't bullshit me. You were there—doing—*whatever* this is."

"I get in the way more than I help."

His face lit up. "You lit those Nazi flags on fire! In Lincoln! Sonofabitch!" I didn't know whether to protest or take the victory lap. "And, of course, throwing those bottles. Thanks again for that."

"Listen, don't get hung up on the obvious here. I need to know about Litton. But before that, I also need to know…are you still a cop? FBI?"

He munched an onion ring. They smelled good. I swiped one.

"It's been made officially clear to me that I'm out of the FBI. Medical separation. They wrote up my pension application for me because I couldn't hold a pen. They gave me lip service about requalifying after rehab, but they'll never… '*tuh-tuh-take back…suh-suh-somone*' who can't string together a sentence." He lifted his right arm and laid it on the table. "Or hold a gun. This arm isn't working the way it should."

"You didn't stammer. And you're not having any trouble with sentences now. And that—" I pointed at his arm "—is probably just a physical therapy problem. But if you're behind a badge I'm not saying diddly to you. Andy's up to her eyeballs in FBI agents right now and she hasn't shared her theory about Litton with them either."

"Fair enough," he said. "Right now, I'm off the clock—and probably out entirely. So, what's her theory?"

I pointed at the flatscreen above the bar. The Fox News talking head hovered over the words BRUTAL HEARTLAND KILLINGS in bold type on a blood-red banner. A photo of Sandy Stone—it looked like it had been taken for her wedding announcement—appeared onscreen. The caption read BEAUTIFUL HEIRESS INVOLVED. I wanted to throw something at the screen.

Donaldson asked, "That's Stone?"

"Senator Bob Stone's daughter. It was her foundation that Litton wrote the check to." I explained about the message attached to the killings.

"And you think Litton's looking for payback? Don't you think that's a little obvious? The hundred million he gave to her little foundation has to be public knowledge."

"Nobody knows it wasn't his idea. He didn't tell you, did he?"

"No. But if he wants it back, he'll just send that school of sharks he has on retainer."

"That's what I thought. My wife thinks otherwise."

"And murdering farm children isn't?"

I started to explain Andy's theory, but he threw a hand up between us.

"Yeah, I get it. Bitcoin. Can't trace it. Makes it deniable. I don't know, Stewart. The old man was ruthless, but these killings?" He pointed at flatscreen. "They had that shit on at the hospital. Brutal. I get what Andrea's thinking, but Litton's more of a boardroom assassin."

"He had Bob Stone murdered."

Donaldson didn't argue.

"So? Where is he? Where's the secret lair? Where's the doomsday retreat stocked with canned goods so the old white rich guy can live out the zombie apocalypse and breed a new human race?"

Donaldson shook his head. "Nothing like that. The desert compound was as close to a fortress as he had."

I started to wonder if I had just played my highest card for nothing. The canary-eating cat sitting across from me suggested otherwise.

"Okay," I said. "Then what?"

"Looking Glass."

20

*L*ooking *Glass.*
 The Air Force named it Operation Looking Glass. Beginning in the early 60s, an airborne command post mirroring the capabilities of the underground national defense system flew constantly. The idea ensured that somebody would fire back if a nuke was launched at the United States. For more than thirty years, one or more aircraft with command authority and communication capability prowled the skies. The program ended in the 90s.

I pulled out my phone and tapped the calculator app.

"Are you shitting me? At 750 gallons per hour...times 24 hours in a day...times 365 days...that's—*holy shit*—over six-and-a-half million gallons of jet fuel per year! At five bucks a gallon, that's more than thirty million bucks a year!" I recognized the absurdity as soon as I said it. "Which is piss-away money for a guy with—what? Forty billion? Fifty?"

"A guy who owns giant oil companies, refineries, distribution pipelines and probably gets jet fuel for ten cents on the dollar. Fuel is not an issue," Donaldson said.

"Wow," I said. "I have to admit, as a security measure, the concept works. Litton has literally left this earth."

Donaldson shrugged. "I was only peripherally involved in setting it up. I never took it seriously. He had the Boeing 737 before you fried his sense of security—the business jet version. He hardly used it. I was only on it once. I expected something posh. A flying party-plane." He shook his head. "Strictly business with a private cabin for sleeping. After I left, I heard from a couple guys who stayed that he added another airplane to the fleet, a duplicate. I assume that one day he climbed aboard and has been in the sky ever since. Untouchable."

"Impossible," I said. "The Air Force can do it because they have air refueling. He has to land for fuel."

"I don't know how he does it. Maybe he had long-range tanks installed. Even before he freaked out, he had the thing loaded with communications gear. Part of the plane looked like Air Force One, but with better gear."

"He still has to land and refuel."

"And if I were to guess where, I'd say either Sky Harbor in Phoenix or Inouye in Honolulu. He owns private hangars at both."

"What about security? Guys with guns?"

"I only know what he had before I got the boot. For the short time I was there after the breach, he wouldn't go into a room alone. He had people with him one hundred percent of the time. Shower. Toilet. Sleeping. Twenty-four seven. He refused to enter any room with a window. I thought it was all nonsense, but then he fired me so what did I care?"

"Jesus," I said. I reached over and stole Donaldson's last onion ring. He had the damned thing coated with salt. I knocked off what I could and ate it.

"It's like you said: He still has to refuel."

"Yeah, but how often?" I asked. "Do you know for sure if he added auxiliary tanks? Because if he did, that thing might be able to stay in the air for a couple days. And he sure as hell isn't going to publish where he plans to land next. It could be anywhere. On top of all that he's in a sterile security environment wherever he puts it down. He has TSA and Homeland guarding him as well."

"No problem for you."

"I have limits."

"I wanted to ask about that. When you did it to me…I felt funny. I mean, obviously! But I felt a little queasy."

"Weightless. It makes you weightless. Don't make me explain about weight and mass and gravity and inertia. I barely get it myself, but I've got a fifteen-year-old who can spin your head."

"Weightless…shit! You can fly! That's how you got in!"

"Christ! Will you let that go? Even with what I can do, the problem of catching Litton when he lands for fuel remains."

He leaned on the table.

"Not if we can dictate when and where he lands."

21

Millard Airport to Sky Harbor in Phoenix flight-planned at 893 nautical miles. I broke the flight into two legs lasting roughly two and a half hours each. Even with a bathroom stop before takeoff, two and a half hours pushes my bladder limit. We landed in Pueblo, Colorado a little before three in the afternoon. Donaldson had trouble climbing out of the passenger seat onto the wing, but he was motivated—he announced that his eyeballs were floating as he took off for the FBO restroom. I followed closely on his heels, then supervised refueling while he explored a vending machine. I used the time away from Donaldson to call Andy.

"How is he?" she asked.

"Oh, I'd say better than we both expected."

"Really? Ohmigod, that's good to hear! Did he tell you anything? Will, if he balks at talking to you, let me talk to him. I think he trusts me."

"I'm sure of that. How are things there?"

"Not good."

"What's going on?"

"It's Sandy. The media. I mean—it was bad with her wedding, but this is insane. They're making it sound like she's involved."

"I saw that."

"She's pushing Janos to let her make the payment. She had a meeting with Mr. Larmond this morning, and I'm sure it was about selling that property. I get it. She feels cleaning out the Foundation's accounts is a small price to pay to save another set of victims—but it's still wrong. Janos has great people on this."

"Is he close?"

"I don't know. I'm not directly involved. He's letting me babysit Sandy, but that's about all. Tom has me dotting the I's and crossing the T's on the Johns arrest. With good reason. His lawyers showed up here this morning screaming bloody murder because we moved him to County. They're going to be apoplectic when they find out we swabbed him."

"How's the girl…Verna?"

Andy sighed into the phone. "About as you'd expect. She doesn't remember much. Hurt. Embarrassed. Scared. Ashamed. I hate rape cases. I hate how they're handled. I got in a shouting match with one of the doctors at Memorial. Insensitive ass. It wasn't pretty, but it scored points with the girl's mother. They're half a hair from suing everyone in sight, including the city. It's probably good that I was there."

"It's always good that you're there," I said.

"Aw, you're my wonderful guy," she cooed, "and a total suck-up."

"I'm getting that printed on a t-shirt."

Her silent smile warmed me through the cellular connection.

"I didn't ask. Where are you?"

"Pueblo," I said. "Getting some gas. We're headed to Phoenix. We—"

"We? WE? Will, what are you doing?"

"Um…I forgot to mention. Your FBI pal wouldn't share unless I took him along."

"He told you?"

"Yeah. We're on our way to visit you-know-who." Mentioning Bargo Litton by name over a cellular connection didn't seem like the best idea.

"My God, Will, the man has been through multiple brain surgeries!"

"Like I said, he's a lot better than either of us expected."

"Okay…" she said in a way that made me cringe, "…and just how do you intend to get to you-know-who with our friend tagging along? Without him learning about *the other thing*?"

"Yeah…that's not going to be an issue."

She said nothing.

I waited a moment.

"Dee?"

I pictured her, feet planted, one hand holding the phone to her ear, the other hand buried in her hair. Face down. Eyes closed.

"Dee? You still there?"

"Tell me you didn't."

My turn to say nothing.

She one-upped me by saying even more nothing than I did. I couldn't stand it. "On the plus side, it kinda fixed his head problems."

"Will!"

"Hey, you're the one that's been trusting his ass all this time!"

Silence.

"Dee?"

"This..." she said it slowly "...is turning into a nightmare. First, Lillian and Lewko, then Johns, then these hideous killings and poor Sandy, and now —*what were you thinking?*"

"The same thing you were," I snapped. "Because if you're right, it might save a family somewhere *and* Sandy, so we're just going to have to take whatever measures we can. Plus, I didn't have a choice." I explained that Donaldson remembered everything that happened in the roadhouse.

"That's impossible. People with head injuries usually don't remember anything. Sometimes for days or even weeks on either side of the event. Look what happened to you, Will!"

She had a point. It made me stop for a moment to look at the FBO office, but I couldn't see Donaldson through the glass.

"We'll do what we need to do, Dee." I didn't want to argue. I looked for a way to shift the subject. "Silver lining...at least the media attention is off the Johns case. Ignore the screaming lawyers. They're only screaming because you have their client wrapped up in a perfect package for the D.A."

Andy hesitated. She didn't want to argue either. Truce was declared when she said, "It's not all that tidy."

"Why?"

"Just some loose ends. I have to backtrack all of Traeger's canvassing, and I can't find the Boardman girl or her car. She took Verna to party with Johns, but she ditched her and now she's gone."

"Probably heard what happened and is scared to death. She'll turn up."

We shared a silent moment. When she spoke, her tone was soft and smooth. "Will you call me tonight?"

I felt the small electric jolt I get in my chest when an intimate signal crosses the connection between us.

"I will. Nothing happening tonight except me hitting a pillow."

"Call me," she said again.

"I will. Love you."

"You, too."

. . .

"Are we good to go?" Donaldson asked when I returned to the FBO office. He had purchased a hat at the front counter and used it to replace the bandage. It displayed the logo for the Aircraft Owners and Pilots Association, and it covered the worst of the damage to his skull. Blotchy red and a few stitches could still be seen above his ear.

"No," I said harshly. "Because you're a horse's ass and I'm an idiot!"

He shrugged. "Of the two, I'll take horse's ass."

"If I didn't think it might turn your brain back into Jell-O, I'd punch you in the face."

"You mean you would try. What has your panties in a twist?"

I stepped closer to Donaldson and lowered my voice.

"You didn't remember shit." I pointed at his skull. "Nobody remembers anything from a head injury. Not one like that. So how did you know?"

"What? Your disappearing act? The bottles?" His smug grin prompted me to reconsider that punch in the face. "I didn't. I never would have guessed it."

"You read the police reports."

"Every word."

"The interviews. That weenie from the State Department. Conway. And that guy who took off before the shit really hit the fan. They both saw the bottles flying."

"Weirdest thing. If one of them said the fight started when the lady cop used her telekinetic mind to start flinging bottles all over the room, I might have written it off. But they both told the same story. And both stories started with you diving over the bar to hide like a coward. However, your wife's version didn't say anything about bottles. Or you. If she left it out, I figured she had a reason. I just opened the door for you."

"And I walked right through it. Shit."

"I wanted to see how far I could get. I never expected—you know. Hell, I still can't wrap my head around it."

"You're an ass."

"Maybe." He closed the space between us and with some effort, lifted his right hand between us. "But my oath stands, Stewart. Semper fi. Exactly as it translates."

Always faithful.

I took his hand. The grip was weak, but he pressed home a solid handshake.

"Okay," he said, "I squeezed every drop I could outta my bladder so let's get this show on the road."

"Please tell me you washed your hand."

22

I checked my watch. It had been close to an hour. Not good.

Donaldson badged his way into an unmarked hanger at Phoenix Sky Harbor Airport just before 11 o'clock. I waited in the car, thinking that if a Crown Vic carrying FBI suits rolled up, I would simply drive away. Or vanish.

His plan sucked. He unveiled it over breakfast at a Denny's just across the river from the airport.

"I spent some time in the hotel business center last night," he said. He pushed a white piece of paper across the Formica tabletop toward me. It bore the Boeing logo at the top.

"What's this?" I glanced down at the two lines of text imprinted on the white sheet.

"One refers to the sensor for air data. The other mentions a control valve for fuel cross feed."

I lifted my eyebrows. "Listen to you. And you even have part numbers here."

"Amazing what you can find online."

I handed it back. "So what? What's that going to get you?"

"That," he said reaching into his pocket and pulling out his FBI badge wallet, "and this will get them to call Litton back from wherever he's flying."

"They let you keep your badge?"

"Only until the paperwork clears. Or until they figure out that I have it."

I pushed the document back at him. "I don't see how a forgery helps. One call to Boeing and they'll know it's bogus—and probably breaking federal law."

"Ye of little faith," he scoffed. "I tell a much better story. About how the FBI has been working with Boeing since that mechanic tried to sabotage an American Airlines 737. About how Boeing and the feds are checking the entire fleet and doing so with a minimum fuss to avoid media coverage and copycats. How the corporate boys want to keep a very low profile—what with all the shit dripping from their fans over the Max 8. About how Litton's maintenance people can make all the calls they want, but they're going to hit brick walls because this initiative comes from people who will not confirm or deny anything."

"Wow," I said, exaggerating false admiration. "That's the worst line of crap I've ever heard."

"But it will work," he said, tucking his wallet away, "because it asks nothing of them."

"You're asking them to call back the airplane."

"Their call, not mine. And all this does is ask them to inspect. Just inspect. And be vigilant. If both items check out, no problem. I'm just the messenger. I don't ask to get on the plane. I don't even ask to go in the hangar. In fact, I don't even wait around."

I thought about it. "So, they inspect the one in the hangar…and it checks out. And then they call back the other one. The one he's on."

"Right. It guarantees he will come back here instead of Hawai'i."

"Why not inspect it in Hawai'i?"

"Because I will tell them to keep a tight lid on this. Limit it to a maintenance supervisor only. No crew. And I happen to know the maintenance supervisor for his flight department is here. Hawai'i is support crew only. Easy."

Unless they correctly assess that you're full of shit and call the real FBI.

Which is what I was thinking as I listened to the air conditioning unit in the rented car fight off Arizona heat. I checked my watch again. A full hour.

Donaldson appeared at the hangar door. He turned and shook hands with someone inside. The door closed behind him and he walked confidently toward the parking lot with his new ball cap pulled down and his face carefully angled away from the security cameras.

He slipped into the car and I pulled away.

"They bought it."

"Says you."

"Oh, they did. I undersold the whole story. Told 'em I was bored silly pounding the pavement in a crap assignment because I'm on a desk thanks to a medical issue." He pointed at his wound. "And I only spoke in terms of the airplane sitting in the hangar. Told them it was lucky the airplane was here. Bing, bang, boom—they can inspect it before the boss needs it."

"They say anything about him being up in the air in another one?"

"Nope. Not a word. Nor did I ask. Good security on their part. Indifference on mine."

"So, what took so long? You were in there for an hour."

"Oh, I knew a couple of the security guys. Guys I hired. We shot the shit for a while. They wanted to know all about the dent in my skull."

"What? Jesus, man! You've been identified!"

He looked at me like I spoke another language.

"They'll know you were here!"

"Uh-huh. So what?"

I was speechless. How could he not realize what this meant?

"The Boeing story is bogus."

"They won't check. The maintenance guy practically talked my ear off about how hard it is to reach the right people at Boeing. And I'm not asking them to change or replace anything. The FBI just wants all 737 operators to be vigilant."

"The FBI? You're walking around with a badge that isn't yours anymore. Pretty sure there's a law or two about that."

"Will, it's an inspection for possible sabotage. Right there, it gets dismissed. Who's going to sabotage these guys? It's a damned formality and waste of time. I laughed about it with their security guys."

"Except that I'm about to breach their security again."

"If we do it right, Litton will never admit we were there. Let's go buy some binoculars and go back to the hotel. My room has a perfect view of the airport."

FOUR HOURS and twenty-four minutes later Donaldson spotted the jet as it settled onto Runway 8.

"That's him!" He sat in a reversed hotel room desk chair. He used small binoculars to look out the window and follow the landing jet.

"You sure?" I hopped off the bed and took up a position behind him. Sky Harbor airport sprawled in shimmering heat, vast and tan. I watched a Boeing 737 roll out on the runway. "It's got no markings."

"Told you, I've seen it before. It's a twin to the one I saw in the hangar." He pointed.

Behind the Litton hangar, another white 737 devoid of markings sat on the asphalt ramp, freshly pulled into the sunlight.

"They're doing a swap!"

"Yeah. I watched them pull it out." He heaved himself out of the chair using his good left arm. He scooped up the rental keys and limped for the door. "Come on!"

The parking garage connected to the Crowne Plaza Hotel gave us rapid access to our rental, which we parked on the top level. We had timed the route. Six to seven minutes from the hotel to the hangar. Donaldson made me test the drive twice. He planned to ambush Litton when he switched planes.

"Shock and awe," he told me on the way from the room to the elevator. "We'll catch him off guard."

"He's not going to tell you anything."

"He doesn't have to. I know the old man. His face will tell me everything I want to know. If he's behind those killings, he can't hide it from me."

The elevator responded to the call button in less than fifteen seconds. Half a minute later we emerged from the fourth-floor door to the hot upper deck of the parking ramp. I jogged to the driver's side and threw my flight bag in the back seat. While Donaldson limped to the passenger side, I pulled what I needed from the flight bag and jammed it inside my t-shirt. The gear was heavy, but the shirt, tucked into my belted jeans, held.

"Keys!"

Donaldson threw the rental keys across the car roof to me. I ducked into the back seat and pulled a pair of power unit and prop combinations from the flight bag.

"Let's go!" Donaldson ordered. He slid in and slammed the door.

I closed the car door and stepped back.

He leaned down and looked out the window at me.

I shrugged and slipped the rental key into my jeans pocket. I held the power units close against my chest and covered them with my hands.

Fwooomp!

I vanished and tapped my toes against the concrete.

"Stewart!" Donaldson threw open the door and pulled himself out. "God dammit!"

"Go get a cold beer," I said calmly, rising. "I got this."

23

An easterly tailwind shortened the flight from the hotel to the hangar. I stayed high to avoid power lines. Litton's jet completed its rollout, turned off the runway and began to taxi back.

I eased back on the power and floated the last couple hundred yards to the peaked center of the hangar roof. Litton's other glossy all-white jet blazed in the sun on the apron below me. I pumped the power unit in reverse to stop. The tailwind that had favored me tried to push me. I used steady low thrust to hold my position.

Litton's jet approached from the east. I expected it to pass across in front of me and continue to my right to the first available runway crossing point. That would bring it to the ramp from the right and allow it to park with the cabin door facing the hangar.

It didn't. The jet crossed the runway while it was still to my left. It turned onto the ramp and approached from the east.

This looked like poor planning to me. His security team would have to take a mobile stairway around the arriving jet's nose to let Litton disembark. Then the stair would have to be repositioned on the opposite side of the backup jet for him to board. Unless they planned to use a vehicle, it exposed him to crossing a wide-open ramp. It made no sense.

And where was the stairway truck? I checked the ramp below me and the spaces on either side of the hangar. No boarding stairs.

Did they plan to leave Litton onboard? Then why bring out the second jet? If they planned to inspect the arriving jet and return it to service, the maintenance supervisor would need to board the aircraft to reach the fuel cross feed control that Donaldson identified in his inspection ruse. He would need a lift to inspect the air data port. I saw no lift, no maintenance supervisor, no crew and no security team.

Litton's jet rolled across the ramp. As it eased to a stop beside its sister ship, the twin jet engines abruptly wound down to silence. Motion to my right caught my eye.

A food service truck rolled onto the ramp. It passed the tail of the backup jet and swung left, then right, pulling up to the nose of the arriving jet.

"What the hell?" I asked aloud.

The answer came quickly. I heard the truck motor rev and a high-pitched electric motor whine. The food service truck box began to rise on a scissors frame.

"Son of a bitch!"

I thumbed the power unit control slide and shot off the roof, over the ramp, and across the high vertical tail of the backup jet. Angling down, I aimed for the nose of the arriving jet. The first officer remained in the cockpit, his head turning, working checklists and switches. The pilot's seat was empty.

Behind the first officer's side window, several yards back, a door cracked open and swung aside—the hatch through which trash would be removed and soft drinks, snacks and meals would be loaded, had this been a scheduled airline flight.

It came together. There would be no stairway truck. Litton planned to exit the arriving aircraft directly into the protection of the service truck box.

The lift ceased rising. The driver eased forward until a platform over the cab came within inches of the aircraft. The forward-facing roll door of the food truck shot up revealing half a dozen men in black tactical gear. Each one carried a sidearm. The presence of weapons within the TSA perimeter of an air carrier airport attested to Litton's power.

The instant the door cleared, four men stepped onto the flat bridge between the box and the jet hatch. They stood shoulder to shoulder in two lines, facing outward. I pulsed my power unit and rose to get a better view.

The pilot of Litton's jet appeared in the open hatch. He wore a standard white pilot's shirt with four-stripe epaulets on the shoulders. A leather shoulder holster showing the reversed butt of a holstered semiautomatic handgun looked jarringly out of place over the white shirt. On the elbow of the pilot, Bargo Litton hunched and hurried between the jet and the truck box. In a matter of seconds, the pilot ducked back into the jet, the security team darted into the truck and the roll door slammed down. The electric motor whined again, and the truck box began to descend.

A perfectly timed ballet of absolute security.

I hung in the air, dazed. Any chance of reaching Litton evaporated.

Ditching Donaldson had been in my mind from the moment he demanded to tag along. All I needed was Litton's whereabouts. I felt sure I could get to him. I once grabbed a prisoner under the noses of an armed guard at a Montana prison. If all else failed, I planned to swoop down on the old bastard, grab him and make him vanish in front of his security team.

This security arrangement killed any chance of reaching Litton. It suddenly made sense that they had parked the jets nose to nose, each abeam the other's right side.

The truck backed away. I looked at the waiting backup jet. The service door opened and swung aside. An armed pilot stood waiting within. In a moment or two, the truck would pull up, the box would rise, and the security ballet would play out in reverse.

Leaving me hanging.

I shoved the power unit control slide forward and launched in an arc that took me toward the backup jet. I curved past the vertical stabilizer. The long white tube of fuselage slid under me and I eased downward until I could have walked on the riveted aluminum. I used the core muscle I feel in the vanished state to pivot my legs behind me. In a prone position, I descended until I skimmed the paint.

Pulsing reverse power, I slowed. I reached out with my left hand and touched the top of the jet. I made contact and used the resistance to vector right, angling toward the top of the open service hatch.

The truck backed away from the arriving jet, executed a 90-degree turn, then another to reverse itself and roll toward the backup jet. The efficient maneuver bore the signature of plentiful practice. The lift motor began to whine, and the box rose, bearing Litton to his high hiding place.

I gave the power unit a shot to push me down, then scrambled to jam the device into my pocket. With my hands free, I grabbed the open lip of the service hatch and arrested my forward movement.

Upside down, I dipped my head below the lip of the hatch, coming almost face to face with the pilot. He waited with his hands clasped. His job, in a moment, would be to escort his boss across the platform, between the security men, into the jet. I would have five, maybe ten seconds.

The truck box rose and stopped. The roll door clattered open. The security men hustled into position and the pilot stepped out below me.

I didn't wait or look. I curled my body around the top lip of the open hatch and pulled myself into the jet. The move took me inside what would have been the forward galley on a commercial airliner. This interior bore no resemblance, with one exception. On the opposite side of the hull, I spotted the standard forward exit. I shoved myself across the cabin, past the open cockpit door, and reached out for the big door handle. I grabbed it and curled myself up against the side of the cabin.

Behind me, I heard footsteps. The captain hustled the old man into the cabin. Litton hurried aft. The captain attended to the service hatch. The truck backed away. The hatch closed with a muffled thud.

I heard the whistle of jet engines starting up.

Oh, crap.

24

These guys operate like it's a damned SAC drill! The moment the engines lit, the pilots released the brakes and rolled. I knew from my flight along the north perimeter of the field that rush hour jets were lined up for departure at all three runways. With luck the heavy traffic would delay takeoff long enough to let me reach Litton.

The forward section of the aircraft served as a galley and crew dining area. Cabinets and countertops had been mounted against the left side of the cabin. The right side contained a large stainless freezer and refrigerator. A table with seating for two anchored one of the counters. The fixtures looked utilitarian—if anything, subpar. Not what I expected on a billionaire's private jet. The carpet belonged to the airliner this aircraft was originally intended to be. Leather upholstered the chairs, but they fell short of plush. Standard plastic built-in shades, all pulled down, covered the windows.

A small divider with an open curtain marked the aft end of the galley. The next section had a single bunk against one wall, suggesting that on round-the-clock flights the pilots took sleep rotations. I didn't think a 737 could legally be flown by a single pilot, but I had only seen two pilots on board so they either flew on a waiver or bent the rules. A small desk and double closet lined the opposite wall. Two blue uniform coats hung in the closet beneath a shelf holding two peaked caps.

A second divider featured a single narrow door that granted entry to the third section. The door hung open, revealing twin banks of electronics, screens, monitors and keyboards. It seemed plausible that the setup enabled

Litton to direct his oil and gas empire from this center section of the plane. I looked for signs of a radio operator or technician and crossed my fingers that Litton's rampant paranoia meant he alone operated the equipment.

The command center ended at a bulkhead with a closed door which I assumed marked the entrance to Litton's private quarters. Between the closed cockpit door and the closed door aft of the command center, I had the aircraft to myself.

I rotated to an upright position, lowered myself to contact the deck, and—

Fwooomp!

The instant I reappeared, Andy's Beretta M.92 broke the seal between my t-shirt and belt and dropped to the carpet. A short black tube followed. I dove after them.

Andy keeps a licensed suppressor for the M.92 in her gun safe. I borrowed it to good effect for my first visit with Bargo Litton. I packed it for this trip, although I reminded myself that my wife's law enforcement career would end abruptly if I got caught with the weapon or the weapon could be linked to a crime.

Dropping it did not bode well.

I recovered the handgun, screwed the suppressor in place, then racked a round into the chamber. I advanced into the cabin and laid the weapon on the dining table. It rattled and moved as the pilots aggressively taxied for take-off. I removed my sunglasses and laid them on the table beside the weapon. I hunted inside my shirt for the rest of my equipment, a black balaclava and a pair of tight Nomex gloves. I located the balaclava eye hole and slipped it over my head, pulled on the gloves and then replaced my sunglasses.

I scooped up the weapon and glanced around for a mirror to see just how badass I looked.

The cabin offered no mirror.

One more item called for attention before I advanced on Litton. I found a box of tissues on the kitchen counter and pulled half a dozen. I stepped back to the handle for the forward exit and wiped my fingerprints clean, then stuffed the used tissues in my jeans pocket.

Weapon forward, I advanced through the cabin, dancing to keep my balance as the jet taxied. A hard turn to the left threw me sideways and told me we were lining up to cross Runway 8. I waited for the inevitable braking and stop, but it never came. A hard turn to the right told me we were clear of 8 and had turned on the parallel taxiway to join the lineup for takeoff. At any moment we would stop to wait our turn.

I felt the seconds ticking away and hurried aft.

The communications center proved even more impressive once I stepped inside. I recognized a full rack of aviation avionics, including Garmin's latest navigation displays, slaved to identical units up front. Stacks of VHF radios, UHF radios, cellular receivers and systems I did not recognize lined the fuselage walls. A rack of servers blinked cryptically. Multiple flat-screen monitors displayed weather data, shifting digital graphs and flowing financial data that could have just as easily been Egyptian hieroglyphics to my eye. Half a dozen news feeds filled additional screens. Most of them trumpeted the Midwest Murders. Sandy's picture hovered on at least three screens.

Seeing her image made me glad for the loaded gun in my hand.

We hadn't stopped. This section of the aircraft had no windows, but I began to wonder. I had estimated a ten- to fifteen-minute wait behind half a dozen airliners before reaching the number one position for takeoff.

I tested the knob on the closed bulkhead door. It turned. Just as I screwed up the courage to throw the door open, the engines surged. The aircraft heaved right. I lost my balance and banged against the bank of equipment on the left side of the plane.

"What the—?"

I knew the answer. We were rolling for takeoff. Litton's plane had been given priority.

As I fought to regain my balance, the pilots pushed the throttles on the roll. The big Boeing jet accelerated, heaving me against the bulkhead.

Too fast! I had no idea how they jumped the line, but I felt the aircraft leap forward on thrust pouring from the big GE engines. Takeoff acceleration pushed me against the wall.

The wheels thundered on the runway. I knew what to expect and waited. The nose broke ground, hesitated, then heaved upward. The jet adopted the high angle all such massively powered aircraft use for initial climb. Acceleration pressed me against the bulkhead. I could have eliminated the effect easily by disappearing, but I held off.

Acceleration dissipated. The pilots stabilized the climb speed.

I moved into position, turned the doorknob and threw the door open. Six-foot-one, black from head to toe, and holding a large handgun with a larger suppressor, I filled the doorway.

Bargo Litton, strapped in a plush leather chair, glanced up. Recognition bloomed on his face.

"Miss me?"

He'd shrunk since I saw him last. His hair thinned along with his body. His designer casual clothes lacked a tailor's touch; they hung loose at his shoulders and knees. The hands I'd once seen confidently working a laptop at his desert fortress looked boney. The face that commanded boardrooms and presidents reminded me of a piece of fruit left on the counter a day too long.

In less than a second, his skin blanched, his eyes bulged, his jaw dropped. A coffee mug slipped his grip and dropped, spreading a brown stain on plush white carpeting that looked more like an ermine pelt than fiber.

I aimed the Beretta at a spot between his eyes.

Failed speech squeaked from Litton's throat.

"I told you what would happen, you son of a bitch. I told you I would return if you ever went back on our deal!"

A sheen of sweat erupted on his forehead.

"Did you think these toys would protect you? Goddamned waste of jet fuel!"

The engines throttled back.

I knew why. The jet had been cleared to climb on runway heading to five or seven thousand feet. The pilots had already contacted departure control and in short order would be cleared to climb higher. I need to conduct my business fast. I estimated I had another thirty seconds.

"I—I—I did everything you asked!" he cried.

"Elbows and ankles. Put your arms out!" I reminded him of my original threat; to use frangible bullets to blow apart all four appendages; to leave him alive and unable to walk or feed himself or clean himself. "NOW!"

He wrapped his arms tightly around his chest. Terror dug into his thin flesh. I felt a twinge of regret for torturing the man, until I reminded myself of the two children murdered by his arrogant political maneuvering and manipulation.

"Christine and Paulette," I said. "Remember?"

"But I did all you asked! I swear!"

"And you came back for it! You couldn't let go of a goddamn dollar!"

His eyes shot to my left. My peripheral vision caught the glow of a rack of flatscreen displays. I didn't need to look to catch the flashy banners and bold brand look of cable news. I didn't need to read the screen to know what story blazed across the top of the hour.

I advanced on him. He cringed in his seat, pressing his skull into the leather. I pushed the muzzle of the suppressor into the parchment skin between his sparse eyebrows.

"That's right! It's all over the news. That's your doing, isn't it?"

"NO! NO! I swear! I'm not the one you want!"

I stepped back, swept the weapon to my right and fired.

The gun issued a *Snick!* and *Click!* The suppressor killed the sound of the shot and the slide racked a new round into the chamber.

The sound of the small window exploding and blowing out was much louder. Litton shrieked. The cabin air swirled.

I bent over and picked up the ejected casing and pocketed it.

The shot and its result were more theatrical than dangerous—nowhere near the fatal event people expect. The jet flew well below cabin pressure altitude. Blowing out a window at this point meant nothing more than some thunderous wind noise and a draft in the cabin.

"IT'S NOT ME!" Litton screamed. His hands flew up and clapped together as if to pray. "I SWEAR IT'S NOT ME!"

The engines abruptly throttled back. Alarms must have flashed in the cockpit. There would be no climb now. I felt a shift as the pilots stabilized the 737 to deal with cabin pressure warnings.

I pushed the hot muzzle into Litton's forehead.

"WHO?! Who's your proxy? Who did you send to do the killings?"

His hands went from prayer to grasping the barrel of the suppressor. I jerked it free, aimed over his head and fired again.

A second window, opposite the first, exploded. Neither blown out window posed much of a threat. Nobody risked being sucked out.

Litton didn't know that.

I lowered the muzzle to his left elbow. He shrank into the seat as far as he could, but I pressed the gun against him.

"You have three seconds."

"I don't gamble! Yarborough! The report! It's all speculation! I told them no! I never—NEVER—I—!"

I caught movement in my peripheral vision. The cockpit door opened.

Shit!

A white shirt with three-stripe epaulets emerged from the cockpit.

I shifted to my left to duck out of sight of the first officer. I needed more time.

Litton twisted in his seat. He flipped open the padded armrest. He stabbed his hand into the open armrest compartment and came up with a shining oversized revolver. I had an instant to think how frail his hand looked holding a .357 Magnum before his finger jerked the trigger.

FWOOOMP!

GO!

Litton fired.

My perspective on the room altered in a blink. From watching the black muzzle of Litton's revolver swing toward me, I went to a high view of him blasting away at the bulkhead where I stood a fraction of a second ago.

Gunshots hammered my ears.

He emptied the gun, blowing holes in the bulkhead. Electronics sparked in the command cabin. A cloud of smoke, plastic, wood and insulation joined the swirling air.

He jerked on the trigger and continued dry firing as my head and hearing cleared. I slapped my hands over my torso, feeling for the holes he had to have drilled through me. I felt no pain, no tears in my clothing or skin.

The instant his finger had squeezed the trigger something gripped me, gripped my center. A split second ahead of conscious thought, I vanished and shot across the cabin.

It took me a few seconds to feel pressure on my chest and realize I had stopped breathing. I blew out a lungful of air and sucked in a new one.

Litton dropped the empty revolver. His hands hung in the air. He blinked at empty space. He quivered suddenly and gasped, then slumped over.

I drifted in the cabin airflow momentarily unable to find an anchor point. I rotated myself and kicked the wall behind me. I shot forward and grabbed the door frame.

Litton had a small black hole in the center of his white golf shirt. The hole slowly flared red.

Oh, shit!

I was about to reappear to examine him when I spotted something worse.

Sitting on the deck with his back to the forward bulkhead, the first officer stared down at a blossom of red on his white shirt. Blood spread down his left side beside his empty leather shoulder holster. He stared at it in dazed wonder. He tried to lift his left arm, but it flopped beside him. His right hand rested in his lap, still holding the weapon he had drawn and fired.

What the hell? It took me a second to realize that the two men shot each other. *Shit!*

Litton may or may not have been beyond hope, but he was firmly beyond my capacity for compassion. I grabbed the door frame and yanked myself through. I shot through the communications bay and into the crew section. I stopped long enough to jerk a thin blanket from the crew bunk and throw it at the first officer. Passing through the kitchen, I stopped again and jerked a towel from a loop near a small sink. I threw that at the wounded pilot as well.

I pushed myself across the small space and collided with the bulkhead above the wounded pilot's head. Gripping the edges of the wall, I dropped beside him and grabbed his belt as an anchor.

His face went slack. His eyes, distant.

"Steady, pal. Hang in."

"I'm shot," he said weakly. "Fucking got shot."

"Arnie! Arnie!" the captain called from the cockpit. "Are you okay?"

"Fucking got shot, John," Arnie answered conversationally.

"Arnie!"

I pulled the towel off the floor, folded it and jammed it into the space between his left arm and his ribs. I grabbed his shoulder and pulled him away from the bulkhead. He cried out, but I had to find out what was going on in his lower back.

The exit wound formed a gory hole the size of a golf ball. My stomach rolled and I clenched to fight it.

I repositioned the towel so that it covered both the entry and exit wounds. Then I folded the blanket and jammed it in over the towel.

"Easy there, man. Can you put your hand here? Can you hold this?" I pulled the gun from his fingers and laid it on the deck. I moved his hand into position on the front side of the wound. "Press. Hard!"

He nodded but I feared he wouldn't remain conscious long.

The aircraft heaved into a turn.

"Mayday, Mayday, White 739—we are declaring an emergency." The captain spoke calmly. I glanced into the cockpit. He held a steady grip on the yoke and throttles. "Shots fired on board. I have an injured first officer. I am returning to Phoenix."

I glanced into the cockpit. The captain's right hand jumped from the throttles to the instrument panel and back. He threw a worried look over his shoulder at the open cabin door.

"Arnie!"

"White 739 you are cleared direct, cleared to land, runway your discretion, advise when able your type aircraft and the number of souls on board." ATC matched his calm tone through the overhead speaker.

"Lift your arm for a second," I told the first officer. He complied. I pulled the elastic strap of his shoulder holster, wound it down around his arm and slipped it free of his hand. I pushed his hand back onto the towel. "Press."

He pressed.

"I can't see you," he said.

"Nope. I'm an angel. Press that sonofabitch, hard!"

"Nice mouth for an angel," he muttered. His head bobbed abruptly.

"Hey!" I lifted his chin. "Focus."

I yanked the shoulder holster halfway down his left arm. The tangle of leather and elastic now lay across the blanket covering his exit wound. I reached behind him and adjusted the back straps over the blanket. In front, I drew the elastic gun-arm strap across his chest. I lifted his limp left arm and hooked the elastic around the arm, working it halfway up his bicep. The half-assed rig formed a belt around his torso and pulled his arm against his side where it pressed on the blanket. I adjusted the back to put maximum pressure on the exit wound. Blood seeped from the edge of the blanket onto my hand.

"Where'd you solo?" I asked.

"Huh?"

"Where did you do your first solo?"

"Little crop-dusting strip in Iowa. My dad had a…"

His chin dropped again. I lifted it and he blinked.

"Your dad had a what?"

"Champ…little red one."

"How many hours? Your first solo—how many hours did you have?"

"Nine."

"Nice. Beat me by an hour," I lied. He smiled.

"Why can't I see you?"

"I told you. I'm an angel." The amount of blood pooling on the carpet sent a cold shiver through me. Too much. "Captain!" I shouted. "Get this damned thing on the ground!"

The captain looked back at the cabin. He searched for the voice. "I can't. We have to dump fuel! We're over max landing weight!"

"Screw that! You took off with it. Grease this sucker on or your first officer is not going to make it!"

The engines abruptly cut. We rolled into a turn. I felt a rumble in the airframe. Flaps and slats for landing.

"Phoenix, White 739, we're landing on Runway 8. Roll everything. I repeat, roll everything. We have injured aboard. Full fuel. Possible shooter aboard," he transmitted calmly and deliberately. "We are landing heavy. We're over max landing weight."

"Roger, White 739, you are cleared to land Runway 8. Emergency services has been notified. Understand you are requesting security as well?"

"Affirmative!"

Arnie's face fell forward again. I lifted his chin and tapped his cheeks.

"How many hours do you have?"

"Huh?"

"How many hours?"

"Nineteen hundred…spent the last four hundred flying in circles over the Pacific…boring as shit. How 'bout you?"

"I'm an angel. We fly so much we don't keep logbooks."

"Am I gonna die?"

"Oh, hell no! I'm here to make sure of that. We're backlogged as shit up there. You're getting a gate hold here on Earth, but you gotta stay with me!"

"It hurts. A lot."

"Good. Keeps you awake."

A deep rumble vibrated the deck. Gear down. My ears popped, signaling a rapid descent. We heaved into another turn. The light on the cabin shades shifted.

"You married?" I spotted the bloodied ring on this left hand, which lay in the blood pool spreading on the deck.

"Uh…"

"Hey! Are you married?"

His head came up again. "Six months…she's…attendant with…Southwest."

"You gonna try to get on with Southwest?"

"Boy, am I. I'm done with this shit."

He tipped sideways. I pulled him back up. His chin sank to his chest. I poked and slapped his cheeks, but he did not respond. I touched his neck and felt blood pulsing weakly through an artery.

"Captain! Your man needs to be on the ground NOW!"

"Base to final! Who are you?"

I didn't answer.

Shadows in the cabin shifted again. He cranked the aircraft in a tight turn no airliner would ever impose on its paying customers. I heard the engines spool up as the captain set up the landing with gear and flaps hanging out. He dragged the 737 across the fence on the back side of the power curve and eased it onto the concrete as smoothly as the best landing I've ever made. Even as the wheels touched, he held it off, letting the overloaded jet settle gently on the struts. I didn't feel the nose gear make contact.

The stop was anything but gentle. He hammered the brakes and threw the engines into violent reverse thrust. The 737 thundered to a halt. The engines wound down as soon as the captain pulled the thrust out of reverse. I heard seat belts snap open. I released my grip on the first officer's belt.

I pushed off and floated backward into the cabin as the captain rushed out, weapon drawn.

He searched in vain for the intruder.

Finding nothing in the immediate cabin, he stepped over the first officer and grabbed the forward cabin door latch. He pulled the big release lever and heaved the door open, then jerked the handle that engaged the escape slide. I heard it blow open against the sound of approaching sirens.

The captain knelt and tested the first officer's pulse. Momentarily satisfied, he stood quickly and started for the rear of the cabin.

"Forget about Litton!" I snapped. He spun around, startled, looking for the source of the voice. "Throw your friend out! They'll treat this like a hostage situation. He'll bleed out before the cops allow medical help onboard! Get out now!"

He looked at the rear cabin, then holstered his weapon. He crouched over the first officer's head and hooked his hands in the man's armpits. He dragged him to the door, hesitated a split second, then simply sat down on the edge, pulled his wounded crewman against his chest, and tipped himself backward. I hoped someone stopped him at the bottom before he hit the concrete.

I grabbed a corner of the dining table and reversed myself. My hand left blood on the surface.

I pushed through the cabin, through the comm section, back into Litton's quarters. The old man leaned sideways in his chair. The red stain on his chest had expanded across his shirt front and onto his pants.

Bargo Litton was dead.

Sight of Andy's Beretta on the plush carpet gave me a jolt. I had no memory of dropping it. I picked it up, then spotted the brass from my second window shot and recovered it.

I tucked the gun in my belt and pulled my shirt over it. An electric snap signaled that it vanished. I pulled a power unit from my back pocket and thumbed the slide. Thrust pulled me up the aisle. I gave it too much. When I attempted to turn, I bounced off the forward bulkhead before realigning and shooting out the forward exit door.

Sunlight momentarily blinded me. Twenty feet above the runway, I cut the power on my BLASTER and rotated to look back.

A streak of blood painted the yellow escape slide. At the bottom of the slide, two firefighters pulled the captain away as two EMTs rushed to the wounded first officer. Fire trucks advanced on the jet. Firemen jumped to deploy lines against smoke that billowed from the burning brakes beneath the white jet.

Word of a shooter on the plane electrified the scene. The EMTs shouted and grabbed the first officer. They rushed him away from the slide to the protection of the nearest emergency vehicle. A trio of police cars raced up the runway. The squad cars heaved to a halt in a rough circle around the nose of the aircraft. Officers in blue with bulging body armor took up positions behind their vehicles, weapons drawn.

I heard choppy breathing and realized it was my own. My heart pounded. The muscles in my arms felt both tense and weak.

I turned and aimed the BLASTER at the airport perimeter.

I needed to get away.

Before my hands started shaking.

25

Litton's wild gunfire unhinged me. Nerves caught up to me as I reached the edge of the field. The power unit became almost impossible to hold steady. I lost my bearings on the baked industrial landscape. None of the landmarks fit my dislocated sense of place and position. I completely ignored Litton's other jet, still sitting on the ramp several hundred yards away. The structures lining the north side of the airport meant nothing to me.

Seemingly endless blasts from Litton's revolver echoed in my head. My memory suggested that I'd seen the muzzle flashes while looking directly down the barrel. It was both terrifying and impossible.

The other thing pulled me out of the line of fire, but the after-effect jarred me out of the moment. I felt like I'd been jerked five feet to the right of reality. It didn't help that I'd failed.

The old billionaire's denials rang neither true nor false, making them worthless on either account.

Moving at roughly ten to fifteen knots over dusty asphalt at a height of thirty feet, I abruptly cut the power. I closed both hands on the power unit and fixed a concrete grip on the device to prevent it from slipping out of my shuddering fingers.

I closed my eyes.

Litton's muzzle flashes waited for me behind my eyelids. I fought them off and concentrated on breathing. Easy in. Easy out.

Sirens competed for my concentration, but I pushed them away.

The delayed shock slowly wore off.

When I opened my eyes, the first thing I saw that made sense to me was the high cube of the Crowne Plaza Hotel.

Donaldson. The rental. My flight bag. The thoughts marched in rapid sequence. I fell in step with them. I felt located again. Centered.

I restored my grip on the BLASTER and fixed my thumb on the power slide. I aimed it at the hotel.

My phone rang.

I don't need a cute ring tone to tell me when Andy's calling. I always know when it's my wife. I also don't have a way of answering a cell phone that I can't see unless I wear a Bluetooth earpiece, which I have a habit of leaving in my pocket or my flight bag.

I let it ring. The old-fashioned bell ring tone sounded weirdly pedestrian and calming as I skimmed across the span of parking lots and industrial buildings lining the north perimeter of the airport.

I aimed for the parking garage beside the Crowne Plaza, specifically for the silver rental parked near the top deck entrance to the hotel. A plan formed as I lined up to land beside the car. Donaldson would be there. He would be waiting, knowing I would return for my flight bag. No problem. I would land, reappear long enough to grab the bag from the back seat, then wrap myself around the bag and make it vanish. After that, a simple push off and short flight would take me across the airport to the general aviation ramp where the Baron occupied a tie-down. Donaldson might anticipate the move, but I had the rental keys and by the time he reached me, I'd have the airplane fired up and on its way.

Unless he called the police. Or TSA. Or FBI.

Why would he? I decided I would deal with that *if and when*.

I crossed the white concrete parking deck feeling steadier when I saw that the car sat empty. I coasted the last fifteen feet and touched my feet to the concrete. At the same instant I reappeared.

Fwooomp!

I trotted a few steps to the car. I tapped the car keys in my pocket and smugly thought, *This is getting easier by the second!*

I opened the rear door to grab my bag.

A sheet of paper—a flight plan form torn from a knee board I keep in the bag—lay on the back seat where the bag had been.

MEET ME IN THE BAR ASSHOLE.

Dammit! At least the sentiment was mutual.

. . .

"Jesus, you've got blood all over you," Donaldson slid off his bar stool. He picked up my bag and moved to intercept me as I entered the hotel bar. "You're just walking around like that? C'mon!"

"Screw you," I reached for the bag.

He jerked it away from my hand. "Before we get all grab-ass here, we need to talk." He hooked my upper arm and pushed me toward the lobby.

"This blood isn't from the old bastard, if that's what you—"

"No, it's not what I want to talk to you about." He aimed us for the elevators. "Well, it is, but there's been a development."

"What?"

He looked around. Two women in golf attire approached the elevator. I checked my right hand, which was spotted where the first officer's blood had soaked through my Nomex gloves. The spots and blotches were half wet, half dried. My shirt and pants had a damp glitter as well, although being black fabric, the blood didn't show its true color. The balaclava and gloves I balled up and jammed in my back pocket were probably full of it, too. I folded my arms and tucked my bloody hand in the crook of my left elbow. When the elevator arrived, we stepped to the back. The two women boarded and faced the door, adopting the nervous silence that dominates elevators. Both women disembarked one floor below ours.

Donaldson didn't speak until we reached his room. He keyed the lock and held the door for me. Inside, he handed me my bag. He closed the door and flipped the latch.

"Get washed up. Then we'll talk."

He had a point about me walking around looking like a serial killer.

Cleanup took longer than I expected. Blood stained my shirt, belt and pants. From my pants it had seeped into my underwear. I had spares in my flight bag, as well as a plastic garbage bag for dirty laundry. I washed first, then stripped off the bloody clothing and carefully laid it in the bathtub. I rinsed the blood off my belt and laid it aside. Andy's Beretta and my power units each had stains. I cleaned and secured them in my flight bag. After putting on fresh clothes, I shoved the garbage bag in the wastebasket and spread the open mouth as broadly as I could. Then I rolled the bloody clothes into a tight cylinder and carefully lowered the cylinder into the bag. I washed my hands again, then lifted the bag and sealed it. I ran the shower for a few minutes. A forensic specialist might find traces, but I didn't think this room would be treated as a crime scene.

"Take that with you." Donaldson pointed at the plastic bag when I emerged tugging my damp belt through the loops on my jeans.

"I figured." I unzipped a flight bag compartment, moved a few things, and stuffed the incriminating evidence inside. "What's the new development?"

"Did you kill him?"

"For the record, no. Litton's first officer killed him by accident after Litton went trigger happy with a .357 Magnum, blew out some windows and shot the first officer. The evidence will sustain all of that," I said.

Most of it, anyway.

"Did you get what you needed?"

"That's not your concern. You held up your end. For that I thank you, but we're done. I expect you to honor your oath. I think you came out ahead on the deal." I tapped my skull and then pointed at his.

"You came up empty-handed."

"Find your own ride home." I lifted my bag to go.

"They're going to hit another farm family." He folded his arms. I wanted to call the look he gave me smug, but it wasn't. To my irritation, it was sincere. "But if you got Litton to confess and you know who's doing the killing, I guess you better be on your way. You can alert your wife."

He knew I didn't.

"Where did you get this?"

"See for yourself." He pointed at the television in the room.

"Why don't you just tell me?"

"They posted half a dozen photos. Isolated farms. Farmhouses. Kids playing in yards. The photos by themselves are harmless, but in the context, they're chilling. Targets."

"Posted how?"

"Some damned social media. I'm sure it's being traced and I'm sure any trace will come up with a burner phone or some other electronic dead end. The pictures went out to the news media along with new pictures from the previous three crime scenes for authenticity. They're going to hit again in three days—they say—unless payment is made."

I dropped the bag and leaned against the chest of drawers.

"Every news anchor and analyst in the country is trying to crawl up your friend's skirt to get her to say whether she's going to pay or not. People are calling on the government to pay the ransom for her. They're setting up GoFundMe accounts. Your friend is probably going through hell. But hey, if Litton set this in motion, and he's dead now…"

Donaldson shrugged.

"He is dead."

"Then the threat's been removed."

"Bullshit. If it *was* Litton, whoever he set in motion still wants the money. If it wasn't Litton, we're at square one regardless." I picked up my bag again, determined to go. "I'm wasting time here. I need to go home."

"Will!" He stood up. "Think for a minute! There's a fifty-fifty shot that you and your wife were right—that Litton set this up to get his money back. If that's true, it's not something you can take to the FBI. Not without admitting that you were the one who set all this in motion to begin with. Or having to explain whatever happened on that jet."

"Fuck you!" I snapped at him. "This isn't on me!" I said it wishing with all my heart it was true.

He waved his hand between us. "I'm not pointing a finger. What matters is the fifty-fifty chance. Half the odds say it's got nothing to do with Litton and for that half of the odds you have the FBI and a zillion different agencies hot on the trail of every possible lead. But the other half says it *was* Litton, and the only people working that angle in the investigation are you and your wife. That's it. And your primary lead is now dead."

"What's your point?"

"Up your odds."

I had no idea what he was suggesting.

"Take me with you."

"Hell, no."

"Look, I can't stop you. But you have no clue where to turn. I do. I was with the old man long enough to know who came and went. Who did the dirty deeds. I know people—people on both sides of the law. I know the next rock to turn over."

"Why? And don't bullshit me. This time, I want to know why up front."

"Simple. I'm not done yet." He lifted his right arm and regarded it. "I don't know if this is going to get better, but I can't accept it."

"That's your problem."

I wished I hadn't said it. It wasn't his problem, not when he wore the injury on behalf of my wife's life.

He said nothing.

I tried to think of what Andy might say, something I rarely anticipate correctly. I had yet to hear her unvarnished thoughts on the fact that I exposed *the other thing* to Donaldson.

Donaldson did have one unassailable point. If I walked out the door and vanished, leaving him, then what? If a next step existed, I couldn't see it.

"Oh, for fuck's sake, stop pretending to think about it! Let's go," he said. He limped past me to the door. "And you better call your wife. Let her know about the reunion tour. Any idea what you're going to tell her?"

"That I've lost my mind."

26

After dislocating myself in space inside Litton's 737, I compounded the problem by losing track of time. It was nearly six in the evening before we checked out of the Crowne Plaza. Making matters worse, we encountered an immediate problem upon reaching the rental car on the top deck of the parking garage.

Donaldson scanned the airport then handed me his binoculars.

"That's a serious cluster fuck."

I looked. Litton's all-white 737 sat on Runway 8 surrounded by vehicles. When I left the scene, the vehicles mixed emergency response equipment with police squad cars. The mix had changed. The emergency response vehicles had been pulled back onto the terminal ramps, which were now empty of aircraft. The vehicles surrounding Litton's aircraft comprised of police squad cars and quasi-military armored vehicles. Nothing moved near the parked aircraft. I looked for a boarding stair, but none had been driven to the aircraft. The emergency escape slide remained in place, looking like a great yellow tongue hanging out in the heat.

"Jesus, I don't think they've even boarded yet!"

"Nope. They're negotiating."

"With who? A dead man? 'Cause that's the only soul on board, assuming he had a soul."

"I'm going to guess we're screwed as far as hopping in your little airplane and flying away from all this."

"It's not a 'little' airplane." I scanned the terminal area. Every jetway hung free, detached from any aircraft. Beyond the terminal buildings, I saw dozens of airliner vertical stabilizers where they didn't belong. "But, yeah, you're right. Everything has been evacuated to the south ramp. It's clogged. The whole airport is shut down. We're screwed. It's going to take hours to restore normal traffic flow…and that's once they figure out that there's nobody on that jet wearing a suicide vest."

"You couldn't just grab the man while they were parked," Donaldson jabbed. Not knowing him all that well, I checked. He wore a stone face, but a smile glinted in his eyes. My impulse to respond angrily melted.

"How's the head?"

His eyes flicked upward to his AOPA cap. "Hurts when I go jogging. Are you hungry?"

"I could eat."

WE PARKED in a remote corner of a strip mall parking lot and ate burgers from bags. A need for privacy prompted the choice of fast food. I balanced my phone on the console and touched the speaker icon.

Andy answered on the third ring.

"Dee, I have you on speaker," I said quickly.

"Hello, Detective Stewart."

"Lee?"

"How are you?"

"How are *you*? Did Will tell you they wouldn't let me contact you?"

"It's okay. I wasn't very conversational anyway."

"Should you be out of the hospital?"

"Oh, Christ, yes! The only Jell-O I will ever touch again better be infused with Vodka. I'm okay. Better than okay."

"Will told me last night. I'm glad."

"No, you're not. At least, not that your husband had to share his little secret with me. But I do appreciate the after-effect. And he played on my sentimental nature and made me swear not to tell."

"We appreciate that. But I am glad. I'm glad I have a chance to thank you. For what you did."

Donaldson gave it a moment, then said, "I get that you need to say that, and you're welcome. But that's the last time we speak of it. Understood? If anything, I'm in the red at this point."

I filled the awkward silence that followed. "Dee, what's going on there?"

"First things first. Bargo Litton is in the news."

"Yeah…about that." I explained what happened.

"That's it? That's all he said? That he wasn't the one you were looking for?"

"Something about—I dunno—Yarbo and a report. I didn't catch it. But yes, that's it."

"His exact words, Will," Andy prompted.

"'I'm not the one you're looking for.' Something like that."

"That makes it sound like he knew who you should have been looking for. If he knew nothing at all he would have said so."

"I agree with that," Donaldson chimed in.

"In any case," I said, "we're stalled here. The airport is closed."

"It's on the news—in between the Farm Family Murder story, of course. They're saying it's a standoff on a private jet owned by the missing billionaire, Bargo Litton. The speculation is that he's being held hostage. I'm in my office and it's on the big screen."

"Well, he's onboard," I said, "but it's not a standoff, because there's nobody but a dead man on the airplane. The airport is on full lock-down, so we may be a while getting out of here. How's Sandy? What's happening there?"

"There's a new message. They're going to do it again in three days. Sandy's decided to pay the ransom. It hasn't hit the news media yet, but she's doing it. The FBI asked that she hold off for 48 hours and she agreed, but not a minute longer. She doesn't want to risk running up against the deadline."

"I thought she was short."

"She's selling that parcel. The buyer saw the story on the news. His attorney reached out and offered to transfer the funds on a signed letter of intent and a full non-disclosure. Dewey Larmond said he would work out the formal closing later."

"Who's the buyer?" Donaldson asked.

"Anonymous. Hence the NDA. The lawyer says it will go through a private holding company. They say they don't want to be associated with the killings."

"Who's the SAC?"

"Janos. Out of Chicago."

Donaldson nodded his approval. "Good man. I did a couple advanced courses with him at Quantico. Is he letting you in? He knows me. Tell him I said he should let you in."

"I'm fine. I have my hands full on another matter. And I've never seen such an abundance of resources on a case. They don't need me. Plus, I'm in a better position to advocate for Sandy."

"They don't know that they need you. And that brings me to business." Donaldson recapped his fifty-fifty theory.

Andy, true to form, saw the issue from all angles. "The downside of your math is the possibility that anything you—"

"We!" he interrupted.

"...we do, is just wheel spinning if it turns out Litton didn't instigate all this. Also, there's not much I can do here without having people ask me questions."

"Let us handle it. As soon as we can get out of Phoenix, Will and I are paying a visit to someone Litton used to use."

"Use how?"

"As a hammer," Donaldson said. "Might be best if you don't know about this part. If we get anything from him, it won't be something you can put in a report. He'll never be a cooperating witness."

"I don't like that."

I sent Donaldson an I-told-you-so look.

"Desperate times, Detective."

"What's going on with Johns?" I asked quickly.

Andy heaved a sigh over my transparent attempt at diversion.

"Still no sign of Stella Boardman but her car was found at the Wisconsin Coach bus station in Madison. MPD is going through their records and video to see if they can track her. Johns' lawyers pushed for a bail hearing for tomorrow morning, so Johns will be out by noon to spin his innocence for all the waiting cameras. Between looking after Sandy and meeting with the District Attorney on Johns, I've been tied up here. I sent Lyle up to the lake to canvass all the houses on the north end again."

"Really? Lyle?" I asked.

"All I want him to do is get a list of names of neighbors who were home at the time, before and after. He's unsure of himself, but he makes up for it by taking great notes, Will. And I don't have time for that kind of legwork. Once he has a list, I'll do the interviews. Saves me knocking on doors."

"Does this have to do with that feeling you were telling me about?"

She paused briefly, then said, "Maybe."

I reached down, tapped the speaker-phone icon to turn it off, picked up the phone and stepped out of the car and strolled away, leaving Donaldson with a surprised look on his face.

"It's just me." I closed the door behind me. "I'm sorry this didn't work the way we hoped."

"It was my idea. Will...you're telling me the truth about Litton...right?"

"Dee, we've both had our moments when either one of us could have pulled the trigger on someone who deserved it, and never given it a second thought. I won't lie. I could have done that with Litton. Both times. But no. It went down just as I said."

She said nothing.

"Dee, it's okay that you asked. It is."

"Thank you."

"I just wish the whole thing had rendered better results."

"You think this lead of Lee's will produce anything?"

"No. I'd rather pack it up and come home. I think he's chasing a wild goose to make himself feel better. They're drumming him out of the FBI and he's not taking it well. Waste of time. Plus, I feel bad not being there for Sandy."

"I told her you were looking into something that I couldn't divulge. She understands. Rosemary II is in a perfect fury, however. You may have to buy her flowers."

"Why?"

"Janos wouldn't let me release the airplane yesterday morning. She had to cancel a charter."

I winced.

"Why?"

"Took me all day to find out. They have you listed as a person of interest and didn't want you flying off somewhere in it."

I laughed.

"I know," she said. "After I told them you were already gone, they still didn't want to release it, but I put up a big stink. They wanted to know where you went."

"What did you say?"

"Omaha. It was both true and sufficient. Oh, and Earl called. He left me a message that you told him to tell me that the Challenger is back on the ramp again and that it belongs to Mermaid Construction. Do you know anything about that?"

"I asked him if he heard about anybody buying property up at the lakes. I think he put on his junior detective hat and got a little overenthusiastic."

"Challenger?"

"It's a business jet." I started to mention that they were courting Pidge but decided that saying it aloud might make it happen.

"How long do you think before you can leave Phoenix?"

I shook my head for my own benefit. "Your guess and mine."

"Get some rest before you go flying all over the place."

"Right back atcha."

We gave the line a moment of silence that transmitted what we might otherwise share with the touch of a hand or a knowing glance.

"Love you."

"You, too."

The call ended. I pocketed the phone, did a quick scan of a cloudless blue sky, then climbed back behind the wheel of the rental.

"You ate all my fries," I said.

"I didn't want them to get cold. Let's go turn this car in. We can twiddle our thumbs at the airport as well as anywhere else. And I want to be ready to go."

"Where?"

"Farmington."

27

While we waited for Homeland Security to lift the temporary flight restriction on Phoenix Sky Harbor Airport, I filed a flight plan to Farmington, New Mexico. The weather forecast offered low clouds and reduced visibilities in light rain showers, but nothing nefarious. With no idea when we would be able to depart and subsequently land, I called the Atlantic Aviation FBO and arranged for a middle-of-the-night arrival, a tie-down and a courtesy car with the keys stashed under the mat.

I found those keys a little after 2:45 in the morning on the rain-slick Farmington ramp. The FBO left the car at the tie-down and taped a note with the gate code to the steering wheel. After tying down the Baron, we drove off the ramp, out the gate and onto the street. The airport and town sit on a plateau. Ten minutes later we descended Main Street, took a right on Highway 170 and in short order drove into the middle of nowhere behind the cone of headlights probing thin mist.

"His name is Walking Bear."

I had been about to ask. During the flight up from Phoenix, I wore my headset but since I didn't carry a spare, we didn't chat, which was fine with me.

"Indian?"

"No. He just uses the name. I would imagine it pisses off some of the Navajo nation around these parts."

"Who is he?"

Donaldson leaned against the passenger door and angled his face toward me. "A fixer. A handyman."

"Are those euphemisms for hired muscle?"

"Not so much muscle. Litton owns—er, owned—a lot of this country's petroleum infrastructure. He didn't own all the gas that went through it, but he owned the pipelines. He didn't own all the oil being refined, but he owned the refineries. The ships. The trucks. Pipelines running through sensitive lands can cause problems that require creative solutions."

"Are you talking about the Dakota Access Pipeline?"

"That wasn't Litton, but yeah. Same scenario. Pushing pipeline through land where half the locals can be bribed either with jobs or flat out bribed, and the other half try to organize and protest. Sometimes, when money doesn't do the trick, muscle does."

"You knew about this?"

"No." I looked at him. "Knowing and guessing aren't the same thing."

"Then how do you know about this guy?"

"Because if it wasn't muscle, it was money. And somebody had to deliver the satchels full of cash. The old man sent me up here a couple times to make the delivery."

"From FBI to bag man. Nice."

"I never said I was proud of it. And after I left Litton, I tried to investigate, but people aren't inclined to chat if it means derailing the gravy train."

"And you think this Walking Bear knows something about the farm killings?"

Donaldson switched his gaze from me to the windshield. He sat for half a mile without saying anything, letting the hiss of the tires on wet black pavement hold the only conversation between us.

"Do I think this guy is a sadistic sociopath hired by Bargo Litton to get his hundred mil back? Killing women and children? No."

I waited for an explanation, but none came.

"Then why are we here?" I finally asked.

"Because Walking Bear was Litton's link in the chain. He knows *a guy* who knows *a guy* who knows…et cetera. If anyone knows, he knows."

28

"Stop! STOP!"

I stomped the brake to the floor. The anti-lock brake system chattered and the wheels ground against gravel. The headlights dipped, then hung beams of light mist over the gravel track ahead of us.

"What?!" I instinctively looked for deer—or a pedestrian—or a woman with a baby carriage in the middle of a one-lane winding gravel road miles from pavement in the rugged New Mexico terrain. My pulse pounded.

Donaldson closed the cover on my iPad, which he'd been using to navigate. He pointed between the headlights.

I saw nothing in the black between the white beams.

"Turn off the lights."

I found the knob and rotated it.

"See it?" He opened his door. I squinted into the darkness.

Red sparkles winked on a line across the road. I hopped out and joined him at the front of the car. He pointed, then swept his finger to the right. He followed the red beam to the side of the road to a post driven into the rocky soil.

"Ever see a Claymore mine?"

"Are you kidding me?!" The red beam emanated from a small black box with a bright red eye. Wires ran from the box to a curved olive-green pack attached to the post. "This place is booby-trapped? With military explosives? Screw this!"

"Easy there, Stewart. Look. It's facing the other way." He pointed. I wasn't sure I saw what he was saying. "It's a shaped charge. He's got it pointed away from the road."

"So?"

"So, it makes a big bang, but it's not lethal. It's designed to scare the shit outta someone without putting the owner in prison."

"Maybe this one is, but are you willing to bet your life on the next one? Let's get out of here!"

"Hang on!" Donaldson bent at the waist and studied the device. "You got any tools in that bag of yours?" He held out a hand and made a gimme gesture. "Back up the car and point the lights over here."

A minute later, after swinging the headlights, I pressed my Leatherman into his palm. He expertly opened it and selected a cross head screwdriver, then leaned closer to the device.

"What the hell do you think you're doing?"

"I'm going to borrow it." He applied the screwdriver to one of the screws holding the device on the post.

"Hold up. Let me get far enough away so I don't get any of you on me when you blow yourself up!" I jogged back down the gravel track until I had fifty feet between us. Then decided to add another fifty.

After several minutes hunched over the post and device, he swung himself upright with the mine in hand. He waved me to join him in the car. I slid behind the wheel reluctantly. I closed the door gently.

"Don't worry." He shook the damned thing. "You can't set it off by jarring it. Walking Bear had this one wired to a laser sensor." Donaldson examined the black box with the laser eye. He struck me as far too fascinated.

"Can I assume you know what you're doing with that?"

"I trained on these in the Corps."

Small comfort.

"This probably isn't the last one," he said. He turned to me. "We should leave the car here. Tell me about this weightless thing that happens when you go poof—and those prop devices you carry."

29

The cabin materialized out of the mist less than a hundred feet away. I cut the power on the BLASTER in my left hand. Donaldson held a grip on my right hand with his left. His shoulder bumped against mine. We slipped into a silent glide just fifteen feet above the gravel.

"This is so fucking amazing!" he whispered.

"Don't get used to it. I'm not into holding hands with other men."

I blipped the power to pull us on a down angle toward a wooden porch. The cabin had a one-room look to it but grew larger than its first impression as we approached. It could have been used as a set for a western. The roof sloped down over the porch, held up by what looked like hand-cut posts. The wood looked unfinished at first, but on closer examination I caught the satin gleam of varnish. This was not a survivalist shack. As we eased under the edge of the porch roof, I could make out prefabricated logs. A single light glowed from a window centered in the front door.

"Grab that light fixture," I told him as we bumped up against the door. I felt us stabilize.

"Deadbolt," he whispered. "I need that Leatherman again. I think I can pick the lock, but it might take me a while left-handed."

"Or..." I pocketed the power unit and pressed my hand on the deadbolt. In my head, I put pressure on the imaginary levers that send me in and out of *the other thing*. Like water spreading on a floor, *the other thing* spread from my hand to the door. In a moment, light escaped from the interior of the cabin through the transparent hole under my hand. I watched it envelop the deadbolt cylinder, then touch the jamb.

"Push the door! Push!" I commanded. I counted on his grip on the light fixture as leverage. Beneath my hand, I felt the door jerk over a slight snap of resistance. "Easy, now. The bolt snapped. Don't let it fall."

He eased the door open. The bolt stayed in the jamb, maintaining silence.

"We have *got* to talk about this!" Donaldson whispered.

"I'm letting you go. This is too awkward. Are your feet touching?"

"Yeah."

Fwooomp!

I released his hand and took in the electric snap that followed. I remained unseen while he settled onto his feet, dimly lit by the interior light, which appeared to come from a kitchen at the back of the house.

"Wait here."

He gingerly advanced, testing the floorboard for squeaks with each step. I ignored his command and pushed slowly into the cabin behind him. The front door opened on a rustic sitting room that occupied half of the building. The room had a fireplace and overlooked the porch through four evenly spaced windows. A narrow hallway led to the kitchen in back. Doors on either side of the hallway suggested two bedrooms. Both doors were open.

The front door area and sitting room offered nothing to grip, but an open beamed ceiling spanned the entire space. I pushed for the nearest cross beam and used it to follow Donaldson.

He moved without haste. I stayed close above and behind him, thinking I might be able to grab him and make him vanish if the need arose. He checked the bedroom on the right, then shook his head. He checked the door on the left and gave a thumbs up signal to the front door where he assumed that I waited.

A grin crossed his face.

30

Donaldson snapped open the lighter and touched the flame to the cigarette he had taken from the pack on the nightstand. He sucked in air to make the tip glow and fill his lungs. He leaned over the bed and blew a cloud of smoke into the sleeping face.

The man in the bed was no bear. Skinny arms clutched a thin sheet over a boney body. He wasn't much larger than Pidge. His head had a narrow, pinched skull that came to a prominent point with a Kirk Douglas dimple on the chin. His hair was either shaved or buzz cut. In the brief illumination given by the cigarette lighter, I couldn't tell.

The smoke caused his nose to wrinkle. He moaned.

"Wake up, Walking Bear. But don't move." Donaldson drew in a lungful of smoke and blew it into the man's face.

His eyes flashed open.

"Uh! Uh! Don't move." Donaldson pointed at the bright red laser beam that appeared in the cloud of smoke. It threaded a line across the bed in the notch between the man's chin and his chest, just above his throat. "See it?"

The eyes went wide, shooting left and right. To his left, near the door, he spotted the red eye of the laser sensor.

"Any questions?" Donaldson asked, sliding onto the mattress.

The man lay frozen.

"Good. Spares me the explanation. I wouldn't sneeze if I were you." He stubbed out the cigarette in a well-populated ashtray on the nightstand.

"Who are you?" The words came out clotted with sleep phlegm in his throat. His eyes shot between Donaldson's silhouette on the bed and the red beam at his throat.

"You don't remember me? I used to bring you special deliveries from Bargo Litton. Payment for services."

The eyes fixed on Donaldson for a moment. Recognition flared.

"Whaddyawant?"

"I want you to stay very, very still because I do not have any desire to be perforated by a couple hundred steel balls, okay? Can you do that?"

He started to nod but sucked in a sharp breath and froze.

"Yeah," Donaldson said. "I repurposed one of your Claymores. Stay very still. Yes, no or answers to my questions. Try not to move your head."

"Motherfucker!"

"You took care of things for Mr. Litton, correct?"

"He's dead. Saw it on the news tonight."

"That he is. Which means he won't mind you filling in a few blanks for me. And since you've been watching the news, what can you tell me about the farm family killings?"

"I don't know shit!" He said it through gritted teeth, holding his chin high.

"We're going to skip the whole 'I don't know shit' part, Bear." Donaldson picked up the lighter. "Or else I'm going to get up and leave. But not before I flick this Bic and touch the flame to the corner of your mattress. Understand?" He snapped the flame alight and held it up for Bear to see. "So, reach into that Rolodex head of yours and give me a name. Who did Litton send after that woman with the Education Foundation?"

He waved the lighter flame back and forth. Bear's wide eyes watched it, glittering with reflections.

"Okay! Okay! Okay! Chill, man."

"A name."

"This is about that babe with Litton's money? That senator's kid?"

"A name."

"Litton did send someone, but that was last year. Guy goes by Artie! But Litton never authorized action! That's all I know, man!"

"What do you mean he sent someone?"

"Litton wanted to scope out that woman he gave all the money to. He was furious. He wanted a way to get it all back. He knew about Artie and he asked for him."

"Why?"

"Artie's a fucking pervert psychopath. It's his thing."

"What's his thing?"

"Creepy shit! He creeps around, man! He went up there and creeped into her house and stood in her bedroom all night. That's his kind of thing. But then Litton called it off. Said he didn't want him to do anything. That's it! That's all I know!"

"Litton hired Artie to gather intel, and that's it?"

"Dude, that's it! Artie took some pictures. Some souvenirs, you know? Some underwear. But that's all. He knew better than to do more unless Litton gave me the word. Word never came!"

My skin crawled at the idea of someone standing over Sandy Stone in the dark, listening to her breathing.

"What's his name?"

"Artie! That's it! That's all I ever had!"

"How do you reach him?"

"Voice mailbox."

"How do you pay him?"

"The last time? Bitcoin." Bear's eyes dampened. His voice hitched. "Look! I seen the news! I know what's going on! And that's probably Artie because he's one sick sonofabitch, but I didn't set that up! I swear! Litton never called me after that one time. I ain't heard from Litton since he disappeared."

"Did Litton make direct contact with Artie?"

Bear looked indignant. "No, man. Strictly through me. But I gotta say—I never want to hear from Artie. Fucking wake up with him standing in my bedroom like you! That's all I got! I swear!"

"Describe him."

"I can't! I never saw him!"

"How did you find out about him?"

"A guy I know who knows a guy. I told you, Artie's a pervert. The guy knew of him from some trouble he got in when he was in college. I had a job in Florida—they wanted someone to scare someone. Artie sounded scary, so I made a call to a guy who made a call."

"Names, Bear. I want names."

"No names! I was twice removed. Strictly voice mail. Artie just called me up and we did a deal. That thing with Litton. But that's it! That was the only time! I got nothin' to do with this shit on TV!"

"His number. I want his number."

"You gotta let me go!"

"Bear, that Claymore is set up on a chair on the other side of that wall. Pointed at you. I want his number."

"Okay! Okay! It's in my phone. Over there on the desk!"

Donaldson eased off the bed and stepped to a desk in the corner of the room. He flicked the Bic.

"You got a dozen phones here, Bear."

"The Samsung. Black case. Sticker on the back."

Donaldson picked up a phone and examined it. "Care Bears?"

"That's it!"

The screen lit up. "What's the passcode?"

"2-3-4-5"

"You're an idiot."

"Fuck! You try and remember all those damned passcodes!"

Donaldson worked the screen. He scrolled and scanned for a moment. "Under AR?"

"Yeah! That's it!"

"Brilliant code system, Bear."

"I gave you what you want! Now turn off that fucking laser!"

Donaldson closed the phone screen and pocketed the device. He stepped back to the corner of the mattress and looked down at the skinny man under the sheets.

"Please!"

Donaldson reached in his pocket and pulled out his FBI wallet. He flipped it open and held it up, then lit the lighter again. He waved the flame near the badge.

"See this? When I get done tracking down your friend, Artie, I'm coming back for you. Unless you decide to save the taxpayers a small fortune and stick your head up into that beam."

"PLEASE!"

Donaldson walked out.

"YOU CAN'T FUCKING DO THIS TO ME!"

I took one last look at Bear who lay frozen in the dark, clutching the mattress and shouting for Donaldson to come back.

I used the beamed ceiling to follow Donaldson out the front door. He stood on the porch with his back to the door. I collided with him, which made him jump.

"Shit!" he uttered.

"Let's go," I said. I worked my way around to his left side, closed a grip on his left hand and pushed.

FWOOOMP!

He vanished. I kicked off the porch and we rose into the mist outside the protection of the porch. I pulled a BLASTER and gave it full power. It accelerated us toward the gravel track.

We were halfway to the car when the explosion ripped through the misty silence. I nearly dropped the BLASTER.

"Christ! You killed him!"

Donaldson said nothing for a moment. Then I felt him shrug.

"Nah. But I blew the living shit out of his kitchen."

31

"Artie," I told my wife.

"Just Artie?"

"That's all we have. That and a phone number. Can you enter it into a computer? Search for any mention of the name? Anybody using it? Variations?"

"Of course, Will," she said. She sounded exasperated. I had expected a different reaction. Donaldson gave me a smug look that I didn't like. "Did you get anything else?"

Donaldson leaned over the phone on the dash. "He might have a record for sex offenses. My CI called him a pervert and said he had some trouble in college."

"Any idea how old he is?"

"No."

I jumped in and told her about Litton sending the man to Sandy Stone's house.

"That's creepy," Andy said. "The thing is…I don't know how much I can do with this right now."

"What do you mean?"

"We have a situation here. It's not good. Lyle Traeger is missing."

Voices broke in the background.

"Will, I can't talk now. When can you get here?"

"Fast as we can."

"Be safe. Text me that phone number and I'll do what I can with this, but I gotta go."

The call ended.

"Who's Lyle Traeger?" Donaldson asked.

DAWN SLITHERED out of the relentless mist when we reached Farmington. I told Donaldson the truth. I was beat. The ForeFlight app on my iPad said I was looking at close to six hours of flying to reach Essex County from Farmington, New Mexico. Nothing out of the ordinary on a typical day, but I'd been up for twenty-four hours and nothing is more dangerous to a pilot than fatigue.

"I need a nap and then a ton of coffee," I said as we reached the city limits. "Just a short nap. Enough to fool my body into thinking it's not tired for a couple hours. I can use the back seat."

"Let's get a room. You can sack out, and I'll go get some food and coffee."

"Get a thermos, so we can take something with us. This would normally be a two-legged trip, but I'm going to make it three. Bladder stops. Then there's only one other problem."

"Which is?"

"There's a low over upper Michigan training a cold front down through Wisconsin, Iowa and points south. It's cooking up rain statewide with a chance for severe storms. I'll see how far I can get us, but we may have to hole up somewhere for a few hours."

"Hey, don't push it on my account. Whatever you need."

The iPad gave us the Silver River Adobe Inn, which we had already passed on the way to the airport. We backtracked, got lucky with the last available room, and I crashed on top of the sheets with my phone set on a one-hour timer while Donaldson took off with the courtesy car.

Sleep came slowly and I worried that the effort would be for nothing. I fell asleep without knowing it and shifted quickly into a dream that someone was standing in the room, in darkness, watching me. It startled me awake. Searching the room in dim morning light, I found nothing. I rolled over and tried again.

A few seconds later, or so it seemed, the alarm sounded.

WE FLEW from Farmington to Renner Field in Goodland, Kansas. Gray mist on the surface at Farmington broke into dazzling sunlight and blue skies at nine thousand feet, which was our flight planned altitude. I didn't want to go higher because the Baron had no supplemental oxygen system. Altitude and fatigue don't mix. We skimmed the tops of the clouds for miles before they gradually broke up beneath us.

Renner Field provided fuel, exercise and bladder relief. We pressed on for Freemont Municipal in Freemont, Nebraska, almost equidistant from Omaha and Lincoln, and not terribly far from Seward, where Andy and I had recently contributed to the crash of a light jet. I briefly contemplated making Seward our destination but decided karma might take it out on me.

Fatigue gnawed at my joints when I climbed out of the cockpit at the Freemont gas pumps. The Baron carries plenty of fuel and could have made the flight all the way to Essex County, but fueling provided exercise and my favorite cargo. More fuel.

Our thermos was empty. The FBO office had the same affliction. Donaldson offered to take the airport courtesy car into town to find a refill, but I dismissed the idea. More caffeine at this point would only add a jitter that I didn't need on the controls.

"The weather does not look good," I told Donaldson after we strapped in. I showed him the graphics on the iPad. "There's a line of thunderstorms moving northeast toward Madison. It thins out near Eau Claire, and we might be able to do an end run into Essex County. Depends on whether we get there first or the storms do. If it's the latter, we'll divert to Green Bay."

"You're the captain."

It was close. The end run added twenty minutes to our flight time. When we reached Essex County, we were in solid IFR conditions with rain pelting the windshield and turbulence jarring my jitters. I regretted the amount of caffeine running through my system, because the flying and the weather were more than enough to keep me wide-eyed.

Approach gave us the GPS 31 procedure and warned of an area of moderate to heavy radar returns just five miles west of the airport. I flew the approach at damn near cruise speed, holding off on the gear and flaps and bouncing against the seat and seatbelt. Already in gray clouds, the cockpit grew ominously darker as I struggled to square the needles on the glideslope. The GPS ticked down to just over a mile from the airport when we broke out of ragged clouds and I spotted the familiar terrain that preceded the runway.

I pulled the throttles to idle and positioned my hand on the gear lever, watching the speed drop to maximum gear extension speed. The instant the airspeed needle passed the mark, I dropped the gear. The landing gear grabbed the wind like an anchor. I rolled the electric trim and reached for flaps, fighting to keep the runway numbers centered in the windshield as wind gusts worked against me. As soon as I had flap speed, I dumped everything. Rapid throttle inputs dealt with wind shear when it pulled the rug out from under us on short final. Donaldson grabbed the dash with his left hand as we plunged toward the runway numbers. I resisted pitching up, preserving speed, until it looked like we would hit hard. At the last second, I heaved the nose up. The wheels squeaked onto the runway. The nose settled. Side gusts tried to jerk the controls in my hands.

Lightning jabbed the earth directly ahead, as if to protest my successful landing. Before we could make the turnoff to the taxiway, the skies opened, and torrents of rain dumped on us.

Donaldson didn't let go of the dash until I pulled up in front of the barely visible hangar. I cut the engines.

"Ladies and gentlemen, welcome to Essex County," I said. "Please push all internal organs back down your throats before you exit the aircraft."

32

"What's that about?" I asked. Andy watched Donaldson and Special Agent Janos huddle at the end of the hall near Chief Ceeves' office.

"That's Lee telling Janos that he's on medical leave, and that his boss, Rayburn, doesn't know he's here and he'd like to keep it that way. And that's Janos telling Lee that he's welcome here and that any thoughts he might contribute are appreciated but that he shouldn't over-exert himself, what with his injury."

"Really? Janos rolls out the welcome mat? I thought the speech would be that whole 'and keep your nose out of my investigation!' schtick."

Andy smiled. "This is why I hate cop movies." She motioned for me to follow her to her cubicle. I sat down in the plastic chair beside her desk. A monster yawn overwhelmed me. She rolled her chair close and brushed a hand through my hair.

"You've got to be exhausted."

"Oh, yeah. I will crash hard tonight. Do not come hunting in my bed for wild sex, woman. Unless you want some, in which case, please do your best to wake me."

"I think you'll be safe. I do not expect to get out of here anytime soon."

"Any news?"

She shook her head grimly. "Lyle's unit is still missing. The tracker is off-line. He's not answering his cell phone."

"How long has it been?"

"He pulled the three to eleven yesterday. I asked him to canvass the Lakes but suggested he do it in the evening when people are more likely to be home. He checked in for dinner at six. Mae said he was heading up after that. We heard nothing. She reached out to him around nine. By end of shift, we had units looking for him."

"No chance he just…forgot he was on duty and went home?"

"That's a bit much, even for Lyle. But we checked. I wish we hadn't, because now his wife is terrified. She doesn't like it when he takes a shift here. Another reason Tom hasn't offered him full time. Tom interviews the spouse, too."

"He didn't interview me."

"Mmmm, yes he did. Before our wedding. And don't think he wouldn't have pulled the plug on the whole thing if he didn't approve of you." She said it with a smile that cracked through the sheen of worry. "We spent the day today going over Lyle's movements. He did the canvass, and we confirmed it with each resident he visited. Most of the homes up there are occupied for the summer. The immediate neighbors to the west are out of town, but we spoke to them by phone. They've been gone all week and didn't know about Johns. The owner is into racing, I guess. Lyle's tracker shows him stopping there, then driving west on Sunset Circle. Then it goes dead."

"Did he maybe go off the road? Maybe into the lake?"

"About the only place for that is where it happened to Lydia," Andy said, recalling her sister's near-death plunge into Leander Lake. "Lyle went west, around the other side of the lake. And there are no signs of a vehicle leaving the road. We checked."

"Don't you still have roadblocks up? Guarding Sandy?"

"We do. But he went the other way around."

I knew Andy would have started pulling video, traffic cam footage, and plate reader data from the highway patrol. She would have half a dozen other initiatives underway. I didn't ask for details. If she wanted to share, she would.

Reading my thoughts, she pressed a hand to my knee and said, "You should go home. But don't take Lee with you. I'm going to see if the Chief will let him use one of our workstations to dig around this Artie character. The phone number was no help. I don't have time for that right now. The department can put him up at the Holiday Inn with the rest of the FBI team."

"How are you going to explain the origin of that lead?" I asked *sotto voce*.

"I'll let Lee own it. Something from an old case he remembers. We're grasping at straws now, so anything from anybody is fair game." She leaned over and put a hand on the back of my neck. She pulled me into a kiss. When it was over, I had trouble climbing out of the deep pool of affection in her eyes. "Go home."

"I hope you find Lyle."

33

I got my third soaking in twenty-four hours when I ran from the station lobby to my car. By the time I reached home, the rain had let up enough that I didn't bother dashing from the car to the house. It hardly mattered.

A hot shower almost put me to sleep. I imagined being found on the shower tiles by Andy late in the night or being jolted awake when we ran out of hot water. The massaging effect of the hot water loosened my muscles and my mind. Dried off, I put on a pair of boxers and hit the sheets. I anticipated winking out quickly as soon as my head hit the pillow, but a lingering afterimage from my nap that morning lurked behind my eyelids. The goose bump creepiness of having someone slip into the house found its way to me —a stranger in my bedroom just standing in the dark. Somehow it seemed even more menacing than the notion of a home invader looking to steal or molest. Andy and I agreed not to tell Sandy what Walking Bear had described. Not right now, at least, and if never became an option, so much the better.

Lying in the dark, I pushed Artie out of my thoughts only to have him replaced with the image of my bloodied hand and the distant, glazed look of the first officer on Litton's plane. I had asked Andy to check before I left the station. She told me he was reported to be in stable condition at a Phoenix hospital, expected to survive.

I fixed on that thought and hoped to ride it into a solid sleep.

My phone rang.

"Shit," I said aloud.

I plucked the phone off the nightstand and hit the green call button without looking at the caller ID.

"Hello."

"Will, it's Lillian. Spiro Lewko has agreed to meet you. How soon can you get here?"

PART III

34

I slipped the Navajo out of the hangar at three a.m. after four hours of restless sleep. Andy never joined me in bed. It came as no surprise that she wouldn't leave the station with an officer missing. Peeling my wife away from her desk would have left claw marks.

I thumbed a text to Andy about having to take an early flight. I wrote that I hoped to be back by "midday," crafting the message to provide just enough information to hold off her curiosity. She had far heavier issues at hand. Admittedly lame, it beat explaining why I ran off on a hare-brained mission at the request of her least favorite hare-brained scientist.

Not that I hadn't argued with Lillian.

"No," I told her flatly.

"You don't understand. I got us in."

"Um, it sounds like you gave me up."

"He knows your name from the NTSB report. He connected the dots on his own."

"How did you get anywhere near him? These guys don't exactly wander the streets unprotected."

"I rolled up to his research facility, handed them my resume and told his security people to take me to their leader," she said sarcastically. "What do you think I did? I told them I had information about his artifact!"

"And they took you to see the man himself?"

"Instantly."

"Jesus! What did you tell him?"

"That I knew about those kids in Wichita. That I knew his people grabbed the artifact. That he needs my knowledge and credentials."

"And me?"

"I told him I knew you through the certifying neurologist on your case with the FAA, and I could get you to tell him your story about the crash."

"Uh…okay…and how is any of this good news?"

"Because if we're going to get our hands on it, we need access. Which I just got us. But I can't just stuff it in my bra and walk out the door. You can."

"I don't wear a bra."

Essex County Airport to Hickory Regional Airport flight-planned at just under three hours in the Navajo. I filed for a direct route, which clipped off the southern third of Lake Michigan and kept me east of O'Hare's airspace.

A cold front—the one that made for a thrilling arrival at Essex County in the Baron—curled from a low-pressure center over Sault Saint Marie. It ran down the eastern coast of Michigan. Storm remnants dragged through Ohio and as far south as Kentucky. I passed behind the front, encountered a few showers before dawn, and arrived beneath clear skies on Hickory Regional's Runway 24.

Lillian waited at the fence as I pulled into a tie-down, guided by a ramp rat who had only just arrived for his day shift.

"I see the appeal," she commented when I finished my business with the FBO, which included a request for full fuel and optimistic instructions to have my bill ready for an afternoon departure. "Driving took me fifteen hours, with fourteen of that stuck in traffic around Chicago."

She feeped her Prius and hopped in. I loaded my bag into the back seat and slid in beside her.

"Do you have a plan? Or are we flying by the seat of our pants?"

She accelerated out of the parking lot.

"A little of both."

"Do I disappear while you get us through the front gate and into the secret laboratory?"

"Nope. We walk in. I've already got your visitor tag, issued by the man himself." She pointed at a glossy badge sitting in her console cupholder. It displayed a photo of me.

"Well, that's creepy," I said. "Where did they get the picture?"

"The world we live in."

"If you already have access, why not let me slip in with you, grab the damned thing, and slip out? I thought that's what you wanted. To get this thing out of his hands as fast as possible."

"I don't get in without you," she said.

I downgraded the half-assed plan to quarter-assed.

Lillian drove east from the airport to Hickory Boulevard, which angled northwest through lazy suburban sprawl, pretty and green. Fifteen highway miles later, Evermore, named after Spiro Lewko's formidable cyber retail empire, sprang abruptly from a landscape sparsely populated by farmland and individual country homes. We drove from rolling fields directly into a Norman Rockwell painting. The highway morphed into a quaint Main Street with angle parking and traditional high façade storefronts. Shops and cafes lined the sidewalks. Notably missing at the edge of town were the big box stores, car dealerships and gas stations typical of American suburbia. Also missing was the twenty-acre distribution center that had been part of the Evermore deal with North Carolina. I asked Lillian. She told me it lay five miles beyond Lewko's pet research village.

Side streets named after trees fanned out from Main Street. Homes with front porches and gingerbread accents nestled beneath the healthy crowns of hardwood trees. Most of the houses looked as if they'd been constructed before World War One, but closer inspection showed crisp new siding, composite porch boards and steps, and tight-fitting energy-efficient windows. Solar panels spread on every rooftop. Many of the yards had been recently sodded. Everything wore fresh paint.

"Disney's Main Street U.S.A.," I commented. "I was expecting a gate with a guard house. I remember your warnings about intense security."

"They know we're here." Lillian dipped a glance at the badge in the cupholder. "Wait for it…"

We slowed to twenty-five and rolled between rows of shops. Pedestrians strolled the sidewalks, some with big cups of coffee which I regarded jealously.

"Wait…"

I waited.

A woman's voice spoke through the car's audio system.

"Good morning, Ms. Farris and Mr. Stewart. Welcome to Evermore!" Her crisp elocution served up a delicate English accent.

"Good morning," Lillian replied.

I mouthed *Farris?* at Lillian. She put her finger to her lips.

"Would you like driving directions to your destination?"

"No, thank you."

"I see you will be meeting with Mr. Lewko this morning. I am to inform you that he will serve breakfast at your meeting. Do you have any special dietary requests?"

"I'm vegan."

"I'm not," I said quickly. "Terwilligy arga bultrimil mobiltras."

"I'm sorry, Mr. Stewart, I did not understand your request."

"I'll have the haggis."

"I will forward your request to Mr. Lewko's chef. Do you have any other requests?"

"No," Lillian answered before I could speak up. She flared her eyes at me in a *shut the hell up* way.

I pulled my cell phone from my pocket. The screen showed a text message from Andy.

Home for dinner?

I had no idea. Nor did I want to explain why I had no idea. I decided the lesser crime would be not to answer. Andy accepts that I often ignore my phone when flying.

I snapped the phone free of its protective case. With a thumbnail, I opened the phone's back and pried out the battery. I twisted around in the seat and unzipped a side pocket in my flight bag, depositing the pieces. I was about to twist back to face forward, but as an afterthought, I pulled out a power unit and prop. I lifted my pants leg and slipped the prop into my left boot, then dropped the power unit into my right. Both were awkward and uncomfortable, but secure. I pulled the jeans back down over my western boot tops.

Lillian slowed and signaled for a left turn off Main Street. We cruised a residential street where lawns like carpets hugged homes belonging to Barbie dolls or Stepford Wives. The closest thing to litter on the street was an errant leaf or twig from the overarching maples.

We passed a school built in FDR's New Deal style. On closer inspection, it proved to be an office building. Similar structures randomly dotted the neighborhood. The plan for this community seemed to be one of housing the workers near the work. I thought of the old neighborhoods in Milwaukee that blossomed around breweries and foundries. Evermore's tech version lacked yeast odor and smokestacks belching clouds against the skyline.

I noted an absence of wires overhead.

A pillared brick building with white trim appeared among the homes. Park surrounded the building. The park featured a baseball diamond and a playground.

Though it lacked a fence around the property, the facility did not lack a gate and guardhouse. I looked for but did not find cameras; I took them for granted.

A uniformed security officer stepped out of the small guardhouse as Lillian turned in the driveway. He raised a friendly wave and brought her to a halt. She lowered her window.

"Morning!" he greeted us while his eyes roamed the car interior. "May I have your identity tags?"

Lillian surrendered both. I expected him to duck back into the small guardhouse, but instead he pulled a smartphone from his utility belt, waved it over each tag and examined the result on his screen. Satisfied, he handed them back.

"Mr. Lewko is expecting you at the main building." He pointed at the pillared entrance. "Just pull up in front. It's valet parking. Have a great day!"

"Better put this on." Lillian handed me the tag. Once in hand, I realized that the tag was not laminated, but had thickness and was in fact a small screen displaying my picture, full name, a bar code and a series of numbers. The screen was the thickness of a piece of cardboard and it flexed without disrupting the imagery. A small clip rode on the back.

"Cute." I dropped it in my shirt pocket. "Does this get Netflix?"

"Probably."

Lillian pulled up to an entrance beneath four columns. To the eternal disappointment of my fifth-grade teacher, Mrs. Wilson, I had no idea whether the columns were Doric, Ionic or Corinthian. If quizzed, I would have answered white.

A young woman in perfectly creased trousers and a white summer blouse hustled to open the car door. An identity tag rode above her left breast. She held out a hand for Lillian to turn over the key fob to her Prius. I stepped out and realized that the objects in my boots were anything but comfortable. The sharp prop tip stabbed the bone at the side of my ankle. The power unit bumped against my leg.

The Prius hummed quietly away.

Lillian gestured for me to follow her through tall double doors. All colonial pretense dissipated the instant we stepped inside.

The interior of the "library" building was a set director's dream for a science fiction picture. White marble, chrome and glass flashed at me beneath a vast sky of blue. It took a second to spot the reflections in the sky. The entire ceiling consisted of digital screens displaying the same sky I stood under moments ago. I looked for seams and found a few, but the panels between each seam were gigantic. Three floors marked by chrome and glass railings rose above a central atrium lobby. From where I stood, I couldn't see walls on any of the floors, suggesting each had the same open concept that spread in either direction from the lobby. The ground floor shared workstation space with a coffee shop and food court. Screens floated at the workstations as if levitated. Circles of plush furniture surrounded low tables where people in corporate casual attire huddled over tablets and laptops, many nursing tall coffees that taunted me.

I expected to see young workers hustling to their duties on hover boards.

"Do you know where we're going?" I asked Lillian, who had paused to take in the sights.

"No."

The atrium offered both stairs and elevators to the upper floors.

"You haven't been here before?"

She shook her head.

"Please proceed to the elevators directly to your left," the woman with the British accent instructed me from my shirt pocket. I pulled out the identification tag. A twenty-something woman with neatly tied back blonde hair smiled at me from where my photo had been.

"You talkin' to me?" I asked.

"Yes. Please proceed to the elevators directly to your left."

"Bultrimil mobiltras," I replied.

"I'm sorry, Mr. Stewart, I do not understand your request. Do you require assistance?" She smiled. I came close to buying her humanity.

"I think we have this," Lillian spoke to her badge, which rewarded her with a smile from the same AI image. Lillian took off in the direction of the elevator; the doors opened as we approached. The walls of the car were glass, which didn't surprise me. That the floor was also glass did surprise me.

Lillian glanced down and sucked in a sharp breath. "Oh, God!" She reached for a handrail, found none, and planted her palm firmly on the glass. "I do not do well with heights!" She squeezed her eyes shut.

"A fitness program for the acrophobic. Makes them take the stairs."

"Annapurna." My tag announced.

The glass doors closed. The elevator rose. I looked for cables or gears or pulleys and wires but found nothing but a silver piston-like tube on each of the back corners of the car.

The car performed a smooth, silent ascent.

"Annapurna," a male voice in the car announced as the car stopped. The glass wall at the back of the elevator slid aside and Lillian hurried onto solid ground. Her ashen complexion explained to me why she had refused a ride with me in *the other thing*.

On either side of the atrium, the top floor of the building sprawled beneath a high ceiling made airy by skylights. Glass walled offices lined the perimeter. Interior glass walls partitioned a maze of workstations. Central to the entire floor, however, was a broad open area with a series of floor-to-ceiling concentric rings of glass. At the center, a wall of brushed stainless steel formed a cylinder. Lighted control panels hung at symmetrical intervals.

"Please proceed on the amber line," our guide instructed us from my shirt pocket.

A set of sequential lights glowed in the floor, throbbing like weird luminescent water flowers sunk in an acrylic pond.

"Follow the yellow brick road," I said in Munchkin voice, falling in step behind Lillian.

The lights led us on a winding path through the workstations, keeping us well clear of the central metallic cylinder. Demonstrating a certain sentience, the lights kept pace a perfect distance ahead of us, whether we accelerated or lagged. I contemplated making a wrong turn just to see if the lights changed from amber to red, or if they formed a new path to put us back on course.

We walked to a conference room centered on the side wall of the building. Glass walls bared the room to outside scrutiny. I noticed a slight tint and wondered if it might be made opaque by an electronic control.

A sense of unease nagged me. It didn't feel like common nervous tension. It felt like unfinished business. It felt like the sixth sense that tells me there's more ice in the clouds than Flight Service predicted, or a line of storms won't dissipate as expected, or a smear of hydraulic fluid on one of the landing gear doors needs serious attention.

The lights led us into the conference room and vanished.

"Cute trick," I said to no one, at least not to any of the half dozen people milling around the conference room with breakfast plates in hand. A few glanced at us. Others chatted energetically.

A buffet had been set up at one end of the room. I smelled bacon, peppers and fresh fruit. A woman in a chef's smock and hat stood at an omelet station. She worked her whisk in a bowl.

"Everyone, this is Dr. Lillian Farris and her guest, William Stewart." The British AI spoke from somewhere within the room. I glanced down at my tag, which had changed back to my familiar mug.

Faces turned. Hands waved. A few people said, "Good morning."

"Please enjoy the buffet breakfast, Dr. Farris and Mr. Stewart. Mr. Lewko will join you momentarily."

We followed instructions, gingerly loaded plates at the buffet and took them to the conference table where our names glowed within the glossy surface. The names disappeared as soon as we seated ourselves. Blessed coffee aroma sought me out from a selection of glass carafes. I picked one, tested the scent, and poured the second-best cup of coffee I've ever had.

"Who ordered the haggis?" a voice behind me asked, carried briskly into the room by an athletic man roughly my age. Shoulder-length light brown hair, fresh-from-the-shower wet, brushed a gray polo shirt. Light blue eyes darted beneath bushy eyebrows. His wide mouth had the constant appearance of someone hiding a joke from the teacher. A bit shorter than me, he carried a weight advantage and precious little looked like fat.

"That would be me," I confessed.

He scanned my plate. "You're not having any? Did we not prepare it properly?"

"Frankly, I've never seen haggis before."

A few of the faces around the table worked to conceal smirks.

"Ah! Challenging our AI! Very good!" He laughed. "Try it! I'll venture it's the best haggis you'll ever taste." He grabbed a small plate from the buffet table, dropped a pair of dark disks aboard and brought it to me. "Stewart?"

"Lewko?"

His hand came out. He pumped a brisk, firm handshake. "The man who fell to earth. Pleased to meet you." He studied me, then turned to Lillian. "Dr. Farris, thank you for bringing Mr. Stewart—may I call you Will?"

"You may."

He darted back to the buffet and filled a small bowl with fresh fruit. "You may call me Mr. Lewko. Not because I'm being snooty, but because I resent my parents for giving me the same first name as a disgraced American vice president. Please, everyone, be seated. Let's begin."

On that cue, all present found places at the table. The omelet chef slipped discretely out of the room and a glass door sealed the entrance. I watched for the glass to turn opaque, but nothing happened.

Last to take a seat, Lewko dropped into the head chair. He placed his palm on the table. A light within scanned it. The names in the glass disappeared. The table surface flashed, showing file folders and rows of text. He worked his fingertips on the surface. Lists appeared and disappeared. In rapid succession, a series of photos spread down the center of the table.

"How's the haggis?" he asked me.

I didn't answer or touch the Scottish dish. Taut strings inside me pulled tighter. Tension ran down my arms. My eyes were trapped by the photos.

I looked from one image to the next.

A vertical stabilizer stabbed into muddy earth. A wing with an engine attached. A roll of incoherently smashed aluminum. A leather upholstered pilot's seat slouching in tall grass that had been beaten flat by emergency workers.

I recognized the photos. Not because I'd been at the accident scene where they were taken—I had been there in darkness, neither alert nor conscious—but because an NTSB investigator named Connie Walsh shared them with me.

The photos documented the remains of the Piper Navajo I'd flown to its destruction a little more than a year ago.

No one spoke. Lewko swept his fingers over the surface of the table and the images changed to broken airplane pieces laid out on a concrete floor. I recognized the floor of the Foundation hangar at Essex County Airport. NTSB stamps marked date and time in the lower right corner of the images. I recognized the pieces because I had visited the reassembled wreck after the accident.

Once.

Lillian's hand slipped beneath the lip of the table and came to rest on my thigh. She squeezed a message of uncharacteristic support. I took in the photos, then looked down at the plate. My hand seemed distant, disconnected, and I wasn't entirely sure I had control of it. I picked up a fork, turned it on edge and cut a piece from what looked like a tiny charred frisbee. I stabbed it with the fork and put the morsel in my mouth while cool blue eyes watched me.

I chewed.

Swallowed.

Looked at Lewko.

He wore the look of someone waiting for a practical joke to unfold, with that permanent smirk trying to bloom into a full smile or heartless laugh.

"That is, without a doubt," I said, "the best haggis I've ever tasted."

The smile escaped the smirk. A few chuckles broke from the small crowd around the table. The release of tension granted permission for all to eat.

"Of course, it is!" Lewko said brightly. "Everyone, you all know who Will is. Will, we're grateful you could join us. We have a lot of work to do here, and your input may be invaluable to our task. But for the moment, please relax and enjoy breakfast!" He dug into his fruit to make the point.

I hadn't taken much from the buffet. I finished it off quickly. The haggis, surprisingly, proved not only edible, but delicious. Finishing it off felt satisfying on several levels.

I closed my plate, leaned back and sipped coffee.

"Let's not cover old ground unnecessarily. You're all familiar with the accident that brought down Will's plane. You have copies of the preliminary NTSB report, along with notes from the FAA investigators, Cyler and Walsh—"

"Walsh was NTSB," I corrected him.

A ripple of unease coursed the table. I made a mental note. The staff did not correct the boss.

Lewko did not look at me. "Of course. NTSB. As I was saying, you have all read the reports. When Dr. Farris joined this effort, she promised to bring Will to us for a personal debrief, which I think is great. Will, if you don't mind, and I hope it's not too painful—would you recount for us the events that led to the accident?"

"No."

The word hung like smoke in still air.

"I don't know what Dr. Farris told you, or promised you, but the answer is No. I can't recount any of the events because I have no memory of those events."

"To be fair," Lewko said, "we knew about your memory loss. I still think there's value in you sharing what you can of your experience."

"I understand you have a fragment of whatever it was that caused the accident. Can I see it?"

The reaction around the table told me I'd jumped well ahead of the script.

"Will, that's a big ask. We're engaged in highly confidential, unprecedented research. I don't think it will be possible to give you direct contact."

"I've already had direct contact. I hit it, or it hit me."

"Granted, but I cannot—"

"I'm aware that the object exhibits exceptional properties."

"I'd rather not comment," he said.

"Well, then let me. I have exceptional properties." Lillian turned to me and I heard her breath catch. "I am alive. I have no idea how or why. I hit something while traveling in a lightweight aluminum aircraft at over one hundred and forty miles per hour. It ripped the left wing off the aircraft, tore open the fuselage like a beer can pop top, and yanked me out at five hundred feet. That photo of the pilot's seat…that's where they found me." I pointed at the table. "I learned all this after the fact. I also learned that a kid at a Tuscaloosa salvage yard found a piece of something jammed in the back of the fuselage near the autopilot servos."

The detail caused another ripple around the table.

"The kid and his friends knew they were on to something big and tried to capitalize on their discovery. Somebody came along and *persuaded* them that they weren't the best people to study this problem. And here we are. Mr. Lewko, if you'd like my help, I'd like a look at this thing. Because I have an itch I can't scratch."

Heads traded glances. Seven people shared the table with Lillian and me, all in the twenty-to-forty age range. Three were men, four were women. And I had just said something that made them each a little more confident that they were smarter than me.

"I'm afraid a 'look' will not be possible," Lewko said, protecting the secret.

"Right," I said. I leaned forward and planted my elbows on the table. "Because it can't be seen."

Once again, the words hung like smoke in the air.

"Well, Dr. Farris, you did not tell us that Will had specific knowledge of the item's unique properties," Lewko said to Lillian.

"Will is unique in his own right," Lillian said. "Let's move past the dancing here. We're all here for the same reason. We all believe that the object you have behind that steel wall may be one of the greatest discoveries in human history. And that the object does not have its origins *in* human history. So why don't we stop tiptoeing around and get on with the research that needs to be performed? Starting with gathering any and all facts or impressions we can from the person who, as he said, made first contact."

"Yes," I said. "First contact."

Lewko stared.

"That's what you think, isn't it?" I asked. "That this isn't some Russian stealth aircraft or U.S. Air Force drone that wandered off course. I have to say, that sounds crazy to me."

Lewko chuckled dismissively.

"Mr. Stewart, do you know how many stars are in our galaxy?"

"A lot."

"Two hundred and fifty...billion, plus or minus a hundred billion. And do you know how many galaxies there are?"

"A lot."

"One hundred billion." He let the number hang for a moment. "My grandmother grew up in a farmhouse that had no electricity until she was in high school. No indoor plumbing until she left for college. Her father used horses for cultivation and harvesting. Think about that. I'm just two generations removed from a thousand generations of our species basically camping on this planet. Go back to my grandmother's generation, and people think steam powered trains are the peak of human achievement! Yet here we sit today with men orbiting the planet, with cameras that can bare the soul of a distant galaxy or the inside of a beating heart! With—and you'll appreciate this—supersonic flight."

"Not anymore, at least not commercially."

"You make my point! Every generation feels it is at the pinnacle. We wonder…have we learned everything there is to learn? Written every song that can be written? Discovered every discovery? Do you believe that a thousand years from now, or a hundred or even a decade from now, life will be exactly as you see it today?"

I didn't answer.

"By any stretch of the imagination, given those hundreds of billions of stars multiplied by a hundred billion galaxies, can you possibly believe that this planet is the one and only rock on which sentient life has evolved enough to invent flush toilets and flying machines?" Lewko answered his own question with a vigorous shake of his head. "I laugh every time the mainstream media breathlessly announces that NASA may have found life beyond our atmosphere. The shocking discovery would be that the vast universe is barren *except for this planet!* Of course, we're told that if there is life out there, it's beyond our reach. It's too far! We will never reach it and it will never reach us. Never in a lifetime of hurtling through empty space—or hundreds of lifetimes!" He leaned over his empty fruit bowl. "We're told that there's a speed limit. We've always been told there's a speed limit. No one could possibly create something that travels faster than a man on a fast horse, right? Or a Ford Model A, right? Or a Boeing 747, right? Or a Saturn rocket, right? No one could possibly come up with a way to prevent the absolute force that is gravity from putting a speed limit on the highways between stars, right? And for damn sure, Einstein imposed the speed of light as the final limit, right?"

He waited for me to speak. No one else around the table dared.

"That thing I hit. It can't be seen. And it has no weight," I said, carefully choosing my words for the superiority it rendered in his eyes.

"No. It has no 'weight' here on Earth. You fly, Mr. Stewart. How fast?"

For a moment I thought he meant *the other thing* and panic welled up. Then I realized his meaning.

"Two hundred…ish."

"Why? Why not go faster? Because you need bigger engines, less drag. You need to overcome forces that line up against you. Friction. Heat. Shock waves. You can't point your airplane straight up and go to the moon because you can't escape Earth's gravity. But what if you could? What if none of those forces lined up against you? How fast do you think you could go between planets, or stars, or even galaxies if you had nothing to stop you?"

I fed him the line he expected. "There are physical limits. Laws."

"Really? A generation ago, supersonic flight was impossible. It was an impenetrable wall. A generation before that, flight was impossible. It belonged only to birds. A few generations before that, travel on a steam train at sixty miles per hour was expected to tear the flesh from human bones. Those are all unbreakable laws that have been broken."

"Then you think that what I hit has the properties to break the next set of laws?"

"You don't?"

I began to understand his appeal with Lillian.

"I want to see it."

A woman sitting across from me objected. "Aside from the fact that you *can't* see it, I have serious concerns about contamination. Not to mention obvious security issues."

"Amy, the 'concerns about contamination' ship has sailed," one of her colleagues scoffed. "This item has been in our atmosphere for over a year. It's been through a collision with an airplane, transported all over the country, handled by those clowns in Wichita, and even mishandled by some of our own people. Get over it."

A brief argument broke out between the woman, Amy, and two of the men. One of the men emphasized the nature and security of the facility now housing the object. He gestured at the concentric rings out on the floor. I hoped he would elaborate. He didn't.

"I have a question," I interrupted. "You've had this thing for a while. Aside from the fact that it can't be seen, either with the human eye or on radar, but it can be detected using sound, what do you know about it?"

"Well, you're better informed than we expected," Lewko observed. "Tom?"

A man across the table from me answered. "We know its precise dimensions. We've been able to map it using the rather old-fashioned method of making molds of its shape and laser-scanning the impressions. We have a 3-D map of the object."

Lewko stroked the tabletop. A luminous 3-D drawing appeared in the surface. It rotated slowly. To my eye, it looked like a broken piece of pottery with several shark fin vanes protruding from a curved surface. Each vane mimicked the appearance of a GPS antenna. I waited for the object to rotate until it revealed the underside. If the vanes were antennas, there might be severed wires.

There were no wires. Opposite the smooth curved surface, the object gave the impression of a jagged, rocky landscape. Of something broken off something larger.

"Does that look like anything you've ever seen, Will?" Lewko asked.

"Yeah. Engine cooling vanes. Or an aircraft GPS antenna, possibly attached to a composite surface, possibly anti-radiation. Any idea what kind of material you're dealing with?" I asked. "Is it like the ceramic heat shield tiles on the Space Shuttle?"

"One of many questions we're exploring," Amy replied tersely.

"Well, if that material came from an aircraft that *isn't* from *out there*, someone holds the ultimate patent on stealth," I said.

"I think we've been forthcoming, Will. Your turn," Lewko prompted.

I glanced at Lillian whose stony expression offered neither encouragement nor permission.

"Fine," I said.

I told what I could. I gave the start and end points of my memory. I said nothing about floating in a hospital room and I did not mention the recurring dream I had, though less of late, in which I piloted the Navajo through a night sky into a darkness blacker than the night. Into a hole. My story was simple, short and unsatisfying.

"Do you remember seeing something? Just before the crash?" one of the women asked. "I listened to the ATC recording. You called them back. Just before impact, after you had been cleared to leave the frequency, you called them back. Was it to report something?"

When I visited the wreck, Connie Walsh, the NTSB investigator, played the recording for me and made the same observation.

I had no memory of it and said so.

"Have you tried hypnosis?"

"No."

"Would you be willing?"

"No." I didn't leave room for discussion.

The team at the table asked a few more questions. Most, I could not answer. A few centered on my flight experience and background. I shared answers to those freely, seeing no reason to preserve secrecy where facts are publicly available. Amy asked for my scholastic credentials.

"I'm a genuine high school graduate," I said without hesitation, granting her the supremacy she sought.

As the discussion progressed, my unease grew. Tension ran to my extremities and made me shift uncomfortably in the chair. I felt a disconnect.

Like shooting across Bargo Litton's jet cabin just before he opened fire.

Like each of the other times *the other thing* took control of me in response to subconscious thoughts issued as commands.

Lillian glanced at me several times. My uneasiness showed.

Amy remained protective. "Mr. Lewko, you're not actually going to let him near it, are you?"

Lewko tipped his head slightly. "He did make first contact."

"My name goes on the t-shirt," I said.

Lillian nodded enthusiastically. Amy shot us a contempt-laden glance. "I repeat my objections. We've discussed this. Looking down the road at practical ramifications in material design and manufacturing, I feel that our ability to fully analyze, and reverse-engineer this object will be compromised by contamination. Just my two-cents' worth."

"You're up to a buck fifty, Ames," one of the men said. It got a laugh.

"I think we can offer a compromise to Will. Look, but don't touch. Can we agree on that?" Lewko offered.

Amy didn't give up. "Then why bother? Why look at something you can't see?"

"Closure for me," I told her. I turned to Lewko. "Maybe it shakes something loose in my memory."

The sneakers-and-jeans-clad billionaire whose math and science aptitude built a retail empire capable of making more money in a single day than most Americans earn in a hundred lifetimes clapped his hands together, satisfied. Excited.

"Then let's have a look."

35

"I have one request before we enter," Lewko said.

He positioned himself between us and the open space that appeared in the curved glass wall. He held out a hand.

"May I have the device hidden in your right boot, Will?"

I shrugged, bent over and lifted my pant leg. I pulled out the compact power unit and handed it to him.

"Nice security," I conceded.

"Yes, a pet project of mine. I see a near future in which people simply arrive at the airport and walk to their gate to board without medieval searches and scans. It can all be done passively." He looked at the power unit. "This is rather…simple." He thumbed the slide control. The power unit whined. He opened the battery door and pulled out my rechargeable batteries. "What's it for?"

I bent over and extracted the prop from my other boot.

"It's a fan," I said. I held out my hand.

He reassembled the batteries and passed me the power unit. I snapped the prop in place and pulled the slide in Reverse mode. I held the unit up and let it blow air in his face.

"You fly around in an air-conditioned jet," I said. "Try sitting in a hold line for takeoff in hundred-degree heat in a light twin sometime. Fits in my flight bag, or my boots." I handed it back. He played with the control.

"That's a lot of power," he commented.

"Yeah, I tried those little plastic fans. They break or don't last. I wanted something solid. I'm thinking of marketing them."

"I might have a few suggestions for you. No disrespect, of course. It's the engineering impulse in me." He handed the power unit to Amy, who examined it with distrust. "I can't allow it inside, of course. To Amy's point, we're doing our best to maintain a sterile environment. That includes the electromagnetic. This—" he gestured at the steel wall ahead "—is shielded from every type of radiation possible."

He led us through the first glass opening, two concentric rings away from the steel cylinder-like wall. Once through, one of the team members handed out lightweight coveralls. We zipped ourselves into flimsy protective suits and slipped booties over our shoes and elastic caps over our hair.

Lewko led Lillian and me forward, leaving the rest of the team behind. Some stayed to watch. Others went to nearby workstations and worked keyboards that altered displays on the many monitors surrounding the ring. Others slipped away. We entered the second-to-last concentric ring. The glass opening sealed behind us.

"You may feel a little pressure," Lewko warned. "We maintain positive air pressure on this inner circle."

An air vacuum system whistled. The air and any particles we had carried in was sucked away and replaced by cool air with a vaguely disinfectant scent to it. Pressure squeezed my eardrums. The air system died down and we heard a sucking sound as the next glass panel unsealed and granted entry.

The metal cylinder forming the next concentric ring rose from the floor and ended at the high ceiling. Roughly the diameter of a farm silo, it had a brushed metallic surface, a series of small control panels set at intervals, and no visible seams. I felt an absurd impulse to put a greasy handprint on the spotless surface.

Lillian remained inscrutable beside me. Had she consumed the Lewko Kool-Aid? Did she plan to remain on the Lewko team to dissect this artifact? Did she intend to sell me out? Or did she still expect me to steal the object right under Lewko's nose?

I had no idea what she was thinking.

Worse, the uneasy feeling spreading down my core had grown. The car stereo wires Dr. Doug Stephenson found on my brain scans seemed to vibrate in my head and down my spine. Not in a physical way, or in a way that caused pain. But in a way that caused *need*.

What it *needed*...I had no clue.

Lewko danced his fingers across a control panel. The steel wall betrayed no sign of a door, but a moment later an entire section slid downward into the floor, revealing an opening.

We stepped through.

Brushed steel encircled a clear tube at the center of a round room. Steel lined the ceiling and formed the floor. Lights mounted high in the wall pointed uniformly at the transparent tube. Andy calls them 'jewelry lights,' bright halogen bulbs that bring out the sparkle in a gem.

The clear tube obviously contained the weightless unseen object. I saw no means of reaching it.

Lights in my peripheral vision began to swim. The air took on a shimmer, like heat on a long stretch of highway.

Tension running down my center multiplied tenfold. I fought to steady tremors threatening my arms and legs.

Something was wrong.

I'm vanishing!

The realization rode a wave of panic.

Whatever this object was, it had been reaching out to me from the moment we entered the building. I felt it now, touching me with tendrils like the wires in my head. I felt the shift coming. I knew the next thing I would feel would be the cool sensation washing over my body, the slip from gravity, the noise that thumps between my ears when I vanish.

This thing was taking me.

Right in front of Spiro Lewko.

I pictured the levers in my head and what I saw supercharged my panic. The levers moved! As if automated, without my imaginary hand, they swung forward, just as they would if I intended to make myself disappear.

Lewko spoke. My ears could have been under water; I didn't hear him. Lillian had stepped between him and me, and I instantly credited her for blocking his view of my face. She'd seen something in my eyes, something happening. It put her on alert.

I had no choice.

In my head, I reached for and grabbed the levers. I felt them moving forward of their own accord. I pulled and felt resistance. I pulled harder. I slammed them back, all the way back, to the stops.

Fwooomp!

Everything stabilized.

In the same instant, a pale white piece of what looked like broken ceramic appeared in the center of the transparent tube. It hung in the air just long enough to catch my eye, then gravity fixed a grip.

The artifact dropped to the steel floor and shattered.

Lewko stopped speaking and stared.

36

"Get them out! Get them out!"

Amy's shrill voice shook Lewko out of his startled stare. He turned and bodily pushed us back through the steel opening. I barely cleared before the door swished up from the floor and sealed the cylinder.

The glass panel for the inner ring opened with the sound of a wet kiss. I felt air rush as we passed through. The door closed quickly behind us.

"What the hell?!" Lewko demanded. He abandoned us and darted to a workstation where rows of screens showed half a dozen camera angles on the same scene. His team scrambled around him.

Multiple monitors showed multiple angles of off-white shards littering the floor of the transparent inner cylinder.

Upturned faces at workstations all around Lewko wore matching expressions of bewilderment.

"What just happened people?!" Lewko demanded, his voice rising.

He turned on his team who met his demands with silence.

Lillian reached for my hand and tugged to gain my attention. She made a face at me that translated to *Do it! Do your thing!*

I hesitated. Lewko lived and breathed tech. Not seeing cameras everywhere didn't mean there weren't cameras everywhere. Lillian's tug on my hand grew urgent when Lewko suddenly turned toward us. For an instant, I wondered if he'd seen something—my face—my posture. Did he make the connection?

I reached again in my head for the levers. I closed my thought hand on the round knobs and readied myself for a push as I tightened my grip on Lillian's hand. I checked the surroundings for something to use for propulsion and navigation, and for a path to escape.

"Get them out of here!" Lewko barked.

"You need to come with me!" Amy broke my grip on Lillian and slipped between us. She closed pincer grips on our arms. She steered us away from the growing confusion.

I looked at Lillian who briskly shook her head at me.

We let ourselves be pushed forward. At the outermost ring, I reached for the zipper for the protective gear, but Amy maintained her grip and drove us away from the rings.

She hustled us to the elevator. She maintained her grip, which I found mildly amusing, considering I stood a full head taller with at least fifty pounds of confidence that she couldn't keep her grip without my consent. The elevator arrived. We rode down and I managed to shed the booties and hair covering. Lillian followed suit.

The elevator stopped. The door opened. Amy briskly escorted us to the front door. It opened the instant she swiped her tag across a reader.

"Out!" she cried. She pushed us through. We staggered into sunshine in all-white coveralls.

She stood in the doorway for a second.

"It's best you think before discussing this morning with anyone, anywhere at any time. Dr. Farris, you signed a substantial NDA. It will be enforced! If information about Mr. Lewko's business seeps into social media or any other outlets, and that information comes from you, the response from Mr. Lewko will define shock and awe. Am I being clear?"

"Bultrimil mobiltras," I said, drawing a blink.

"Very clear," Lillian said. "I'd still like to be a part of this project, Amy. Please tell Mr. Lewko. It would be contrary to my—"

Amy slammed the door.

Lillian stared at me. I stared at her. I clamped my jaw against what might have been a laugh, although it felt mildly insane. She threw her finger to her lips and began to tear off her coveralls. I unzipped and jumped out of the suit, leaving it in a heap.

"Dr. Farris, will you be leaving now?" Lillian's badge spoke up.

"Just going for coffee." Lillian spoke as if she were standing on a land mine. She unclipped her tag. "Please have my car brought around."

A moment later, the valet arrived with Lillian's Prius. The young woman leaped from the driver's seat and held the door open.

Lillian rounded the fender and handed the startled valet her tag. The valet tried to protest but then saw me pull mine from my pocket and flick it like a playing card across the broad concrete pad in front of the building.

Lillian pantomimed something about the car's audio system. She enforced silence until we reached the airport.

"Grab your bag!" I told her after stepping out and pulling my flight bag from the rear seat. "Then lock it and leave it!"

"What? No. You go, and I'll—"

"Grab your bag, Lillian. This is not the time to be on the road in a part of the country where Lewko owns half a county. You can come back for the car some other time. Any second now, he's going to pull his head out of his ass and figure out what variable just changed to cause that object to suddenly appear and drop. I don't want to be here when he comes looking to have a conversation."

"And how does running away from this not look guilty?"

"Who's running away? They kicked us out. Besides, you said it the day you met me. Run. Get off the grid."

She surrendered and went for her bag in the hatchback. I dashed into the FBO office and paid the fuel bill. The guy behind the counter took forever. I watched the road for a line of SUVs to come charging after us.

"What about you?" she demanded.

"If he comes looking for me, I can disappear a lot easier than you can."

"He'd love to see that. Will, what did you do back there?"

"Nothing."

"Liar."

"Did you mean it? That you still want in?"

She allowed a clipped laugh to erupt. "With that pompous icon of greed? Why would I do that when I have you?"

I wasn't sure that made me feel better.

"What was that? What you said. Bilious mobility?"

"Bultrimil mobiltras?" Now I laughed. "I have a cousin, a bit of a genius. When he was a little kid, his mother kept referring to 'making a BM' when he was being potty trained. She never told him what BM meant, so he made up his own words."

"Well," she said firmly. "Spiro Lewko is full of bultrimil mobiltras!"

Ten minutes later I pushed a different set of levers to the wall and the Navajo engines responded with blessed thunder.

We raced down the runway and lifted into the sky. As the wheels tucked into their wells, I banked on course for home.

37

I dropped Lillian off in Madison where, she said, she planned to crash with Doug Stephenson for a while.

"He will come after your skinny ass," she warned me after I shut down the engines on the Wisconsin Aviation ramp. She sat for a moment in the copilot's seat, regarding me with sharp concern. "Lewko."

"Me? I doubt it. I was the dumbest guy in the room."

She shook her head. "Lewko was the second smartest guy in that room—after me. Which means he won't underestimate you."

"Did you just compliment me?"

"No. You're still a dumbass."

"Do you think he really believes all that UFO...stuff." I nearly said *crap*.

"It's not a question of him believing, Will. It's a question of everyone else refusing to believe. That includes you, dumbass."

That strange, brilliant, fervent woman gave me a hug after we stepped from the airplane to the ramp. She hurried to the glass FBO building without looking back.

I nearly followed her. Haggis notwithstanding, I was hungry and the Jet Room restaurant that shares space with the Wisconsin Aviation FBO serves one hell of a hamburger. But I had not yet reassembled my phone and called Andy. I decided the short hop home to see her in person made more sense than an awkward conversation via cellphone.

Less than half an hour later, I rolled off Runway 31 and onto the main ramp at Essex County Airport. In an unusual fashion, half of Earl's air charter fleet stood nose to tail in front of the hangar.

I taxied past the three aircraft, then killed the Navajo's engines and rolled to a stop facing the Foundation hangar. A few minutes later, driven by curiosity, I strolled across the grass toward the air service office, mindful that Rosemary II might have a bounty on my head.

While I schemed a way to avoid Rosemary II, a stream of SUVs swerved off Highway 34 into the airport parking lot. The gate to the ramp had been locked open. The parade, led by Chief Ceeves' big SUV, shot through the gate and disappeared around the hangar. Five vehicles followed. A moment later, the caravan pulled up beside the waiting aircraft. Doors flew open. Men and women from the ranks of the visiting FBI spilled out. Special Agent Janos climbed out of the Chief's SUV and began directing his agents to line up to board Earl's small fleet.

I diverted to the ramp as Earl Jackson and three Essex County Air Service pilots emerged from the hangar and met the FBI teams. Dave Peterson waved at me, then headed for the King Air parked in the lead. Janos ordered seven of his team to follow Dave.

"Pidge!" I called out as she hurried toward the Piper Mojave parked behind the King Air. She held up one hand with five fingers splayed.

"I can take five!" she announced to the armed and body-armored agents on the ramp.

"Pidge!"

She turned to me without stopping. I trotted to catch up to her. I blinked when I spotted a yellow and purple bruise on her cheek, starting at the eye socket.

"What happened to you?"

"Later, Stewart! I gotta go." She pulled open the Mojave airstair. Four men and a woman wearing FBI gear and carrying a variety of packs and bags lined up. She climbed aboard and called back to me, "Get the door!"

Dave Peterson spun up the King Air's turbine engines. Earl closed and latched the big airplane's door, then backed away. I did the same for the Mojave. Props turned and engines fired on the Baron, the third in line. I joined Earl beside the Chief at the corner of the hangar. Pidge lit up the left engine of the Mojave and surged after the taxiing King Air. She fired the right engine on the roll. We watched all three aircraft taxi quickly away for takeoff. I retreated to the hangar.

"What's going on, Chief?"

"The feds think they have a hot tip on these farm killers." The Chief did not explain, and I did not ask.

I turned to Earl. "I just saw Pidge. What's up with the…?" I pointed at my cheek.

Earl Jackson's standard expression is anger. For variety, he switches it up with rage. What flowed under the rugged landscape of his face and in the menacing glare of his eyes made me take a step back. Tom Ceeves put one of his big hands on Earl's shoulder.

"One of them fuckers from that Challenger," Earl growled through clenched teeth.

"Pidge?"

Veins jumped at his temples. If Earl's gargoyle looks had turned to stone in that instant the title of the statue would have been Murder.

"Motherfucker!" was all he could say, and that was a struggle. Tom Ceeves leaned toward me.

"I guess the guy offered to show her the cockpit. Only it wasn't the cockpit she expected."

I felt my own blood boil. "Where is he now?"

"Over t' the hospital getting his nose removed from somewhere down around his asshole, I imagine," Chief Ceeves replied.

"Jesus." I looked at the business jet sitting on the ramp. The Essex County Air Service tug, a square propane-powered tractor, sat near the aircraft's sleek nose. A heavy chain connected the tug and the nose gear. "Is she okay?"

"Might'a bruised her fist."

Earl muttered something about goats, intercourse and hellfire, then said, "I get my hands on him…" He didn't finish. I decided no matter what damage Pidge had done the offender could count himself lucky that it had been administered by Pidge, and not Earl. Chief Ceeves spared me a look that suggested we best keep an eye on Earl.

"Is she in any trouble?"

The Chief shook his head. "Not in this county. Andy's at the station, Will. You want a lift?"

38

I braced myself. Mae Earnhardt, the night dispatcher, happened to be returning a stack of files to the cabinets along the wall near Andy's cubicle. She dished out a friendly smile, which I returned, thinking she would make a good human shield if necessary. Unless, of course, she fled the scene.

Andy looked up from the monitor on her desk. A lock of auburn hair fell across one eye. War flag.

"I can explain," I said. I held up the pieces of my phone, which I chose not to reassemble as a show and tell gambit.

She brushed back the descending hair and waved for me to sit in the plastic chair beside her desk. She leaned toward her desk phone.

"There's a second book to the spreadsheet. Do you see it?"

"Hang on." Donaldson's voice came from the intercom speaker. "Got it."

"That's everything I pulled from the VPF file. I don't think there's much there, but maybe you can cross it against what you already have from NCIC?"

"Will do."

"I included Arthur as a first name and as a middle name and as a last name."

"Not my first rodeo, Detective."

Andy poked the blue button on her phone and the light went out.

"It was Lillian's fault," I said.

"Hold on," Andy poked another button on the phone. "Jeff, do we have Madison PD's summaries yet?"

"Just came in."

"And?"

"Hang on…wait for it…wait for it…" Jeff Parridy's cubicle was close enough that I could hear the senior detective's voice slightly out of phase with the intercom. "Nothing."

"Seriously? How is that possible?"

"I'll call them."

Andy stood up suddenly and called across the tops of the cubicle dividers. "Ask them why it took the whole damn day!"

Andy forgets that while Jeff is not her superior in any way, he remains her senior officer in the two-person detective pool. She sat down and poked the blue button to kill the intercom connection.

"The good news is that I think we're done with Lewko," I said.

She leaned back in her chair and stared at the intercom. I knew the look and the move. If not for having her hair in an intricate French braid, she would have buried her fingers in the lush locks. I often think she uses scalp massage to shake loose answers to difficult questions.

I saw an opening for a diversion.

"What's not possible?"

"Stella Boardman's car. Madison police found it at the bus station," Andy said. She sounded more like a woman talking to herself than to me. "Yet Madison PD can't find her on bus station security video or street cam video…anywhere. No images of the car or of her. It's like the car just dropped out of space."

"I know someone who would buy that theory."

"She used her credit card to buy a ticket online for Chicago, but they have no record of her boarding."

"I think you're right. That doesn't sound possible."

"I have the same problem with Lyle."

The Chief had filled me in on the way to the station. Traeger and his patrol unit were still missing.

Andy said nothing. I took the time to put my phone back together.

"No word on him?"

"No video. No tracker. No plate reader data. Will, I truly do not know how Lyle can be missing this long. He's driving a damned black and white with our name plastered all over the side. We have everybody looking. *Everybody.* That is, everybody who isn't on the farm thing."

Her focus remained fixed on a point somewhere between the fabric wall of her cubicle and the nearest star, searching not only for Lyle Traeger and Stella Boardman, but for the clue she blamed herself for missing.

"The Chief told me the feds have a bead on the farm family guys."

She turned to me as if seeing me for the first time. "I'm glad you're here." She reached for her cell phone, which she tucked in her shoulder bag. "Come with me. I need to go up to Sandy's."

I stood. She drew close and pecked my cheek with a kiss. Her scent filled my senses and the way she pressed herself against me renewed hope that my running off with Lillian had been forgotten, or at least downgraded to a misdemeanor.

She spoke to me over her shoulder as we walked out. "You can explain yourself on the way."

"LEWKO IS all over the UFO theory," I told Andy as she drove. "It's why Lillian was able to get in with him."

"Big surprise."

"I mean, yeah, she's got a ton of abbreviations after her name—which, by the way, is Farris—but I don't think any of that means much to Lewko. He can buy all the talent he needs. I think she got in the door because she's a kindred spirit. A fellow abductee."

"She got in the door because she used you! God! I hate that she gave you up to him! What was she thinking? After all that ranting about getting us off the grid!" Andy gripped the wheel and as her anger rose, her foot descended on the gas pedal. "You remember that? How she wanted us to just abandon our lives and live on some island? Can you imagine if we'd fallen for that?"

"Could'a been fun for a few weeks..." I pictured my wife in a bikini.

"Please tell me you didn't have to—you know—right in front of anybody."

"Close, but no. Actually, the opposite." I explained what happened. "Dee, I felt something from the moment we entered that building. It pulled on me—tried to make me vanish. I think if I had done nothing, I would have."

Her jaw clenched and her lower lip, prominent thanks to a slight underbite I find exotic, signaled new worry.

"Is there any chance he saw you do it? Make that thing appear?"

"I don't see how."

"Empirical data, Will. They've had possession of it for weeks and made no progress. You show up and it suddenly appears."

"If that's their thinking, they're a day late and a dollar short. Their first impulse was to hustle us the hell out of there."

"Doesn't mean they won't review the facts. You're still the miracle at the origin of this story."

"A miracle with no memory. I had nothing new to offer and they were not impressed by my scholastic credentials. Besides, they now have something they can sink their teeth into. That debris is no longer hidden. They can analyze it and figure out where it came from. My money is on Bed, Bath and Beyond."

"Makes sense, since Toys 'R Us went out of business."

Her willingness to play improved the overall mood.

"I'm sorry about the communication blackout. Blame Lillian's paranoia —which, to be honest, wasn't unfounded. Dee, they had AI talk to us through the stereo in her car! And you should have seen their ID badges. Like little TV sets. After everything you've told me about phones, and with Lillian's paranoia and Lewko's tech, I decided to pull the battery on mine."

"It's fine. It's been crazy here all day."

And you're a big boy. You can take care of yourself, I added using her voice in my head.

"Usual disclaimer. What's the deal? Are the feds really going to get these bastards?"

"Usual disclaimer. Maybe."

"Did that thing with Artie help?"

She shook her head. "No. Lee's been on that all day. You heard him. He took over the workstation downstairs in Processing. He's been chasing that name up and down all the NCIC files. Right now, he's combing the Violent Persons File to check everyone with a first or middle name that starts with A. The guy is relentless. He should be resting instead of chasing a dead-end lead."

"You really think it's a dead end?"

"I don't know. But I worry about him. He's not well."

"He's better than he was," I said.

Andy reached across the console for my hand. "In my heart, I know what you did was good. But it scares me, Will. That part of all this truly scares me."

I looked for a change of subject. "What made the feds reenact the Normandy airborne invasion?"

"The photos that were released two days ago."

Had it been two days? I tried to remember when in the recent whirlwind of flights and events the conversation in the Crowne Plaza Hotel room took place.

"The FBI dove deep into those photos," Andy said. "The lab at Quantico ran them against millions of images on the internet. Don't ask me how. For all I know they waved a magic wand. That tech is so far beyond me. It paid off, though. Out of twenty-one images, nineteen were copied from web sources and matched up."

"To a geographic location?"

She nodded, but with qualification. "All over the lower forty-eight. One from Anchorage. One from Spain."

"Chaff."

"What?"

"Chaff. Originally, the husks and waste product sifted off the grain by a threshing machine. More recently, the name of the material thrown off by an aircraft to fool radar. Sounds like they were throwing up chaff to screen what they're really doing."

"That's what everyone here concluded."

"Yet you have a location."

"They feel that the nineteen matched images are false leads. But the perps think they're being clever by including two genuine images of their next target—so they can point back and say, 'We told you so.'"

"What were the two images?"

"One was of a mailbox. The other was a rural landscape. In the landscape, there's a grain silo."

"The feds found them?"

Andy nodded, looking impressed. "Rumor has it that Google stepped in to help, but that's absolutely confidential, Will. Seriously."

I did the lip zip gesture.

"It gets better. The two outliers stood out because they came from the same device."

"They can tell that?"

"The FBI lab can. Both images came from a device belonging to a lot of pre-paid phones delivered to a Walmart in Springfield, Missouri. The rural landscape matched a location sixty miles west of Springfield. From there, they found the mailbox. It pinpointed a family-owned dairy farm. Identical victim profile. A father, mother, teenaged daughter, two little boys."

"Wow. I think…but…"

"You're going to suggest it's a diversion? Because everyone here said the same thing."

"Wait! You said the phone was bought at a Walmart. There has to be security video."

"I didn't say bought. The device went to the Walmart, but it's gone—yet it doesn't show up on sale records. Hence no checkout cam video."

"Stolen?"

Andy issued a sly grin. "Possibly. Or purchased by switching bar codes with a different item, and then shoving it through a very busy checkout line with a ton of other stuff. How many kids, single moms or retirees working a Walmart checkout do you think are cross-referencing each purchase against the scanner beep? Especially if the price is close. Let's say a Virgin phone rings up with a bar code for a T-Mobile phone. Who's going to catch that? And even if they did, our perps would act surprised and ask to reverse the purchase. If they're smart, they'll make it look like the error costs more. That way, if they're caught, it doesn't come off as theft."

"Jesus, Dee, how did you come up with that?"

"I busted Jamie Wildeen and his kid brother when they used it a couple months ago. Only they tried to sticker an X-Box with the label from a nineteen-dollar pair of ear buds. Idiots."

"Still, it seems like a lot of trouble to go to."

"It beats getting caught for shoplifting. And it guarantees them an anonymous way to obtain a device without us being able to pin them down on video."

"Do you think Janos and his strike team are chasing a wild goose?"

Andy squinted. "I have no idea. Truly. And it doesn't matter. We have an obligation to protect the family—who are now under guard. The airborne invasion you saw is Janos gambling that he can catch the killers on site."

I whistled softly. "I don't think I'd go anywhere near a farm this weekend. With what's been covered by the media, trigger-itchy farmers are probably packing heat while they milk the cows."

"Packing heat? Who are you, De Niro?"

I let my mind wander.

"Dee…where was the first one?"

"West Virginia."

She looked sideways at me. "I know what you're going to say. The FBI had a team on that idea days ago."

"An airplane."

"It would explain some of the regional movement, but we still don't know how they got to the farms and played on their victim's trust. They didn't land an airplane in the farmer's field. Even so, the feds ran computer analysis of every flight plan filed and flown relevant to each of the crime scenes. Nothing came up as a pattern or repeat."

"You don't have to file a flight plan," I said, "but I agree on the logistics. You still need ground transportation."

We rolled up to the Sunset Circle roadblock manned by Essex County Sheriff's deputies. Andy dropped her window and traded small talk before being waved through.

"Does this ambush plan mean Sandy has changed her mind about paying?"

Andy shook her head.

"She doesn't know yet. Which is why I was sent here. Sandy wants to pay—and I can't blame her. It could save a family." She glanced at her watch. "She plans to make the payment at 8 tonight. Janos wants me to talk her out of it—or at least into waiting until tomorrow morning. He wants to give the ambush a chance."

"Are you? Talking her out of paying?"

"I'm not sure I can."

Neither of us spoke again until we reached the Stone house on Leander Lake.

39

Sandy met us at the door. I tried to remember what she'd been wearing the last time I saw her but drew a blank and dismissed the idea that she hadn't changed or slept. She wore flat sandals that slapped her feet when she walked, and a pair of white jeans under a gray t-shirt without text or a logo. As Andy does around the house when she doesn't want to invest time in her hair, Sandy trapped her blonde locks in a functional ponytail.

My wife held her in a hug for a few seconds longer than would have been warranted by mere formality. I gave a nod to the Wisconsin State Trooper on guard duty. He checked me over, then scanned the sidewalk and the circle in front of the house where we had parked. He closed the door behind us and remained at his post when Sandy led us into the great room overlooking Leander Lake.

The sun had another hour to shine before kissing the treetops on the far side of the lake. Back light gave the trees between the house and the water a green luminosity. Reflections off the lake made the leaves shimmer and appear to wiggle, even though the evening air hung still.

Arun jumped to his feet as Andy and his boss entered. I would have taken odds that he slept in the clothes he was wearing. A stubby love seat and accompanying end table had become his office. Piles of files occupied a nearby coffee table.

A pair of FBI agents sat in an adjoining room facing laptops across Sandy's dining room table. Andy had warned me they were there, monitoring Sandy's landline and cell phone. In a movie, wires and cables would be snaking across the floor; headphones and cryptic devices in suitcases would clutter the room. Except for the laptops, their station was tidy. These two could have been playing World of Warcraft. At the sight of visitors, one of them rose and politely closed a set of doors separating the two rooms.

"Where's Senator Keller?" Andy asked after greeting Arun and releasing him from his gentlemanly obligation to stand. Andy folded herself onto a sofa beside Sandy.

"A county planning commission meeting."

"On a Saturday evening?" I asked.

"It was rescheduled from last Monday, I guess," she replied.

"She couldn't find something to binge on Netflix?"

"I don't know. Lorna got excited when she heard a deputy secretary from the DOT is coming. I'm not sure. She seemed to think it was important enough to stop smother-mothering me for a few hours. I don't think she wants to be here when I make the payment."

Arun looked like someone just murdered his puppy. Sandy paid him a commiserating glance, reminding me that paying the ransom ended Arun's short career as manager of her Education Foundation affairs.

And mine as pilot for the Foundation airplane.

"Mr. Larmond will be coming soon. He spent time today preparing," Sandy said. "I'm not sure I understand it. We had to set up accounts—er, a Bitcoin account, make transfers and—I guess—purchase the bitcoins, which seems to be controlled by passwords. And of course, the bank is closed today, but when you're moving around millions, I guess they make special arrangements."

"Keys," Arun corrected her. "Mr. Larmond set up a Bitcoin wallet with public and private keys."

"What about the land sale?" I asked.

"Done," Sandy said. "All very rushed, but the money has been wired."

"We now have enough," Arun added. "Although I still do not understand why you're paying this, Miss Stone. I don't understand why this isn't a matter for the government."

"Our government doesn't pay ransom."

I asked, "The code in their message provides a—what is it?"

"An address," Arun said.

"An address to send the bitcoins," Sandy said. "You'd think the government could trace it, but I guess there are infallible ways of masking or encrypting the address."

"The keys," Arun interjected.

Sandy waved a hand in the air. "It depends on the recipient. The two agents in the other room say they will try to trace it, but they said not to count on it. Chances are the money will vanish as soon as payment is made."

"About that," Andy began.

Sandy saw it coming. "No. My mind is made up."

"I understand. But something is happening." Andy spelled out what she told me about the images, the FBI conclusions and the decision to mount an ambush. As she spoke, Sandy's tension grew until she took to her feet and paced the wide room.

"I can't take the chance, Andrea. Can you imagine what it might mean if they're wrong? I pray to God they're not and they can arrest these people—but we have no guarantee! What if they set up this ambush in—where was it?"

"Missouri," I said.

"And while they're waiting another innocent family is murdered. I can't—I can't let that happen if there's something I can do about it."

"And if they do it anyway?" Andy asked. "Are you ready for that?"

"I have to be. But I will have done all I could."

"They might come back for more," I said. "If you pay."

Sandy shrugged weakly. "Then they'll just have to wait until the second week in September when I get my first school district paycheck." She laughed weakly.

"Sweetie," Andy pulled her back onto the sofa and squeezed her hands. "They sent me here to convince you to wait. From behind my badge, I can tell you that it's the best opportunity we have of ending this with an arrest. Just twelve hours. But as your friend—and I shouldn't be telling you this—you're not wrong. You do what you need to do. Understand?"

"I know."

"Have you slept? Have you eaten?" Andy asked.

"The last three days have been a dieting windfall. I call it the Trauma Diet."

"Let's get you something. I'm starved."

I didn't need to be told twice and took to my feet anxious to raid Sandy's kitchen. I wondered if Keller left any of that Scotch.

Andy's phone rang as she stood.

"It's the Chief. I have to take this." She stroked her phone and strolled toward a set of French doors that opened onto the deck where several nights ago she and I had decided Bargo Litton was responsible for this nightmare. I gave Arun a surreptitious head gesture toward Sandy and then the kitchen. He folded his laptop and set off after her. I followed Andy into the evening air to listen to her side of a conversation with the Chief.

"When? Where?"
"Was he with it?"
"Nothing?"
"I should go. I can have Will fly me. I can—"
The Chief spoke for a while during which Andy grew agitated.
"Which one, Chief? Johns? This Farm Family case? How do we know it's not that? I know they're stretched thin, but—"
The Chief explained.
"You can't be serious! Illinois CID?"
She shook her head, harsh but silent judgment of the Chief's instructions.
"But he's been missing for thirty-six plus hours!"
I heard the Chief's deep voice rise.
"I know. I'm sorry."
Andy listened. Then the call ended. She looked at me in pain.
"They found Lyle's unit. In Rockford." She answered my question before I could ask it. "No sign of Lyle."

"Arun has an idea," Sandy said as we rejoined her and Arun in the vast Stone family kitchen. Arun had produced a plate of fruit from a gigantic refrigerator. My stomach rolled over, reminding me that my last meal included haggis. Sandy gestured for Arun to speak up.
"We already have the transfer address. The transfer protocol allows for a message to be sent—like a memo for a check."
"What's wrong, Andrea?" Sandy asked, reading Andy's expression.
"Our officer. Lyle Traeger. His unit was found. In Rockford, Illinois."
"What was it doing there?" Arun asked.
Andy said she didn't know. That no one knew.
"He hasn't been found?" Sandy asked.
"No."
"Dee, does Tom think this is related?" I asked.
"We don't know." Andy cleansed her thoughts with a deep breath. "I'm sorry. You were in the middle of saying something."
"At 8 p.m. Miss Stone plans to make the payment," Arun said. "What if she pays one bitcoin at 8 p.m. and tells them in the memo that she will pay the balance at 8 a.m. tomorrow? It forces them to issue a new address because the address we have can only be used once."
"A new address doesn't necessarily help us," Andy said.
Sandy said, "I know I'm not law enforcement, Andrea, but this might hold them off of hurting anyone—"

"And they might make a mistake. Get impatient," Andy mused. "Or disrupted. Maybe they'll move into position or get caught doing a pass on the target. If I know the feds, no vehicle will be able to move in a fifty-mile radius of that farm without them knowing who's at the wheel."

"Do you agree?" Sandy asked Andy.

"Let me call Janos's deputy at the station and run it past her." Andy pulled out her phone. She turned to me on her way to the privacy of the great room. "And then you and I have to go. I want to look at something."

She hurried away, working her phone.

I turned to Arun, who had brightened at the possibility of preventing the destruction of the Education Foundation fund.

"Arun, a question."

"Yes!" he chirped. He wore his excitement like a fresh shower.

"Was that sliced ham I saw in the fridge?"

40

Andy ate the sandwich I threw together. I finished mine too quickly and wished I'd made another. She ate and talked as she drove.

"When Lyle first started solo patrols, he did a couple shifts with almost nothing in his notebook and next to nothing entered in the shift logs. Tom reamed him out about it, and ever since the guy practically writes a novel every time he goes out. He goes too far. He'll make a call or a stop, and then spend twenty minutes by the side of the road writing it up. It's one of the issues Tom holds against him."

"That he's too thorough?"

"No. He doesn't process his learning and adapt. He's all or nothing on things. He's not making judgments and adapting input to advance himself."

"Yeah," I said. "I've seen it in student pilots. Tell 'em they're not using enough rudder and they're suddenly Fred Astaire on the pedals."

Andy steered with her left hand and held her sandwich in her right.

"Do you think there's something in his notes that points to what happened to him?"

I waited for her to finish chewing.

"We all thought that. We've been over his entries a dozen times, starting with the night we arrested Johns. If there's something there, we're not seeing it. Or he made pocket notes but never had a chance to transcribe them." She finished off the sandwich and followed it with water from a bottle she keeps in her car.

"Then what are we looking at?"

"His notes again. But I want to look at them in the environment. His last assigned duty was to re-canvass and list the names of Johns' neighbors who were present that night. He entered all the names before he disappeared. I've already called most of them. My phone interviews didn't add anything to what we already know. Almost all of them heard the music. Most of them closed their windows and went to bed. The immediate neighbor was out of town. Now I'm starting to rethink my approach."

"How so?"

"I spoke to each of them in the context of the Johns case, not in the context of a missing officer."

"You think someone Lyle talked to knows or saw something?"

She wouldn't say, saved by her phone, which signaled an incoming text. She found the device in her bag and lifted it, gave it a glance, then returned it.

"It's done. Larmond made the first transfer. Just one."

"Do you really think this is a good idea?"

Andy shook her head. "There are no good ideas in this."

WE SPENT the next two hours retracing Patrol Officer Lyle Traeger's steps. Andy worked from the volume of notes Lyle entered in the CPU mounted against his unit's dashboard before he disappeared.

Andy connected to the Essex PD system via tablet. I looked at the screen with her.

I pointed. "He's got notes that one residence had garden gnomes."

"That's actually helpful. Some of those gnomes come with cameras."

"An entry that says, 'Four bicycles.' What's that about?"

"If I ask how many people live at that residence, and it's just a married couple, it means someone was with them the night of the incident. See what I mean? The guy is nothing if not thorough."

He may have been thorough, but the door-to-door visits provided Andy with no hint of what had happened to her fellow officer.

We left the home belonging to Clayton Johns' immediate neighbor for last. Andy expected no one to be home.

"He races cars," she said after we parked in front of the seven-car garage. "He wasn't home that night."

"Then why are we stopping here?"

"He might have come home. That's why I left it for last."

She started up the sidewalk, but I caught her arm above the elbow and stopped her. I pulled her around to face me and pulled her against my body.

"Are we about done here?" I hoped something tactile might inspire her to say that, Yes, we are about done here, and I want you to take me home.

I moved against her, trying to emphasize the point.

"Honey," she warned me, "I'm on duty." Yet she did not pull away. We stood in shadow on the sidewalk leading to the front door of the wildly oversized lake cottage.

"It has been a dismal week for us. I'm having PTSD flashbacks of my bachelor days."

She hummed. "Most guys long for those days."

"Long periods of celibacy are overrated. And by long periods, I'm talking hours. Days, even. God forbid, as much as a week."

She made a move against me that only added to my argument.

"Hold that thought."

And she was gone. Or at least no longer in my arms. It took me a moment to catch up to her.

She pressed the doorbell.

"Who's this supposed to be? Stockbroker? Hedge fund manager?"

Andy checked the tablet.

"Lyle has the owner down under the name Santi. Derek and his wife Ariel." She glanced at me in the light of the motion-sensing carriage lamp beside the front door. "What?"

"I know that guy."

She tried to look inside, but prismed glass on either side of the door protected the interior.

"As in?"

"I told you about him. The guy. The drunk guy. Muscle-bound asshole? Remember?"

She tried the doorbell again. "Should I?"

"Yes! I told you all about him." This proved it. She had slept through the whole story. "Forget it. It doesn't matter. Looks like no one is home."

She checked her tablet again.

"What else does the Shakespeare of police reporting say?"

"There's a third name. Roger Duwyllen. And a note that says, 'Fins Wet.' I have no idea what that means, but if he got names, someone must have been here when he did his canvass. Funny, though...all the other entries run on like prose that needs a good editor. This is just the three names and that note."

"They must have been here when he visited. How else would he have gotten the names? I'm going to look in the garage."

"Will! No, you can't!" She chased me down the sidewalk to the garage.

"I'm not going in!" I told her, pulling out my phone. I switched on the flashlight app. "I just want to take a look." I folded the phone in my hands. I checked for cameras and line-of-sight to the windows.

Fwooomp!

I vanished and tapped my feet on the pavement. I rose under the garage roof overhang until my face reached a series of small windows high in the garage door. I held up my phone. The light probed the garage.

"Empty," I said.

"I told you. They're out of town."

"Well, if they're out of town at a race, they forgot to take their race car with them." I swept the light over a low, tarp-covered vehicle in the only occupied bay of the garage. Beneath the hanging tarp I made out bright red body panels and racing tires. The body suggested Corvette.

"Probably the spare. Rich people have a spare everything. Let's go." My exploring made Andy nervous.

"Damn. I wish my garage was this neat. You could do surgery in here. It's empty."

"Will!"

I pushed against the overhang and drifted back down until my shoes touched the asphalt.

Fwooomp! I flicked into view. I touched my phone screen and killed the flashlight app.

"Let's go," Andy suggested.

"This guy was a client in Lyle's other job."

"We're already on that. Jeff got a complete list of clients Lyle has driven. In case there was a complaint or if there was an altercation."

"And?"

"And nothing. His clients loved him. I don't remember this name on the list, but I can check it."

I climbed in the car beside her. "Actually, I don't think Lyle ever actually drove this guy. The customer was a no-show that night."

"Makes him that much less important. Hang on," Andy said, pulling out her phone, which growled on vibrate. She checked the screen, then touched to accept the call.

"Rosemary?"

"Andrea, thank God! Is Will with you? You need to come to the airport!"

"Why? What's going on?"

"It's Earl. He's going to commit murder."

41

Leander Lake is forty minutes of pleasant country driving from downtown Essex; thirty minutes from the airport which is located east of town. Andy covered the distance in twenty-two. We arrived three minutes after nine-thirty. She parked in the Essex County Air Service lot. We spotted several people near the airport tug, which remained chained to the Challenger. A second visiting jet, a Citation, sat near the gas pumps. A dark-haired woman paced back and forth near the nose of the jet, watching the confrontation from a distance. Her fashion statement screamed Spandex. Silhouetted against the hangar building lights, she might have been wearing a superhero costume—except for the high heels.

Andy cut across the lawn directly for the tug. I spotted Earl Jackson and looked for bodies on the ground.

As we approached, Rosemary II detached herself from the cluster around the tug and pointed at the badge on Andy's belt.

"As I promised, here are the police," she said loudly.

A man in a dark suit turned his attention to Andy. Roughly my height, he had a small, pursed mouth, fleshy jowls and a belly that tried to hide his belt. I made his age to be in the late sixties or early seventies, despite dark dyed hair arranged in a comb-over. His suit, probably expensive, looked loose and lumpy, unable to overcome the body beneath it.

"Officer arrest this man," he ordered Andy. His mistake. Compounding the error of issuing a command to my wife, he folded his arms across his chest, planted his feet and lifted his chin. The pose said *Il Duce* and bought no favor with Detective Andrea Stewart.

Earl sat on the tug seat with one foot propped up on the headlight bar. His affect gave me a chill. There was no mistaking his intent.

"And you would be?"

"I'm the owner of this airplane, which that man is unlawfully detaining."

"Why don't you give me a chance to decide what's lawful and not lawful here, sir?"

"Why don't you do your duty," the man snapped back. "If you won't, I can easily reach out to a very good friend of mine, a close friend and a very high-ranking official with Homeland Security. A top man with authority over aviation matters."

Second mistake.

"You've now told me what you are. I asked who you are." Andy stepped unusually close to the man. He had to depress his upraised chin to look at her. "May I see some identification?"

"I'm Emilio DeSantorini," he announced, but he made no move to produce ID.

"Maybe you are. I still need to see that identification."

"Don't be ridiculous! Everyone knows me. That's my airplane. That man is clearly detaining it. You should be dealing with him!"

Earl said nothing from his perch.

"That gentleman," Andy said calmly, "I know. You, I do not. Now either you produce the identification I asked for or we can discuss all this at my station house."

Two men behind DeSantorini—pilots by the look of their matching white shirts, black ties and light jackets—exchanged glances with a third. I pegged the third as The Assistant.

"I can help with that!" The Assistant chimed in. "If you'll just wait a moment, officer—"

"Detective Stewart."

"Yes, of course, Detective. If you'll just wait a moment..." he backed away. "It's in the other airplane. I'll just be a moment!" He broke into a trot across the ramp, chased by his own long shadow. His boss did not acknowledge him or turn to watch him.

One of the pilots held a bolt cutter half hidden behind one leg.

"Sir, I need you to put that down," Andy told him. He didn't question. He dropped the tool to the asphalt; it still bore the price tag.

Andy turned back to DeSantorini.

"While your friend is fetching your wallet, maybe you can tell me what this is about," Andy said.

"Are you blind?" Third mistake. DeSantorini took an abrupt step back, exactly as Andy had intended. He pointed at Earl. "He's blocking my aircraft. He has it chained to that tractor, which is causing damage to a very expensive nose wheel!"

Andy turned her head and examined the heavy chain running from the rear hitch to the nose gear strut.

"I don't see any damage, sir."

"I don't see how you could. You're not qualified to make that judgment." At that point I stopped counting mistakes.

"What's your business here, Mr. DeSantorini?" She closed proximity to him again. It gave me a nervous twinge, the same as I might have felt if she stepped to the edge of a cliff. Once again, DeSantorini took a step back.

"Not that it's any of your concern, young lady—"

"*Detective.*"

"My business here is not your concern. I want that chain removed, this tractor gone, and that man arrested. If you can't resolve this, I'll call your boss."

I looked at Earl, then at Rosemary II, whose worried expression mirrored mine. We held our breath, anticipating calamity.

Andy glanced at her watch. "I think you will not like the result if you drag my boss out here in the middle of a Packer pre-season game." Andy turned to Rosemary II. "Is there a reason the aircraft is being detained?"

"The gentleman has not paid a seventy-five-hundred-dollar fuel bill," she said. "He also has an open invoice for repair to a nosewheel tire for two thousand, four hundred and eighty-three dollars."

"You've been given all of the appropriate billing information," DeSantorini said.

"Sir, that's not how this works," Rosemary II replied. "I will not send an invoice to a P.O. box in New Jersey for a ten-thousand-dollar bill."

"You'll get your money."

"Liar." Earl said it so softly he might have been speaking only to himself.

"What did you say? Did you just call me a liar?"

"Mr. DeSantorini," Andy said, "do you have a credit card you can use to settle the bill?"

"This is insane. Do you know who I am?"

"That's the problem," Rosemary II said, gaining confidence. "We do. We spoke to your FBO at Teterboro. You have a history of not paying your bills, and those that you do, you take a very long time."

"You'll get your money, but I will be deducting for damage done to my nose wheel."

"As I see it, Mr. DeSantorini, that chain isn't touching the nose wheel. Nor has it damaged the oleo strut, the camber counterweight or the retract braces."

DeSantorini blinked at Andy. "What do you know about it?"

More than you, I thought, although I had no idea where she came up with camber counterweight.

"Do you plan to fly out on this jet?" Andy asked. She pointed. "Or on that jet?"

"What business is that of yours?"

Andy shrugged. "It's a simple question, but if it's that difficult to answer, then let's go to my office where we can have a comfortable chat over a cup of coffee."

DeSantorini stared. He lowered his chin and shook his head. "Detective, you will regret your treatment of me. I plan to press charges against the woman who attacked my employee. I can easily add you to the list."

"If you're referring to the young woman who was sexually assaulted by your employee—"

"*She* committed assault and battery."

"Liar. That's twice."

Everyone looked up at Earl. His posture remained unchanged. I wondered if I could stop him, or at least slow him down. Either way, it would hurt. I didn't think Earl, in his present state, would hesitate to go through me to get to DeSantorini.

"Ridiculous. She attacked my employee and put him in the hospital."

Andy said, "The district attorney is reviewing the matter. Last I heard, he's considering charges against your employee."

I had no idea that Andy was aware of the incident with Pidge—or that it had escalated to criminal charges.

DeSantorini scoffed. "Why am I not surprised. If you people choose to shield a criminal, then I will bury that woman in lawsuits."

"Anyone with a checkbook can file a lawsuit. However, the recording that the young woman made on her cell phone, which begins at the point where your employee lures her onto the aircraft under false pretenses and ends at the point where she calls 9-1-1 *on behalf of your employee*, suggests you would be better served spending your money paying your vendors."

As if on cue, The Assistant arrived out of breath. He held up a black wallet. Andy asked him to produce a credit card. He looked for release to do so from his boss, then scrambled to pull out an American Express card. Rosemary II dove into her purse for her cell phone. She attached a small cube to the side of the device and held out her hand for the card. The Assistant looked at DeSantorini for permission.

Rosemary II didn't wait. She snatched the card from The Assistant's hand, tapped her phone screen, swiped the card through the cube on her phone, and waited. We all waited.

After a moment, satisfied by the result, she handed the card back.

DeSantorini curled his lip. "Detective, you have no idea the shit you've stepped in here."

He turned to his trio of associates.

"I want that fucking chain removed!"

Not waiting for a response, DeSantorini marched toward the second jet where the Spandex woman paced, radiating impatience. The Assistant hustled after him with both pilots close in trail.

"Get the fuck on the plane!" he snapped at her.

Her body language ricocheted his attitude right back at him. I decided they deserved each other. The pilots jogged ahead of their boss and performed one of the fastest startups I've ever witnessed for a business jet.

They taxied quickly for departure with the cabin shades drawn.

Earl climbed slowly off the tug. He sauntered past us, stooped and picked up the bolt cutters.

"Nice," he said, hefting the heavy tool in his rugged hands.

He strolled toward the hangar without looking back.

"My God!" Rosemary II breathed relief as she laid a hug on my wife. "Earl was going to kill that man. Thank you so much for coming!"

Andy watched Earl disappear into the hangar. "You did the right thing."

"You saw it?" Rosemary II asked urgently. "You both saw it?"

Andy nodded.

Me, too.

Earl had never stopped grinning.

42

Andy dropped her keys in the dish by the door, pulled her service weapon from her satchel and left the bag on the kitchen countertop. The weapon would go in the small gun safe mounted on the nightstand beside our bed.

I locked the back door and stepped into our kitchen, our home. I tried to remember when she and I had been here together after dark.

"What a week," I said. I reached for her, but she put a hand up between us.

"Just one more thing," she said. "A work thing."

I made a face at her. She gave a heavy sigh, then drew up close. Her lips approached my ear, near enough to brush and tickle it. She whispered something indecent and pulled back with the devil in her eyes. "I'll only be a minute."

She pulled out her phone. A moment later her call connected.

"Mr. Larmond? It's Detective Stewart. I'm sorry to call you so late...yes, that was a good idea, thank you for your help...I didn't think so, the agents said there's little chance it can be traced...no, I'm afraid I can't tell you anything about the FBI's plans. The reason I'm calling, I wonder if you could go back and look at the land sale for me...I understand that, but I have some information for you and I'd appreciate if you would take another look. I want to know if the anonymous buyer is or is associated with an Emilio DeSantorini or a New Jersey company called Mermaid Construction or any other entity under DeSantorini's name...I assume the way it sounds, but I'd have to look it up…yes, I understand, Monday should be fine but sooner if you can…Thank you."

She ended the call and closed the screen. She pocketed her phone, picked up her weapon and walked across the kitchen to me.

"Are you sure you're not too tired?" The devil in her eyes taunted.

I scoffed at her foolish notion.

She closed a grip on my belt and led me to our bed.

ANDY'S PHONE.

It rang in my dream, which vividly involved facing a choice between fighting Earl Jackson and—I'm not sure what the other option was. A rabid badger? A tyrannosaurus? In the dream, I couldn't make up my mind. Andy's ringtone signaled time was up and I had to pick.

She untangled herself from my arms and rolled over. I heard her paw the nightstand for her phone. The screen illuminated the entire room and gave her skin a sleek glow as she read the caller ID.

"Lane?" She held the phone to her ear and listened, then lowered it and double-checked the screen. She tried again. "Hello? Lane?"

After a moment she looked at me.

"Is that Lane?" I stupidly asked.

"There's no one there."

"What time is it?"

She read the screen. "Twelve-forty-two."

We hadn't been asleep long. On one hand I resented the interruption. On the other, we were both awake again, which inspired fresh mischief.

"Hello?" Andy tried a few more times. With no response, she hung up. She stretched to put the phone back on the nightstand. I put my arm around her and pulled her back to me, determined to prove that unbridled love tops utter exhaustion.

Her phone rang again.

This time Andy drew herself up and swept her legs off the bed. She picked up the phone.

"Lane? Hello?"

I sat up and scooted closer. Andy angled the phone to share the audio with me.

"Lane? Are you there?" We listened. No one spoke.

Andy tapped the screen to put the call on speaker.

"Did she butt dial you?" I asked.

"At this hour?" She keyed the volume control and ran the bar to full.

We listened.

I heard breathing. The whisper of breath drawn in and out chilled me.

We leaned closer, straining to hear more.

"...nnn...truder..." It was less than a word, less than a breath, barely the sound of a tongue touching teeth to form words, but it launched Andy from the bed. She whirled and pointed at me, then at my phone. She gestured for me to toss the phone to her. I did, then grabbed my boxers and pants.

Andy laid her phone on the nightstand, keeping the connection to Lane open. She jabbed her fingers at the screen on mine.

It rang.

"Mae!" she said as soon as someone answered, "This is Andy! Who's there? Right now, who's in-house?"

"Chief Ceeves is in his—"

"Get him! Tell him to go to Amanda Franklin's house. Right now! Critical! Possible home invasion! He knows the address. Go!"

Andy didn't wait. She dropped the phone and dove for her clothes.

In the race to dress, Andy beat me by a split second. She threw my phone back across the tangled sheets. I pocketed it as she pulled her weapon from the gun safe beside the bed. Half a step behind her, we pounded out the door, down the stairs and through the house.

She grabbed her keys and threw open the back door.

I hesitated.

She looked back and saw me pulling BLASTER units and props from the mudroom cabinet.

"Will!"

"Go!"

She didn't argue. She dashed for her car door, jumped in and slammed it. The engine cranked and she kicked up gravel as she shot backward down the driveway.

Ordinarily, I would have given odds that she would reach Lane's house ahead of me. Between her heavy foot on the accelerator and the light bar in the grille of her car, she had the speed advantage. I rarely press beyond thirty miles per hour when flying.

Tonight, I felt something different—a visceral sensation. The same sensation I felt at Lewko's Evermore facility. A vibration inside.

A *need*. An overwhelming need.

I knew instinctively that throwing myself into *the other thing* would fulfill that *need*.

I jammed the power units into my back pockets and broke into a run. I darted through the back door, leaving it open and unlocked. I hit the back step once and leaped.

FWOOOMP!

GO!

The image of Lane's house flashed across my consciousness.

The sensation I had tried for months to replicate slammed a grip around my center, around the unknown muscle that allows me to flex and turn within *the other thing*. It pulled/pushed me forward. For a moment I thought this burst of forward force would throw me into the trees lining the edge of our yard.

The grip altered and lifted me. I shot over the trees, then leveled off, accelerating. My heart thundered. The relative wind tore at me.

It felt exhilarating and familiar.

When I pulled Andy's sister Lydia from the icy waters of Leander Lake, this same sensation hurled me halfway across the county to the ER entrance at Essex County Memorial.

I struggled in vain for months to repeat the effect. I tried varying combinations of concentration and impulsiveness. I tried when I was dog tired, and when I was freshly awake. I even tried it after consuming—in the name of science—half a six-pack of Corona to induce a comfortable buzz. Nothing happened, other than to discover that drinking and operating my BLASTER was ill-advised.

Now, months of frustration melted away as I effortlessly shot across the Essex landscape. If not for the terror I felt for Lane, I would have probed and studied this new sensation.

Wind rippled my clothes and slapped my hair against my forehead. I started to reach for a power unit, then realized I flew with more speed than I had ever achieved using batteries and a propeller. I tucked in my arms and rotated my body to present minimal wind resistance.

The black night air swept past me. A vast field of stars hung above me. I feared I was too low. I worried about power lines.

On that thought, I rose another hundred feet and leveled off.

The lights of Essex glowed directly ahead. To my right, Andy's car flashed down the highway, leading with bright headlights and her flashing blue and reds. I overtook her and crossed the road. The roof of her car angled under me.

Trees and homes and open fields swept below me. My night vision improved. Details gained clarity. A herd of deer loitering in a cut hayfield bolted abruptly when I streaked overhead. An owl flushed from a dead tree and flapped madly away, confused by the sound of a much larger, much faster unseen predator in the night.

There was no guessing my speed. Wind watered my eyes. I wished for my ski goggles.

The airport, a broad black space beneath the slowly spinning green and white airport beacon, passed on my left. The pilot-activated runway lights slept.

A twenty-four-hour gas station on the edge of town glowed up at me. I shot over it, squinting at bright high-pressure sodium lamps that woke up sleepy drivers and discouraged crime.

My flight path scribed an arrow-straight line to the small Essex neighborhood where Lane Franklin lived with her mother. Homes marched in rows beneath me. Streetlights drew dotted lines at orderly perpendicular angles. Almost nothing moved on the streets below.

What about stopping?

I grabbed a BLASTER, jerked it out of my pocket and instantly fumbled it. It bounced off a roof and disappeared.

Close ahead, I spotted Rosemary II's tiny house. Chief Ceeves' SUV sat on an angle across the sidewalk in front of the house. The vehicle's bright lights painted the structure. The driver's door hung open.

I approached at high speed. If stopping failed, I had the consolation of knowing the chief was already there.

STOP!

Raw thought outpaced my mind's ability to form the word. I stopped so fast that the change in perspective made my eyes lose focus for a moment.

I hung in the air above the Franklin house, twenty feet above the peaked asphalt-shingle roof.

Down! I thought.

Nothing happened.

Shit! I don't have time for this! I pulled out my second power unit, snapped a prop in place, and buzzed myself forward in a spiral that ended on the sidewalk in front of the house.

The front door hung open. Lights glowed inside. I did a quick survey to check for witnesses, then—

Fwooomp!

—I flashed into sight on the run. I pounded out three steps and filled the doorframe of the small Franklin home.

Rosemary II crouched over a body that took up most of the small living room floor. I had just long enough to recognize that the huge frame didn't belong to Lane.

"Will! Help me!"

I hurried to her. Lane stood in the corner behind her mother, clutching a robe to her chest, shivering.

"You okay?"

She jerked her head up and down.

I dropped beside Rosemary II. She worked her fingers on Chief Ceeves' neck, probing for a pulse. She dropped her ear to his nostrils.

"What happened?"

"Someone was in my room!" Lane blurted out.

Rosemary II lifted her head. "He has no pulse! He's not breathing!"

She grabbed the front of his shirt and jerked it open. Buttons split and popped. The shirt halves tangled with wires. Rosemary II jerked them aside, leaving two bleeding welts in the Chief's white chest flesh.

Taser.

Rosemary II formed a fist and leaned into chest compressions.

"His heart stopped!" she said through clenched teeth, working her weight against his diaphragm.

"What can I do?"

She didn't answer, but dropped to his face, pinched his nose and blew air into his mouth. Then again. Then again.

I pulled out my phone.

"I already called!" Lane blurted out.

Sirens woke up in the distance. A car rushed to a halt in front of the house. I heard a car door slam. A moment later, Andy dashed through the front door. Her hand lifted her phone to her face. She reported herself as a plain clothes officer on the scene.

She hopped over the chief's legs and pulled on my shirt to move me up and aside. She fell in beside Rosemary II, who urgently pressed home mouth-to-mouth resuscitation.

"Heart stopped!" Rosemary II said between breaths.

Andy took up a position to resume chest compressions. I stepped slowly backward, transfixed at the sight of the two women desperately reaching out to pull life back into the chief.

Lane slammed into me from the side and wrapped her arms around me. I pulled her tight.

Sirens screamed. A vehicle roared to a stop in front of the house. Doors slammed.

Al Thorson, a City of Essex EMT, appeared bearing a heavy case.

"Christ! Is that—?"

"He was tazed. His heart stopped!" Andy called out.

"GIDDDOFFFFAMEEE!"

The chief's booming voice blew Andy and Rosemary II backward. Rosemary II bumped up against my legs and nearly took me off my feet.

The chief heaved a gigantic gasping breath, drawing air for three men into his lungs. He coughed it out. His arms waved in the air and he did a creditable impression of a beetle trapped on its back.

Al dropped to his knees opposite Andy and Rosemary II. He planted a hand flat on the chief's chest and pressed down.

"GIDDDOFFFFAMEEE!"

"Down, big guy! Take it easy!" The chief struggled against Al's restraining efforts. Andy and Rosemary II joined in. "Easy! Easy!"

Rosemary II sobbed. I swallowed a sharp lump in my throat, feeling the wave of relief that flooded the room. A second EMT rushed through the front door and nudged Andy and Rosemary II away. The women stood, backed up and turned their attention to Lane, who released her death grip on me and fell into her mother's arms.

Andy herded us all into the small kitchen set off the living room. "What happened?" she asked Lane and Rosemary II.

"Someone was in my room!" Lane blurted out.

"I saw him come out," Rosemary II said. "When the chief broke through the front door, it woke me and I came out, and someone came out of Lane's room and threw me backward." She touched the back of her head, then checked her fingertips for blood. "I fell. But I saw him come out."

"Who?"

"I don't know. A man. He came out and bumped into me and then went down the hall and he ran into Tom! I heard Tom shout and I heard a loud noise, but I ran into Lane's room."

"I was under the covers—I was really afraid—Mom grabbed me and I thought it was him and I—Mom! I'm so sorry!"

"Honey! It's okay! Did he hurt you?"

"No! Did I hurt you?"

"No, sweetie! No, I'm fine!" They hugged each other again.

"You said he used a Taser on the chief?"

"There were wires. When I did CPR there were wires."

"Al!" Andy cried out. "Did you get that?"

"I see the marks," Al replied from the living room.

"How long ago? How long before Will got here did this happen?"

Rosemary II's face strained. "A minute? Three? I don't know! I was so scared! I came out and saw Tom. I thought he was dead."

"Did you see or hear a vehicle?"

Rosemary II's face lit up. "Yes! Yes! When I went in Lane's bedroom, I saw through the window—a van—a minivan! I saw the shape through her curtains. A minivan! It drove off!"

"Color? Make?"

She shook her head. "I'm sorry."

"No, no...it's okay. That's a good start." She grabbed my arm and pulled me through the kitchen and out the front door.

A police unit pulled up and a patrol officer stepped out. Andy waved him back in. "Minivan. Go. Maybe a four-minute head start. Possible home invasion suspect." The officer slammed his door and roared away.

Andy pulled me to the back of the parked rescue squad, to a space between the big wagon and the chief's SUV, a space hidden from the gathering gawkers. "Can you?" She lifted her eyes to the sky.

"On it." I realized I still had my BLASTER in hand. I pushed it under my shirt. I looked around for witnesses and saw none.

Fwooomp!

It felt different this time, but only by degrees. Normal—if vanishing and losing my connection with gravity could be called Normal.

Normal because the sensation of *need* was absent.

I tapped the pavement with my toes and launched upward. The EMT van fell away, then the street, then the house. I pulled out the power unit and pushed the slide forward.

Fifteen minutes on an expanding-spiral search yielded no sign of a minivan. I chased anything with headlights or taillights. Service trucks. Lumbering eighteen wheelers. A pickup pulling a fifth wheel trailer. Cars carrying last call bar patrons home for the night.

No minivans.

I searched on the assumption that the intruder had raced the first few blocks, then dropped to an obedient speed limit, gradually zigzagging his way to a main road. As each minute passed, his escape margin grew and my chances of finding him diminished.

After ranging as far as Highway 34 and the airport perimeter, I returned to a crime scene populated by multiple vehicles, officers and onlookers. The crowd forced me to glide one block over to land and reappear behind a free-standing garage. I walked back and rejoined Andy who stood in Rosemary II's kitchen with someone I did not expect to see.

"What are you doing here?" I asked Donaldson.

"Couldn't sleep. Decided to stay at the station for the play-by-play from Janos' team. I heard the commotion."

"Will," Andy said urgently, then she looked around, "let's take this outside."

Donaldson and I followed her out the back door, onto the lawn. Andy looked over her shoulder to confirm that we were alone. She spoke directly to me.

"Lane said she dreamed someone was in her bedroom. It scared her and she woke up and laid there, you know, frozen. Then she realized it wasn't a dream; there *was* someone there. Just standing in the corner of the room. She said she couldn't move. She keeps her phone under her pillow—I know, don't ask me—so she pulled her covers up over her head to hide the light. That's when she called me."

"Why you?" Donaldson asked. "Why not 9-1-1?"

"She couldn't see the keypad, but she has my name on voice-activated dial. She put it on mute so he wouldn't hear my end."

"Wow. Smart kid."

"You can't imagine," I said.

Andy grabbed my arm. "Will, the guy was just standing there. Who does that sound like?"

I looked at Donaldson, who already knew the answer. "Our guy."

"Artie."

"We are not getting any sleep tonight, are we?" I asked. I held out a mug. Andy poured coffee.

"You had your chance," she said coyly.

"Ah, the sacrifices I make for true love."

"Mmmm…is that what that was?"

I followed her, letting my lustful eyes fall to her alluring form. We walked back to the police department's larger interview room. Chief Ceeves had been alert when Al Thorson and his partner hauled him off to the hospital. Al threatened to sedate the chief when he tried to climb out of the rescue squad. Duly warned, the chief cooperated, but not before issuing orders, one of which commanded Andy to "handle this." The department's main conference room temporarily belonged to the FBI team Janos left behind, led by his second-in-command, a woman named Richards. Andy set up shop in the interview room, which offered privacy, a whiteboard and a table.

Andy handed a cup of coffee to Donaldson. He shuffled a stack of printouts. Yellow highlighter tracks journeyed through the stack.

The night patrol supervisor interrupted to ask Andy about calling in part of the day shift. Andy said that with nothing specific to search for, there wasn't much point.

A moment later, Mae Earnhardt poked her head in and asked about the chief. Andy described his refusal to be placed on a gurney, which satisfied Mae that he would live.

Andy closed the door behind her.

"What's Artie doing in Lane Franklin's bedroom?" Andy asked.

"I am out of ideas," Donaldson admitted. "It's like I'm back in neuro-disconnect. I mean—you're probably right, that creepy shit had Artie's MO all over it. But I don't have diddly to help us identify him. I dunno, maybe it's time to visit Walking Bear again."

"The guy's probably deaf," I said.

"There is that."

"I have to be honest, Lee, I thought the whole Artie thing was…well, a side trip."

"Something to placate the disabled FBI guy who won't let go?"

"No! Not that," Andy protested.

"If that really was Artie, holy shit…" I said.

Donaldson leaned forward. "I'm asking again—what the hell was he doing in that girl's bedroom? She's the one, isn't she? From that thing with the Milwaukee councilman last year?"

We nodded.

"Christ, that kid cannot catch a break."

"I think she did tonight," I said. "Still…why Lane? Is she some sort of pervert magnet?" I felt the cold weight of hate in my heart.

"We had Artie tagged as part of the farm family killing team because of his connection to Litton. How does that connect him to that girl?" Donaldson asked.

"What if it doesn't?" I asked. "The guy sounds like a sick puppy. What if he visited Lane just because he happens to be in town and needs to feed his disease?"

"You mean 'just happens to be in town' for his role in the farm case?" Andy asked. She shook her head. "You know how I feel about coincidences."

"And unicorns," I said.

"No…I believe in unicorns."

"It's too crazy," Donaldson said firmly. "Too completely crazy. What? He just picks her out of the Universal Victim's Catalog? Sorry. No. It has something to do with the case. We're not seeing it."

"But Lane's not part of the farm case." Andy sat back abruptly. She shifted a startled look back and forth between Donaldson and me.

"What?" I asked.

"She's not part of the farm case," Andy repeated. "But she *is* part of the Johns case."

"Your NFL player?" Donaldson asked.

"Stella Boardman originally wanted to serve up Lane to Clayton Johns," Andy said. "She talked her up to Johns. Maybe even showed him a photo."

"Are you suggesting Johns has a connection to Artie?" Donaldson asked.

Andy's fingers dove into her hair on either side of her head. For a moment she looked like a woman trying to contain a wild thought. When she let go she said, "Johns leased his lake property from Sandy."

"That doesn't explain Artie. His path into all this is through Litton. He already knew about Stone. Artie did this creepy bedroom thing with her first."

"I'm not getting this," I confessed.

Donaldson held up a finger, claiming the floor. "Maybe it's just one pervert sharing tips with another. Maybe Clayton Johns, who has a thing for underaged girls, crossed paths with Artie, who happens to be up to his neck in the farm case because Litton sent him to get back his hundred mil."

"Or it was Colonel Mustard in the parlor with the candlestick holder." Andy ignored me.

Andy pushed to her feet and shouldered her bag. I took it for granted I was invited and followed suit. She looked at Donaldson. "Let's go ask Johns if he knows Artie. Are you coming?"

"Hang on, Hot Shot," he said. "It's two in the morning. You're talking about shaking a soon-to-be-arraigned celebrity pro sports player out of bed for a police interrogation. How do you plan to plow past his army of high-priced lawyers?"

"It's two in the morning. They're all in their earth-lined coffins."

"You have night and day backward," Donaldson said, "but I get it. Lemme think out loud for a sec. Artie came to us via the assumption that the whole farm thing was concocted by Litton. Artie was our proof that Litton wanted his money back. Litton denied it to Will, of course—"

"Not worth the spit needed to say it," I said.

"And now Litton is out of the picture, but his team is going ahead with the scheme for the cash. Artie's on that team. If you think there's a new connection to Artie—through Clayton Johns—then I need to start over with NCIC, and maybe shake some of Johns' associates and teammates out of bed. I'll stick here and work the keyboard and phone."

Andy started for the door.

"Andrea," Donaldson stopped her.

"What?"

"I have to read in Janos about Artie. This isn't our pet theory anymore."

She agreed with a firm nod. "Do it."

ANDY SPENT twenty minutes with the night patrol supervisor, then logged out with dispatch. She signed out a marked unit, number twenty-three. I asked why. She said she preferred not showing her personal car to a suspect on bail pending arraignment. Particularly one with a lot of money and a lot of friends. And certainly not in the middle of the night.

"Whoa, back up. You think someone would try to come after you?" I asked, suddenly feeling wary.

"I don't."

She hesitated.

"What?" I demanded.

"Nothing. It's nothing. It's just…"

"Spill it, Dee."

"The DA called me as soon as he heard that Lyle was missing."

I felt a chill. "Oh crap."

"Don't get all freaky on me." She warned.

"Jesus Christ, Dee! Are you telling me that the DA thinks Lyle has been 'taken out' to weaken the case against Johns?"

"He's way more worried about his case than he is worried about me. Okay, that didn't come out right. No. I don't think that's what he's thinking. He just wants to make sure nothing disrupts the case he's building."

"Still not making it sound right. Come on!"

"Okay! It was talked about, okay? Everything was talked about."

"Dee, you have to take this seriously! Look at what OJ pulled off, and Clayton Johns has way more money! His last contract was for eighty-seven million! God, I never considered this!"

"That's my job. That's what I get paid for," she smiled at me as she wheeled out of the department lot.

A list of reasons to turn around and go back to the station raced through my mind. Andy's probable stubborn response to each popped up just as fast. I found myself in a familiar spot with my wife. Lacking words for the argument I wanted to make, I went with the first thing that came to mind.

"This car smells like french fries."

. . .

Clayton Johns did not return to his leased home on Leander Lake. The City of Essex Police Department considered it a crime scene. Andy and Jeff Parridy had searched the house twice already, but the district attorney wanted state crime scene investigators to conduct a down-to-the-foundation search and evidence collection. Andy said techs weren't due to arrive from Madison until early in the coming week.

If the city's embargo on the property wasn't sufficient to keep Johns away, a small flotilla of paparazzi parked off the end of his pier, fixing a constant camera watch on what they called his "sex palace."

Without permission to remove his personal belongings but restricted to a twenty-five-mile radius of the court that had released him on bond, Johns took up residence in a rented townhouse in an expensive new development on the north side of Essex. Andy told me it had been set up by Johns' Chicago-based team of attorneys, and that she wasn't sure one member of the legal dream team hadn't been assigned to babysit him.

"What do you want me to do?" I asked when she pulled up.

"Wait here."

"Not a chance," I said.

"Will, no! I don't need you distracting him."

"Then why did you bring me along?"

"Because I planned on dropping you off at home. Or letting you off so you can use that propeller thingy to go home."

"It's called a BLASTER." I pulled it from my pocket.

"Only in your comic book mind, dear. Stay put. This needs to be handled delicately. If his lawyer is bunking here, I won't get past the front door."

"At least roll down the window for me."

Andy hit the window button, slipped out and walked to a gated entrance to a Mediterranean-style courtyard. A magnetic lock on the gate demanded a keypad code. Andy pulled out her phone and called dispatch. The police and fire departments keep a database of secured entrances to private residences within the city limits. Dispatch told Andy the code, which she entered. The gate issued a satisfying metallic *clunk*. She pulled it open and edged through.

Fwooomp!

I vanished, released my seatbelt, and pulled myself through the open window. The BLASTER responded to my thumb and pulled me upward until I could see over the gate and wall. Andy crossed the tiled courtyard, rounded a running fountain, and angled toward one of the six ornate doors marking the townhouse entrances. The front door of each nestled beneath a broad balcony with a cast iron rail. I took aim, set a course, then let a glide take me to the railing above my wife.

Andy thumbed the button beside the door. I rotated to watch. A buzzer growled inside the townhouse.

She pressed the button relentlessly.

After several minutes, a voice addressed her through a remarkably good speaker system.

"You can't be here, and I can't talk to you."

Andy looked up and searched the door frame until she found the camera lens.

"I'm here without a witness. You can deny this conversation ever took place."

"Go the fuck away."

"You say you were drugged. I think you're right."

No answer.

"Mr. Johns."

No answer. Andy stared at the camera, unmoving.

A minute passed. Two. I would have given up. Anyone else would have given up. She stood like a school principal waiting for a confession from the kid with the spray can in his hand.

The front door clicked and opened.

Clayton Johns formed a silhouette within a rectangle of soft yellow light. He wore a t-shirt and workout shorts, but his body overpowered any other impression. Known for having the build of Jerome Bettis and the moves of Barry Sanders, Clayton Johns had been called "the new mold" for a running back in the National Football League.

To me, he was coiled violence, a dangerous force that could swallow up and crush my wife without taking an extra breath. His arms and legs would have sent Michelangelo hunting for more marble.

I didn't like this situation. I pushed myself lower and fixed a grip on the lip of the balcony that gave me a shot at reaching Andy before he did. If he went for her, my only hope would be to cause her to vanish and confuse him.

He didn't speak.

"Mr. Johns, I'm not here to make your situation worse. I'm not here to build a better case against you. A young woman was attacked tonight. I'm here to help her."

"What does that have to do with me?" he asked. His voice was deep and clear, his enunciation excellent. The man had a future in broadcasting, if he escaped a future in prison.

"If I promise not to report this conversation to the district attorney or my superiors, will you let me ask you a couple questions?"

"And who's here to witness that promise?"

"Who's here to witness your answers?"

He did not move.

"I can only offer you my word of honor."

He looked her over in the dim light.

"You can ask. I can't guarantee I'll answer."

"Fair enough. On the night we arrested you, were you alone? I don't mean Verna. I mean, was someone else partying with you?"

He said nothing. I expected the door to close in her face, but he held it open and simply stared at her with a stone face.

She waited.

"God's honest truth, Detective, I do not remember. I do not remember anything about that night. I know that sounds like a lame defense, but I have been trying and trying and I do not remember."

"Were there other times? Other parties with other people?"

He chuckled, but it was a sad sound. "There's always other parties, other people. Lots of people. Most of the time you don't even know them. That's why I liked The Lakes. It was away from all that. I like to read."

"You like young girls, Mr. Johns."

This time I knew he'd slam the door on her.

He didn't.

"I like women. People introduce them to me. Most of them want the same thing—since I was fourteen. I never forced myself on anyone, and I NEVER looked for girls who were underaged. They came around. People brought them around."

"What people?"

He didn't answer.

"What people?"

Andy waited.

"Look, there have been some parties. With people from my days. With folks I met up here."

"What folks from up here?"

"Couple of neighbors on the lake, that's all."

"Do you know a man who goes by the name Artie?"

The big head on the bigger neck shook.

"Nobody by that name came around?"

"Nobody by the name Artie."

Andy likes to create silence for other people to fill. She waited.

"Is that it?" Johns moved the door slightly.

"I know you think of me as the enemy, Mr. Johns, but you will be held in higher regard by my office and the district attorney if you are able to furnish information about someone named Artie. You have my word."

"And you have my word. I don't know anyone named Artie."

The door began to swing shut.

"Mr. Johns." Andy stopped him. "I think one reason you don't remember will be found in the results of the toxin screening. I think you may have been drugged, just as you said. Certain anesthetics cause memory loss. It doesn't change what you did or who you were with, but it may explain your memory."

He hesitated, then closed the door.

Andy turned and took a step. She stopped and surveyed the dimly lit courtyard. Her chest rose and fell, collecting and releasing air that cleared the tension she had deftly hidden.

"You were supposed to wait in the car," she said softly.

"Who says I'm not?" I replied. "Are you really helping him, Dee? He raped a fourteen-year-old."

"Of course, he did. He also just told me what I needed to know."

43

Andy checked her watch, which made me check mine. Almost 3 a.m.
"The theory is that the killers drive up to the farmhouse in broad daylight. Their arrival is non-violent. Friendly, even." Andy gripped the steering wheel but made no move to start the car. "Which means we have a few hours. They're not going to hit during the night. Also, we now have reason to believe that Artie is here in Essex, not in Missouri. If he's part of the team..."

"Then either he's sitting this one out, or the whole Missouri ambush is a bust."

"And that means either there is no attack today, or it's happening somewhere else. Somewhere around here, since this is where Artie is."

"They won't walk away from the money. When is Sandy planning on giving them the rest of it?"

Andy checked her watch again.
"She said 8 a.m."
"Are you going to tell me?"
"What?"
"Johns. You said he told you what you needed to know."

Andy stared blankly at the darkness ahead. When she spoke, it was like someone waking from sleep.

"Sorry! I was just—I don't know which case to think about, Will." She turned the key and put the car in gear. "What did you ask me?"

I repeated the question.

"He did. Johns told me that he partied with some people from around The Lakes. Neighbors."

"Okay. What does that mean?"

"It means that someone else may have been there that night. Somebody on Lyle's list." She pulled out of the condo lot.

"Where are we going?"

"Good question. I want to go through Lyle's list in depth, and for that I need to be at my desk with access to department and city records. I also want to go back up to Sandy's. She's not going to sleep tonight—she'll be up waiting for word from Janos or waiting for the next transfer instructions. I also want to take you home—"

"I love you, too, but if you get me in bed, I'm just going to fall asleep."

"—and drop you off!" She laughed. I liked the sound.

"Yeah…no. I'm sticking with you. Let's compromise and go back to the station. You can play at your desk. I'll get us some breakfast. And we'll both head back up to Sandy's around dawn. If anything's going to happen in Missouri it will be after the sun rises, which is early on a farm."

"Fine, but we have one stop to make first."

"HE'S GONE." Dr. Sam Morrissey shrugged. "It's not like we were going to stop him." Morrissey looked me over. "How are you doing? Are you okay?"

"Me? I'm fine," I said warily. "Why?"

Morrissey gave a sly grin. "Because you're a member of our frequent flier program, Will. When I see you walk, crawl or get carried into our ER at 3 in the morning, I never know what to expect, or if it can be explained."

My status as a miracle remained undiminished with the doctor who treated me after the crash of Six Nine Tango. I didn't know whether to be proud or scared.

"Did Chief Ceeves give you a chance to examine him? His heart stopped," Andy said.

"They told me. I would have loved to have given him a full workup. All I got was blood pressure, pulse and a quick listen to that nuclear reactor he has in his chest," Morrissey said. "It was a fluke, you know."

"The heart stopping?"

"I mean, it happens, with Tasers. Not often, but it happens. The thing hit him just right, I guess. Otherwise, I'm not sure a Taser would have much effect on Tom Ceeves. I wouldn't want to rely on it if he was coming at me."

"The man is unstoppable," Andy agreed. "I came to see how he's doing."

"Well enough to march out of here. I want to ask, since you're here. How's Verna Sobol?"

"Not great. It's not something any fourteen-year-old should have to deal with."

"Uh-huh." Morrissey looked around the empty ER admin station. He lowered his tone. "I heard about you. That night. With one of my colleagues."

"He was an insensitive ass," Andy said flatly.

"I'm sorry I wasn't here." Morrissey pulled a pen and small notebook from his pocket. He wrote a note and tore off a sheet. "This is the name of an excellent counselor. She does a lot of good work for the Sojourner women's shelter. I think she would be invaluable to Verna."

Andy pocketed the slip. "I'll see that her mother gets this. Thank you."

"And you," Morrissey turned to me. "How's the pelvis?"

"It aches when the Packers lose."

"We all do."

"I take good care of it. No overexertion. Avoid contact sports. Running, jumping. Leaping tall buildings."

"At this point, exercise is good for it and good for you. Go ahead."

"Does this mean he can go running with me in the morning?" Andy asked.

"No, I can't," I answered quickly.

"Yes, you can," Morrissey betrayed me just as quickly. Andy wrinkled her nose and made a face at me.

"Any good news for our friend Miss Stone?" Morrissey asked Andy.

"Not so far."

"That media circus is out of control," he said. "We had a couple news crews show up here yesterday on a rumor that another family had been attacked and was being brought in by helicopter."

Andy shook her head. "When they're not interviewing each other, they're making things up. I hope this ends soon. I've been busy but trying to stay close to Sandy as a friend."

"Give her my best."

"One more thing as long as I have your ear, Sam," Andy shifted gears. "What kind of drug can induce memory loss?"

Sam Morrissey never speaks without thinking first. He took a moment, then asked, "Do you mean date rape drugs?"

"Inclusive, but not exclusive."

"Rohypnol, of course. Gamma hydroxybutyric acid—or GHB—which is also called Liquid Ecstasy. And ketamine. They all have side effects. Memory loss is one. Seizures and death round out the list."

"What if you want to guarantee memory loss?"

"Well, it's a real problem with Propofol, which is the most common general anesthetic. We're learning more all the time. It's not just short-term memory that's affected. There can be long-term effects. The classic 'Grandma was never quite right after her surgery' story."

"How is that administered?"

"Typically, through an IV. Or injection." Morrissey waited for Andy's next question. Andy pulled her business card from her bag.

"I know you're busy, but if you have a moment, would you mind jotting down a list of what to look for and sending it to my email?"

"Will this help Verna?" he asked, taking the card.

"Indirectly. I'd appreciate it."

Morrissey pocketed the card and stuck out his hand for me to shake. "Good to see you when you're not on a gurney, Will. I need to get back to this raging television medical drama that is the ER." He waved a hand at the silent, empty emergency room. To Andy he said, "Tell the chief if he doesn't show up here within a week for a full heart workup, I'm coming after him."

"I will, but he might start carrying a gun," Andy said.

44

NEED YOU HERE.

I looked at the text message on Andy's phone. Arun, precise in his practice of digital communication, did not use all caps lightly.

We were within sight of the section of street in front of the station that had been closed and turned into a parking lot for media trucks, vans and assorted vehicles. Andy slowed, but did not stop.

"Are you turning around?" I asked.

"If something's happening, I better check in," she said. "Text him back. Tell him we're at the station and will head up there soon."

I tapped out a reply. Andy turned in the service driveway and drove around the city maintenance shed. She stopped to open a gate that had been set up to prevent news vans from entering the parking lot behind the station. As we parked, her phone rang in my hand. I didn't recognize the number.

"Detective Stewart," Andy answered.

I heard a familiar voice but couldn't make out the words.

"I'm outside. Be there in a minute." She killed the engine and pushed her phone into her bag. "That was Donaldson. Something is happening."

We hurried inside. Donaldson had abandoned the small interview room. We found him in the main conference room, which was crowded with plainclothes FBI and uniformed police. In addition to suits and ties, I saw brown shirts belonging to county deputies, blue shirts belonging to City of Essex police, and the signature Smokey Bear hats belonging to State Patrol.

Everyone focused on the flatscreen TV mounted on the back wall. The classic bands of news graphics, boxes, and never-ending crawl filled the screen. In one box, a reporter stood on what appeared to be the shoulder of a road. The night anchor for CNN filled the companion box. Behind the reporter, emergency lights flashed their tragic fireworks in the distance, lighting up lines and structures belonging to a bridge.

A "Breaking News" screen band stretched across the top of the frame.

"What's going on?" Andy asked Donaldson the instant we entered, keeping her voice low. Everyone in the room hung on the words of the reporter.

"...authorities have closed the interstate highway in both directions..."

Donaldson spoke softly, "They answered the short payment." He looked shaken. Muscles in his jaw flexed. "Couple of kids. Teens. It looks like they ran them off the road and then—" He choked on it. I felt my own throat close, seeing this veteran of countless crime scenes unable to find the words. He struggled on. "—tied them—threw them off the bridge. An overpass."

"Hanged?" Andy asked.

"No. Tied them together, but not at the neck. Threw them over so they were—dangling. A truck hit them."

No one in the room spoke. The reporter droned on, providing no concrete facts, at least none as devastating as the few words Donaldson managed to string together.

"Do we know it's the same people?" Andy asked.

Donaldson nodded.

"It's them," Chief Tom Ceeves said. He'd been standing behind us.

A woman at the front of the room aimed her arm at the screen and hit the Mute button. She commanded instant attention.

"Alright people, this is what we know. A phone matching the one found in Baraboo was found at the scene. It had pictures. It had a message. Another Bitcoin address. Same as the last one, but with something extra." Special Agent Richards—Janos's second-in-command—pulled a notebook from a pocket in her dark blue blazer. Lack of sleep and a severe expression hardened her face. She read in a clipped, precise monotone. "Stop fucking around in Missouri and pay."

"They knew about the ambush," one of the FBI agents said. "How the hell did they know?"

"I've already informed Special Agent Janos. He's folding up the operation. This follows the same pattern as before. Everything has already been released to the media via social. Pictures—of those poor kids—the message. We've asked them to withhold, but the photos were also sent to fringe websites who consider any request from the FBI proof of a new conspiracy, so the images are already on the web."

"Motherfuckers," somebody muttered.

"God, their families!"

Special Agent Richards held up both hands, commanding silence. "We stay on task. The phone is already on its way to the lab in Madison. State CSI is at the scene and our team is on its way. The highway is closed. State DOT has given us full authority. There's next to zero chance of any highway camera footage. The overpass was a county two-lane. But we start there and map every possible route in both directions. Then we check cameras." She pointed at two of the FBI people in the room who immediately ducked out. Richards addressed the rest somberly. "We were set up, people. Let's not let it happen again."

"Where was this, Chief?" Andy asked as the meeting broke up and people began filing out.

"West of Madison on I-94. Listen, Andy, Will, I need to see you in my office." He dropped a huge hand on my shoulder.

"Chief, I know I'm not assigned to this, but I think I need to get up to Sandy's place," Andy said as he led us out and down the hall. "I'm sure she's been up all night, waiting for word from Missouri, and now there's this."

Chief Ceeves said nothing. He lumbered into his office, then paused at the door to usher us in. He closed it behind us.

Two county deputies stood waiting. I didn't recognize the badges sewed to their shirtsleeves. To my deep discomfort, they fixed their attention on me.

"Chief, what is this?" Andy asked, quickly reading the room.

"Will Stewart?" one of the deputies asked. He took a step toward me.

"Yes."

"Would you turn around and put your hands behind your back, please?" He detached a set of handcuffs from his belt.

"Chief!" Andy said.

"Detective, please step aside," the second deputy held out a hand against the possibility that Andy might intervene. The first deputy closed a tight grip on my arm and turned me around. He pulled my arms back and I felt the cold snap of handcuffs around my wrists. Despite the presence of a fellow officer, there was no courtesy in his treatment. I sensed anger.

My pockets were emptied. The deputy put my wallet, phone, Bluetooth earpiece and two BLASTER units on the chief's desk, paying the latter a moment of curiosity.

"Stop!" Andy said sharply. "What is this about?"

The lead deputy ignored Andy.

"Will Stewart, you are being arrested on charges of simple assault, assault and battery, trespassing and unlawful conduct with intent to cause harm under a duly served warrant issued by the City of Brainerd, Minnesota, and executed by deputies of the Crow Wing County Sheriff's department. I have here an extradition consent signed by the Wisconsin Department of Justice." He pulled a card from his shirt pocket and read the Miranda Warning. It rang in my ears.

"You're not taking him anywhere until you explain this!" Andy stepped between me and the two deputies.

"You're the wife?" the lead deputy asked. Andy's jaw clenched and her posture stiffened.

"I am Detective Andrea Stewart, and this is my husband, and you need to show some respect to a fellow officer, deputy. Start explaining!"

The deputy stepped face to face with Andy and gave no quarter. "Your boss has a copy of the warrant. Read it. We've got a long drive ahead. We're leaving."

Andy looked at me, confused. "Will?"

I wanted to confidently tell her that everything would be all right, but my knees felt weak and my voice failed me.

"Hey!" the chief stopped them cold. For an instant I felt salvation. "You take him through the sally port and out the back, understand? If his face shows up on television, I will come for you, badges off. Got it?"

I sensed that the deputies had planned just that, a full-frontal departure through the Essex PD main entrance, letting the cameras have their way with me.

"Don't fuck with me," Chief Ceeves warned.

"Chief!" Andy argued. "You can't!"

The chief said something low and soft to Andy, but my pulse hammered in my ears and I didn't catch it. The deputies took me out of the chief's office, picked up the pace and led me through the offices. Curious eyes followed me out of sight. We went down a set of stairs and into the police garage. One of them stayed with me. The other fetched a vehicle.

Andy broke through the garage door and ran up to me. She shot a hard look at the deputy and ordered him to step away. He hesitated, then wandered a few paces off.

"Will, what is this?!"

I swallowed. "Dee, I need to figure this out."

Her eyes pleaded with me, but there were ears close by.

"Not here," I said.

Her phone buzzed. She automatically pulled it and read the screen.

PLEASE HURRY

Andy started to ignore Arun's message.

"Go. Take care of Sandy. If she saw what happened on the news…"

Andy shook her head sharply. The sally port door began to rise. Headlights painted us. Andy's eyes glistened. The helpless look on her face tore me open.

The deputy returned and took my arm again.

"I love you!" Andy said suddenly. She pulled my face to hers for a kiss. The deputy pulled me away.

I left her standing on the gray concrete.

45

Neither deputy spoke during the first two hours of the drive. They radiated anger, expressed the moment they buckled me in the back seat of a big Ford Expedition with a Crow Wing County Sheriff's badge on the side.

"Sit. And shut up." I deemed the instruction worth obeying, at least for a while. They made no move to unlock the handcuffs.

Around two hours into the trip, the sun shifted the chroma of the sky behind us, hinting at dawn. We rolled on the relentless hum of oversized tires and a truck suspension that made this luxury SUV anything but. My shoulders ached from having my arms restrained.

The men in front remained stone cold and silent. I decided to test their mettle.

"Hey!"

Neither moved. Neither spoke.

"Hey! I've got a question."

"Shut the fuck up!" the deputy riding shotgun barked without looking back.

I gave him a mile or two to feel satisfied with his unquestioned authority. Empty Wisconsin scenery sailed by.

"How is she?" I asked.

Nothing.

"Angeline Landry. How is she?"

Nothing.

"Come on, at least tell me that much."

Deputy Driver glanced at his partner. Shotgun Deputy sniffed loudly and turned to face me.

"She's dying, you piece of shit. The girl is dying, and you fucking terrorized her. Who does that to someone like her? Sick son of a bitch!"

"You know her personally?"

His face reddened. "Yeah. I know her. A lot of folks in Brainerd know her. They know what she's going through. They know about her two little boys. God damn! What did you think you were doing?"

"Terry…" the driver warned.

Shotgun Deputy ignored him.

"The girl only has a few weeks, maybe less. And you come along and attack her. For what? Did you cop a feel? Is that how you get your rocks off? Do sick people turn you on?"

"The Foundation I work for can help—"

"I don't know what kind of scam you're into, but nobody's buying that crock of shit. If you were there to help, where's the fucking money? You put her back in the hospital, shithead! Who's gonna help her pay for that?"

"Terry, can it," the driver said. "My partner is a little sensitive in this matter, sir, on account it's his best friend's cousin you assaulted. With a little luck, maybe he'll be on the jury." He flipped a saccharine smile over his shoulder.

"Asshole," Shotgun muttered. "Instead of spending her last days with her little boys in her own home, she's plugged into tubes in a hospital room at St. Michael's."

I took that as a gut punch. The idea that I'd accelerated the woman's decline had not occurred to me. I had expected another miracle—or worst case, no change.

Doug Stephenson's statistics suggested that over eighty percent of the time the bodies I wrapped in *the other thing* emerged cleansed of the killer.

An eighty percent chance of life means a twenty percent chance of death. One in five.

Angeline Landry must have been the one in five. Maybe she was too old for *the other thing* to work its molecular magic. Maybe she was too far gone. I should have been more careful, but my shameful hubris walked me right down the path to this.

And I'd been clumsy. Finding me had been easy.

I wondered what she told the police, and then hated myself for wondering. She had every right to tell the police what happened. It's not like I stopped to explain why a stranger was grabbing her in her own back yard.

Empty miles spun beneath the big SUV's wheels. I added up the damage I'd done. To Angeline. To her family. And to Andy. Fresh waves of regret came with recognizing that I'd just done one of the worst things the spouse of a police officer can do.

I got arrested in front of her colleagues.

Andy's role in the Johns case, in the farm case, and as a friend to Sandy at a moment of desperate need, had been impacted if not shattered by my actions.

I saw only one way out of this.

46

My bladder screamed at me from Eau Claire to the Twin Cities, but I kept silent. I imagined peeing through the screen all over Shotgun Deputy, who tossed silent sneers at me every ten miles. I imagined simply vanishing and slipping out the door when they stopped to investigate my disappearance, then peeing on them from a floating hover above their SUV. In fact, just about everywhere my mind wandered, I factored in peeing.

I thought about asking them to stop but guessed the deputies would use an urgent request as a malicious reason to keep going. I stayed silent. Sooner or later, they, too, would need a respite. Two empty coffee cups on the console told me so.

Relief came twenty miles northwest of Minneapolis. Deputy Driver swerved onto the rest stop ramp without comment or warning. Shotgun muttered something I didn't catch. He stretched in his seat, however, and universal body language told me he'd reached his limit as well.

Deputy Driver parked in one of half a dozen handicapped spots nudging a flat-roofed rest stop.

"We go first, then you," Shotgun told me.

"That's okay," I said. "This backseat smells like urine anyway."

They traded looks and decided to shift priorities. I got escorted to the men's room first. Shotgun held my arm while Deputy Driver checked each stall. The facility proved empty. They led me to the farthest stall, the one with the oversized door and handicapped assist rails. I understood why when they released my right hand from the cuffs, but then snapped my left securely to the handrail.

"Don't wander off," Deputy Driver said. They stepped out and closed the door behind them.

I took care of urgent business first. It was close, working one-handed. Things got a little comical when the splashing sound seemed to go on forever. Zipping up posed a challenge, until I figured out that a simple side-step put my left hand in play again.

I listened. The deputies took care of their own needs, exchanging few words. I made plans to vanish. Once gone, I would extend *the other thing* over the metal chain connecting the handcuffs. It would weaken the links, letting me break free. After that, it was a matter of rising above the stalls and watching the confusion until they went away.

And then…

I was still thinking about the *and then…* part when a phone rang. Deputy Driver answered.

"Yes, sir."

"Yes, sir."

"Uh-huh."

"About an hour and fifty."

"Yes, sir."

The call ended. He said to Shotgun, "Boss wants us to take him up to St. Mike's for a positive ID. He wants that logged before booking him."

The stall door opened. Both deputies examined me, then the stall. I had been a fraction of a second away from vanishing. In my mind, my hand gripped the levers that make me disappear, ready to push forward.

I released the thought.

Shotgun hid no disdain. "Are you a pig? Flush the damned thing!"

St. Michael's Hospital in Brainerd would have barely qualified as a small clinic in a large urban setting. The red brick single story building had not aged well. The trim needed paint. The asphalt driveway needed resurfacing.

The deputies rolled the unit under a flat overhang. A small SUV bearing the badge of the Crow Wing Sheriff's Department occupied a Reserved space in the front row of the parking lot. The owner of the second vehicle, a round-bellied man with heavy jowls and bushy eyebrows, stood beside his vehicle. My deputies disembarked and met him with the deference demanded of rank. They spoke for a few minutes before Shotgun approached the rear door to release me.

Timing is everything.

I waited until he closed his hand on the handle. I heard the latch snap.

I rolled to my back, kicked with both legs and—

Fwooomp!

I vanished and—

FWOOOMP!

I pushed *the other thing* harder, down the length of my arms behind my back. The effect spread over the handcuffs until they vanished as well, leaving only the chain.

I jerked the cuffs. Nothing happened.

I jerked again. A soft snap, like a strand of yarn breaking, rewarded my effort. The link between bracelets snapped. Both hands came free.

Shotgun took the full force of my door kick in his hand and wrist. He uttered a sharp outcry and jumped back. He grabbed his right wrist and pulled it to his belly, bending over and swearing.

The door snapped fully open.

Behind him, Deputy Driver and his commander turned abruptly.

I grabbed the passenger assist grip just above the door. I raised my legs and heaved myself out of the vehicle.

My move fired me directly at the belly of the senior officer. At the last second, I hooked the open door and stopped. This left me hanging off the door, which was an instant from being kicked shut by a howling mad Shotgun Deputy.

I twisted awkwardly, pushed and rose toward the underside of the overhang.

Shotgun kicked the door shut.

"Motherfudge!" he cried. He clutched his right wrist.

Deputy Driver chuckled. "Jesus, Terry." He strolled over to check out his partner. "Lemme see it. Come on. Lemme see it."

I bumped against the white overhang, using my hands to cushion the collision and avoid a rebound. I floated above the black and white SUV. A huge number 6 lay below me in black on the white roof. Or a 9, if they drove in reverse.

"Don't be such a big baby," Deputy Driver jeered at his partner.

The senior deputy stepped past the two men.

"Where is he?" He pointed at the empty interior. "*Where is he?*"

Both deputies looked through the rear door window. Deputy Driver jerked open the door.

All three men stared into the empty space.

Shotgun lunged forward and stuck his head down. He searched under the seat, which struck me as ridiculous.

"*Where the hell IS he?*" The ranking officer's voice hopped an octave.

All three men stepped back. Deputy Driver dropped to his knees and looked under the car. Shotgun dashed around to the other side, looked in the window, looked in the front seat, then tried to look through the privacy glass hiding the rear compartment.

The search expanded to the entrance. Then the driveway. Then the parking lot. They dashed out and came back. They searched behind bushes hugging the front of the building. They searched inside the entrance, checking a hall that ran in both directions.

I monitored their futile search and drifted slowly to the edge of the overhang. Gripping the edge, I traveled hand-over-hand to a post at the corner. The post took me down to the concrete surface of the entrance where I remained while the deputies regrouped.

Deputy Driver suggested a call to the Brainerd Police Department.

"Goddammit, Milt, what exactly am I supposed to tell them?" his boss fired back. "Go in and make sure this clown isn't terrorizing Angie, fer chrissakes!"

The broad glass doors swept open. Deputy Driver trotted inside.

I pushed off the post on a vector that took me to the edge of the door. A grip on the frame let me adjust and aim myself higher through a second set of doors.

I floated into a small lobby. The lip of a recessed skylight offered a handhold. From a high vantage point, I watched the deputy hurry down the hall. Halfway to the end, he eased to a walk, then leaned cautiously into a patient room. He slipped out of my sight.

A fire suppression sprinkler pipe ran the length of the hallway. I shoved myself away from the skylight and grabbed the pipe. One of my first excursions through a public building employed sprinkler plumbing, back in the day before I discovered power units, which I dearly wished I had. I rotated to an inverted position. The ceiling became my floor. I pulled on the pipe and sent myself gliding down the hall.

Essex County Memorial belongs to a large medical corporation and provides its patients with amenities. Carpeting. Paneled rooms with second-rate hotel furniture. Nice lighting. This small clinic looked like it operated on the fringe of insolvency. A linoleum floor and walls coated in glossy paint offered no warmth. Fluorescent lights leeched color from everything passing under them. Carts parked along the hall looked old and worn.

The more I saw, the worse I felt for putting Angeline Landry in this place.

Deputy Driver emerged from the patient room. He left the door ajar behind him. He hustled back down the hall, I presume to report that, no, I wasn't attacking the young woman again.

The recessed door offered nothing to grip. I settled on applying opposing pressure to the sides of the opening with my hands. I probed one foot forward until it touched the door, which I eased open, hoping that if anyone saw it, they would credit changing air pressure or an unseen breeze.

With the door open enough to slip in, I repositioned and pulled myself through, headfirst.

She lay on a hospital bed, attended by an IV stand without any fluids, kept company by a dormant electronic monitor. Where a normal bed would have had a headboard, she had stainless steel fixtures, oxygen connections, and plugs for a variety of devices.

The room contained two chairs, vinyl refugees from a 1960s motel. A stainless-steel sink and some cabinets lined the interior wall. A pair of double-hung windows dominated the outside wall. Old yellow shades ineffectively blocked the morning light.

Only five days had passed since I saw Angeline sunning herself. Yet those five days had cost her. Her skin scarcely contrasted with the white sheets. Her bones were prominent. The sunshine in her back yard may have deceived me, but five days ago she had been a woman holding on to life. Now she looked as if life had forsaken her.

I floated above her bed and the sharp contours of the sheet that covered her thin body, and I hated *the other thing* for letting me think I could reverse the disease consuming her. In that moment I decided I would never again administer this *thing* to another sick human.

Ever.

The door opened. A small bald head wrapped in a colorful silk scarf probed the room. An impish girl leaned in, studying the room's occupant. She wore a pink sweater over turquoise tights. She watched Angeline for a moment, then ducked silently out, taking my new and short-lived promise with her.

I pushed off the ceiling and rotated my legs downward. When my feet touched the floor—

Fwooomp!

—I reappeared, settled onto the leather soles of my boots, and closed the door, careful to turn the knob so the latch wouldn't snap.

I walked around the bed and sat down in the chair beside it.

She lay with her head angled toward me. The orbs of her eyes enlarged the thin skin of her eyelids.

We sat trading nothing but the whisper of our breath.

After a moment, she spoke softly.

"It's okay, Daddy, I'm awake. I'm just resting my eyes."

"That's alright," I said.

Her eyes popped open. She stiffened.

"Wait." I held up my hands to show I meant no harm, but then realized handcuff bracelets dangled from my wrists.

"You!" She looked around the room for someone, anyone else.

"Yeah. It's me. Please give me a minute to explain. Please."

She swallowed.

"Just one minute. I'm begging you."

A debate raged behind the guarded look on her face. She glanced down at the call button.

"I want to show you something," I said quickly. "I wasn't trying to hurt you. What I did—it was meant to help. That's all. I was trying to help you. May I show you?"

The expression didn't change. "What do you want?"

"Just watch me. Closely. Watch my face," I said.

Her eyes, so large within the thin contours of her face, fixed on me like spotlights.

Fwooomp!

"Do you see?"

Fwooomp!

Disappearing surprised her. Reappearing frightened her. She shrank back against the pillow.

"It's okay. It's okay, really."

"What the hell?" she said hoarsely. She lay frozen, staring.

"I know. It's a lot to take in. But you're not going crazy. Want to see it again?"

She hesitated. A little of the rigid tension in her posture melted. She nodded.

Fwooomp!

Her lips parted but no words came.

I tried hard to sound matter-of-fact. "The crazy part is that when I do this, I start floating in the air. That's what you felt the other day. Remember?"

Fwooomp!

Returning to her sight was either less disturbing or mildly reassuring. Her rigid posture eased slightly.

"This is what I did. I made you disappear. Do you remember feeling weightless?"

The words came, broken and choppy. "What—? How—?"

I forced myself to relax. I sat back and crossed a leg. "Ah, now that's a bit of a story. Got a minute?" I tried a smile.

Something amused her. More tension melted.

"Depends on who you talk to."

She remained frozen, as if she feared movement might provoke me.

"I'm a pilot" I said. "You already know that, don't you, because that's how the cops found me. They must have told you." She nodded. "Well, I was in a bad crash—about a year ago."

I told her the short version of the crash of Six Nine Tango. With each word, I wondered how upset Andy or Lillian would feel about me sharing my secret with a stranger.

"As if this isn't weird enough, it comes with a side effect. Something I didn't expect. Something…good, I guess." I slipped from my story into the story of delivering a little girl in a fog-bound Angel Flight to Marshfield. "…which did something to her. It made her better. Don't ask me what it did. I am clueless. But I've got a doctor friend, and we've been trying it on people—mostly kids—with Leukemia. And sometimes it works. Statistically, most of the time it works."

She listened, not moving.

"I saw your photo at the restaurant."

"Those pickle jars," she said. "They're sweet to put them out. I worked at the Wings Café for a while."

"That's what they said."

"So…what? You go around and try to help sick people by—I don't know—making them disappear?"

I shrugged. "I try. Mostly at night, with children, when they're sleeping. Yeah, I know how that sounds, but you saw what happens when I tried it in daylight with an adult who was awake."

"And it cures them?"

"Sometimes. I don't understand how it works. I just know it happens."

"This is crazy," she said.

"Tell me about it. I haven't gone public with this. I'm afraid to." I uncrossed my leg and edged a little closer. She didn't recoil. "I'm sorry. I'm so sorry for scaring you. You were right to call the police."

She pushed herself up a little higher against the pillow. I felt a barrier fall, or at least lower, between us.

"I didn't. That was my dad. I kinda blurted out to him that somebody was in the yard and grabbed me, and he freaked out. He said some guy had come to the door looking for me. He called the cops. I told him not to make such a big deal."

"Well, I did break your lawn chair. I'll pay for that, by the way."

She laughed. "It was a piece of crap."

"Your dad was just trying to take care of you."

"If I hadn't seen you do that…thing…a minute ago, I would call bullshit on all of this."

"Yeah, well, you'd be entitled. I'm just—I'm so sorry for scaring you. I got a little full of myself. I did more harm than good. They said you took a bad turn, because of what happened."

She shook her head.

"No. I mean, yes, things got bad. But it wasn't you. I felt it coming on. That day. I knew when I got up that morning that it was happening fast. I asked my dad to take me outside so I could feel the sun. It was such a nice day. I just wanted one more day outside."

"Even so, if you want to press charges, I get it. But I came to explain, and to ask if you could maybe leave out the part about me doing—you know. I can't afford to have that made public, for a lot of reasons. If you tell that part, I would have to pretend I don't know what you're talking about. And I don't think anyone would believe you. It would break my heart, because you'd be telling the truth and I'd have to make you look like a liar."

She shrugged. "I'd sound like a loony."

"To be clear, you're not. This is real."

"Assuming I don't wake up suddenly." She reached for the bed control and pressed it, slowly bringing her head higher. "I'm such a mess." She brushed at her head where there should have been hair, then laughed at herself for it. "Crazy. I keep doing that."

We hit a moment of awkward silence, until she said, "I'm sorry. About the cops."

"No, please, forget it. It'll be fine."

We stared at each other.

From what I could see, *the other thing* had done nothing for her. And she knew it, too.

"I know it sounds crazy, but it really does seem to help. I'm willing to try again," I offered. "But only if you don't get your hopes up. I can't promise anything."

She put on a rueful smile. "It does sound crazy, but not crazier than dosing myself with deadly radiation or taking poison. What you did hurt a lot less than all the rest of it." She spent a long minute looking at me. I had the feeling she was just now seeing me, not a stranger who could wink out of sight.

"I guess we can try again."

"Okay, but no promises."

"No promises," she agreed. "What do you want me to do? Do you want these covers off?"

I stood up. "Let me."

I lifted the light sheet and folded it away beside her. She wore a thin cotton nightgown with tiny flowers sewn on the neckline and sleeves. She quickly arranged and straightened it, and I saw what her father had told me, that she had been a pretty girl, and now felt self-conscious.

"Your dad said something to me and—well, I don't mean to creep you out, but…you still are, you know."

She looked up at me. "What?"

"Pretty."

It earned me a smile and the faint blossom of a blush in her thin cheeks.

"Okay, I want to give this the best possible shot," I said. "I can do this by just holding your hands, but if you'll let me, it might be more effective if I wrap my arms around you."

"Do you want me to get up?"

"No, stay there. I'll come to you. Remember, when it happens, we're no longer affected by gravity."

"Does that mean you can fly?" An expression of wonder lit up her face.

"More like an astronaut in weightlessness. I have no real control. You ready?"

"I guess…"

"I'm going to do it now. I'll talk you through it, okay?"

She tidied her nightgown again.

"This is the craziest thing I've ever done," she said. "Let's do this before I think too much—or wake up."

Fwooomp!

I vanished. She released an involuntary laugh and quickly put her hand to her lips. "What if someone comes in?"

"There won't be anything to see." I grabbed the side of the bed. "Okay, I'm going to take your hand. Hold it up for me."

She lifted her right hand. I closed my left around it. At the touch, a smile broke out on her face. I used the bed and her hand to lift myself. Then I used the inner muscle to rotate until I was fully extended over her.

"This is going to get a little personal, okay?"

"I'd tell you to keep your hands where I can see them, but that would be silly."

"I'm going to put my arm around your waist."

She arched her back slightly as I slid my hand into a position that reminded me of a boy-girl dance in grade school.

"Here goes. You're going to feel a cool sensation."

"Should I close my eyes?"

"Hell, no. You'll miss the fun part. Ready?"

"Ready!"

I pushed the levers full forward, hard.

FWOOOMP!

She vanished, leaving a wrinkled depression in the hospital bed. A laugh sparkled up from the place on the pillow where her head had been.

"Oh, my! Oh!"

"Easy. Just breathe." I pulled her toward me. It had the effect of lifting her from the mattress while pulling me down toward her. A balanced exchange of force. She bumped against me.

"Let go of my hand. Put your arms around me," I said.

She wiggled her fingers free. I felt her embrace, the thin arms of a child. I reached around her and closed a gentle grip on her back. The bones of her spine and ribs met my fingers. I pulled her against me, then reached down and pushed on the mattress. Even weightless, I could tell she was light as a feather.

We rose. She laughed again and I could feel her turning her head back and forth to watch the room fall away below us.

"Oh, God! We're flying! Oh, my God! Is this real?"

"Shhhhhh. We don't want to attract a crowd."

"Like anyone could see us! I don't know what to say! This is wonderful! This is amazing! William—do they call you that, or are you Bill?"

"Will."

"Sorry. Will, I mean it. Oh, this is incredible!"

We bumped into the ceiling. The light fixture jabbed me in the back. I freed a hand and found a grip on the frame. I pushed us toward the foot of the bed, then rotated us so she could see the room without having to crane her neck.

She suddenly applied surprising power to her arms and pulled me into a tight embrace. I responded with light pressure, pulling her closer. Her cheek touched mine. Her breathing deepened. I felt a gentle jolt. Then another.

"Are you okay?"

She sniffled and I realized the jolts were sobs.

"It's—it's—!" The sobs grew deeper and stronger. She pressed her face against my neck.

I patted her back gently and tried to let her know it was okay. But it wasn't. And even if it was, I couldn't push words past the sour knot in my throat.

"It's just—!" She released a sudden, loud cleansing breath and whispered, "It's been so long since anyone held me."

She cried.

47

It wasn't attraction, but it was love. Not a love that threatened Andy in any way or had a life beyond this moment. It was the love poets profess for their fellow man. The kind John Lennon sang about. The kind that hides beneath the skin of humanity and peeks out when tragedy reminds us that everyone around us reflects the face we see in the mirror.

She cried for a long time. I held her and absorbed her helpless sobs, thinking that all along she'd probably worn the brave face. For her children. For her father. For the friends that collected coins in a pickle jar on a restaurant countertop. That Angie, she's a fighter, they said. Fighters don't cry. At least not until they can be sure no one can see them.

I tried to sense if anything passed between us via *the other thing*. Was there a chance that prolonged exposure would work? I couldn't tell. Absent evidence, I prayed.

The room door opened. This time, it wasn't a small girl with a flowered scarf around her head and a shared illness. I recognized the old man, her father. She saw him and stifled her sobs. He ventured in, noted the empty bed, then checked the bathroom. Bewildered, he left.

I felt her swallow. I heard her clear her throat.

"I'm sorry."

"I suppose we better get you home before I get in trouble with your old man," I said. "Again."

She giggled, cleansing the last sob away.

"It's been a lovely date," she said. It helped that we were both in a vanished state. I would have blushed terribly.

I had to claw my fingernails into the metal strips between acoustic ceiling tiles to generate movement. I gave it a shot and lined up for a landing on the bed. During the short glide, I rotated, putting her beneath me. My aim was off, but I reached out and grabbed the side rail, righted us, and lowered her to the sheets.

She squeezed one last hug and I felt a kiss hit my cheek. Then her arms slipped away from my body.

"I'm going to let you go now. You'll pop back in sight and drop a little on the mattress. Are you ready?"

"No," she said. "It's like a ride at the fair. I don't want it to end."

"Here goes."

I released my grip.

Fwooomp!

She reappeared and dropped, issuing a startled gasp. Her hands gripped the sheets as if she feared she might float away again.

"You okay?"

"I have no idea." She lifted her hand and reached for me. She found my chest, probed up my neck and touched my cheek. "Thank you."

I grabbed the side of the bed and levered myself into a standing position beside it.

Fwooomp! My feet planted.

"I am such a mess!" she declared again upon seeing me. She scrambled for tissues to wipe her glistening cheeks. "God!"

I sat down beside the bed again.

"I can't fucking believe that!" she declared. "Excuse my French. I mean—did we really do that? What am I saying! I'm babbling now. I look horrible and I'm babbling like an idiot!"

"No, you don't and you're not," I said. "Let's face it—this is impossible to believe."

She touched herself. "Should I feel something? Different?"

I shrugged, largely because I didn't trust myself to speak.

She read the expression on my face.

"Oh," she said, reigning in hope. "Yeah. You were probably right. I don't think it worked for me."

I didn't know what to say.

"Well, the ride was worth it." And there it was again. The brave face.

I don't remember ever feeling so helpless or insignificant. Ever.

The door opened again. Her father appeared. A series of almost comical shifts in expression transited his face. Blank curiosity. Surprise at seeing her. Discovery. Fear. Anger.

"You! Get away from her!" He leaned back out the door. "HE'S IN HERE!"

"Daddy, stop!"

"HE'S IN HERE! HE'S IN MY DAUGHTER'S ROOM!"

"Oh, for God's sake, Daddy, stop shouting!"

Her father threw the door open and boldly took a step and pointed at me.

"They're coming! You just stay where you are! Don't you touch her!"

Heavy footsteps approached in the hallway. Deputies Driver and Shotgun entered the room behind Angeline's father. Their leather utility belts creaked with each step. They hustled the old man aside. Shotgun rounded the bed with malicious intent painted on his squarish face.

"Terry, STOP!" Angeline cried out. "Goddammit, stop! It's not him!"

If he heard her, he didn't care. His big hands closed on my shirt and pulled me out of the chair. He tried to whirl me around to lock a grip on my arms, but this time I stood firm. A button popped from my shirt.

"TERRY, I SAID IT'S NOT HIM! HE'S NOT THE GUY!"

"Terry!" Deputy Driver shouted at his partner. "Let him go!"

Shotgun didn't like what he was hearing. He reluctantly released what was about to become a very painful grip on my arm and wrist. I shook him off and stepped away.

"What are you talking about?" Shotgun demanded. "This is him! Stewart! He's the pilot!"

"That's the guy!" her father joined in. "That's the guy who came to the door!"

"Yes," Angeline said, "but he's not the guy who grabbed me! Are you deaf? For God's sake, leave him alone!"

All three men hesitated. Angeline dropped against her pillow, breathless from the exertion. "I'm telling you, that's not the guy! Listen to me!"

They stared bullets at me. A moment later the senior officer appeared at the door, gasping. He pushed past the father and Deputy Driver.

"What's going on?" he demanded. "Why is *he* in here?"

"She says he's not the guy," Driver explained. Shotgun maintained malice in his eyes and his posture.

"Terry, just leave him alone," Angeline warned.

"That's not the guy?" the boss asked her. She shook her head.

They all stared at me.

"I wasn't lying. I'm from a foundation that would like to help. That's why I visited the house."

Angeline snapped, "Can you all just back the fuck down!"

"Angie!" her father said sternly.

"Daddy, I'm sorry, but this has gotten out of hand. He's just a nice man who wanted to help." She turned and looked at me. "And I will always be grateful, no matter what happens. Always."

I found it hard to look at her. I turned to Shotgun and lifted my wrists.

"Do you mind?"

He studied the broken handcuffs.

"Take 'em off, Terry!" the boss ordered. "Sir, I'm sorry about all this. Truly. If she says you're not the guy…well, I guess that's that."

Shotgun produced a key.

"I think you need a new set," I said. He shot me a *this ain't over* look and I pegged him as a bully who found a home for his cruel streak in a uniform. Andy would make short work of him in her department.

"I need to talk to Mr. Stewart," Angeline said. She sounded tired. I saw, to my deep regret and against all prayers and hope, that there appeared to be no change in her, and that the exertions had sapped her. "Alone! Would you all just leave, please?"

The uniformed officers muttered apologies, wished her well and shuffled out.

"You, too, Daddy," she said to her father who still didn't and probably never would trust me. "And Daddy, would you do something for me?"

THE GIRL'S name was Jillian. She was eight. She poked her head in the door after Angeline sent her father to fetch her.

"Hey you!" Angeline brightened at the sight of the child. "I want you to meet someone. This is Mr. Stewart."

The girl stepped around the end of the bed and gave me a proper handshake.

"Hi!" she said brightly.

"Hi, back!"

Angeline beckoned the girl to come closer. "I met Jillybean in treatment. We were chemo pals. She's been my bud here, too. Haven't you?"

"BFFs!" The girl rushed to the bed and dished out an uninhibited hug. Angeline held her for a moment, then squared her up and looked her in the eye.

"Honey, can you keep a secret? A super-serious secret?"

Jillian nodded enthusiastically.

"If you can, then Mr. Stewart has something that might help you."

The girl looked me over. I tried looking trustworthy. It must have been a bad effort because Angeline quickly said, "He's my friend and you can trust him."

I didn't think Jillybean was buying it.

"Will you?" Angeline asked me.

"If she says it's okay. But I think it's better if we all go together. Can you sit up?"

Angeline worked her way upright and swung her legs off the side of the bed. Without prompting, Jillian hopped up beside her and fell into Angeline's arms.

"Okay," I said. "Let's do this."

I stood up and leaned over them. I closed my arms around them.

"Group hug!" Jillian cried out happily. She threw her free arm around me.

FWOOOMP!

48

"It was all a misunderstanding," I lied. Andy knew it, but she had me on speaker phone. Chief Ceeves and Donaldson shared her end of the call. "I was in the wrong place at the wrong time. The assault happened shortly after I left, but a witness thought it was me."

"They're dropping the charges?" Andy asked.

"They took me to see the victim. She stated positively that it was not me."

"So, they didn't book you?"

"It never got that far."

"Thank God, Will!" Andy's relief carried through the phone I borrowed from Angeline. The chief muttered something about one less headache and left the call proximity.

"Yeah, so I called Pidge to come and get me. Can you make sure there are no snags with her using the Foundation Navajo?"

"She'll be fine. Are you okay?"

"Are you asking if they beat me with rubber hoses?"

"I just—Will, I was worried! Those guys were angry." I knew she wanted to say more privately, but she also wanted other ears in the department to hear the outcome.

"I'll tell you all about it when I get home, Dee. If you don't hold up Pidge, she can be here by noon, and I'll be home by 3."

I heard something bump. It sounded like a chair.

"Hang on!" Donaldson's voice joined the call loudly. I pictured him leaning unnecessarily close to Andy's phone. "What did you call her?"

"Who, Pidge?"

"No. What did you just call your wife, Will?"

"Uh...I don't think I called her anything." I didn't think it possible for this day to get any weirder. Then it hit me. "Dee? You mean, did I just call her Dee? Yeah. That's short for—"

"He doesn't need to hear the story, dear."

"Short for Deeply Embarrassed, which is what she said she felt after falling for me."

"D.E.?" Donaldson asked.

"Yeah. Dee."

The chair bumped and rattled.

"What just happened?" I asked.

"I'm not sure. Our pet FBI agent just ran off." Andy's voice changed. Closer. More intimate. She switched from speaker phone to hand-held. "Hey, are you really okay?"

"I'm really okay. They're giving me a ride to the airport. Minus the handcuffs, this time."

"Did you, um, you know?"

"I'll tell you about it. No worries. How's it going there?"

"I'll tell you about it. No worries."

I laughed. "You wouldn't tell me if there were worries."

"Of course not."

"Love you. See you soon."

"Love you."

49

Deputy Driver, whose name was Milt Lindstrom, drove me to Brainerd Municipal Airport. He rolled to a stop at the curb beside the entrance to the Wings Café after a short and wordless ride. I planned to reciprocate the wordless part, but when I reached for the door handle, he spoke.

"Hold up a sec."

He flexed his hands on the wheel at ten and two. I tried to read his affect. Anger? Resentment? He didn't seem the hothead his partner was, but this shaped up to be an unfriendly sendoff.

"I'm gonna ask you, Mr. Stewart, did you buy your way out of this? Tell me straight up."

Like many cops I've met, the eyes he laid on me served double duty as lie-detectors.

"No," I said to his face. "I didn't give her anything." And I hadn't. By the time I left the sad little hospital room, despite Jillian's cheerful company, it was clear to me that *the other thing* had changed nothing for Angeline. Doug Stephenson would catalog it and consider it and tally it in his statistics, but this dismal failure would stay with me long after Angeline Landry had gone.

Deputy Lindstrom offered no sign that he believed me.

"That said," I added, "would you do something for me?"

"Depends."

"She has two children."

"Her boys."

"Yeah. Do me a favor and wait a day or two, then stop in and see her and tell her that she will be contacted by a man named Larmond. He's an accountant for the Foundation. He'll be setting up a college trust fund for her two boys. Full ride."

"Why didn't you tell her?"

"Because, Deputy, I didn't buy my way out of this."

I didn't know if the Foundation would still exist when I reached Essex. This promise might carry less weight than I do when I vanish, but it didn't matter. If the Foundation had no money, I'd obtain it elsewhere. I'd done it before.

Milt didn't say anything. I don't think he could.

He nodded.

I nodded.

I opened the passenger door, stepped out and closed the door without looking back. Before I reached the café entrance, I heard the electric window drop.

"Mr. Stewart!"

I turned around. Milt leaned across the console.

"Tell that Larmond guy not to wait too long."

"I will."

PIDGE ROLLED the Navajo across the ramp and braked in front of the café. I twirled a finger in the air to signal her that I would jump aboard with the engines running. She ignored me and cut both engines.

She met me at the cabin door.

"No, no," I said, waving for her to go back to the cockpit. "Let's go."

"Fuck you, Stewart," she scrambled down the airstair. "I smell the best hundred-dollar hamburger this side of Lone Rock! It's lunchtime, baby!"

I pulled a carryout bag from behind my back and dangled it between us. Her face lit up.

"You are a god among mortals!" she cried, grabbing the bag. "Raw onions?"

"Hell no. You're not stinking up my cabin. Grilled onions."

"That'll do. And guess what! You're flying!" She climbed back into the airplane and took a seat in the cabin, flipping open one of the small tabletops and spreading her riches. I threaded my way past her and slid into the pilot's seat after sliding it all the way back.

"Did you file?"

"Mmmrmph!"

I looked at her. She flashed a thumbs-up and wolfed another bite of bacon double cheeseburger.

Twenty minutes later I cruised at nine thousand feet among solitary puffs of rising cumulus. Pidge dropped into the copilot's seat licking salt off her fingers. She pulled on a pair of headphones.

"When were you going to tell me about that Challenger asshole?"

"Nothing to tell."

"Really? You rearranged his face."

She shrugged. "He offered a walkaround and a tour of the jet's front office. Said he was authorized to offer me a job on the spot. Turns out it was a blow job. He whipped it out. I told him I'd bite it off. He took a swing. I punched his nose through the back of his head. I guess I got fired before I got hired."

"I guess. You could have gotten in some hot water. Good thing you recorded the whole thing."

She looked sideways at me. "What the fuck are you talking about?"

"On your phone. The recording."

She made a face. "I didn't record anything."

"But Andy said—" I stopped and smiled. "Never mind."

We flew in silence for a few miles. I weaved between cloud tops that reached for the blue above us. I could have let the autopilot haul us through the vapor, but it's more fun zipping around the puffy walls, something I don't do with paying customers aboard.

"Are you okay?" I ventured to ask.

She looked at me again. "Seriously? You think I'm supposed to get all girly because some dick flicker ruined my Pollyanna world? Fuck that. Am I supposed to be all 'Me, too' and 'power to the p—'"

"Don't say it!"

"I mean it, Will!' Am I supposed to go lesbo because one guy is a pig? Fuck that, too. Lemme ask you a question."

"Shoot."

"Guy offers you a job if you'll do a job on him. How would you take that?"

"I don't punch as hard as you."

"True."

"But I'd come close."

"Well that's my point."

I had no idea what her point was. She figured that out quickly.

"Look, shit like that happens only because there are stupid fucking idiots in the world. It doesn't indict the whole system. Does it mean that men should not be attracted to women or women attracted to men? Look at you and Andy!"

"What about us?"

"Oh, please! You two sexually harass each other all the time. I'm getting you a bib for your birthday, to catch the drool whenever you're around her."

"So?"

"Exactly! It's what we do! You. Her. Men. Women. I don't want to change that dynamic. It's what the species does. It's how we're built. If I'm single, and that Challenger captain is ten years younger and he buys a few rounds and shows me he has a heart and some respect and a sense of humor—and I'm not otherwise involved with someone—then I'm gonna bang the shit outta the guy and enjoy the ride. But if he pulls that Harvey Weinstein crap on me, I'm punching his lights out. Simple."

"Not otherwise involved?" Pidge ordinarily sidestepped any discussion of her interest in Arun. "My turn for a question. How did Arun take this whole thing?"

"Whaddya mean?"

"Arun. Some guy assaulting you." I pointed at the bruise under her eye. "Does he know about this?"

She shrugged. "I dunno. He's been busy. I've been busy."

"You're avoiding telling him."

"It's not a big deal!"

I fixed a skeptical look at her.

"What?"

I said nothing.

"Okay! I haven't mentioned it!"

I shook my head. "You better think it through. You said you don't want to change the dynamic. How we're built. Arun's a guy. He may not be an action hero, but he's programmed to protect."

"I can take care of myself!"

"Obviously. And you know that's not the point."

She didn't argue, which told me she understood.

"I wouldn't have taken the job anyway," she said curtly, ending my probe into her personal life.

"Why not?"

"It's a fucked up outfit. Family business. Some rich real estate developer in New Jersey. His jet crew spends most of their time flying the guy's kid around. I don't see myself hauling some entitled bimbo with a handbag full of yappy dog back and forth to Vail."

Probably best for all concerned, especially the dog.

50

I asked Pidge to take over and perform the approach and landing at Essex County Airport. Deep fatigue caught up to me. I pulled some oxygen from the supplementary system, but it didn't help. My math on the last time I hit a pillow for anything more than a glorified nap was fuzzy.

Pidge greased the landing. "Pull it up to the pumps?" she asked on the rollout.

"No. I'm too tired to deal with it now. Just swing it around in front of the hangar. I'll gas her up in the morning."

"Is Arun in the office?"

"I doubt it. He's been babysitting Sandy. He's probably still at the lake."

"Oh."

"You should call him. He needs a break."

She seemed to ignore my idea, but a few minutes later, with the engine exhaust system ticking and cooling on the silent ramp, I saw her pull out her phone and hold it to her ear as she marched away.

"You're welcome," I said to myself. I reached for my own phone.

Shit!

No phone. No car keys. I wasn't all that sure where my car was. I had a key to the hangar on the ring in the Navajo's engine ignition, but after extending the thought I realized I had no reason to go inside. I left my only two power units on the chief's desk. The rest were recharging at home.

"Pidge! Hey, Pidge, wait up!"

. . .

"Are you going up there to meet him?" I asked as she drove me to the police station.

"He wants to go home and shower. He says he hasn't changed in a couple days."

"I don't suppose you asked if Andy was there?" It seemed unlikely to me, since any action related to transferring the payment would have taken place hours ago.

Pidge shook her head. "Didn't ask." She turned onto Park Street and stopped. "Now what new machinery of Hell is all this?"

"Jesus Christ, they're multiplying."

We faced a City of Essex barricade. A big Road Closed sign leaned against a row of striped sawhorses. To one side, a police cruiser angled into the street from the curb.

Beyond the barricade, rows of television news vans gave up all pretense of finding parking. They simply filled both lanes of the street. Masts were raised. Cables snaked around the tires. People milled around between vehicles. I spotted a Taco Truck that ordinarily parked farther down the street at the Library Park on Tuesdays for Farmer's Market. One or two of the vans pointed blazing lights at reporters standing in front of shoulder-mounted cameras. Someone had set up a line of portable toilets near the curb.

Del Sims, the smallest officer in the department, walked from the cruiser to Pidge's side window, which she lowered.

"Hi, Will," he greeted me, then looked over Pidge. I tried to think whether they'd met or not. His expression said not.

"This is Pidge," I told him. "She's my ride."

"Out!" she ordered. "I'm outta here."

I joined Sims outside the car. She backed quickly away.

"Thought you were on paternity leave," I said. "Congratulations, by the way."

"Thanks. I thought so, too. But all this...and Traeger still missing..." He spread his hands. "The chief called me in, and I'll be honest, it's nice. Peaceful. I may hang out here all night. No crying infant."

"Something happen?"

"Yeah," he said grimly. "Couple kids were killed. Pretty gruesome. What cave have you been in all day?"

"I knew about the kids. Anything else?"

"Half of the North American agents of the FBI have taken over the station house. We've been holding our shift briefings at the library. And the number of media trucks doubled this morning. That's why we closed the street. Oh! And the chief died and came back to life."

"I knew about that, too. Do you know if Andy's inside?"

"Should be." He waved for me to try my luck. "You may want to call her and have her meet you at the door."

"Don't have my phone," I said over my shoulder. "Would you let the desk know I'm coming?"

He gave me a thumbs-up and pulled out his cell phone.

AFTER THREADING my way through the carnival of television trucks—recognizing some of the local and a few of the national on-air reporters along the way—I entered the lobby of the station. Ordinarily the lobby is only visited by the occasional citizen buying a bike or dog license or paying a citation. This afternoon a pair of state troopers guarded the entrance. They stopped me and asked a lot of questions until Mae Earnhardt came to the rescue.

"I'm so sorry! Del called but I got busy!" Mae's mainspring seemed a little tightly wound.

"I need to get in the chief's office," I told her. "I left my phone."

"I've never seen anything like this," she fretted after unlocking the door and ushering me past the front counter. I followed her through the reception area and down the hall toward the chief's office. "My sister called to tell me she saw me on television! They had a camera looking in the front window. Can you imagine!"

We passed the staff offices. The cubicles, including Andy's, contained federal agents I did not recognize. Most worked desktop keyboards. Some held phones to their ears. A few hurried in and out on urgent errands.

"Jesus, where'd they all come from?"

"They came back from Missouri this morning while you were gone. Will, I heard about Brainerd. I'm so glad that wasn't you they were after!" I agreed and thanked her.

She opened the chief's office. I found my phone, earpiece and two BLASTER units. I stuffed the works in various pockets. Mae eyed the power units suspiciously.

I headed off her question. "Have you seen my lovely wife?"

"She left to be with Sandra. They scheduled the payment for noon. Andrea wanted to be there. The chief told her to stay out of all this other business—except, of course, looking for Lyle. I'm worried that Lyle is being given less attention because of all this."

"He isn't," I said. "Andy won't let that happen."

We left the chief's office. Mae seemed a little uncertain about what to do with me. I asked, "Do you know where that Donaldson guy is? Is he still here?"

"Is he the one with the limp?"

"That's him."

"Well, if he's still here, he'd be in Main Interview."

Right where I left him.

"Will," Mae looked up and down the hall, "I don't think they'll let you wander around here. I know you're family, but it's different with all these federal agents here."

"Not to worry. I'm going to talk to Donaldson. Then I'll call Andy and either connect with her or go home."

"Take her home with you. That girl of yours needs rest…and I need to go back up front." She hustled off.

I didn't find Donaldson. He found me. He rounded the corner of the hallway just as I poked my head into the empty Main Interview room that he, Andy and I had occupied what seemed like days ago.

"Damn, Stewart! I hear you beat the rap!" He hurried toward me ignoring the reluctance of his right leg to keep up. Aside from the limp, he looked full of energy.

"It wasn't a raging success, but I stayed out of jail." I looked him over. "By the way, how are you doing?" He had abandoned both his bandage and his hat. I wasn't sure how comfortable people were seeing his Frankenstein crosshatched stitches.

"Great! Why?"

"Are all the neurons still firing? No brain farts?"

A line on his brow deepened and he lowered his voice. "Yes, why? Are you telling me this might wear off?"

"No," I said. "Well, actually, I have no idea. It doesn't come with a warranty."

He pulled me into the interview room.

"Well, I can tell you that the neurons are kicking ass. I figured out why we were coming up empty on Artie, and it's a hot lead. About a third of the agents here are working it under me."

I wondered if his energy sprang from the lead or the leadership.

"We had it wrong. We weren't looking for Artie."

"I don't follow."

He grinned. "Not Artie. RD."

I didn't hear it the first time. He enunciated. "Are…Dee. RD! It hit me when you called your wife Dee! We heard it wrong from Walking Bear! The guy goes by RD!"

"Do you have a name?"

"No. Not yet. But we're all over NCIC. We're looking at cases where a person of interest was identified as an 'RD.' Some of them fit the mold of our weirdo. But think about it! We can place him at Sandra Stone's home at least once on orders from Litton. Walking Bear said Litton backed off, but obviously RD knew about the money and decided to score it on his own. Or with a crew. And after last night, we know he's here in Essex! Progress!"

"Did the ransom go out?"

"Yeah. She paid it. And the official word is that it's gone. Not traceable. I don't know if I buy that. I asked Janos if we didn't have some tricks up our sleeve at NSA or CIA. He gave me schtick about domestic intelligence and congressional mandates, and blah blah blah. I have a few connections from the old days. I'm reaching out to them. But this is good news, pal!" He slapped me on the back. "There's a team out in New Mexico picking up Walking Bear. That'll piss him off."

"Maybe not as much as blowing up his kitchen. Does Andy know about this?"

"Yeah, I told her before she took off. Thought it might give her friend some comfort."

Not if it means telling her that RD spent a night watching her sleep.

"Listen, I gotta get back to it." He ducked out. Halfway down the hall he turned. "Hey! When this is over, we gotta talk."

I really didn't think so but chose not to say it.

51

The chief agreed with Mae. I passed him in the hall. He told me that Andy had gone to lend support to Sandy Stone. I tried her cell. My call jumped to voicemail. I had no car, but I had two BLASTER units and a sparkling summer evening. The decision to take the scenic route came easily.

I needed to disappear. Not so easy.

Doing it inside the station wasn't an option. I would still need to get out the door and state troopers guarded the main entrance. Doing it outside the station presented issues, too. Half a dozen news cameras fixed their lenses on the front entrance, providing B Roll footage for 24-hour news outlets. And the back entrances were likewise covered by the department's non-stop video monitoring.

The question frustrated me until I remembered my walk through the Park Street media carnival. I thought of the perfect place to disappear.

Ten minutes later, I took the self-conscious stroll everyone takes when approaching a row of portable toilets. Business at the relief station was slow, with no lines. I found a door with a green "Vacant" sign above the handle and slipped in, confident in being unobserved. Most people choose not to stare at someone entering a public toilet.

I latched the door, then waited long enough to ensure that anyone who had randomly seen me enter had forgotten or moved on. I took time to text Andy a "Call me" message. I pocketed the phone and then pushed the Bluetooth earpiece into my ear.

Fwooomp!

I pushed the door open and slipped out, easing it quietly shut. Using the handle for leverage, I lowered myself until my feet made flat contact with the pavement. I checked for wires and tree branches overhead, then bent my knees and kicked off.

A rapid ascent took me above the canopies of the elms and maples lining Park Street. Media trucks and vans stretched the length of Park, all the way to the city library. A trio of Essex PD squad cars at the library affirmed what Del Sims had told me about the department using the library to stage its patrol officers.

As I rose, I pulled a BLASTER from my back pocket and snapped a prop in place. I held the unit up and thumbed the slide forward. The resulting thrust pulled me higher. I angled my wrist toward Leander Lake, a silver sliver in the distance.

I CRUISED above treetops and power lines. The route took me past home and I momentarily considered stopping to pick up a set of ski goggles. The wind waters my eyes and I can go faster with goggles, but I decided that any time gained by flying faster would be zeroed out by rummaging around our mudroom for the eyewear.

I cruised on over fields of late summer wheat stubble and woodlands flush with green leaves.

Upon reaching the southern tip of the long, narrow Leander Lake, I shifted my flight path to skim the water. By approaching the Stone property from the lake, I avoided overflying the sheriff's department roadblocks. I didn't want the buzzing power unit mistaken for drone surveillance. Half of the media vans had deployed drones, a practice quickly shut down by the chief. Speedboats pulling water skiers drowned the BLASTER's hum.

I reversed power and slowed over the Stone pier. I tipped my wrist and rose above the broad sunset deck, then over the house, then into a spiral that took me to the front sidewalk. Andy's car was nowhere to be seen. Arun's car and two others sat on the circle driveway in front of the house. I recognized Senator Keller's Cadillac, but not the third car. A driverless state patrol unit sat at the end of the driveway. I saw no sign of vehicles belonging to the FBI. I wondered if they pulled up stakes once the ransom was paid.

Fwooomp!

I reappeared between two upright arborvitaes gracing the walk to the front door. The state trooper on guard duty inside answered the bell just ahead of Senator Keller.

"Will?" Keller matched the trooper's scrutiny of me. "What are you doing here?"

"I'm looking for..."

Sandy Stone appeared behind Keller. Her eyes, swollen and red, met mine. Without exchanging a word, she pushed past Keller and put her arms around me. I pulled her into a tight embrace, ignoring the impatience simmering in Keller's protective posture.

"I'm so sorry," I spoke into Sandy's blonde hair. "It's not your fault." She didn't move. She maintained the pressure of her embrace, tight and unyielding, taking what she needed from human contact. I thought she might cry, but she only breathed deeply, as if each breath challenged her to take the next.

"I know," she whispered. "Still..."

The trooper minced his feet and moved discretely to a post by the door. Keller waited.

Sandy backed away and looked up at me.

"God, you're a mess," I said.

She laughed—a spasm of relief. She stepped away, rubbing her eyes with the back of her hand.

"Thank you."

"I always know just what to say to a woman," I said proudly. "I didn't mean to interrupt. I'm looking for my wife, but I see that her car isn't here. Do you know where she went?"

Arun appeared, car keys in hand, shouldering his laptop bag. "Andrea left about an hour ago."

"She told me she had an interview to conduct," Sandy said. "For the Johns case. That poor girl."

"That's a story that fell from the headlines quickly," Keller observed.

"Miss Stone, I have an appointment this evening, but if you'd like me to come back, I'm happy to."

Sandy took both of Arun's hands. "No. You've done so much, Arun. Go and relax. I'll be fine. We'll regroup tomorrow." She pecked a kiss on his cheek. He stiffened and blushed.

"After noon, please," Keller warned.

"I'll be here at noon," Arun promised.

"Call. Call here at noon," Keller ordered him.

"I'll be at the office in the morning. I will call at noon," Arun promised Sandy. He slipped out the front door.

"Did Andy say where or with whom she had the interview?"

Sandy shook her head. Keller saw an opening and swept in to take her charge by the arm. "We should get you something to eat. Will needs to find his wife and Mr. Larmond should go."

"Dewey's here? Can I get a word with him?"

"I'll fetch him for you," Keller said. Translation: Stay here.

Sandy gestured for me to follow her. "He's in the kitchen. Headquarters, these days. Come." Keller frowned.

I didn't begrudge Keller's attempt to insulate Sandy. A bulldog at the door wasn't the worst idea.

I followed the women into the kitchen. Dewey Larmond sat on one of the stools at the island, looking morose.

"Will," he stood and shook my hand formally.

"Mr. Larmond, I wonder if I might have a word?" Angeline Landry hovered in my thoughts. Having made a promise in Brainerd, I hoped to find out what, if anything, remained of the Foundation's resources.

"Yes, I missed your wife. I have the information for her. It's not concrete. Not yet. I expect to have documents on Tuesday," he said. He paused and looked at me. "You're aware that Andrea asked me to make an inquiry?"

"I was there when she called you."

Larmond cleared his throat. "I believe that the company, or series of companies, backing the anonymous buyer of Miss Stone's property ultimately originates with Mr. DeSantorini, just as your wife suspected."

"I will let her know." I had a feeling this news would come as no surprise to Andy.

Keller, startled, looked at Larmond. "Are you talking about Emilio DeSantorini? From New York?"

"Most of the gentleman's holdings are in New Jersey, but he never misses a chance to claim status as a wealthy New York developer."

"You know him?" I asked Keller.

"Hardly." She stopped herself and placed the palm of one hand on the granite countertop for a moment. Perfectly painted nails tapped out runaway thoughts in code. "I saw him at the county planning commission meeting last night."

"Then that confirms it. Why else would a New York—"

"New Jersey," Larmond corrected me.

"—developer attend an Essex County Planning Commission meeting if he hadn't recently acquired land here?"

Keller remained distant. "I hadn't intended to go, but our darling Sandy here made it clear that I was becoming annoying."

"Lorna, no!"

"Don't be silly, sweetie. I can read a room. Besides, I was curious. The Deputy Secretary of the State Department of Transportation decided to come in person. When an official like that ventures into my territory, I hear about it."

"Sounds salacious," I said, thinking it anything but.

"It was a rescheduled meeting. DOT just completed a two-year highway expansion study. The full report was to be presented a week ago, but the engineer who conducted the study and wrote the report did not show up—or send the report. Rather embarrassing for DOT."

"So, the no-show embarrassed the office and the boss had to make the big presentation himself," I said. I abandoned my plan to corner Larmond and decided to call him in the morning. "That stings. Listen, I'm going to head out."

"No," Keller said, planting a hand on my forearm. She stared at me. "No, he didn't make the big presentation. And he didn't provide the report. He provided a summary."

"You make it sound out of the ordinary." I looked for an opening to pull away. Keller tightened her grip. She stared directly at me, but it felt like she wasn't seeing me at all.

"A summary that green-lighted the next phase, which is to allow private party proposals."

"For what?"

"Land use proposals. To WISREGPC." She reeled her focus back in and read my dumbfounded expression. "Wisconsin Regional Planning Commission. Long range land usage planning. They sign off before bringing in the federal Department of Transportation."

Keller abruptly turned on Larmond. "Are you certain?"

"Of?"

"DeSantorini is the anonymous buyer."

"I am certain he is not. What I am certain of is that DeSantorini companies are behind the anonymous buyer. It's quite complicated, but—"

I interrupted him. "Then he might as well be the buyer. Are you telling me that this DeSantorini guy just happens to close a deal on Sandy's land the day that the state gives their blessing to new highway projects that may benefit the owner of that land?"

"I cannot account for the timing, or guarantee the future value, but it does represent an opportunity for a significant windfall," Larmond observed. "The parcel is largely agricultural, woodland and wetland. It has little value as is, but that can change dramatically if a new highway is planned."

"I think it already has…" Keller said, her wheels turning rapidly.

"Why?" Sandy asked.

"The engineer conducting the study was tight-lipped about it to prevent land speculation—but frankly, no one expected it to be an issue. The proposal didn't have a future. The summary surprised me because it keeps the project alive. Politically, cutting through this part of the state with a new freeway spur has enemies. The tourist lobby for one."

"Citizens here in Essex, for another." I remembered Sarah Lewis's father making a pitch for Andy to join the protest cause.

"Why?" Larmond asked. "I should think the tourist lobby would embrace new highway development."

"Not if the project gives Milwaukee, Chicago and Green Bay traffic a destination that *isn't* Wisconsin Dells, which is the beating heart of this state's tourist lobby. That's why I haven't followed this proposal closely. It was a non-starter."

I looked at my watch. "This is all very interesting, but I really do need to catch up with my wife." Keller paid no attention to me. She sank into thought again. I took a step toward leaving but stopped. "Okay. I'll bite. Why does this all hinge on Essex County?"

Dawning realization spread on Keller's face. "Because it has The Lakes."

I met her gaze and remembered thinking something.

A perfect spot for a hotel.

"Oh, lord," Keller said. "Sandra, I'm so sorry. We were caught up in all...*this*...and I never thought about the land. I should have seen it. I should have seen it last night."

"Seen what?" I asked.

"It was a *summary*."

"So?"

"A summary written by the Deputy Secretary—a political appointee."

"One of pinhead's appointees?" I nurtured no love for our governor.

Keller shook her head in grudging admiration. "That sonofabitch rewrote the report *as a summary*!"

"Are you saying that the summary contradicts the full report?" I asked. "Isn't that easy to expose? Just have the author come forward and call this for what it is—a complete crock of shit."

"Really? A career civil servant is going to call the Deputy Secretary of the Department of Transportation, his boss, full of shit?"

Keller marched across the kitchen. She pulled her phone from her purse and dialed, tapping one foot impatiently until the call connected. "Casey!

What's the name of the engineer doing the DOT study for central? The one going to WISREGPC?"

Keller listened.

"Yes, that one. He was supposed to present the study here in Essex County last week, but he never showed up. Has the report been filed with the—"

She stopped.

She listened.

Casey, presumably an assistant happy to jump through hoops for her boss on a Sunday night, spoke for a long minute, during which Keller's expression darkened.

"Thank you," Keller said. She ended the call.

"My lord," she said. "His name was Dennis Yarborough!"

Like we were supposed to know who that was.

Keller's eyes expanded for emphasis. "Yarborough!"

Something about the name hung just outside my memory's reach.

Keller had the answer—but not the answer I stretched to find. "His entire family was murdered on the farm in Baraboo."

"No," Sandy protested. "That was the Williston family."

Keller shook her head. "The family was Williston. The engineer's daughter was the wife and mother. Dennis Yarborough was the father-in-law. He was killed, too. That's why he didn't show up last week."

52

"Donaldson."

"It's Will. Got a minute?" I lingered near Dewey Larmond's car, hoping the trooper in Sandy's foyer wasn't watching or noticing that I did not have a car of my own.

"Not really. Things are moving fast here. We have a line on RD. What's up?"

I tried to explain. Donaldson listened.

"Lemme get this straight. You're saying that a Wisconsin DOT highway engineer was the target of all these farm family killings? That all the rest of it was meant to hide this one victim? Because of a report he had written?"

Putting it that way, he made it sound highly implausible.

"Must've been some report!"

"No one knows."

"Will, you're watching too many conspiracy movies. Victims of crimes have a thousand tangents in their lives, you know what I'm saying? The mother just announced a run for PTA president. The father's brother has a history of drug abuse. The farmer in Michigan had a prison record. Every human being is a cluster fuck of entanglements and motivations. Don't think we haven't been digging through all of them. We already knew this. This guy happened to work for state government. What was his name?"

"Yarborough."

"Right!"

"Whose job was to write a report that ties to land that was sold under duress in order to pay the ransom!"

"Will, the Bitcoin payday was worth ten times the value of the land. The land sale has been in the works for months. Plus, selling the land was Miss Stone's idea."

"C'mon, man!"

"I'll put it in the hopper, okay?"

"Good. One more thing. Do me a favor and go find the chief."

"Why?"

"Andy's not picking up her phone."

Saying that aloud induced a sharp pang of worry.

53

Fatigue. Good pilots recognize it for the insidious danger it represents. Unlike aviation thrillers in the movie theater, where an emergency is marked by shaking controls and whining runaway engines, fatigue is the silent emergency that forgets to lower the landing gear, descends below a published minimum altitude, or misreads a clearance and puts an aircraft on a dark, wet runway in the path of another.

One remedy for fatigue is crew rest. That's why air carriers enforce strict duty time limits for flight crews. People who tell me their flight was delayed because they had to change crews at the last minute often express disgust when they should be expressing gratitude.

Another remedy for fatigue is a jolt of undiluted fear.

That jolt hit me when I tried Andy's number again with no answer. I've been down this road before with Andy. She can take care of herself, and sometimes that scares the hell out of me.

I pocketed the phone and pulled out a BLASTER unit. Not caring whether the state trooper inside saw me or not, I broke into a run across Sandy Stone's lawn. At the corner of the house, I cut to the right, toward the lake. Three strides in, I hugged the power unit to my chest and leaped.

Fwooomp!

The power unit vanished with me. I extended my arm and pushed the slide to the stop. Immediate acceleration shot me past the house, past the deck and over the lake. The hour had grown long, and Leander Lake's curfew on motorboats had taken effect, rendering the surface glass smooth and silent in honor of imminent sunset.

The BLASTER screamed like an angry cicada.

I aimed for the north end of the lake. Enroute, I passed over the spot Andy described—the spot where she found Clayton Johns spent and unconscious after raping an underage girl.

A woman can be forced into sex when unconscious. A man can't. That fact more than any other ensured Johns' conviction, despite Andy's certainty that he had also been drugged.

But if Johns was drugged, how and by whom?

Andy hadn't been looking for a confession from Johns. She had been looking for him to slip and he had. Johns' comment that he partied with people who lived on the lake sent Andy back to Lyle's notes. On the way to the station after speaking to Dr. Morrissey, she told me she planned to spend the day digging through property records and retracing Lyle's steps, putting together a list of who might have been Johns' accomplice.

But that was before two teens were murdered on a bridge.

And before I'd been arrested.

I'll tell you about it. No worries.

Andy and I traded the same line. I used it to delay a difficult discussion about Angeline Landry. She used it to channel her worry into work. For the six hours between my arrest and my call to tell her I had escaped justice, she had been coping the way she always copes with stress. By diving into work headfirst.

Which told me she knew where to look for Johns' accomplice. And I had a solid notion of where that was.

Approaching the shoreline, I skirted the half-dozen boats still anchored off the Johns property, laden with cameras hoping to catch a shot of the NFL superstar and accused child rapist. I shifted aim to the immediate neighbor to the left. The same home Andy and I had fruitlessly visited earlier.

Derek and Ariel Santi, and their third-wheel friend Roger.

If their performance at Detroit Metro Airport was any indication, Derek and his dominoes were perfect party animals for latching onto a former NFL star's libido. To seal the deal, they brought something special to the party—young girls looking for exciting and a little dangerous summer fun.

My conclusion sprang from seeing the Santi couple first-hand. Andy would have arrived at the same place by cross-checking property records, registered deeds and tax rolls against Lyle's list.

Lyle's detailed list.

The list that contained a short essay about each visit on Lyle's routine canvass. Except one. The stop that merely listed three names and a single note.

A jolt of fear can paralyze, but it can also evaporate fatigue and shake bits and pieces into place.

Lyle's detailed list.

Except for a single note, he had written nothing about Derek and Ariel Santi. I tried to remember his note, but even with the jolt, that piece eluded me. But now, as I approached the million-dollar summer home on Leander Lake that neighbored Clayton Johns' leased property, I understood something I should have realized from the outset.

The significance of Lyle's notes wasn't what he had written about each visit. It was in what he *hadn't* written about the Santi couple. He hadn't written anything.

Lyle's notes, transcribed into the department server, ceased with the Santi couple and I feared I knew why. It wasn't because they weren't at home during the crime or when Lyle came calling. It's because someone *was*. And Lyle had asked one too many questions or penciled one too many observations in his pocket notebook—which never made it into the system.

Because this was where Lyle Traeger's investigation, and possibly his life, ended. Someone had been at this lake house when the patrol officer came to the door with his routine questions about the incident next door. Someone had realized that this overweight, over-eager officer had inadvertently recorded a fragment he didn't recognize—but one which he could not be allowed to leave with.

I prayed I was wrong. For one thing, it didn't explain how Lyle's vehicle could go from Leander Lake to Rockford, Illinois without being seen. Or how Stella Boardman's car got from a party on Leander Lake to the bus station in Madison. Could that have been the piece that Lyle tipped to?

I felt a desperate need to hear Andy recite "Usual disclaimer" and tell me I had it all wrong. Because if she knocked on this summer home door with the same questions as Lyle, and tipped to the same knowledge as Lyle…

I shunned the thought and dove toward the sprawling, multi-level structure.

Clayton Johns' leased property had a vast deck with an infinity pool overlooking the water. The Santi property next door sat on a lot one quarter the size, though the houses had similar dimensions. Homes on Leander Lake range from Williamsburg colonial to Frank Lloyd Wright stacked slabs. From McMansions to original 1940s cottages. The Santi house, like the home owned by Andy's sister Lydia, paid homage to the Frank Lloyd Wright school. It sat on a sloped lawn like a trio of pizza boxes knocked askew. The top tier walls made a forty-five-degree angle to the next level, giving a two-story all-glass space the look of a ship's prow. The middle level jutted out below the ship's prow. Comprised largely of glass, it had sliding panels that opened the interior to the adjoining deck. The bottom tier had been built into the slope almost at water level. It opened onto a white plank pier.

Andy and I had visited the building from the land side, where the driveway joined a huge garage. I approached from the lake and aimed for the peak of the ship's prow. I crossed over the building's centerline, returning to the spot where my wife had admonished me not to peek into the garage.

There were no vehicles in the driveway.

Good. I felt the grip on my gut relax. The absence of Andy's car suggested she had come and gone. Did she make an arrest? Did she leave the impression that her visit was routine, planning to return with the Essex PD swooping down on the occupants like Sitting Bull on the Seventh Cavalry?

I used reverse thrust to stop above the perfectly sealed asphalt, then lowered myself to the level of the garage door windows. I pulsed the BLASTER unit and drew close to the high windows.

The garage remained sterile, but now three of the six bays were filled. The tarped Corvette sat unmoved. Beside it, a large fifth wheel trailer, and beside that, a bland-looking Chrysler Town and Country.

I looked for the requisite Porsche 911 or Maserati. Or, given Derek Santi's physical height, a black Hummer. Except for the Corvette, none of money's macho symbols parked in the garage. The Town and Country looked several years old and utterly unremarkable. It needed a wash. Hardly the daily driver I expected of someone involved in racing.

I scanned the rest of the space.

A pristine acrylic floor emphasized the near-surgical cleanliness of the place. White walls. Canister lighting. And something missing. In fact, everything missing. No lawn mower. No garden tools. No garbage cans or tool benches. No stacked boxes yet unpacked after the last move. Thinking of my cluttered garage and looking at this sterile space spawned serious garage envy. What I couldn't do with a space like this! Which was the point. Nothing had been done with this space.

How does someone involved in racing not have a space filled with spare tires, cases of oil, stacked tool chests on wheels? How did they not have a spare engine, a second chassis? Racecar owners wallow in extra wheels and tires.

The fifth wheel trailer underscored the racing theme. I'd seen others like it. Room to transport the race car. Walls lined with cabinets filled with spare parts, service manuals and supplies. I'd seen similar rigs at Road America in

Elkhart Lake, crammed with power tools. Rolling garages filled with tens of thousands of dollars' worth of parts. Perhaps the Santi trailer carried everything. Every tool. Every part. Every can of oil.

I pushed back and cruised along the eaves, calculating my options. If Andy's car had been here, I would have found a way to connect with her, even if she was still interviewing—especially if she was still interviewing. With her car gone, my second choice was to call her again, or call the station.

A third choice propelled me around the perimeter of the house.

I floated above the slope to the water. Gliding downward, I passed blank empty windows revealing empty rooms.

I rounded the next corner and crossed the lakeside façade, the ship's prow. Glass rose high above me. A vast furnished great room offered the owners a million-dollar view of the lake. The furniture was new and expensive looking, yet something felt off.

For a brief period in the spring, Andy suggested we consider buying a house. I had zero enthusiasm for the project, but she curled up with her laptop and found a few listings around Essex. She called it testing the waters. I called it a colossal waste of time, yet she dragged me to several open houses. The homes were spotless showcases of modern living. I finally asked an agent hosting the open house if anyone lived there. She laughed and said, No, the house had been staged. Rented furniture gives an empty house sales appeal.

This house looked staged. The furniture coordinated, the lamps and knick-knacks posed in all the right places. Proper magazines fanned out on spotless glass coffee tables—tables without a single condensation ring.

No television. No remotes scattered on the arms of the sofa. No Cheeto crumbs on the carpet.

The bar at the back of the room had no liquor on the shelves.

No one moved within. I pulsed the power unit and arced away from the glass wall, down to the next level.

Another wall of glass faced the lake—huge motor-driven glass panels capable of opening to merge a broad room with a tiled patio overlooking the water. The room featured a scattered array of leather sofas and chairs. Patio furniture carried the casual theme in wrought iron summer furniture with pastel cushions.

I had planned on entering the house here using a trick *the other thing* provides—the same trick I used on the handcuffs. By extending *the other thing* over metal—a doorknob or latch—the metal becomes weak. Frayed. Under pressure, it snaps.

The motor-driven glass walls foiled my breaking and entering scheme; there were no latches.

A light came on in the room on the other side of the glass. Legs appeared on a wide staircase. The legs were male, tree-trunk-like and wrapped in a light, silky fabric. Some sort of pajama bottom. To my surprise, two central wall panels—floor to ceiling glass—slid silently apart.

Derek Santi descended the stairs with a cocktail in one hand and a cell phone in the other. He tucked the phone against his ear. His bleached white hair flashed as he passed under canister lights.

I reversed the power unit to reduce forward movement. My glide continued at roughly the same speed as the parting glass panels. As the panels opened, I caught a faint scent coming from within the house.

Santi wore a muscle t-shirt, gold on both wrists, and dark glasses. He trotted across the carpet on bare feet in loafers, through the yawning wall and onto the tiled deck. He set his drink on a glass tabletop and dropped into one of the deck chairs.

"Ugh!" he grunted into the phone, stroking his hand over his pale hair, "I know how he gets! But you can handle him."

A female voice on the other end had a lot to say, but the words eluded me. I drifted farther and farther away with nothing to grab. Evening rules about motorboats on the lake are made for a reason. The residents want quiet, and this deck delivered. Using my power unit to stop would have sounded like someone firing up a dishwasher. I had to ride it out.

He held the phone to his ear and used his free hand to lift his drink.

I listened to half of a conversation.

"No. Not here...Because twilight here is practically forever and those goddamned boats probably have infrared...Ambulatory, babe, just walk right up the stairs...Doesn't matter on the other end...No, he's not making a fucking mess on the carpet...Okay, yeah...Okay, babe, call you when we get back here for the wheels."

The call ended.

The wife?

Spandex Woman.

I suddenly placed the woman waiting at DeSantorini's airplane, pacing, throwing female curves around like judgment. Derek Santi's wife or girlfriend or whatever she was. I remembered her cavorting down the aisle of the Delta flight. She had changed her hair, but her shape was unique and hard to miss, easily defined by the way every stitch of her clothing adhered directly to skin.

What was she doing with the New Jersey real estate developer who now owned the plot of land next door? Or was that the point?

Santi sipped his drink and stared at the lake. The sun set fire to the eastern shore. The western shore fell into shadow and would soon be a silhouette against a splash of vibrant sunset colors.

A second figure arrived in the opening between the interior and the deck. Third Wheel. The man I'd seen on the Delta flight wearing the tiny suit. No man bun tonight; black strands of hair hung uniformly around his head, touching his collar. He had a boyish face and small pale eyes.

"Did you tell her?" Third Wheel—Roger something—asked.

"Fuck no. She'd freak."

"What *did* you say?"

Santi picked up his phone and poked at the screen. He found what he wanted and held the device to his ear.

"It's me. We're doing this…Yes, now…I don't give a shit how he feels, tell him if it hurts, I'll amputate the fucking thing and be done with it …Just out and back. We'll be there in an hour. Work it out so I can drive right up, okay? Good."

"What did you tell Ariel?" Roger asked.

Santi stood up abruptly. He finished his drink and tossed orphaned ice cubes across the deck. They skittered off the edge.

"Told her it was just a nosey neighbor. No point in worrying her."

He regarded the tumbler in his hand for a moment, then wound up and hurled it high over the water. It splashed down and left placid ripple rings expanding on the glassy lake.

"I can't wait to be out of this fucking plastic bubble."

Roger lifted his hands and for the first time I noticed that both men wore tight clear latex gloves.

No furniture. No fingerprints. And that scent from within was cleanser.

T0LD *her it was a nosey neighbor.* I wondered. Did he mean Andy? Had she been here? If so, my bet was that she dished out a hypnotic smile, played to Derek Santi's gymnasium-toned ego, and left to get reinforcements.

The urgency I felt to find her relented, replaced by a need to tell her that these men were leaving town.

I wore my Bluetooth earpiece, but when I vanish, my phone screen vanishes with me. I can pull my phone out of my pocket. I can touch the screen and it radiates light. But I can't see icons or lists. I have no way of swiping through menus to find a contact. Voice command might work, but it's generally not an option when I'm trying not to be seen or heard, and I never bothered to set it up.

I completed my drift across the lateral dimensions of the patio and reached a railing that ran along the side. I lifted my legs to float across the railing. Santi and Roger disappeared into the house.

I cleared the railing and pulsed the power unit, curving right and rising at the same time. The roof of the house spread below me. I drew low thrust from the power unit. Crossing the flat asphalt and pebble roof, I rotated the unit, reversed thrust and fought the ascent until it stopped, hesitated, then turned into a descent.

I dropped and touched my feet to the roof.

Fwooomp!

I pulled my phone from my pocket and crouched to finger the screen and the necessary icons. The Bluetooth woke up in my ear and her phone rang. And rang.

Andy didn't answer.

"Christ, Dee! Dead battery or what?" I muttered when her voice told me to leave a message. I worked the screen and dialed the police station. Dispatch answered. I didn't recognize the officer.

"Dispatch, this is Will Stewart, calling for my wife Andrea. Is she there?"

"Hold on a sec, Will." Whoever it was knew me. He came back a moment later. "The log shows she logged out to spend time with Miss Stone. You might want to try her there."

"I've been trying her cell. Can you raise her on the radio?"

"Can you hold?"

"Actually, no. Give her a message. Tell her the two men she interviewed are leaving town. She'll want to know. And have her call me! I gotta go!"

I killed the connection and shoved the phone in my pocket. I listened. A new sound reached my ears—the sound of the garage door opening.

Fwooomp!

I pushed off gently. A shot of power pulled me toward the circular driveway behind the big house. Clearing the roofline, I looked back and saw the second door of the garage rise and expose the grille of the minivan. I heard vehicle doors close and an engine start.

These guys weren't kidding about being packed and ready. I wondered if they'd even taken the time to close the glass wall to the deck.

Headlights flashed on. The van pulled out of the garage. I faced a snap decision. Go high or go low.

Low meant diving after it and grabbing the roof rack. The maneuver guaranteed going wherever they went, and it saved battery power, but what if the destination was Chicago? Then what?

High meant easier surveillance and greater room to maneuver. It gave me better options if Andy called.

I chose high. It's worked before.

The garage door reversed and closed behind the minivan. I pushed the power slide control and accelerated straight up.

Their first move would say a lot. If they turned right on Sunset Circle Road, it meant they planned to angle east and south, joining Highway 34 which eventually joined I-43, which suggested Milwaukee or Chicago.

They turned left. That meant Essex.

Santi's voice echoed in my mind.

We're leaving

Who needed to know they were leaving? He'd already talked to the woman.

I don't give a shit how he feels, tell him if it hurts, I'll just amputate the fucking thing and be done with it

It hit me. I knew where they were headed.

The Town and Country accelerated. I pushed the power control on the BLASTER to the max to keep up. Sunset Circle Road runs all the way down the west side of the lake, the side currently free of law enforcement roadblocks. I cut the corner. I soared over the placid water, climbing and accelerating, keeping watch over the minivan headlights to my right.

I didn't know what Andy knew at this point. Or what she planned. But these guys were about to leave Essex County at jet speed aboard Emilio Santorini's Canadair Challenger.

I needed to reach Earl.

Simple. Land and use the phone. Except landing and stopping meant losing sight of the vehicle and running the risk of not reacquiring them. The sun had already set, and one dark vehicle looked a lot like another. What if I was wrong? What if the airport wasn't their destination?

I've been in this position before. Hard experience taught me that following a vehicle isn't easy.

Neither was dialing my phone. Time to choose. Call for help or maintain contact with Santi and his lap dog, Roger.

The minivan wound its way south down the tree-lined pavement of Sunset Circle Road, swinging back and forth with the curved contours of the lake properties. One or two other cars moved on the road, but far enough away from my target to make tracking easy.

I needed height.

I angled my wrist and climbed. My calibrated aviator's eyeball read the altitude as five hundred, then a thousand, then two thousand feet. The Lakes Region spread out below me, bathed in twilight. The last rim of fire from the sun dipped below the horizon, leaving a stunning pastel sky with a short lifespan.

Three thousand feet.

I reached in my pocket and pulled out my phone. Climbing straight up at full-speed—roughly sixty miles per hour—translates to a climb rate of around five thousand feet per minute, roughly five times a normal aircraft climb rate.

Four thousand feet. I struggled to keep an eye lock on the moving vehicle. It had grown tiny—easy to lose or to confuse with another vehicle. I realized I hadn't noted the license plate again. Dammit. Andy had been trying to drum that into me lately. If Santi and Roger found a neighborhood soccer game and mingled with a dozen moms in minivans, I was screwed.

For the moment, they continued south alone.

Now or never.

With a sixty-mile-per-hour wind tearing at me, I killed the power and jammed the BLASTER in my pocket. The wind resistance quickly took effect and I decelerated.

I held up my phone and positioned my right hand at the ready.

FWOOOMP!

I snapped out of *the other thing* and reappeared—along with my phone.

Gravity, ruthless bitch that she is, wasted no time. I felt my body acquire its full one hundred and eighty-three pounds of weight, plus boots. My upward momentum died fast. At the top of the climb, I stopped, went weightless momentarily, then dropped—a terrifying carnival ride sensation.

I held up my phone and swiped the screen. Icons appeared.

Gravity dug in its claws. I accelerated in free fall, gaining speed faster than I anticipated.

Focus! I stabbed the phone icon. Then the Contacts icon. I stroked the list. More. More. More—dammit! Too far!

It would only take a few seconds to reach terminal velocity. Wind tore at the phone in my hand.

I jabbed the name I wanted.

Yes!

The screen changed to show the call connecting. I pressed the device against my chest to avoid having it torn from my hand. My earpiece woke up with a dial tone, clicks, then the silence that comes like a breath held before the first sound of the phone ringing at the other end.

I didn't wait.

FWOOOMP! I hurled myself back into *the other thing* but now I was descending at near terminal velocity, roughly one hundred and twenty miles per hour, twice the speed I had been traveling on the way up. The earth came up at me with a vengeance.

Ring. Ring.

I grabbed the power unit in my back pocket, carefully closing a grip on it and thinking not for the first time that I needed to have straps for these damned things. Top of the To Do List.

I pointed the power unit skyward but stopped. The relative wind of my fall spun the prop furiously. Had I pushed the slide control, chances were excellent the shaft on the small electric motor would have sheared and the prop would have flown off on its own.

Trees and fields magnified in that way objects do when they're racing directly at you, trying to kill you.

I twisted the power unit to a horizontal position, then slightly down. The vibration from the pinwheeling prop stopped. I applied power, slowly. The unit acknowledged and hummed.

I shoved the power full forward.

My fall gained a lateral vector. Less than a thousand feet to go and the earth, instead of simply bursting upward at me, shifted beneath me.

"What?"

Earl's irritated voice in my ear joined the roar of the wind around me.

Seven hundred feet. I held my arm out, perpendicular to my descent line. I desperately wanted to lift my arm over my head to make the power unit arrest the fall but feared it would destroy the prop/motor shaft or tear the unit out of my hand.

"Will, is that you?"

Five hundred. The carpet of farms and forest swept below me. I cut a curved path through the air, a pendulum swing that looked like it was going to end in the side of a barn.

"Will? God dammit, is this one of them butt calls?"

The barn came up fast. Pulling out of the dive seemed to take forever. I would either plow into the ground or plant myself on the side of the barn like Wily Coyote. Had I been in an airplane I would have been pulling the yoke for all it was worth and praying the G-forces didn't warp the wings.

Neither the ground nor the barn took me. I angled through the space between the barn and a cluster of grain bins. I leveled off so low I had to pull my knees up to clear fences. The speed dropped off enough to raise my arm and let the power unit begin a climb.

"Earl!" I shouted.

"Jesus, Will! Are you flying with the door open?"

"The Challenger! Chain it up again!"

"What?! I can't hear you over all the damned racket!"

"CHALLENGER! CHAIN IT UP! DON'T LET THEM LEAVE!"

I reversed thrust to kill my speed. The roaring wind died around me.

"Earl? Earl?" My earpiece fell silent.

The connection was gone. So was the Town and Country.

I floated above a dairy farm, low enough to smell cow manure. Fields subdued by twilight spread in all directions.

I oriented myself to the sunset and aimed the power unit, thumbing the slide.

Essex County Airport lay that way.

54

Earl Jackson lives two minutes from the airport in a plain ranch-style house on a single acre of land. The diminutive property suggests that the millions he'd made when he sold his hole-boring engineering company and subsequently invested in Essex County Air Service are long gone, but that's not true. He simply doesn't express himself with money. He mows the lawn, but there are no gardens or lawn ornaments. He keeps the house up, hiring painters as needed, snow-blowing the driveway in winter. But his life is Essex County Air Service and his real home is the cramped, too hot or too cold little office down the hall from Rosemary II's office. He probably views the two-minute commute from his house to the airport as a minute and a half too long.

He must have covered the ground in half the normal time, because when I arrived at the airport and cruised the length of the ramp, I found the gleaming white Canadair Challenger jet's left main landing gear shackled to a worn-out Army surplus office chair. Nothing would stop the jet from taxiing away with the chair trundling after it, but no pilot in his right mind would attempt to take off with a length of chain and a chair dangling from one landing gear.

More to the point, no person in their right mind would approach that chair with Earl Jackson sitting on it, grinning.

I didn't see the crew or Santi and his Chrysler minivan. Just Earl, slouched with his fingers intertwined behind his head, one leg crossed.

I needed to reappear and regroup. I continued my glide down the flight line, then eased left into the first row of hangars. I descended behind the largest, rounded the corner and checked for eyes. Sunday night shrouded the airport in silence.

Fwooomp!

I dropped to the pavement beside the metal building. My pulse continued hammering, an after-effect of my high-speed descent. I renewed a vow never to skydive.

I lacked keys but getting into the Foundation hangar presented no problem. I tapped a code into the side door keypad. A car-sized garage door rose. I ducked in. Since the Navajo remained parked outside, an empty hangar greeted me. I hit the button for the main door. While it ponderously opened, I stopped in the office, splashed water on my face and drank a few gulps.

As I strolled outside to the parked Navajo, I scanned the parking lot. No Chrysler minivan. My sense of timing said it might take Santi another minute or two to reach the airport, but I began to feel a knot of worry. If I was wrong, they were long gone.

I turned my attention to the main ramp. The answer unfolded roughly a hundred yards away. Earl remained seated, comfortable and casual. A young man in a uniform jacket faced Earl while backing cautiously away. Between them, prone on the asphalt, another man lay writhing, his hands clasped to a huge bandage on his nose.

Oh, boy, I thought. Calling Earl might not have been the best idea. I watched Earl stand and jerk the captain with the broken nose to his feet. Santi's flight crew had reported as ordered.

"I wouldn't have gone near that old bastard," a voice behind me commented.

Derek Santi walked through the empty hangar. Taller than me, built like one of the current crop of muscle-bound movie stars, he looked like menace afoot. A cold smile graced his face.

The knot of tension in my gut solidified.

"This your airplane? You fly it?"

"Yeah."

"Is it for hire?" He closed the distance between us to a few yards. His corded arms hung loosely at his sides. I looked beyond him at the open hangar side door for his partner. No sign of a vehicle or anyone else.

I did the math. Any physical confrontation with this man came up as a zero sum for me. Disappearing offered an easy escape. I had no qualms about letting him see me flash out of sight if it meant saving my neck.

"Sorry. Not for hire."

"Can I see inside?" He gestured at the Navajo cabin door. "Just a peek. I love airplanes."

This wasn't the drunken, brash bully act I'd seen in Detroit. A cold streak ran down the center of his words, spoken softly, tonelessly.

"Can I? Get a peek? I was thinking about buying one of these. What is it? A Cessna?"

"Piper Navajo."

"Thing is…I'm a big guy, and I don't know if it would be big enough."

"You wouldn't like it. I'm six-one, and it's not big enough for me."

"Let's have a look anyway," he said.

We stared at each other. I reached for the levers in my head. Maybe I could get him to look away. It would add an element of doubt when I vanish. I wondered if Earl caught sight of this unfolding drama. I glanced back to see the copilot running toward the FBO building. Earl stalked behind him, pulling the broken-nosed pilot by the collar of his jacket.

No help there.

Santi made no move to approach me. His smile did not waver. His hands remained at his sides.

"Just a friendly peek, pal," he said.

At that moment, the Chrysler minivan rolled boldly through the side door of the hangar and stopped in the center on the polished concrete floor. Santi's companion stepped out of the vehicle. Santi did not turn his head. He held his gaze on me.

"I know you," he said. For a moment, I wondered if he remembered me from the Delta flight. The notion evaporated instantly. "You're Stewart. The pilot. You fly the blonde hottie around. Your wife is the cop investigating my former neighbor."

I didn't respond.

"What a crazy-assed coincidence. I think you're going to want to show me."

"I don't think so."

Santi didn't move. "RD! Show the man why he should be more hospitable."

Third Wheel grinned.

Roger. Roger Duwyllen.

Shit.

RD jerked open the minivan side door and reached in. He pulled Andy from the floor of the cargo area and swung her around. Her feet hit the concrete and she stumbled to gain footing. He held her by the arms, which were bound behind her back with duct tape. A silver band of tape cinched a pillowcase over her head. A pair of yellow headphones covered her ears. From thirty feet away I could hear, just below the thundering of my pulse, tinny treble rock music blasting from the earphones.

Tunnel vision closed in on me. Everything grayed out except a circle of light around my wife. She struggled against the restraints and jerked her head against the headphones. She staggered on uncertain footing.

RD clamped one hand on her shoulders. In the other, he held a small black box-like object.

Taser.

My pulse thundered and cold electric lightning shot through my arms and hands.

"That's your wife, right? The cop?"

Santi's toneless voice slammed everything back into focus. I felt my teeth clenching, jaw muscle locking, fists closing.

"My friend over there may look like a millennial waste of space, but I guaran-damn-tee you, he is a stone-cold fucking psychopath, sociopath and straight up nightmare. I have seen him do things to men, women and children that would make you shit your pants, pal. If that was my wife in his hands, I would be painting my shorts for sure. So, let me ask you again, nicely. How about showing us the inside of that airplane? Or maybe he digs out one of her eyeballs with his bare fingers."

RD stroked the pillowcase over Andy's head. She recoiled at the touch. I imagined him dead. Dismembered. On fire.

This animal had been in Lane's bedroom.

In Sandy's bedroom.

Against what he'd done on the farms, Lane and Sandy were blessed. But now the woman that meant the world to me strained against his grip.

Disappear.

Don't disappear.

I played out possibilities with a mind choked by the sight of Andy trapped.

Disappearing offered nothing. I had no inertia, no weight. I had no weapon to use against either of them. I might grab Andy and make her vanish with me—but RD's hold on her complicated that option—and they were forty feet away.

I needed to get close to her.

I found words. "I take it you're leaving?"

"Yes. No muss, no fuss if not for that old fart. Granted, you would have been looking for a new wife, and she's a tough act to follow, but maybe you could hook up with blondie. Point is, pal, I'm about three seconds from giving my friend the high sign to start hurting your wife. You're not going to be happy when that happens, so why don't you open that door and climb aboard?"

He moved his hand behind his back and returned it with a bright silver handgun that swept up and stared at me with one soulless eye.

I opened the airstair.

Santi came up behind me. He held out his hand.

"Your phone."

I slipped it from my pocket and laid it in his palm. He reached for me and jerked the Bluetooth earpiece away. He turned and tossed both into the hangar, giving the phone a nice high arc. It shattered on impact.

"After you," he said. He gestured for me to climb aboard.

In my head, my hand closed on the levers that make me disappear.

Santi stepped close behind me and pressed his pistol into the small of my back.

"Right in the old vertebrae. My first shot guarantees you never piss standing up."

I might vanish but it wouldn't take me out of his line of fire.

I climbed the airstair. He followed me. His weight sent a tremor through the cabin.

"Up front," he ordered me. I moved forward and slipped behind the controls, then twisted to watch the cabin. He slid into the rear-facing starboard front passenger seat.

Andy climbed awkwardly into the cabin, pushed and prodded by RD. With arms bound, she stumbled and fell forward on her knees. From behind, RD lifted her, turned her and pushed her up the aisle. Santi shoved her into the seat facing him. The headphones jarred loose. He reached across and squared them over her ears. I heard the headphone music from where I sat. The noise had to be agonizing and disorienting.

"Turn 'em down, for God's sake!"

He lifted the gun and pressed it against her head. She recoiled in the seat.

"How about if I make it really quiet for her?"

I said nothing.

Vanish and poke his eyes out.

Vanish and rip his testicles off.

Santi held the weapon against Andy.

"Whatever you're thinking, Stu old buddy, just know that my bullet gets there first. RD, get the bags and close up that hangar. And move that van outside somewhere. Leave it in the parking lot."

RD backed out of the cabin.

Vanish and stab him in the throat with a pen. I closed my left hand around one of the spare pens in the side pocket.

The bullet gets there first.

I wanted his attention away from Andy.

"Is that how you approached the farms?" I asked. "Your wife? Soccer mom driving a minivan?"

Santi turned his head.

"We're not going to do that, pal. That thing where I can't help myself— where I just *have* to tell you all the details, all the little things that your cop wife and the FBI and the fucking whole world missed. You want to live. More than that, you want her to live, right?"

I nodded.

"I didn't answer her questions. I'm not answering yours. Besides...if I'm you, I want to know absolutely *nothing*. I want the bad guy telling me zip, zero, nada about what he did or how he did it. Because telling you a lot of shit makes it harder for you to believe me when I promise you that if you do what I want, I'll let you and your wife go, right? I mean, you see that shit all the time on TV, and you're yelling at the screen for the guy to shut up because you know they absolutely have to kill him once they spill the whole plan, right?" Without lowering the gun, he looked over his shoulder at me. "Why don't you go the 'Please don't tell me shit' route? And I'll let you both live."

"I'll take you wherever you want to go," I said firmly. "Just keep your friend's hands off her."

He dipped his head. "Fair enough. You fly us someplace quiet. I'll leave you and your wife with this airplane. Of course, I'll shoot up the radio, but you can still take off and fly away, and that will give me plenty of time to get far away and we'll never have to see each other again."

Utter bullshit.

"Deal."

I heard the hangar door rumble. RD appeared at the cabin and heaved a trio of bags aboard. He climbed up and reached back to pull the airstair closed. He fumbled with the latch. I had to instruct him. Eventually he managed.

At last, Santi lowered the weapon. He squeezed between the seats and took the copilot's seat beside me, but only after he found the seat release and ran it all the way back.

"Christ, do you fly around with children in this seat?"

"That child broke your pervert pilot's nose." I instantly wished I hadn't said it, but as Santi settled into the seat, he smiled.

"That was pretty fucking funny." He looked over at the Challenger, the chain and the chair. "A little inconvenient, though."

I glanced back. Andy sat rigid in the right-side seat, facing forward. RD faced her and bent over, pulling her seatbelt across her lap. She stiffened at his touch.

"Tell your friend to keep his hands to himself."

"Or what?"

I looked at Santi, then at the gun he held on his lap, loosely pointed at me.

"Well, I'm going to guess you don't know how to fly this thing or you would have taken it without me. Here's the deal. I'll take you at your word about letting us go. But I'll also flip this airplane over and fly us into the fucking ground and end us all before I'll let dipshit back there play out his sick fantasies on her."

"RD! You hear that? He says you have sick fantasies."

"Picasso said, 'Everything you can imagine is real.'" RD replied. "And I can really imagine!"

"Just the same, RD, let's let Stu here be a good pilot and not go all kamikaze because you're cutting body parts off his wife, okay?" Santi smiled at me again. "Fair enough?"

"Where to?"

"You get us up there. I'll point."

I RAN through the startup checklist, fired the right engine, then the left. As the engines warmed up, I reached across the panel and tapped the fuel pressure gauge. I looked at it suspiciously, then tapped it again. Santi eyed me but I paid no attention.

I glanced at Andy and wondered what she could be thinking. RD sat facing her. Their knees bumped and she jerked away from him.

Did she recognize the engine vibration? Did she recognize the seat? The unique scent of the cabin? If she did, would she know I sat at the controls?

I tried to think of a way to tell her.

A light easterly breeze lifted the windsock and informed me that Runway 13 was active. I taxied past the main hangars. Sunday night. All quiet. The hangar door hung closed. I looked for Earl and didn't see him. I glanced at the big man beside me.

How much do you know about flying?

I skipped putting on headphones. A set hung behind my seat and behind his. Speech in a piston twin-engine airplane is difficult without noise-cancelling headphones and an intercom. If Santi was accustomed to flying around in the plush cabin of a Challenger, the only headphones he used would have been ear buds to watch a movie. He didn't ask and I didn't offer.

I lingered on the pre-takeoff check, looking busy and serious, but wasting as much time as possible.

Controls. Checked.

Instruments. Altimeter and directional gyro set. I reached for the radio stack. I thought I'd turn a few knobs, then set the transponder to the code for Hijack. Santi poked his gun at my hand.

"No radios."

Foiled, I pulled back my hand and went on with the checklist. The transponder, which sent a signal to air traffic control radar, remained on the standard code for visual flight rules.

Gas. I reached beneath my seat and set the handle for the left engine on the left main tank, and the handle for the right engine on the right main tank. Both were low from the Brainerd flight. Running the tanks dry might give me an opening. I turned on both auxiliary fuel pumps for takeoff, then reached across the panel and tapped the glass over the fuel pressure gauge with my finger.

Santi threw me a questioning look, but I went about my business.

Attitude. I set the trim for takeoff.

Run-up. I stood on the brakes and advanced the throttles for both engines to 1900 RPM, tweaking them until the engine sound harmonically synchronized.

Santi watched me. I skipped the magnetos and went directly to the levers that control propeller RPM. Normally, on a warm day, I check each prop control once.

I cycled each one three times.

One. Two. Three.

One. Two. Three.

I eased the throttles to idle. The evening had grown dark.

"I need the radio to turn on the runway lights. It's activated by the radio."

"No radio," Santi replied. "The runway's right over there. I can see it fine."

He wasn't wrong. I checked the ramp and taxiway. If Earl noticed anything, if he called the cavalry, now would be the time for them to ride in.

Nothing moved between us and the runway.

"Let's go!" Santi lifted the gun muzzle for emphasis.

I had no choice. I checked the final approach course for traffic, then rolled onto the runway. We accelerated rapidly under full power.

"Head east," Santi called out after we rotated and began to climb. I pulled the gear handle and trimmed the airplane. "Michigan."

Gear up, we climbed rapidly. I checked on Andy. She pressed herself against the fuselage and twisted her legs to avoid contact with RD. He behaved himself for the moment.

Santi said nothing until I leveled off at nine thousand five-hundred feet. The last remnant of twilight lit the western horizon behind us. Black sky lay across the nose.

"Listen," Santi talk-shouted at me. "I want to keep the sanctity of your ignorance intact, pal. I don't want to tell you things that make me want to kill you. Live and let live, right?"

"Right."

"But *you* can tell me everything you know, and everything your wife thinks she knows."

"I don't know shit and she doesn't tell me police business."

"See," he said, pushing the smile again. Perfect teeth. "That's what I mean. That's the kind of shit that's going to make me turn old RD loose on her. Did you hear what he did to that farmer's wife in—which one was it? Pellston? Or Baraboo? With the frontend loader? Impaled the bitch. She was up there, God, about half an hour, just begging. We brought her kids out to see it."

I moved my hands around to give myself something to do. Something not driven by fury or the impulse to plunge my thumbs deep into his eye sockets. I adjusted the prop controls. I leaned the mixture on both engines. I tapped the fuel pressure gauge again.

"Fine," I said. "What do you want to know?"

Outside the windshield, the eastern horizon blended black with black. Ground lights distinguishing land from sky abruptly ended at the approaching shoreline of Lake Michigan.

"I already told you. Don't make me repeat myself. Repetition is tiresome, Stu. A warning."

"Okay," I said. "I'll tell you what I think I know. You partied this summer on the lake with your friend back there and your wife."

He chuckled. "Go on."

"And with Clayton Johns, next door."

"Did you see the pecs on that guy? I mean, I got a set, but that man rocks it."

"I wouldn't know. You connected with some kids in Essex. Young girls.

Not sure how, but you invited them to party. And Johns has a taste for under-aged girls. You gave him what he wanted."

Santi wore a Sphinx face. "And?"

"You got Stella Boardman to bring Verna Sobol for Johns."

"And?"

"On the boat, it wasn't just Johns and Verna. It was a double date. You and Stella were there. Verna wasn't up for the full play, so you persuaded her with Rohypnol or GHB. I'll guess you shared with Stella, too." I reached over and tapped the fuel pressure gauge. "And then you dosed Johns somehow. You put together that whole little tableau and cranked up the music. And then you took Stella for a swim, right?"

Santi didn't answer.

"She's still in the lake. So's Lyle Traeger."

"Who?"

"The cop."

Santi didn't answer. Lake Michigan crept toward us, black beyond the last lights of the land below, a matter of seeing something because you can't see it.

I tapped the fuel pressure again.

Santi finally reacted. "What the fuck are you doing? What is that?"

"Fuel pressure. It was unsteady on the last flight. It's either a faulty gauge or it's the cross-feed valve."

"Don't fuck with me." The gun came up again.

I gestured toward the back. "Why is she here?"

Santi shook his head. "You tell me."

"She figured you out. You weren't supposed to be home, but Lyle—the cop—made note of a set of wet swim fins on your deck. He asked you about them—and then she did."

"She's a tenacious bitch. We would've let her go on her way, only she asked if we do any scuba diving—like fucking Columbo, you now? All casual like. Walking away. Then, she says, Oh, one more thing..." Santi shrugged. "Thought she was being clever. What else?"

"That's all I know. Well, that and you've been killing people on farms in three states."

Santi broke into a grin. "Yes, well, there is that." He grinned. "But I gave you that one."

"I already knew."

"How?"

"The minivan."

"The hell you did. Nobody suspects a fucking minivan."

I tapped the fuel pressure gauge for the right engine and made a serious face.

"Did you see that?"

"What?" Santi followed my worried look down to the tip of my finger on the glass above the needle.

I leaned closer. "It's surging. See it?"

As he squinted at my finger and the instrument, my left hand slipped off the yoke and found the magneto switches. I flicked off the left mag for the right engine. Half the sparkplugs in the cylinders went dead.

The right engine staggered. The fuel pressure gauge wiggled.

"There!" I shot an exaggerated look at it, locking Santi's attention on the gauge.

"There!" I pointed. "It did it again!"

On my side of the cockpit, out of his sight, I snapped the right mag to Off. The engine quit instantly. The fuel pressure gauge needle dropped to zero.

"Son of a bitch!"

I leaned back in my seat, returned my left hand to the yoke, and slammed the throttles forward, props forward, mixture forward. The left engine surged, making the cabin yaw. Santi grabbed the top of the instrument panel.

"What?!"

"Son of a bitch!" This time I reached over and pounded on the fuel pressure gauge with my palm. "Look! We've lost fuel pressure on the right engine!"

He could feel it. The dead engine wound down, windmilling. The airplane pulled right, heaved by the asymmetrical power of the left engine. Santi stiffened in his seat.

The gun came up and stabbed my temple. He pressed.

"Don't you fuck with me! Did you do that?"

"Hell, no! And I can guarantee you that shooting me isn't going to make things better!"

He drew back. "Fucking explain!"

I pointed at the split needles on the fuel pressure gauge.

"We lost fuel pressure to the right engine!" I went through a series of rapid and completely senseless moves. I pulled and pushed the right throttle lever as if pumping it would make it run. I pulled the mixture control for the right engine all the way back. It made no difference since the engine was dead already. I pulled the right prop control all the way back. It turned the blades into the wind and feathered the prop, which came to a halt. This widened Santi's eyes.

"We can't cross the lake on one engine," I said.

"Then get it fucking started again!"

I fixed a look on his eyes and heaved a deep breath. "Look, I told you, it's the cross-feed valve. I think it's stuck."

"Fucking unstuck it!"

"It's in the back, behind the seat, in the floor. I can do it, but you're going to have to hold this thing." I gestured at the control yoke.

The gun came up. It touched my forehead.

"You do not strike me as a stupid man. If this is you making a play…"

"What? Where am I going to go? Do you think I'm going to fight you? In here? Or anywhere?"

He applied slow pressure to the weapon, pushing my head sideways.

"Fix it. Now."

I swallowed and tried to look terrified, which didn't take much effort.

"The cross-feed valve is in the floor behind her seat." I jerked my right thumb at the cabin behind us. "I can get to it and I can knock it loose, but you have to hold it steady." I gestured at his side of the dual controls. "It's easy. Just like Microsoft Flight Simulator."

"I don't play games," he said coldly.

"Does that dead engine look like a game? Believe me, I want to get it running more than you do."

"Put it on autopilot!"

"Autopilot won't hold it with one engine. Someone has to work the controls. Or I can try to talk you through fixing the valve, but it's touchy. If you break it, we lose the other engine."

Santi took time to think. He lowered the weapon. He tapped the control yoke with the muzzle.

"Show me."

"Put both hands on the controls."

He shook his head and waved the gun at me.

"Fine. One hand on the controls," I said.

Keeping the gun in his right hand, he closed his left fist around the control yoke. He flexed and squared himself in the seat.

"Okay, now look at this instrument." I reached up and pointed at the attitude indicator in the center of the panel. "Don't look outside, there's nothing to see. Look at the artificial horizon."

He looked out the windshield anyway. The black lake merged with the black sky. He brought his attention back to the attitude indicator.

"This is us," I pointed. "See how we sit right on the horizon line?"

"Yeah."

"Alright. I'm gonna let you take it—but be ready. The left engine is pulling hard. You have to fight it. It's going to make you turn, so fight it, okay? Also. The nose wants to drop. Hold it up. Pull. Pull hard to keep it up. You let the nose down and we're all screwed."

"What about the foot pedals?"

"What about them?" He flared his eyes at me. I said, "Push with your left foot. You'll feel it. Ready?"

I touched the electric trim switch on my yoke and rolled in nose-down trim, adding unnecessary pressure to the yoke—more for him to fight.

"You ready?" I asked again.

"I'll fucking shoot her first if you're screwing with me!"

"You do this wrong, and we're all screwed! Here goes!"

I relaxed the controls and lifted my feet from the left rudder pedal I'd been using to keep the nose straight.

"WHOA!" he cried out. The nose dropped. The airplane rolled right.

"Pull up! Turn left! Left pedal!"

I helped him out a little, dramatically jerking the controls back and rolling in left aileron. "Give it some muscle!"

He followed me on the controls. I eased up again and this time he took up the slack. He rolled in left aileron to fight the roaring left engine. He pulled the column back toward his belly to keep the nose up.

"Good! That's good!" I cried out. "Look at the instrument. At the horizon! See it? Keep the nose up just like that. Whatever you do, no matter what, don't lower the nose!"

"Alright! Alright! Alright! I got it!"

Barely. At least he had the muscle for it.

"Here," I said. "This will help! I'm putting the landing gear down to stabilize you." I reached over, found the control knob with the wheel shape, pulled it out of the lock and dropped it.

Like throwing out an anchor. The wheels dropping caught the slipstream.

"WHOA!"

"Nose up! Keep that goddamn nose up!"

He pulled and rolled in left aileron. "Go fix that fucking thing!"

I unsnapped my belt, satisfied that I had him doing everything wrong.

RD's face took on a pale glow. He twisted in his seat. When he saw me start to squeeze out of my seat he shouted at Santi.

"What's he doing?!"

"Let him through! He's got to fix some damned valve behind the seat! Let him the fuck through! And watch him!"

Bewildered but obedient, RD shrank aside and let me into the passenger cabin. I dropped to my knees facing aft between the two rear seats. I twisted and reached behind Andy's seat with my right hand. In doing so, I dropped my left hand on her thigh.

She jolted and jumped and fought against the touch. I closed a tight grip. She recoiled. RD pushed his legs against hers to lock them against the bulkhead. She stopped fighting but remained rigid.

Knees on the floor, face pressed against the side of Andy's seat, I twisted and reached. I pawed at the carpet.

"Hold it up!" I shouted at Santi. I could feel the airplane's nose fall. I felt it rolling right. The speed bled away.

"I AM!"

He pulled the yoke to keep the nose up—the best way to reduce airspeed.

He rolled in hard left aileron, cross-controlling—the worst way to counter asymmetrical thrust.

And he fought to fly on one engine with the landing gear down—the worst configuration during an engine failure.

He had it all going for him…straight to hell.

I glanced at RD, who stared at me, horrified. Good. He did not see my hand move on Andy's thigh. I prayed she would understand.

I squeezed twice quickly, then lifted my hand. With one finger I stroked a single capital letter.

I

I waited a moment. Santi shouted at me to get on with it. I pretended to struggle with an unseen panel deep beneath the seat.

On Andy's thigh, I stroked a second capital letter.

L

"It's turning! Fuck! It's turning!"

"Hold it straight!" I shouted. The left wing rose higher. I stroked out a third capital letter.

Y

At once, Andy's tension eased. Her whole body shifted. I patted her leg, then began a new sequence.

"I can't hold it! God dammit!" Santi shouted.

"Almost there!"

I lowered my hand and closed it on her thigh again. This time she did not flinch. I squeezed.

Three times.

The nose swung to the right. I could feel the airspeed bleeding away.

Two times.

The airplane shuddered and the rate of turn increased.

One time.

Even I didn't expect the degree of violence when it happened. Pulled by the full power of the left engine, dragging the extended landing gear, slipping below Vmc—the minimum speed at which the vertical stabilizer remained effective—cross-controlling and running out of effective rudder—

The big cabin class twin torque rolled.

We flipped.

FWOOOMP! I gave it everything I had, using my grip on Andy to pull her with me. A cool sensation snapped around us just ahead of fierce unleashed forces. I felt her raise both legs to her chest and kick. RD—gaping at the empty seat before him—slammed back in his seat. Unseen, the heels of her shoes hammered his chest. She stomped and pummeled him while I threw my arm around her waist to maintain the connection and keep her in *the other thing*. RD gripped his seat against violent G-forces, unable to fight off blows from a woman who vanished before his eyes.

The nose whipped over and plunged.

RD screamed.

I found Andy's seatbelt release and snapped the belt open. I grabbed her by the upper arm and locked a rigid grip on her, knowing that if I lost contact, gravity and centrifugal force would steal her from me.

The airplane spun viciously—a dead engine on one wing chased by a runaway engine on the other. Distant lights from the Wisconsin shoreline whirled past the windows, exchanging places with the black lake every few seconds.

Santi screamed at me from the copilot's seat. I ignored him.

We didn't have long.

RD jerked up and down against his seatbelt. His head slammed against the cabin wall. He fought to brace himself against the ceiling with both arms. His face knotted in terror and pain. I suspected broken ribs. Andy's kicks had been merciless.

Only one thing on this flight would save it, and I had other plans. I grabbed the frame of the seat and hauled Andy toward me. I expected to fight impossible centrifugal forces. Unseated, we should have been thrown around the cabin like a pinball.

We weren't.

We were part of the spinning cabin, utterly unaffected.

No weight. No inertia. Nothing to be thrown or tossed.

I pulled her free of her seat and heaved us to the rear. We bumped against the aft bulkhead. I twisted to put my back to the cabin door.

"STEWART! FUCKING GET UP HERE!" Santi screamed.

I turned Andy to face me. Her legs closed a vice grip around my waist. Her head tucked against my neck. I reached behind me and found the door latch.

From the space between the two front seats, Santi's face appeared. The muzzle of his silver handgun hunted for me. His wild eyes searched the empty cabin, flashing between fear and utter confusion. The black muzzle flashed. The gunshot thundered in the cabin.

I jerked the door latch. The door behind me fell away and slammed against the stops. I felt the impact in the frame, yet we weren't thrown out.

No weight. No inertia.

Santi screamed. The muzzle flashed again.

GO!

Something gripped us at our center and launched us into the black sky. The warbling sound of a Lycoming engine running at full power, winding around itself in a fatal spin, climbed away from us, rising ever higher.

How was that possible?

Then I realized we were inverted.

I tipped my head back and followed the twirling navigation lights of an airplane that I loved. They grew smaller as the howling engine sound grew distant, penetrating black emptiness.

It took forever.

Then it stopped. Something flashed, then winked out. Silence wrapped around us. There hadn't been much fuel in the airplane after the return from Brainerd. She didn't burn.

Cold water swallowed the airplane.

Andy coiled against me and locked her ankles behind my back. She squeezed and it threatened my breathing. I reached behind her and ripped into the duct tape binding her wrists. The instant her hands came free she clawed into the tape around her neck. It took a few minutes. It might have gone faster if she had let me do it, but I didn't want to fight her. After a violent struggle the collar came free and she whipped the headphones and pillowcase from her head.

Both items snapped into view and flew away. Familiar grinding hard rock music faded quickly.

Hands free, head free, she slammed her arms around me. She uttered a sharp gasp and outcry, relief or pain, I didn't know which and didn't care. I pulled her as hard as she pulled me.

We hung upside down. The distant lights of Wisconsin formed a plateau of stars above us. Galaxies lay at our feet.

"Hey," I said after our breathing evened out.

"Hey."

I rotated us so that up was up and down was down.

"Did you know it was me?" I asked.

"I hoped, but I wasn't sure. Until I was. I love you, too." She kissed me. I kissed back. "Where are we?"

"About ten miles northeast of Manitowoc."

I felt her looking around. Her hair brushed my face. Her scent filled my senses. Her unseen firm flesh met my unrelenting grip. The need to maintain contact notwithstanding, I vowed never to let go.

"Over the lake?"

"Not that far from Essex."

"We're a long way from Essex."

"Well, for once I came prepared." I slowly reached in my back pocket and pulled out a power unit. I flicked it to make the prop whine so she would know what I had in hand. "I thought of a new name. Thrust and Heading for Will's Aeronautical Propulsion."

She said nothing.

"THWAP," I said.

"The sound we will make when we hit something. Absolutely not."

I thumbed the slide control. We moved.

"Please don't fly us to Essex," she said wearily. "Just down. I just want down."

I squeezed and kissed her.

I advanced the power.

On the BLASTER.

Hell, yes.

55

Andy and I landed outside the FBO at Manitowoc County Airport. The field lay silent. The doors to the office were locked. I counted on the emptiness of a municipal airport at night for privacy.

Fwooomp!

The instant we reappeared, I examined her. "Are you okay? Did they hurt you?"

"He tased me. Lord!" She rubbed her abdomen, then took a moment to appreciate gravity and the sensation of her feet on solid earth. She rubbed her arms and flexed her shoulders. "I need a phone. And a bathroom."

I pointed at the south perimeter of the field and offered her my arm.

A short flight later we landed and reappeared beside a rack of propane tanks stacked against the wall of a brightly lit Kwik Trip.

Andy headed for the restroom. I went to the counter and ordered two cups of coffee. Andy returned and pulled me out of earshot of the girl behind the counter.

"We can't tell anyone we were on that plane."

I handed her a cup and sipped some of the dreadful fuel oil. "Yeah...I was wondering about that."

"There's no way to explain it. There's no way to explain us escaping."

"Come," I said. "Outside."

We stepped out into the humid night air. Insects swirled around the lights above us. The gas pumps stood vacant.

"What happened?" I asked.

She made an angry face. "I was an idiot."

"Unlikely."

"I let myself be ambushed." I gave her a moment. "Lyle's canvass—of the next-door neighbors—I wanted to know if they'd seen anyone partying with Johns. But they've been gone. We even had them registered with dispatch as being out of town. Remember me telling you I felt like someone was watching?"

I did.

"I thought someone may have been hiding at the empty place next door. I went up there tonight to look around, but the owners were home. The garage door was open when I got there. The big guy was doing something near that trailer. I asked him about Johns, about the partying. He said he and his wife heard it from time to time but were gone most of the summer and didn't see anyone they knew. And the whole time, I'm standing there looking at that trailer, thinking *that thing is made for carrying a car*."

"You mean like—"

"Yes! Like Stella Boardman's car. Or Lyle's unit!"

"Or a minivan used to approach the farms."

"Twenty-twenty hindsight, yes. And suddenly it didn't feel right. I decided to get out of there and call for backup. Muscle man didn't have a weapon on him, but he didn't need one to be threatening."

"No, he did not."

"I made it all sound routine—you know—call me if you think of anything—and I was leaving. God! I was *so stupid!*"

"I doubt that."

She shook her head, not wanting to hear it.

"I had to ask one more question, something that bugged me, something from Lyle's notes."

"The swim fins."

"Yes! God damn it! I stopped and turned around and asked, trying to be cute, like, hey, you're into racing and all…ever do any scuba diving? So stupid! Because in that instant I knew it was him—them. And he knew I knew. I was at the entrance to the garage. His partner came in behind me and hit me with his Taser. And by the way—"

"I know. RD."

She abruptly put her arms around me and pulled me into a rigid embrace. Her muted words came from lips pressed to my shoulder. "And all I could think was that they would kill me, and I'd never see you again. Because I had been such an idiot."

"You weren't."

"Don't."

Nothing I said would stop her from beating herself up about this. I did the only thing I could. I held her, trying hard to smother the terrifying realization of what might have been.

After a wordless moment, she pulled back and tried to shake it off.

"I thought they would kill me right then and there. I don't know why they didn't."

"I do. I think Lyle and Stella Boardman are in the lake, but they couldn't do the same with you because of those paparazzi boats."

"They wanted me mobile."

"*Ambulatory.*"

"They put that damned pillowcase and those headphones on me. God! I hate Kid Rock!"

I laughed. She laughed. It was abrupt and nervous, but it broke the tension.

"What now?" I asked.

"We lie. We cook up a story for Janos." She looked around. "We have to get back."

"Uber."

"No. It will leave a trail. There are a dozen federal agents waiting to pick apart whatever story I tell them, so it must be ironclad." She glanced reluctantly at my hip pocket. "We have to get back to my car. I need to find my keys, my ID and my weapon. How much battery do you have in that thing?"

"We're at a convenience store. Batteries aren't an issue."

She huffed an unhappy sigh, failing to identify a travel alternative.

"You get batteries. I need hair ties."

56

It took forty-five minutes with one battery change stop to reach the Santi house on Leander Lake. We landed windblown and tired. We broke into the garage where I used *the other thing* to snap the padlock on the trailer. The grille of Andy's car greeted us. I tossed the snapped pieces of the lock in the back seat and set up the trailer ramp. She found the keys in the ignition and drove the car out. I closed the trailer and the garage door. I found her searching the car interior, gradually growing frantic until she found her weapon, badge and shoulder bag stuffed under the right front seat.

"Why would they leave that here?"

"They didn't want ID found with the body," she said, "but it makes no difference if it's found in my car—which they probably planned to ditch the same way they did Stella's and Lyle's. I think they meant for my body to be a Jane Doe found in Ohio or Alabama. Bureaucratically buried in a local investigation. DNA might eventually connect back to Essex, assuming the body gets found and someone makes the effort." Her matter-of-fact analysis of her own murder gave me a chill.

"Are we going to search the place?" I asked.

"*We* aren't. Let's go."

WE DROVE TO THE STATION. Andy marched through the sally port and set a course for the main conference room. Halfway there we passed the interview room. From within, Donaldson called out.

"Hey! Guys! I got RD! His name is—"

"Roger Duwellyn," Andy said without stopping.

Donaldson hurried after us. "Uh, I was going to say Randy Demarco, Ray Denning, Ron Daschell and—how did you—?"

She didn't stop. She swept into the main conference room where Janos and Richards held court over half a dozen FBI agents working at laptops and on phones. All eyes met hers.

"Derek Santi and Roger Duwellyn killed officer Lyle Traeger and Stella Boardman. They abetted Clayton Johns in the rape of Verna Sobol, then set him up for it. They're also the men you want for the farm killings and the killings of the kids on the bridge."

No one moved.

Mae Earnhardt bustled into the room and tapped me on the shoulder. I was about to brush her off when she hooked my neck and whispered in my ear.

"Earl Jackson is in holding." Everyone heard her.

Andy said, "Mae, get the chief and tell him to release Mr. Jackson. He acted to assist a police officer. Then ask the chief to join us, please."

Mae hurried out.

"Sir, I have reason to believe they've stolen the airplane my husband flies for the Education Foundation and are on the run.

Andy's claim made Janos blink.

"What makes you think those two stole your airplane?" Janos asked me.

"Um…it's gone."

He didn't like my answer.

"They stole it because I asked Mr. Jackson to disable theirs," Andy said.

Janos turned to his second-in-command, Richards. "Contact Chicago Air Traffic Control to see if any flights departed Essex County Airport."

I gave Richards a description of the aircraft and the N-Number. She headed for the door. Janos called after her.

"Get someone from our Chicago office over to the ARTCC to lock down all their recordings and start mapping radar tracks," Janos ordered. "If they did fly out of here, I want to know where. And find out if either suspect has a pilot's license."

"On it."

Janos said, "Okay, Detective, you have the floor."

57

We told our concocted story to the chief, Janos and his team. Andy began with the truth—with Lyle's notes from the night of the rape and her subsequent canvass of the neighbors. She explained the 3 a.m. interview with Johns—how it confirmed the involvement of a lake resident, and how she returned to question the immediate neighbors. She described the red flag she saw where Lyle's detailed notes contained a void. She explained arriving at the Santi house and finding Santi and Duwellyn. She said the interview with the two men heightened her suspicions, fueled by hints that they planned to leave.

"I set up surveillance on Sunset Circle Road."

I jumped in. "That's when she called me. She asked me to see if the Challenger—the jet—was still on the ramp at the airport."

"Why?" Janos asked Andy.

"The Challenger belongs to a real estate developer who hid behind a string of shell companies to buy the Stone property. Sir, I think the land sale is the key—and was always intended as part of the extortion."

"Doesn't track. The buyer has been after that land for months," Janos said.

"Unsuccessfully. Sandy refused to sell."

"What does this developer's jet have to do with your suspects?"

"Two nights ago, Will saw a woman leave on another jet with the Challenger's owner—Emilio DeSantorini. We think it was Ariel Santi."

Richards, just returning, caught the name and held up one hand. "Wait! DeSantorini? The billionaire?"

Janos raised his eyebrows at her.

"He's a New York developer," Richards explained. "King of the tabloids for a while. Not so much lately."

"He's the buyer—for the property Sandy was forced to sell," I said. I relayed Dewey Larmond's findings. "Senator Keller thinks tourism is—"

"What do your suspects have to do with the jet?" Richardson asked Andy.

"I believe the jet may be how they moved."

"And you know this...how?"

"The jet had an incident a week ago—a flat nosewheel tire. It grounded the aircraft for a few days."

I took my cue. "Right about the time I ran into Santi, his wife Ariel and their traveling companion—"

"Who we think is Artie—or RD," Donaldson interjected.

"—on a commercial flight out of Detroit, headed for Milwaukee."

"That was two days after the Pellston killings," Andy pointed at the white board timeline. "Which puts this trio in Michigan when we were told they were on the racing circuit. I think the nose wheel issue forced them to fly Delta. That's why—if Santi and Duwellyn were leaving—I thought there was a chance they might use DeSantorini's plane. That's why I asked Will to confirm it was still there."

"But I had already left the field, so I asked Earl Jackson to check it out—and maybe see if he could prevent them from leaving."

"The guy you arrested for punching the pilot?" Janos asked the chief.

The chief shrugged. "We now think the pilot's injury was a pre-existing condition."

Janos rolled his eyes.

"I never heard back from Earl, so I drove over to check for myself. That's when I found the Education Foundation's airplane—the one that I fly —missing. I called Andy—Andrea—right away."

"If that's true, how did they get past your surveillance, Detective?"

Andy dropped her gaze. "I screwed up. I set up to the west of the Santi property on the assumption that Santi and Duwellyn would avoid our roadblocks on the east side of the lake. I can only guess they got past me in a vehicle I didn't recognize—a vehicle they hid in the trailer. The only vehicles I observed at their home were the racecar and a pickup truck—and, of course, the trailer. None of those passed by me. I checked with the sheriff's department. They didn't see them either."

On this point, I caught the chief looking sideways at his junior detective, but he said nothing. Instead, he dispatched an officer to the airport to check the registration of all the vehicles parked in the lot.

"Observing three people on a commercial flight is a pretty goddamn thin connection between the land sale and the farm case," Janos pointed out.

"It's them," Andy said. "I know it. Santi partied with Johns and procured the underaged girls to set him up. The rape violated the lease. The lease violation made selling possible. The extortion made selling necessary. And the highway expansion report makes the land a gold mine."

Janos looked at Donaldson who said, "Told you."

Andy abruptly turned to the chief. "Sir, we need to search the lake for Lyle and Stella Boardman."

"I was just thinking that." The chief reached for the nearest phone and called the fire department, who told him they would call the Coast Guard and arrange to bring in a boat equipped with special scanning equipment.

Donaldson said, "We have a few more pieces of the RD puzzle. He did dirty work for Bargo Litton—which establishes a connection to Stone—but his bad acting goes back to his college days. There were at least three allegations of sexual assault brought against him, all of which fell apart when the victims withdrew the complaints."

"I wonder why," Richards muttered. "I'd be willing to bet if we run a profile on this guy it will fit with the sadism at the farms. Someone with that capacity could intimidate any witness or victim."

"And you think the three of them have been spree killing farm families, just to cover up killing the highway engineer—Yarborough—as part of this land scheme? If it's true, that's cold," Janos said.

"*If* it's true?" Andy asked.

"Yes. *If*. It's a stretch, detective."

Donaldson surprised me, given his earlier dismissal of the idea. "Sir, I think that's exactly what happened. I think the ribbon tying up this sick package was Yarborough. I think that with a new highway, that land is worth way more than the sale price or the bitcoin."

"We need to find the wife," Andy said.

"She's likely with the other two," Richards said.

"No, ma'am," Andy said. "I didn't see her at the house. I think she's with DeSantorini."

"Why?" Richards challenged Andy.

"They're using his jet."

"Supposition. You have no proof."

"I saw her," I said. "In Detroit, and again two nights ago. It was dark.

She was silhouetted. But she has a distinct figure. I side with Andy on this. She left with DeSantorini two nights ago."

Janos passed the question of Ariel Santi to the FBI office in New York who tracked down the developer. The answer came back in under an hour.

"You got it wrong," Janos told us after a lengthy call. "DeSantorini says he never heard of Derek or Ariel Santi—or let anyone use his jet. Your New York guy was traveling with his daughter. He alibis her for all three farm killings."

"I talked to New York, too," Richards said. "They said DeSantorini has a daughter and a son. The son got the boot. Disowned. That makes the daughter the golden child, in line for the family fortune. Doesn't sound like someone who needs to go spree killing in the Midwest for money—if that's what you were thinking."

Janos said, "DeSantorini claims that except for this business trip, his daughter has never been to Wisconsin."

Liar, I thought.

"Which goes back to what I said," Richards asserted. "The wife wasn't with the developer. She's with Santi and Duwellyn."

Andy didn't argue. "We need to talk to that flight crew."

"There's another hole in your theories," Richards said. "If you're suggesting they traveled by airplane to the farm scenes, we've already looked at that. There's no FAA flight plan data identifying any single airplane at each crime scene on the dates of the murders."

Andy shook her head and pointed at the white board where photos taped beneath a timeline represented the three crime scenes. "They didn't fly in. They approached the farms with a benign vehicle. Something nonthreatening—probably driven by Ariel Santi—a woman alone in a subcompact or sedan—no threat in that."

"We've got a lot of image data on vehicles. We checked every repeat—vehicles that appeared before and after the crimes. Nothing like that popped," Janos said.

"You have images from highways leading to the scenes, but nothing within a few miles of each scene," Andy said. "I think they delivered the vehicle to within a short distance of the farm using the racecar trailer—then loaded it again for the departure from the immediate area. That avoids highway cameras. And who questions a pickup pulling a trailer in farm country?"

"We would. We would have seen the pickup and trailer leaving the scene on the highway cameras. We didn't," Richards argued.

"Because they didn't leave. All three crime scenes are close to rural airports. Rural airports are quiet and remote," Andy said.

"Parking a pickup truck and trailer at a small airport for an extended period wouldn't spark questions," I said. "Let it sit for a few days or a week. Nobody cares."

"They came by air to retrieve it outside the window we used for checking highway cameras," Andy said. "I think that was their plan in Pellston, but the jet had the tire mishap here in Essex and they were forced to fly out of Detroit."

"If you searched flight plans before the crimes were committed, you won't find them," I said. "The jet would be used after. Only it failed them in Michigan. I bet the Pellston airport is missing a crew car or rental car."

Janos dispatched a pair of agents to find out and then collect the jet crew.

Donaldson circled back to the Yarborough connection and urged Janos to probe DeSantorini about his business in Wisconsin. "He's lying. The land sale is key," he said. "That makes the asshat a prime suspect."

Before Janos could respond, one of the FBI agents rushed in and turned on the television. CNN broadcast Breaking News that the FBI was investigating the New York developer and billionaire Emilio DeSantorini for a possible role in the nation's top story, the Farm Family Murders. New reports linked the extortion of Sandra Stone's Foundation fund to a DeSantorini land deal.

"What the fuck!" Janos exclaimed at the screen. "We just found out about this!"

Andy glanced at me.

"Wasn't me," I said. I wondered what dark magic Lorna Keller worked, since the media reports specifically cited allegations of a doctored state highway report and false summary issued by the Deputy Secretary of the Wisconsin Department of Transportation.

Janos dispatched Richards to track down the Deputy Secretary in Madison. He issued an indignant denial. He offered to support his position by submitting a copy of the highway expansion report showing that Yarborough's conclusions did not kill the project, but rather endorsed the new highway, a conclusion reflected in the 4-page summary released.

Almost simultaneously, DeSantorini found his way to a CNN camera and loudly denied the claim.

Andy called the father of Lane Franklin's friend Sarah. Robert Lewis launched into a speaker-phone rant. He insisted the DOT summary was a fake—the antithesis of what Yarborough himself had verbally expressed to the citizens land preservation committee. Yarborough's real report, Lewis believed, killed the project.

Andy said to Janos, "Sir, we need to find out if the engineer, Yarborough, had a laptop or saved a copy of the original report to the cloud."

Janos ordered another search of the Williston home in Baraboo.

WHILE ANDY HELPED Janos assemble bits and pieces in the main conference room at the City of Essex Police Department, the FBI swarmed Leander Lake. With Chief Ceeves' blessing, Janos ordered his agents to take command of the Clayton Johns crime scene as well as the Santi property beside it. The roadblock perimeter was expanded to cap the entire north end of the lake. The FBI declared the lake a crime scene and ordered the paparazzi boats to leave.

Agents invading the Santi house used body cameras to stream their search back to the conference room HQ. As expected, they reported that the suspects were gone. Andy asked Janos to instruct the agents to look for swim fins. They located a pair—dry—hanging in the back of the trailer.

A deeper search of the trailer uncovered a cache of syringes, and vials of Rohypnol and Propofol.

THE HOURS at the station wore on and I wore out.

Eventually, Andy handed me the keys to her car and ordered me to go home. I put up token resistance and a lame effort to persuade her to join me. She refused and I understood why. She drew life-affirming energy from the surge of activity around the investigation. The bits and pieces flying about spun my head but energized her. She needed proximity to law enforcement professionals along with its action and activity.

Entering our silent rented farmhouse, I placed my remaining BLASTER unit on the shelf beside several of its older companions. I took a cold beer to bed with me but found it less than one third finished when the sun jarred me awake on Monday morning.

Sometime during the night, Andy crawled between the sheets and slipped under my arm. The sensation of her warm breath tickled my chest. I remained still for a long time, grateful that action and activity weren't the only things she needed.

Eventually, she stirred and pressed closer.

And closer.

. . .

In the morning, we lingered in bed. I like to think it was because she can't keep her hands off me. More likely, we both felt a need to renew our bonds to each other. And to life.

After untangling ourselves from the sheets, I attended to the coffee maker while she called the station for an update. I crossed my fingers that she wouldn't find a reason to dash off and felt relief when she joined me on our screened front porch.

We sipped a perfect brew while I let her brief me. She rehashed everything, shedding each twist and turn as if emptying a backpack full of stones. When she ran out of words, we enjoyed the midmorning serenity of our yard where just a few weeks ago Donaldson appeared and disrupted our lives. I hoped we'd seen the last of him.

Which perversely explains why, simultaneous with that very thought, the Special Agent maneuvered an FBI SUV into our driveway.

"Go away," I said when he climbed the steps to the porch. Andy, who had been deliciously dressed in nothing but a long t-shirt, quickly retreated to put on something more substantial. I held that against Donaldson.

"Nice to see you, too. Is that coffee?" He pointed at the carafe on the table.

"Strychnine."

"Don't mind if I do," he limped into my house, rummaged through my kitchen and came back with my second-favorite mug. He poured and sat down, taking in the late-summer scent and scenery.

"Good morning, Lee," Andy said, joining us a moment later. She had brushed and tied her hair and slipped into white jeans and a light sleeveless blouse, a sign of no immediate plans to go to the station. She refreshed her coffee mug, then sat on my lounge chair beside my outstretched legs.

"I thought you'd want to know," Donaldson said. "We found Officer Traeger and Stella Boardman."

"Where?" Andy asked.

"In the lake. They were chained to the Santi pier. One of our guys saw gas bubbles. Our guess is that they planned to move the bodies after the law enforcement presence and paparazzi boats went away." To Andy, he added, "I'm sorry about your guy."

"It wasn't going to end any other way. At least we know." She started to rise. "I should go and help with the notification."

"Sit," Donaldson said. "Chief Ceeves is already there."

Andy settled.

"Every time you come here, you want something," I said.

"I've only been here once before."

"Like I said—a perfect record. What gives?"

"You and I *do* have a little unfinished business, Will."

Andy stiffened. "You made a promise. You swore an oath."

Donaldson's hand went to his heart. "Semper fi. You have nothing to fear. But you two need to think about what you've accomplished, and how you've had to go about it. You need to think about how many more bullshit stories you're going to have to come up with like the one about those two clowns stealing that airplane."

I glanced at Andy, who held Donaldson's gaze with a stone face.

"Yeah, I didn't buy it, but Janos had to because nothing else would make sense—and because ever since 9/11 the idea of someone stealing an airplane is the nightmare scenario. I assume they're going to find the plane with the cabin door open."

Neither of us spoke.

"Doesn't matter. I'm just saying, there's a better way—when you're ready to talk about it."

Andy changed the subject. "What's going on at the office?"

"Janos and his team are hanging everything around the necks of Santi and Duwellyn, and the missing and mysterious Ariel Santi—"

"She wasn't on the plane," Andy said.

"I figured. Our profiler is arguing that a woman doesn't fit with the violence and sadism of the farm killings."

"That's sexist," Andy commented.

"Did they find the plane?" I asked.

"Radar tracked it over Lake Michigan where it suddenly lost altitude. Some debris has been spotted, but that's deep water. The bureau and NTSB are putting together resources to investigate. The FAA has no record of either man holding a pilot's license. Janos flies. He thinks they lost visual reference the way JFK Junior did."

"Sounds about right."

"Janos is holding up an announcement that those two are the Farm Family Killers. He wants to bring up the bodies, and he wants to firm up connections to the trailer and the minivan. The techs are swarming both now."

"They're your guys," I said.

"I know. But holding off a couple days is good because I say this ain't over."

"Why does that worry me?" I asked.

"Okay. Hear me out. Derek Santi, from what we can piece together, was a body builder with a bad temper. His personal history is dodgy. A couple of

Janos's guys—smart people—are suggesting Derek Santi may be a false identity. A good one, mind you. A long-standing one. But it's a little frayed around the edges. His early years seem too…stock. Roger Duwellyn had a head full of worms. Identity was a revolving door with that guy—with good reason. But we found one piece of his sick life that's consistent—his friendship with Derek, or whoever he was. They go back as far as college together for sure, possibly beyond. The thing is…RD was a sick puppy but, except for his perversions, he wasn't a creative thinker."

Andy paid close attention. I itched for a conclusion.

"I'm sure you'll work it all out," I said.

"I already have."

"What?" Andy asked.

"Santi brought the muscle. RD brought the sadism. So, who brought the brains and who got the bitcoins?"

Neither of us spoke.

"How about coming to New York with me to finish this?"

"You mean DeSantorini," Andy said.

"I thought the FBI was doing a proctological exam of the guy," I said. "Number one suspect."

Donaldson made an equivocating gesture with a flat hand. "The guy's a media motormouth with connections and alibis up the wazoo. He's a moving target. SDNY says they've been looking at him for years—taxes, dirty land deals, cheating contractors—but nothing sticks. Janos likes him for the land scheme but is lukewarm about pinning the farm killings on him—especially with everything pointing at RD and the Santis. DeSantorini wrapped the jet pilots up in lawyers and he buys a lot of political influence that he's using to make himself untouchable. Janos has to tread lightly." Donaldson looked at me. "You…not so much."

"Absolutely not!" I said.

"We'll go," Andy said.

I glared at my wife. She didn't blink.

"Good!" Donaldson rubbed his hands together. "There's just one more thing we need."

"Which is?"

"Do you know anybody with a hundred million dollars?"

58

"That's the Dakota." Andy pointed at the ornate façade with cathedral-like blocks at the corners.

"Is that where we're going?" I asked.

"No. Just pointing it out. Yoko Ono lives there."

"We're going a couple blocks up," Donaldson said, pacing the tree-lined sidewalk and watching traffic on Central Park West. He looked uncomfortable in a suit and tie.

I studied the riot of high dormers and knobby protrusions on the building. "Expensive?"

Andy laughed. The sound brightened a street already bejeweled with antique sidewalk lights. I thought once again, as I had at our hotel, that if anything went wrong tonight, the fault would be mine for being distracted by her.

She stunned me, and that's saying something.

On any given day, my wife effortlessly sucks the air from any room she enters. Her auburn hair can be pulled into a functional ponytail or sculpted into a work of art. Her slender waist accents curves above and below that are magnetic to both men and women. Her gold-flecked green eyes flash like magic from a wand, sometimes hiding beneath long lashes, sometimes wide, warm and inviting. With other life choices, her face would have graced perfume ads in *Vogue*.

Tonight, she took it over the top. Wrapped in a snug and shimmering purple-black dress that plunged at the neck and sloped across her thighs, the movement of her body sent ripples of light across the fabric. Her warm, always tan skin, glowed. Exotic colors swept from her eyelids, painted into sleek, rising French curves at the corners. Tendrils of curled hair danced at her temples while the rest of it had been braided and wound in a combination of spirals and twists. To call it a bun would be to call Canova's sculpture of Cupid and Psyche a lawn ornament.

When she emerged from the bedroom of our hotel suite, I thought my blood might boil.

"How do I look?" she asked in a voice hesitant with genuine uncertainty.

I never saw lips so red.

"If I could talk, I would tell you." I went to her and slipped my hands gently around her waist as if this delicate ornament might break. "Kill me now, because I don't think I can do this thing with you looking like this on the arm of another man."

I leaned in for a kiss. She backed away.

"Lipstick."

She smiled and her eyes sparkled. She picked up the black shoulder-strap purse that replaced her daily bag. It looked expensive. She drew and checked the weapon within. "If it makes you feel any better, I'm armed. Let's go."

Half an hour and a short cab ride later we waited in warm evening air on the sidewalk bordering Central Park. Underlit trees glowed above us. Traffic hustled up and down Central Park West. Donaldson paced. I stared at my wife.

"The financial guys tell me he's tapped out," Donaldson said, largely to himself. "The only bank that will take his calls is a shady Austrian outfit that's probably laundering Putin's money."

I half listened. I had the feeling that Donaldson was building his case largely to convince himself. His phone chirped. He pulled it and read a message. "From Richards."

"She knows we're here?" I asked, surprised. I didn't think the woman was a fan of Andy and me—or of anything that didn't originate with her boss, Janos.

"We get along," he said without explanation. He read. "Oh. Huh. This is juicy."

"What?" Andy asked.

"She sent some background. Depending on what tabloid you believe, DeSantorini booted his kid after he caught him and his sister…you know…"

"Maybe," Andy said, offering doubt. "What? I Googled him. There are half a dozen tabloid versions. Drugs. Scandals. The son's been out of the picture a long time. The daughter became the face of the company. She's the one still in the will. It's not unlikely there would be stories. Happens every time a woman ascends to power. The more salacious, the better."

"Well it ain't much of a fortune anymore," Donaldson said. "Except for the hundred million that just came his way. That's why we're here to nail his ass."

"That's what we're here to find out," Andy corrected him.

Andy checked her watch, but before she could comment, Donaldson said, "He's here."

A stretched Escalade limousine angled through the bike lane and pulled to the curb. The driver let the engine run. He jumped from his seat and hurried around the polished grille.

"Good evening, ma'am! Sirs!" He opened the door for Andy.

Elegant as she was aboard high, spiked heels, she remained a cop and leaned in to clear the vehicle interior before entering. Satisfied, she slid onto a plush leather seat and glided across with her long legs angled. I joined her. Donaldson followed and took a side-facing seat.

"Holy shit!" Lillian's frank assessment greeted us from an aft-facing seat. "You look like a billion dollars-worth of trophy wife!"

I caught the permanent smirk on Spiro Lewko's face as he took a little too long to dwell on the same conclusion. Andy sensed the murder seeping into my mind and put her hand on my thigh.

"Dr. Farris, that hardly begins to cover it. Mrs. Stewart, a pleasure to meet you." Lewko extended a hand and shook with Andy. "Will, nice to see you again."

I waved without enthusiasm.

"And you're Agent Donaldson."

"Special Agent Donaldson."

"Of course."

"Goddamn, woman!" Lillian said, giving up a rare smile. "Did you fall in a vat of *haute couture?*"

"Mr. Lewko sent a small truckload of packages to the hotel this afternoon. Thank you for that, sir," Andy replied. "I'll see that everything is returned."

"No need."

"It's not up for discussion but thank you again for doing this."

"Dr. Farris told me to make it convincing," he said.

"The plan is for drinks and business first," Lillian said, "then you're scheduled for dinner and some event at the Hampton Gallery—hence the reason for playing dress-up."

"It won't get that far," Donaldson said.

"Probably not," Lillian agreed, "but that ass practically wet himself at the idea of being seen with Lewko here."

I remained both impressed and worried that Lillian had jumped in the middle of this when asked. Claiming to be Lewko's administrative assistant, it had been Lillian who made the arrangements with DeSantorini.

Lewko double-checked his price for participation. "I'd like to confirm something before we go any further. Will, you were not forthcoming last time we met."

"You threw me out."

"You broke my toy." It was a question.

"Evidently, I did."

He seemed satisfied, hearing the confession directly from me. "In agreeing to do this with you, can I be assured that you will not hold back on me this time?"

I glanced at Lillian, searching for a sign of resistance or suggestion of deceit. She gave up nothing.

"Whatever Dr. Farris promised you. But don't forget you owe that kid in Tuscaloosa twenty million."

Lewko shrugged. Nonchalance over a sum I could barely fathom reminded me of who he was.

"Do you know all your lines, sir?" Andy asked politely.

"I was the lead in my high school play."

I didn't doubt it.

"Don't get carried away. Nail down the money." Donaldson made his point directly to Lewko. "Then Andrea takes over. Got it?"

"Let's go fight some crime!" The billionaire tapped on the smoked glass behind his head. His driver accelerated into traffic.

59

DeSantorini's building stood taller than the Dakota but lacked the ornate elegance. The architectural lines stroked the vertical. Narrow windows hugged plain columns of stone. Its signature on the expensive border of Central Park was more block letters than cursive. DeSantorini regularly claimed—albeit falsely—that his rooftop apartment at this address was the most expensive real estate in New York City. Andy, who had done the research, noted that the DeSantorini terrace overlooking Central Park often appeared in New York society pages. Celebrity selfies taken at the railing with The Lake in the background graced DeSantorini's self-aggrandizing web page.

The doorman who lent Andy his hand as she emerged from the limousine greeted Lewko by name and said, "Mr. DeSantorini is expecting you." Noting Lewko's tailored suit and Andy's elegant attire, the doorman spared my black jeans and black t-shirt a dubious glance.

"S'okay. I was just leaving." I leaned close to Andy. "Good luck."

"You, too."

Lillian stayed in the limo. Donaldson loitered near the front fender of the behemoth. It had been decided that he would wait outside rather than risk recognition. He had been caught on camera several times by the media covering the FBI investigation in Essex. One network tried to ambush interview him, and pointedly identified him as the wounded hero in the General Pemmick story.

"Call me the instant you have confirmation," he ordered Andy for what might have been the tenth time. He turned to me. "If you get a chance to grab the file or passwords or keys or whatever…"

"Roger that," I said, thinking it the dumbest part of this plot. I saw zero chance of spying over someone's shoulder and memorizing device keystrokes.

I waved to Andy and ducked around the rear of the limo looking for a gap in traffic to jaywalk four lanes to the park. Spiro Lewko disappeared into the building with my wife decorating his arm.

Central Park triggered a sense of *déjà vu* I attributed to the many movies shot in and around the iconic location. I crossed between cars and hopped onto the sidewalk. A set of benches hugged the low stone wall bordering the park. Lush trees formed a canopy above. The landscape behind the wall dropped off sharply, offering a perfect place to disappear.

I checked both directions.

Two young women pushing a stroller approached, absorbed in animated conversation. I let them pass, then veered right and planted a hand on the stone wall. I hopped over. Anyone else might have come to harm on the rocky downslope. In mid hop—

Fwooomp!

—I vanished. Gravity gave up trying to dash me on rocks below. I floated with one hand gripping the stone wall. With the other, I pulled a BLASTER and prop from my back pocket. I snapped the prop in place and gave the unit a test pulse. It whined happily and pulled me slowly upward. I eased clear of the overhanging tree branches. Night-darkened leaves spread in line with the street, broken by pools of light from sidewalk lamps.

I pushed the power unit slide control and gained speed, angling across the busy street and climbing. The imposing building fell away in front of me. I quickly reached the top.

DeSantorini's rooftop landscape dropped into view. There was no mistaking the apartment. In contrast to the plain walls of the building below, the top of the building gave the impression that someone built a baroque mansion on the roof. The effect relegated the building below to the role of pedestal. Tall windows showcased an interior space reminiscent of a museum exhibit, the chamber of an ancient king bent on showing off plundered treasures. Parts of the interior rooms featured paintings hung frame to frame, like the crowded walls of an English castle. Statues choked random spaces, with no apparent theme or design statement other than "I have statues."

Tiny lights lined the border of the rooftop terrace. Potted trees at the corners sparkled with embedded lights. Illuminated statues overlooked a sprawl of plush leather furniture, which prompted me to wonder what happened to the expensive-looking chairs and sofas when it rained.

A polished granite table graced the central axis of the terrace's largest open space. Flickering electric candles ran down the center. Canister lights on gilded posts cast warm pools of light on leather office chairs that waited for a board of directors.

The chairs didn't wait long.

"...absolutely fantastic!" Emilio DeSantorini's overly loud voice preceded him. He guided his guests through the adjoining living space onto the tiled deck. He spread his arms. "Best view in the city. It never disappoints."

Lewko, walking with Andy beside him, spread his smirk. "That it does not."

Andy scanned, clearing the space, searching for someone.

A white-coated waiter appeared.

"What can I offer you?" DeSantorini asked. "Anything."

"Pass," Lewko said.

"I'm fine, thank you," Andy demurred.

"Really? Nothing? I have an excellent cellar."

"Let's get straight to business," Lewko said, gesturing at the table.

"Of course! Please, take any seat you like." DeSantorini closed his hands on the chairback at the head of the table.

Lewko took a chair to his immediate left. Andy took the seat to Lewko's left.

As they settled, one more guest walked onto the patio tiles over hard, purposeful strides on clicking high heels. She marched directly to Lewko, who stood quickly.

"Spiro," DeSantorini said, failing to see his guest wince at the use of his first name. "My daughter Luciana."

Ariel Santi, her red hair now a coal mine black with glinting gold highlights, swept toward Lewko, extending a hand.

She wore a stark white dress that balanced style with business-like lines. A pencil skirt gripped her thighs to her knees, yet she moved confidently against the smooth and shape-defining fabric, a trick I've seen my own wife do yet failed to comprehend. Her breasts rose against a modest square-cut neckline, tastefully contained. A thin gold chain dangled an outlandish diamond and gold bauble between them.

"Mr. Lewko, I am delighted to meet you," she said in a smooth, warm voice. From my perch at the railing, I did a double take.

The voice was not giddy or high or the sign of an echo chamber above the sinuses. The essential physical form left no doubt, but the affect could not have been farther removed from the spangled arm candy who begged Derek Santi for another drink at Detroit Metro Airport. This was the boardroom version of the woman who paraded down the aisle of Flight 1931 daring men to resist the gravitational pull of the two round bodies on her chest.

"As am I," Lewko said. "May I present Miss Taylor, my associate."

Greetings were exchanged and hands shook. Ariel conducted an assessment of Andy from hair to high heels.

I pushed off the low wall at the edge of the terrace and floated toward Andy. Using the chair beside her to stop, I reached and tapped her shoulder three times as we had arranged.

It's her.

Andy signaled acknowledgement with a shallow nod. I pushed away and took a position on the terrace railing again.

"Have you been offered something?" Ariel asked.

"We have," Lewko said. He waited for Ariel to take her seat before sitting again. "Mr. DeSantorini—"

"Emilio, please," he said. "The Vice President of the United States sat in that very chair, Spiro, and he called me Emilio."

Ariel gave no sign she noticed her father's crass name dropping. Her feline gaze swung slowly to Andy.

"That's alright," Lewko said, "I sat in *his* chair in D.C. a couple weeks ago. Can we get right to it?"

DeSantorini paid Lewko a respectful nod.

"First, thank you for seeing me on short notice. I appreciate you taking my call. And thank you for meeting me privately. It's difficult in New York to connect with people without prying eyes. If our discussion is fruitful, then being seen together in public tonight will serve as something of an announcement."

"I think, Spiro, you'll find that the press and I—"

Ariel's hand found her father's arm. "Daddy, why don't we let Mr. Lewko speak. I'm fascinated to hear what he has to say."

To my surprise, DeSantorini relented.

Lewko began again. "I'm here to discuss a venture in which we, you and I, have crossed paths. Miss Taylor will explain."

"The Lakes of Essex County," Andy said. "You recently extorted a land purchase on Leander Lake in concert with bribing a deputy secretary of the Wisconsin Department of Transportation to alter a highway expansion report to ensure development of a major highway spur." DeSantorini's expression froze. Andy gave him no time to protest. "Your plan is to leverage this new superhighway into a resort, gambling and entertainment complex serving Chicago, Milwaukee, Green Bay and the Twin Cities. Did I miss anything?"

DeSantorini fixed a cold stare on Andy. "Extorted is a strong word. It approaches libel, young woman."

"Would you prefer 'murder?'" Andy asked. She didn't let him reply. "Stone wouldn't sell to you, but you found out about the clause in the Clayton Johns lease."

"You can't seriously believe those news reports."

"Please," Lewko said. "Let's be direct. I would have preferred that the press not tip to your plans, because they are my plans as well. It happens. I've found the best response is not to react, but to move boldly forward."

"How do you—?"

"Know? Really? Men like you and me? We are where we are because we know things before anyone else."

Andy resumed the narrative. "You bribed a deputy secretary of transportation to manipulate the state engineer's report. His intervention prevents the highway project from being summarily killed—which it would have been. Then you acquired the keystone property at the head of the lake, perfectly situated a few miles from the path the proposed highway will take."

"Well played, Emilio."

DeSantorini could not suppress a self-satisfied smile.

"You should know, however, that I have acquired ownership of most of the properties on the largest lake, including tracts on both sides of the Stone property you just acquired. In fact, I have you surrounded."

The smile faded.

"I'm a step ahead of you. However, I don't view you as an adversary. You bring something to the table that I lack. I need a public face for the project. You relish the spotlight that I abhor. I can use that. Your vision for the Lakes Region of Essex County is in lockstep with mine. Together, you and I can do for the Midwest what Steve Wynn did for Las Vegas. There's nothing left to build in America. The time has come to help rich Americans spend what they have earned."

"How much of the property do you own?" Ariel asked.

"All of it that matters—excluding your prime piece," Andy replied. "Mr. Lewko planned to make an offer to Miss Stone at twice what you paid but didn't anticipate the events you recently orchestrated—"

DeSantorini lifted an admonishing finger toward Andy. "Those terrible killings? I had nothing to do with that. Absolutely nothing. Bad things happen—through no fault of mine."

Andy continued, stone-faced. "Those 'bad things' meant an offer of that magnitude became too high-profile for us."

"Then the property is mine. My gain."

Lewko smiled. "Emilio, I can force you out. And I will. Unless…" Lewko paused to take in the ruddy anger blossoming beneath DeSantorini's skin. "Unless you buy in. Here. Now. Tonight."

"*Force* me out?"

"Or you can buy in. Call it a pooling of funds if that makes you feel better. I'm giving you the chance to be the face of the greatest resort development in this country's history. Sin City on steroids, set in the heart of the heartland."

Lewko produced a tablet from the flat case he carried. He touched his thumb to the print reader. The tablet flashed to life. He tapped icons and opened a page.

"This is my Bitcoin wallet. One of them. As you can see, the balance stands at over one hundred million. Meet my investment with your own and I will let you in with a sixteen-point share and make you the public face of the project. And before you argue that matching funding makes you an equal partner, let me remind you of the obvious. I hold all the land in the deal. Or soon will. And something else."

"Which would be what?" Ariel asked ahead of her father.

"Buy in, and I won't allow the press or any investigative body to come to the same conclusion that I have about recent events. I'll see to it that no one will ask why you have one hundred million in untaxed, *very discretionary* funds."

DeSantorini chuckled. "I'm a billionaire like you. I can put up a hundred million just like that." He snapped his fingers.

Lewko smiled. "A good partnership demands honesty, Emilio. You're leveraged beyond reason. There isn't a bank in New York that will take your calls and I'm aware of your liquidity limits. But let's not quibble. I not only believe you have the money to join me, I believe you have it at your fingertips, right now, tonight. It is, however, an offer with a short time limit."

"How short?" DeSantorini asked.

"Three minutes," Andy replied

"That's ridiculous!"

"Fortune favors the bold," Lewko said.

DeSantorini's skin reddened.

"Right." Lewko reached into his case and produced a single sheet of paper. "A simple contract. The simplest. We don't need an army of lawyers for this. It's spelled out clearly. You're in for sixteen points—and please don't waste our time trying to negotiate—math is my thing. You can even put your name on the flagship hotel, the one you plan to build on that parcel you just acquired."

"Two minutes, sir," Andy warned.

Lewko slid the paper to DeSantorini, who snatched it up. Ariel moved her sharp gaze from Andy to Lewko while her father read the proposed contract, his lips moving.

"Impossible," DeSantorini muttered. "My bank—"

"The only bank that will have anything to do with you—your Austrian bank—is under investigation," Andy said. "This transaction cannot involve banks. This transaction will be conducted away from federal eyes. At the bottom of that paper is a Bitcoin address. Send one hundred million to that address to join Mr. Lewko's one hundred million and it forms the capital base for the venture. From that Mr. Lewko will continue funding until reaching half a billion. The highway breaks ground in a year. The infrastructure breaks ground in six months. When the last lane of the highway is paved, the first hotel doors will open. One minute, sir."

Andy's calm delivery left no room for question.

Lewko pulled a pen from his case and slid it to DeSantorini.

"Half a billion in working capital, Emilio. Think of the contractors you can screw over with that kind of leverage."

DeSantorini picked up the pen.

"Daddy, stop." Ariel, without moving her gaze from Andy, reached for and pressed the pen from her father's fingers.

"Thirty seconds."

"Enough," Ariel said.

"Luciana, what are you doing?"

She handed the pen to Andy. "Who are you?"

Dammit! I tensed.

Andy assessed the woman. I waited for her to reinforce the story—to bring DeSantorini back on track—but the cold exchange between Andy and Ariel dashed my hopes.

"My maiden name is Taylor. My married name is Stewart. Detective Andrea Stewart."

Ariel shook her head slowly. "We're done here."

"Luciana!"

"Daddy, there is no deal. This—" She scooped up the sheet of paper and crushed it. "This is a con. She's a cop. And you're a fool."

DeSantorini reddened. "You do *not* talk to me like that. Not in front of these people."

Ariel paid no attention.

"Detective Stewart, your play here was…cute. But if this is all you can bring to bear…well…" She spread her hands. "I think you will leave here with nothing while I will still have what I walked in with."

"You don't have what you walked in with. You've lost something."

"Whatever that is, I'm sure it doesn't carry the significance you're giving it in your mind. Time to go." Ariel stood.

"Your husband is dead," Andy said.

"I'm not married."

"Let me put it another way. Your brother is dead," Andy said flatly.

Ariel froze. Her head tipped slightly, a fraction of a gesture betraying a stressed machine that clicked and clattered behind her unblinking eyes. Her entire affect altered as if rigidity drained from her bones while every muscle in her body tightened to compensate.

"Your brother, Ariel. Your brother Derek."

Ariel didn't move.

DeSantorini pushed back from the table. "That's ridiculous. My son has no part in this, or in this family."

Andy stood. She put her hand on the flap of her bag. "Your son called himself Derek and he was living with your daughter."

DeSantorini turned a harsh stare on his daughter. She did not meet it. She locked her eyes on Andy.

"He killed a girl named Stella Boardman and a police officer named Lyle Traeger, and with your daughter and another man, he tortured and murdered three innocent families."

"Lu, tell me you are not—*seeing* him," he said hoarsely.

Andy spoke directly to Ariel. "I was assigned the Clayton Johns case. I'm the one who found him that night. I was afraid your father would recognize me when I walked in here tonight—from that night at the airport—but he doesn't look much beyond a woman's body, does he. And you didn't recognize me, either. Which tells me that you and your brother were already gone when I arrived at the lake. You left with the trailer and Stella Boardman's car. Someone was watching me, though. Was it RD? That was his thing…when he wasn't torturing and killing. He liked to watch. He couldn't help himself."

Color drained from Ariel's skin.

"Spiro," DeSantorini said, "you've been deceived by this woman."

"Oh, no. I'm totally in on it. And this might be one of the coolest things I've ever done."

"It was your scheme," Andy continued addressing Ariel. "I believe your father when he denies the murders. This was all you, Ariel. West Virginia. Pellston. And finally, the one that counted—the highway engineer at the farm in Baraboo. You. Your brother. RD. What you did was unspeakable, utterly inhuman. I saw the medical examiners' reports. You tortured and murdered children in front of their parents. Parents in front of their children. Wives in front of their husbands."

"Stop it!" DeSantorini snapped. "I want you out of here. Both of you!"

Ariel reanimated slowly. She drew a deep breath, turned and walked to a service cart parked a short distance from the railing I gripped. She closed her hand on a bottle of champagne nesting in a silver urn. She stroked the neck and held up her hand. Beads of condensation rolled down her palm, glittering. She watched them track down her forearm.

"Luciana! Tell me you're not *seeing* him again!"

"Shut up, Daddy," she spoke softly. "For once." She lifted her wet hand to her neck and massaged the moisture into her skin. She closed her eyes and went somewhere distant for a moment.

Veins embossed DeSantorini's forehead. "Tell me you have not seen your brother, Lu!"

"I'm with Derek, Daddy. We've been together for years."

DeSantorini's flushed complexion quivered.

Ariel slowly turned to face Andy. "Detective Stewart, I'm glad you're here. I'm glad a woman is here. A man would never understand. What we need. The feelings that flood us. Do you have a husband?"

"Yes."

"Is it love?"

I shifted my position at the railing, drawing a bead on Ariel, prepared to launch.

"Yes," Andy said.

"I fell in love," Ariel said. "With my brother. With Derek."

"Shut up, Luciana!"

"MY NAME IS ARIEL!" she screamed. She froze, closed her eyes, and composed herself. She said, "And his name is Derek. I fell in love with Derek, Detective, because when he came to my bed at night, it was to give the comfort and pleasure I needed."

"That's—not—true—" DeSantorini gasped. "Lies! Tabloid lies! Get out. Both of you get out!"

No one moved.

"Detective, would you say I have a killer body? That's what my father told a reporter for *The Post* when I was fourteen. It took weeks of backpedaling and payoffs to make that story go away, didn't it, Daddy? Of course, it never went away at my school. But then Derek grew big, and he began to hurt people who spoke behind my back. And I loved him even more for it. I loved every bit of the pain he caused." Ariel spoke in a wistful tone, drawing warmth from the memory. I imagined her brother breaking open lips and scraping skulls against brick walls while she watched, breathless. "I rewarded him for what he did for me."

"She doesn't know what she's saying," DeSantorini insisted.

Ariel closed her eyes and stroked her wet palm on her neck, spreading a sheen across the top of her chest.

Andy's hand slipped into her bag.

"Mr. Lewko, you have more money than God. My father is just one of a thousand wannabes who hate you for it—who think you fell into a fortune because you played video games as a kid. You probably encounter that all the time. No recognition of the work that went into the fortune you built, am I right?"

"It happens," he said.

"It happens to me, too. I have the killer body, of course. You looked at it when we met. Men do. Women do. It's a drug. My father's drug of choice. He never saw past it. He thought he owned it—but I gave it to Derek."

"That's—!"

"Oh, shut the fuck up, Daddy. We're past lying here. You're about to face a truth beyond incest. That I'm smarter than you. Better than you. This Essex deal—it was all me—and Derek, of course. My Derek. My husband. My lover." Her eyes blazed.

"No," DeSantorini muttered. "No, it's not true. You were a child. You made a mistake. We fixed everything. We killed the stories."

"Oh, God, that's right!" Ariel exclaimed. "The only absolute measure of truth and reality—did you control the narrative. And when those on camera airheads parrot your lies back at you, well then, they aren't lies anymore. I think you actually believe them."

"Stop. Luciana, just stop. You cannot undo this."

"Detective, my father caught us—my brother and me—making love when he was nineteen and I was sixteen. And he did what he does. He protected his asset. He made Derek go away. Permanently."

"What your brother did was—it was—sick! I saved you! I saved you from that getting out!"

Ariel laughed. "Who do you think let it get out? Who do you think started the rumors, Daddy? I did. You took away the only real love I've ever known!"

"I saved you!"

"For yourself! To parade me around! To display me!"

Andy's hand remained static inside her bag. I knew she had her palm around the grip of her Glock, her finger on the trigger.

"Why are you telling her all this?" DeSantorini pleaded.

"I'm not telling *her*. I'm telling *you*." She jabbed her hand between her breasts and lifted a gold orb crusted with diamonds attached to a chain. "This! This is one hundred million in bitcoin! The keys are all here!" She snapped the bauble open to reveal a thumb drive. "Did you think this was a confession for the cop in the room, Daddy? This is all about showing you what a worthless, bloated ego you are. You were about to sign his sham deal knowing you don't have the money to make it work. It's MY money they were after." She laughed. "I have more money THAN YOU DO!"

DeSantorini blanched. He swung his head sharply and fixed his rage on Andy. "You! You caused all this. Your lies and fake theories have caused my daughter to have a breakdown. That's what this is. It's all your fault!" He took an unsteady step toward Andy, balling his fists.

Andy's hand came up swiftly. She pointed her Glock at his face.

"Do not take another step, Mr. DeSantorini." She took her own step back.

I pushed off the rail and grabbed the corner of the long table, prepared to launch myself at DeSantorini.

"You can't—you can't speak a word of this. My lawyers—"

"Are as crooked as you are, Daddy. Please shut the hell up," Ariel said. "And you, Detective, please put that weapon on the table."

Andy held her gun steady, but slowly turned to look at Ariel.

I had been fixed on DeSantorini. I missed Ariel's move.

Ariel held a black semiautomatic handgun in a professional two-handed stance. Mounted directly below the muzzle, a red laser sight sent a beam across the terrace. The red target ball danced in Andy's hair, just forward of her ear.

I shifted my grip on the table.

"I shoot ninety-seven percent in the ten ring at thirty feet, Detective. With this laser sight, I can put the second round through the hole from the first. Shall I demonstrate?"

"I have five pounds of pressure on a seven-pound trigger. My gun goes off when yours does."

Jesus, Andy! No!

Ariel gave it a beat, then asked lightly, "Mr. Lewko, is this more excitement than you've had in a while?"

He swallowed hard. "Uh-huh."

"Baby, we can figure this out," DeSantorini pleaded. "These people came here to threaten us. We can handle this."

"Daddy, I think I can solve all your problems…and mine."

"Anything, honey, any—"

The shot snapped open the air and hit DeSantorini in the cheek below his left eye. A fan of blood and brain matter expanded from the back of his head. He collapsed in a heap.

The red laser sight instantly returned to Andy's chest.

"I guess that trumps your play, Detective."

Andy slowly lowered her hand to her side. My heart hammered.

I collected my wits and pulled myself to the end of the table near Ariel.

Ariel sighed. "Detective, before I arrange all of this for the cameras… let's be clear about one thing. *Derek is not dead.* You're lying!"

Andy turned to face Ariel. She held her weapon at her side. She had no chance of lifting it and firing before Ariel's bullet would reach her.

I bent my knees and rotated, I coiled with my feet against the edge of the table.

Lewko sat frozen in his chair. The laser dot shimmered on Andy's heart.

Andy spoke slowly. "I interviewed Derek. At the house. He saw that I was close to understanding what Officer Traeger learned. RD got behind me with his Taser. They took me to the airport and planned to leave on your jet, but your pilot was disabled."

Ariel laughed without mirth. "That idiot is so fired."

She stood eight feet from me. I calculated an approach. Her finger on the trigger owned the moment. Nothing guaranteed she wouldn't squeeze off a shot if I tried to slap the pistol away.

Andy continued. "They took me to the airport. Derek and RD. I assume I was to be randomly disposed of." Ariel didn't answer. "But the jet was disabled. They stole a different airplane."

Doubt clouded Ariel's expression. She shook her head. "You're lying. My brother wasn't a pilot. Neither was RD."

"They took another airplane and it crashed. Your brother and RD are both dead."

"No."

"Have you heard from Derek? Has he answered your calls?"

Ariel jerked the pistol to the right. The laser sight dropped and stopped on Spiro Lewko's forehead.

"Whoa! Stop! No! No!" He put up his hands.

"Tell me the truth in five seconds or his brains ruin those fantastic shoes of yours."

Andy shook her head.

"Four!"

Andy stood, stoic, hand at her side, gun in hand. Lewko twisted his head back and forth rapidly. "Hey! HEY! You've got to stop this!"

"Allow me." Andy finished the count. "Three…two…"

I kicked off on Two.

I collided with Ariel on One.

The instant we touched I slammed the levers in my head.

FWOOOMP!

She vanished. Trapped with me in *the other thing* she had the same absent inertia as me. I hit her like a linebacker sacking a quarterback. The geometry of my shoulder beneath her outstretched arms forced the weapon upward. I prayed it was enough to clear both Lewko and Andy.

Ariel shed gravity's grip. I drove her into the narrow ornate rail. We ricocheted upward. Beneath us, on one side of the rail, glossy patio tiles; on the other side, the sidewalk and street ten floors down.

I shoved her arm toward the stars.

She fired.

BANG!

Lightning struck. My world went white. Pain dug into every joint, every fiber, every hair on my body.

FWOOOMP!

I reappeared and lost my grip on her.

The sensation of falling swallowed me. I imagined the sidewalk rushing toward me, but something hit me square in the back, adding to the electric jolt running through every nerve.

A woman screamed.

Cold tiles administered a hard, flat slap to the side of my head and body. Stars flashed across my vision, which had transitioned from blazing white to all black.

Ariel's desperate shriek faded and ended abruptly.

I lay in agony.

Not falling. Thank God, not falling.

I knew I wasn't encased in *the other thing* when Andy's hands found me. Firm and professional, she patted and searched my body for wounds.

"Will!" She concluded her search and brought her hands to the sides of my head. "WILL!"

I tried to see her through water filling my eyes. My ears rang. My teeth hurt. My tongue didn't want to make words and my throat refused to help.

Andy stroked my head. I felt her turn. I heard her tell Lewko to call 9-1-1 to report a shooting and possible suicide.

"*Now!*" she snapped at Lewko. She put her lips to my ear. "Honey! Honey, are you okay?"

I broke the rigid grip on my neck muscles and nodded. My vision cleared enough to see her shape. I heard Lewko carrying out her command, then saw his silhouette behind my wife. He drifted in and out of focus. He stared down at me with a mix of wonder and blossoming awareness.

"You…" his lips formed the word. I barely heard him through the ringing. His lips formed another word. *Sonofabitch.*

Oh, boy, I thought. *Lillian isn't going to like this.*

EPILOGUE I

Andy took my hand, as she often does when we walk together.

"It's supposed to be raining," I said.

"I didn't see rain in the forecast."

"No. At a funeral. It always rains at a funeral. Ever notice that in the movies? The camera backs away for the long shot of everyone under their black umbrellas. Of course, if you look a hundred yards away, you see dry pavement and the sun is shining."

"These things bother you, do they?"

"Immensely."

Dimples appeared, which I know bothered her, because she takes a funeral seriously. I've tried to tell her that the first word in funeral is Fun.

I know I'm irreverent, but she understands why. It's the only brick and mortar I can use to build a wall against hard, wordless grief. She's aware that I hide the pain. She held my hand as we walked between marble markers.

There was no rain. There wasn't a cloud in the sky. The blue deployed above us only appears on special occasions. Close to, but not quite the blue Angeline Landry saw the day she sunned herself in her back yard.

Most of Brainerd emptied out of their homes for Angeline's funeral. I wondered if they knew her before or after her face became famous on pickle jars. The line of mourners at the Fourth Street Elementary School gymnasium grew so long that eventually firefighters in uniform stood in for her weary father. He had been a firefighter as well, and he wore his old uniform proudly. There were pictures of him, much younger, beside a firetruck with a

EPILOGUE I

smiling little girl clutching the safety rail. The child reminded me of Angeline's two boys, who divided their time between meeting sullen strangers and stealing from a vast dessert table.

The procession from the elementary school to the small cemetery felt more like a parade. Families and children lined the streets. There were flags and firetrucks.

For the most part, Andy and I hung back. We were strangers to everyone. Well, almost everyone. After the graveside burial service, Deputy Milt Lindstrom approached. Like others from his department, he wore his dress uniform. Andy recognized him from my arrest. The unpleasant memory must have shown in her face.

"I'm sorry about how that went," he said after a reintroduction. "We got a little heated over the idea that someone might do something to Angie."

Andy said. "My husband said she was a special girl."

Lindstrom turned to me. "I just wanted to say, when we heard what happened, when we heard about your Foundation getting hit like that, losing everything, we didn't think you would come through. It gave some fellows around here cause to think they could badmouth you. If you heard about any of that, I apologize."

"I didn't."

Dewey Larmond got a nasty phone call, but I told Dewey to let it go.

Lindstrom absorbed an uncomfortable silence intensified by Andy's unblinking stare. My wife may forgive but she is not quick to forget.

"That said," he extended his hand. "I just want to thank you for coming through after all. It's a really nice thing you did for those boys. For her."

I returned the handshake, firm and full of honesty.

"It wasn't me. It's the Foundation. I just fly the airplane."

The lie-detector eyes made short work of that statement. Lindstrom nodded at us. "Detective…Mr. Stewart."

Andy watched him weave through the headstones, joining the dispersing crowd.

"Guys like him wouldn't last under my command," she said.

"Oh, he's okay. His partner's an ass. But he's okay. Your command?" She issued a coy look. "Is there something I should know?"

"No."

"That wasn't a heart attack Tom had."

"I didn't say it was."

"Hmmmm…Chief Stewart…"

"Stop it!"

EPILOGUE I

We walked slowly against the flow of the crowd drifting toward cars lined up for blocks around the cemetery.

I needed one more thing before we joined the exodus.

The fresh grave occupied a corner of the small cemetery, well away from the shade of old maples on the property. People talk about how they want their grave in the shade of the old this-or-that tree, but I thought Angeline Landry would agree with whoever picked her spot—out in the open, in the sunshine.

A knot of people lingered around the grave. Some stood with heads bowed. Some cried. Millie from the restaurant, and what looked like a collection of girls who work there or may have once worked there, formed a circle, chatting and occasionally laughing between bouts of weeping.

"Is that her?" Andy asked.

She pointed.

A small, short-haired girl stood at the fringe of the group, holding the pose all children hold while their parents engage in grownup talk. Bored. Distracted. In her own world. She stared at the open grave. Her expression enchanted me—the word that came to mind was *serene*. DaVinci would have understood her face. The hesitation before a smile breaks out. The sparkle in an eye before it blinks at beauty.

She wandered a few steps from the grownups, toward the grave. I don't think she saw a hole in the earth or the last resting place of a friend. From the look on her face, I think she saw a montage of memories. The flicker of a pre-smile at the corners of her mouth suggested she saw Angeline, a big friend brightened by the presence of a little friend.

Jillybean bent at the knees and plucked a white clover flower from the grass at her feet.

"Come on, Jillian!" a woman called to her. The woman looked a lot like the girl. She also looked like a woman who had been through dark clouds and long days and was just now feeling the sun again.

Jillybean tossed the clover flower to her friend, then turned and hurried after her parents, bouncing and skipping.

"She looks good," Andy said. She squeezed my hand.

"Yeah. She does."

EPILOGUE II

Two weeks before Angeline Landry's sundrenched funeral, it did rain. Without umbrellas, we hurried from the cab into the Jacob Javits Federal Building, ducking as if the falling drops could be avoided. Inside, we wove our way through security aided by Donaldson's FBI credentials. We crossed the wide and hollow-sounding lobby. While Andy and Donaldson summoned an elevator, I slipped around a corner to an empty hallway. I checked for cameras. Finding none, I vanished.

Andy pinned the Visitor badge on the lapel of her jacket. Donaldson attached his to his belt. Mine stayed in my pocket.

They stepped into the elevator and held the door open for me. I used a power unit to maneuver, then grabbed the strap on Andy's shoulder bag. Donaldson pushed the button. We rose within the spine of the building.

I felt exponentially better than I had fourteen hours earlier, lying on the tile of Emilio DeSantorini's rooftop terrace. I didn't know if it was possible to hit a wall that breaks every bone in the body, but the sensation had been successfully imprinted on me when Ariel Santi fired her weapon from inside *the other thing*. The energy reflected, causing us both to abruptly reappear. I don't know where the jacketed slug went, or if it escaped at all, nor did I care. Andy wasn't hit. That was all that mattered to me.

Not that I needed the lesson, but for the second time I learned that a weapon cannot be discharged within *the other thing*.

Regaining motor function took time, during which I made no effort to answer Spiro Lewko's barrage of questions. Andy eventually told him to

EPILOGUE II

back off or she would put him in handcuffs. She helped me sit up. I let her massage my hands, my arms. She asked if this was the same thing that happened when I tried to shoot Garrett Foyle in Montana. I must have nodded. The knowledge relieved her. I hadn't been shot and this, at least, she had seen before.

When I stood up, I promptly fell to the floor. Andy knelt and pressed me to remain down, but I resisted. I needed to do something.

I rubbed the liquid out of my eyes. I made my mouth work, finding words, if not vocal sounds.

"Stay here," I whispered.

"No! You need to rest!"

I shook my head. "Get him—outta here. I gotta—"

I decided an argument would take too much time. I had just minutes.

Fwooomp!

I vanished.

"Will!" she protested. Behind her, Lewko's face locked in surprise.

I grabbed the railing and pulled myself up. My grip felt electric and weak at the same time. My entire body tingled as if I'd been sleeping in a bad position. Only weightlessness and lack of inertia allowed me to move. I couldn't have lifted my own leg, let alone my full weight over the railing.

I heaved myself over and saw what I needed far below.

Ariel Santi lay on the pavement, sprawled like a snow angel. Dark red blood seeped from every part of her once perfect body.

I aimed and pulled. My descent took me directly to her. I rotated on the way down and reached. I planted my hands on the sidewalk not painted in her blood and stopped. A crowd formed a circle, aghast, yet jostling each other to see. Phones snapped pictures and recorded video. Donaldson hovered at the periphery, using his phone to make a frantic call. I heard him speak my wife's name. I was glad no one could see me positioned over her like a last lover. The thought made my stomach roll.

I found the diamond-studded bauble resting between her breasts. I closed my hand around the orb and felt an electric snap when it joined me in *the other thing*. The chain dangled for a moment, then fell away as if melted. I slipped the jeweled flash drive into my pocket.

Close enough to kiss her, I took one last look and searched for a pang of sadness for her. I found none. I pushed off and ascended, skimming the front of the building. At the top I reached for and caught the railing. I stopped. I pulled myself over and took up a position beside Andy.

Fwooomp! I reappeared.

EPILOGUE II

Lewko, standing at her side, jolted. A ripple of emotions coursed his face.

"Detective, I believe this is stolen property." I pressed the drive into her hand.

Lewko gawked. For the first time in what I would guess to be a long time, he struggled to speak.

Andy didn't give him the chance. "Not a word from you. We'll hold up our end, but you have to wait." She gave him the choice of being patient or being shot.

He decided to wait.

Fourteen hours later he had only called my phone nineteen times.

The elevator stopped. An office reception area spread out to welcome us. Luxurious—at least by government standards—the office featured rich burgundy carpets bordered by walls of old, dark wood. A woman behind an expansive hardwood desk examined us.

"Can I help you?"

"Nope," Donaldson said cheerfully. He hooked left and led the way. Andy matched his stride, firmly gripping the straps of her shoulder bag, pulling me behind her.

"Sir! Do you have an appointment?"

"Don't need one!" Donaldson called after her.

He found a door with a brass plate that said, Deputy Director Mitchell Lindsay. He grabbed the knob and hobbled in.

Another reception area, another old desk, and another protective gatekeeper greeted us. This one took her job to heart and quickly mustered herself to block entry to the office within. Donaldson skirted past her. Andy followed him, pulling me with her.

"Sir, I don't know who—" the office assistant hurried in after us.

"Special Agent Donaldson, Sioux City office," Donaldson limped to the desk and put out a hand.

The Deputy Director—a sixtyish man who might have passed for a seasoned diplomat or United States Senator—looked up suspiciously. "Did we have an appointment?"

"No," Donaldson said. He backed up and dropped into one of two leather occasional chairs, relieved to take weight off his reluctant leg. "This is Detective Andrea Stewart of the City of Essex Police Department."

Andy respectfully extended a hand and said, "Honored to meet you, sir." Lindsay studied her for a moment, pulled himself to his feet and accepted the handshake. "It's alright, Marie."

EPILOGUE II

The assistant backed out of the office and closed the door behind her.

"Please sit down, Detective," the Deputy Director gestured at the other chair. She took it. He returned to his seat and placed both elbows on the desk, folding one fist in the other.

"Alright, Special Agent, it's your show."

Donaldson cleared his throat. "I want my old job back, sir. Well, actually, I want a way better job."

Lindsay fixed a penetrating gaze on his brash subordinate. He took a moment to assemble his thoughts.

"Pemmick, right? Under Rayburn?"

"Yes, sir."

"How's the head?" Lindsay asked, leaning slightly to examine Donaldson's stitches.

"Rock solid—or so I'm told."

He turned to Andy. "And you…" He narrowed the space between silver eyebrows. "Olivia Brogan, correct?"

"Yes, sir."

"And Parks before that, if I am not mistaken."

Andy nodded.

"Well," Lindsay leaned back. "Aren't you two a pair."

"We're not a pair, sir," Andy quickly pointed out. "We're colleagues."

"Am I missing something? Is there a reason for you to think that a few high-profile arrests give you leave to barge into my office making demands?"

Andy looked at Donaldson. Donaldson looked at Andy.

She turned around and asked the empty air behind her, "Are you sure you about this?"

FBI Deputy Director Lindsay blinked. I didn't give him time to wonder.

"Yes."

Fwooomp!

DIVISIBLE MAN: THE THIRD LIE
Friday, August 23, 2019 – Saturday, November 9, 2019

ENJOY A PREVIEW OF THE NEXT ADVENTURE

DIVISIBLE MAN: THREE NINES FINE

A mysterious mission request from Earl Jackson sends Will into the sphere of a troubled celebrity. A meeting with the Deputy Director of the FBI that goes terribly wrong. Will and Andy find themselves on the run from Federal authorities, infiltrating a notorious cartel, and racing to prevent what might prove to be the crime of the century.

Available in print, digital and audio.
Visit us at **HowardSeaborne.com**

DIVISIBLE MAN: THREE NINES FINE

— 1 —

"What happened to you?"

Earl Jackson leaned farther back than usual on his Army surplus office chair, challenging it to throw him over backward. He leveled his left leg on the only other chair in his tiny office. Ordinarily, I wouldn't have asked an intrusive personal question of the boss, but his open office door guaranteed a quick exit if any of the objects on his desk became projectiles.

"'S my goddamned arthritis. Woke up Sunday morning with that knee all swolled up. Hurts like a hot poker."

Rosemary II, the Essex County Air Service Office Manager and Goddess of The Schedule, leaned in the open doorway and gently nudged me aside. "He's not supposed to be here. And he's supposed to use this." She leaned a cane against the chair supporting his leg.

"Yeah, I'll use it alright," Earl muttered.

I grabbed the cane and handed it back to Rosemary II. "Best not to arm the man in this condition." She scoffed at me and returned it.

"I'm calling your doctor, Earl. I'll take you myself if I have to." She breezed out of sight, ignoring the withering glare that followed her.

"What's going on with the new bird?"

I shrugged. "They finished the pre-buy inspection on Friday. Dewey Larmond is wiring payment today. I planned on picking her up this week, but the pre-buy recommended a new set of tires and replacing one of the brake lines. Probably next week."

The search to replace the Piper Navajo belonging to the Christine and Paulette Paulesky Education Foundation unfolded quickly after the FBI confirmed for the insurance company that the aircraft had been stolen and subsequently crashed in Lake Michigan. The Feds listed the cause of the crash as Dumbass Without Pilot License Loses Control in Non-Visual Flight Conditions Over Water at Night. My role in causing the crash that killed two mass murderers did not make it into the report. I mourned the loss of the airplane but had to admit to some excitement over her replacement, which had been found in San Diego.

"Compressions good?" Earl asked.

"Tip top."

"They check the lifters for pitting?"

"Yup."

Earl's blessing mattered. Earl Jackson has bought and sold more airplanes than I will ever fly. He can smell a good or bad deal across half a continent.

The new Navajo, a powerful cabin-class twin-engine airplane with seats for up to eight, would transport Sandy Stone and Arun Dewar on the Education Foundation's business, which typically meant day trips to small towns for on-site assessments—towns well beyond the sphere of commercial airline service. The aircraft would also fill in flying charters for Essex County Air Service, my previous employer, thanks to a lease/maintenance agreement. I planned to fly the Navajo for both the Foundation and Essex County Air, occasionally returning to my old job to take a charter when demand ran high or pilot staff fell short.

I figured being shorthanded had prompted Earl to call me to his office early this Tuesday morning, although it struck an off-key note that the call came from Earl, and not Rosemary II, who governed the air service booking schedule.

"So, what's up, Boss?"

"Close the door." I did as commanded. He made no move to shift his leg. I remained standing. "I need a favor. Off the books."

"Anything."

Earl glanced at the door as if he detected Rosemary II pressing an ear to the other side. He reached up and rubbed the sun-baked surface of his bald head with a gnarled, calloused hand. He lowered his voice.

"I need you to fly down to La Crosse and pick up a passenger. I was gonna do it, but…"

I pointed at his knee.

"That? Hell, I can fly one-legged. I flew for two months in South America with t'other leg in a cast."

Another Earl Jackson story noted for future inquiry.

"Then what do you need me for?"

Earl scratched his scalp. "They asked if you were available."

"Somebody I know?"

"Nope," he said sharply. "Prob'ly picked up your name from when you were famous. Can you take it?"

I didn't like being famous. I was less happy with the idea of someone thinking they were fixing the odds of a safe flight by choosing a pilot who fell out of the sky and lived. I imagined the passenger rubbing my head for luck—and me punching their face for fun.

"Sure. Out to LaCrosse and then what—back here?"

"Nope. Make the pickup and then she'll tell you where to go from there. Let her do her business. Then take her back."

"Back to La Crosse?"

"Yup."

Earl wears a perpetual scowl, but something in the granite angles and crevices of his face shifted. This request carried a personal priority.

"Wherever you take her, don't file. No flight plan. No record. Got it?"

"Okay. But I'm not doing this without asking questions."

"I wouldn't. Shoot."

"Her? Who is she?"

Earl checked the door again.

"Lonnie Penn."

I blinked. "*The* Lonnie Penn? The actress?"

"Actor. Don't call her an actress unless you want an earful."

Why on earth would an A-list Hollywood name call Essex County Air Service when she surely owned her own jet?

The answer jumped at me. "You know Lonnie Penn?"

"Knew her dad."

"Okay." I wondered if I would ever stop being amazed by the slowly revealed threads of Earl Jackson's life. "Equally impressive. You knew Dahl Penn? *The* Dahl Penn? Ran with John Wayne and John Ford? Said to have drunk Peter O'Toole under the table?"

"I knew some of 'em. I was a snot-nosed kid building time, taking right seat jobs for peanuts with the old Honeymoon Express—Paul Mantz's air charter company." I added the famous Hollywood stunt pilot to the list of people I planned to ask Earl about. "Hauled Dahl Penn out of a Tijuana jail one night after we got the deputy hammered on tequila. We stayed in touch after that."

"Jesus Christ, Earl!"

He waved it off. "Get your head back in the cockpit, Will. This has to be done quietly."

I forced the bald wonder off my face. "Lonnie Penn called *you* for this?"

"Yup. Fly to La Crosse. Park at the FBO. Wait in the airplane for her and then fly her wherever she tells you. She takes care of business. You fly her back to La Crosse. Don't ask her any questions and don't pester her. Got it?"

"I guess."

"Take the Arrow. I had Pidge put it out on the line. Stay off the radio, except for La Crosse." He drilled me with a serious expression. "What? Spit it out. I gotta know if you're all in on this."

"I am. It's just...I have a thing on Thursday. With Andy. How long is this mission supposed to take?"

"You meet Lonnie at ten in La Crosse. A couple hours out. Wait for her. A couple hours back. If it all goes right, you'll be home rubbing your wife's feet for beddy-bye."

If all goes right. In every hare-brained scheme I've ever joined, there's always a moment when a gremlin peeks through the fabric of the plan. I felt sure its arrival had just been announced.

Earl stared at me.

"Okay, Boss."

"Good. Get moving."

Pidge spotted me heading toward the flight line. She told the passengers boarding the Essex County Air Service Piper Mojave to go ahead and take their seats, then she ducked under the wing and trotted after me.

"Stewart!" She caught up as I dropped my flight bag on the wing root of the Piper Arrow, a four-passenger high-performance single-engine airplane. "What the fuck is this all about?"

No secret goes unnoticed at Essex County Air.

"You hauling drugs now? Smuggling guns?"

"Can't tell you. I'd have to kill you."

"Oh, c'mon!"

I shook my head. "Nope."

Pidge propped her fists on her hips. At twenty-three, she holds every rating on the books except seaplane and helicopter. She's the best pilot I've ever seen. Better than me, and I trained her. Her pixie size and appearance mask a stubborn streak that rivals that of my wife. She'll tear into you if you slide onto her bad side, but her loyalty is carbon steel. Pidge is one of a handful of people who knows I can disappear at will. Trust wasn't an issue. I simply didn't want to tell her about Lonnie Penn until I met the woman. The whole thing seemed odd.

"Honest truth? I don't know what it's about. I'll tell you when I get back."

"Fuck you," she replied, living up to the nickname she earned as a teenaged student pilot. Pidge is short for Pidgeon, so named because she talks dirty and flies. "Hey, are you still meeting up with the feds on Thursday?"

Pidge had been hammering me to do something meaningful with *the other thing* for months.

"If it doesn't get put off again."

"What?"

"It was supposed to be today, but the guy we saw in New York stalled it," I said. "Or his secretary did. Miss Carlisle-Plinkham, or some such. Sounds like a British nanny. Anyway, we got the call Sunday. She said her boss had meetings in Washington."

Pidge laughed. "Probably testifying before a Senate subcommittee on dumbshits who can disappear."

"Don't even."

She glanced back at the twin-engine Mojave crouched by the gas pumps, waiting for a pilot. "I gotta go. Call me tonight! I have GOT to hear about this!"

"You and me both," I said. She darted away.

I conducted a thorough preflight inspection of the Arrow. Fuel had been topped. I planned to refill the tanks in La Crosse. Without destination information, the best fuel status would be full tanks. I checked the weather again, using the iPad rather than calling Flight Service for an on-the-record briefing, adhering to Earl's mandate that the tail number of the Arrow only be used with LaCrosse tower.

The Foreflight app on my tablet told me a trough of low pressure extended from the Canadian province of Saskatchewan all the way to Tennessee, causing widespread areas of marginal VFR and in some places IFR conditions—low clouds and poor visibilities in drizzle and mist. This did not mesh with Earl's admonition not to file a flight plan. Getting to La Crosse from Essex didn't pose a challenge but depending on where my passenger wanted to go from there, I might run into lousy conditions for visual flight.

I tabled my concerns. Earl wouldn't have asked me to do this if he didn't think it could be done.

I loaded my flight bag and dropped into the pilot's seat of the Arrow. After plotting a course, I pulled the checklist and settled into pilot mode. Ten minutes later I lifted the landing gear and banked in a climbing turn toward La Crosse.

— 2 —

"Hey."

"Hey, you," Andy replied. Her warm voice came from somewhere in the center of my head, thanks to the Bluetooth connection between my headset and phone. I sat in the pilot's seat of the Arrow on the ramp adjacent to Colgan Air Services at La Crosse Municipal Airport. A light mist fogged the windscreen and glossed the wings. I landed under Visual Flight Rules, but the weather was marginal. The airport reported an overcast ceiling of 1700 feet and visibility of four miles. "What did Earl want?"

"Run an errand. I'm in La Crosse right now. How about you?"

"Office. Paperwork." The Clayton Johns prosecution was making the county DA as nervous as a bride's mother before the wedding. The former NFL star accused of rape mustered a high-powered defense team. At least one of the attorneys practically owned a box as a talking head on Fox News. The DA, in turn, applied constant pressure on Andy to ensure that nothing in the conduct of the investigation would blindside the prosecution. Andy described it as playing nursemaid to controlled hysteria. "Will you be home for dinner?"

"Better not plan on it. However, I hope to be there in time to rub your feet."

"What?"

"Something Earl said."

"That's gross...although..." I pictured dimples appearing at the corners of her lips.

"No. I'm not rubbing your smelly feet."

"What a thing to say to your wife."

I felt a strong urge to say more about my mission, but also knew that whatever story unfolded, it would be better whole. "Anything new about Thursday?"

"God, I hope not." Andy had been disappointed by the delay. We had discussed to death the decision to meet with the Deputy Director of the FBI.

The call from his assistant lent it a feeling of low priority that made us both insecure. Andy more than me.

I tried to brush off her doubts. "Dee, what's the one thing we know about plans?"

"They change," we said in unison. I added, "I thought you might have heard from Donaldson."

"Not since this was set up. It's been radio silence."

"That's over two weeks. Makes me think he's got something up his sleeve."

"Will, you have to get over your distrust of the man," she said. Andy placed firm professional faith in FBI Special Agent Lee Donaldson, who had been the conduit to Deputy Director Mitchell Lindsay. She was wrong about me. My distrust of the man was long past its expiration date, chiefly because Donaldson had saved Andy's life, for which I owed him a deep debt. He also ranked among the handful of people aware of my ability to vanish.

"I think I've shown trust."

"Well, I expect he'll be there on Thursday as planned," Andy said. She paused for a moment, then asked, "Am I getting a hint that this errand you're running for Earl might disrupt our plans?"

"No," I said quickly, feeling a vague sense that I had just lied to my wife.

"Will! You can't. It's been postponed once. We can't just not show up."

"Dee, it's two days away. I told you. I plan to be home tonight."

"Rubbing my feet."

"It could happen."

I watched the jet touch down. Symmetrical curls of spray spun into the air behind each wingtip. I had been watching the approach path to Runway 18. The landing light emerged from the low clouds about a mile out. That told me the ceiling was dropping. Not good.

Something else not good was my passenger's decision to arrive in a Gulfstream G650, the current pet jet and status symbol among Hollywood A listers. Not exactly discreet, although I was mildly amused by the idea of a pampered queen of the screen jumping out of her leather upholstered executive jet and into my single-engine Piper Arrow. I glanced at the seat beside me. No duct tape patching the upholstery, but the forty-plus-year-old airplane had seen better days. Champagne service on this flight consisted of two plastic water bottles lying on the back seat waiting to be served with a warning not to drink them early in the flight because there's no onboard toilet.

The G650 made a stately entrance to the general aviation ramp, enthusiastically waved to priority parking by a ramp rat wearing a reflective vest over a yellow rain slicker. The jet's nose bobbed to a halt and the ramp rat hustled to the unfolding airstair. He produced and opened an umbrella.

There was no mistaking Lonnie Penn. Blonde and trim, she wore a white leather jacket over black tights that advertised her figure. She followed a crewman down the steps and accepted his hand for the transition to the ramp, quickly ducking under the proffered umbrella and paying the ramp rat with a red-carpet smile. A cadre of young men and women hurried down the stairs after her. A woman wearing a ball cap and a long dark ponytail took the star by the arm to guide her forward. The entourage disappeared into the FBO.

If she wanted discretion, she had a funny way of showing it.

I waited in the cockpit of the Arrow. Earl's instructions had been clear. She'll find you. Sit tight.

I obeyed Earl for a fruitless fifteen minutes, maintaining watch over the jet and the FBO. I also had a partial view of the road fronting the FBO offices. When a pair of stretched black SUVs pulled away, I decided the whole plan had gone seriously wrong.

I let another ten minutes tick off the clock. Nothing moved on the ramp. No one emerged from the office. The jet crew eventually disembarked and made their way to the building. A fuel truck rolled up to fill the thirsty jet.

You learn patience as a charter pilot. Customers promise to be back at the airport for departure at a certain hour and then leave you twiddling thumbs for another two hours. It's tempting to call and ask what they're thinking, but I don't bother. Nothing I say or do alters their schedule, their momentum, or their perception of time. On several occasions I met the client at the door hours late and calmly explained to them that they could make hotel arrangements, since the weather window for departure had closed, precisely as I had explained to them upon arrival. Of course, such news is always my fault and the flight home the next day tends to be cold and quiet.

I waited, using the time to check the weather, which continued to deteriorate. Earl's restriction on filing an instrument flight plan weighed heavily on any outbound planning. If Her Hollywood Majesty needed a kale and cappuccino lunch before dashing off on her mystery mission, she was well on her way to screwing things up. I'll fly in marginal weather up to a point, but the derogatory term for it is "scud running" and the practice often generates an accident report.

I checked METAR reports for a two hundred-mile radius—since I had no idea in which direction my passenger would point. Head down in the cockpit, I nearly missed seeing the woman cross the ramp toward me. She wore a brown leather flight jacket over jeans. A ball cap and dark ponytail suggested Penn's assistant—no doubt headed my way to deliver bad news. The mist had turned to a drizzle, but she did not hurry or duck under an umbrella. Despite the low-hanging clouds, she wore aviator sunglasses.

"Come to tell me your boss is getting a pedicure?" I muttered to the empty cockpit as she rounded the wing. I leaned over and pulled the door latch. The door issued a shabby squeak as it swung open. I felt her mount the step behind the trailing edge of the flaps, then watched her jeans, artfully sliced and frayed at the knees, climb the low wing. A heavy leather attaché case dropped into the back seat. In one gymnastic move, she lowered herself into the seat beside me.

"Are you Will?" I instantly recognized the voice from a dozen movies. She put out her hand. "I'm Lonnie."

ABOUT THE AUTHOR

Howard Seaborne began writing novels in spiral notebooks at age ten. He began flying airplanes at age sixteen. He is a former flight instructor and commercial charter pilot. Today he flies a Beechcraft Bonanza, Beechcraft Baron and a Rotorway experimental helicopter he built in his garage. He lives with his wife and writes and flies during all four seasons in Wisconsin, never far from Essex County Airport.

Visit www.HowardSeaborne.com to join the Email List
and get a FREE DOWNLOAD.

ALSO BY HOWARD SEABORNE

DIVISIBLE MAN

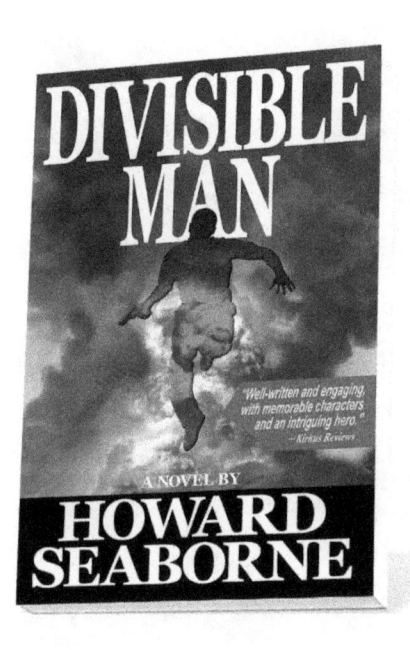

The media calls it a "miracle" when air charter pilot Will Stewart survives an aircraft in-flight breakup, but Will's miracle pales beside the stunning after-effect of the crash. Barely on his feet again, Will and his police sergeant wife Andy race to rescue an innocent child from a heinous abduction—*if Will's new ability doesn't kill him first.*

Available in print, digital and audio.

Learn more at **HowardSeaborne.com**

ALSO BY HOWARD SEABORNE

DIVISIBLE MAN: THE SIXTH PAWN

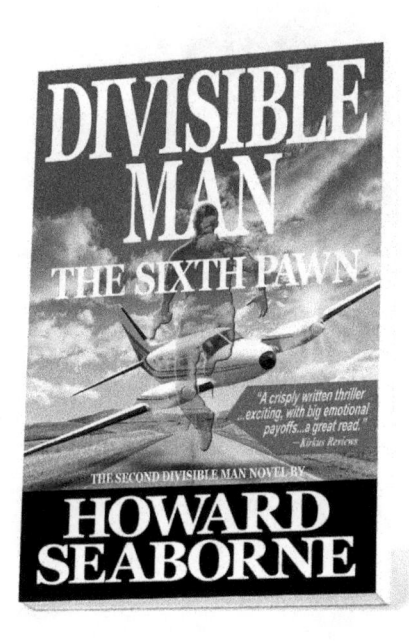

When the Essex County "Wedding of the Century" erupts in gunfire, Will and Andy Stewart confront a criminal element no one could have foreseen. Will tests the extraordinary after-effect of surviving a devastating airplane crash while Andy works a case obstructed by powerful people wielding the sinister influence of unlimited money in politics.

Available in print, digital and audio.

Learn more at **HowardSeaborne.com**

ALSO BY HOWARD SEABORNE

DIVISIBLE MAN: THE SECOND GHOST

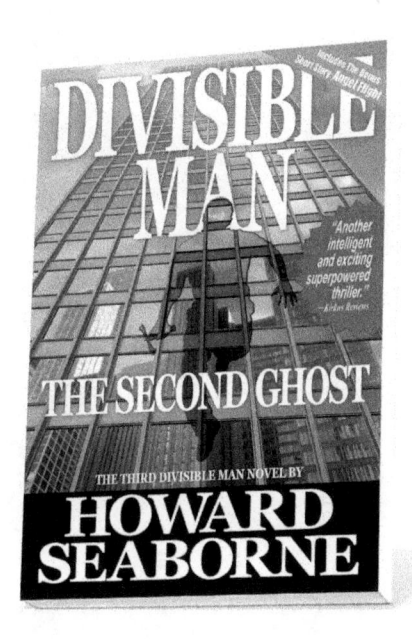

Tormented by a cyber stalker, Lane Franklin's best friend turns to suicide. Lane's frantic call to Will and Andy Stewart launches them on a desperate rescue. When it all goes bad, Will must adapt his extraordinary ability to survive the dangerous high steel and glass of Chicago as Andy and Pidge encounter the edge of disaster.
Includes the short story, "Angel Flight," a bridge to the fourth DIVISIBLE MAN novel that follows.

Available in print, digital and audio.

Learn more at HowardSeaborne.com

ALSO BY HOWARD SEABORNE

DIVISIBLE MAN: THE SEVENTH STAR

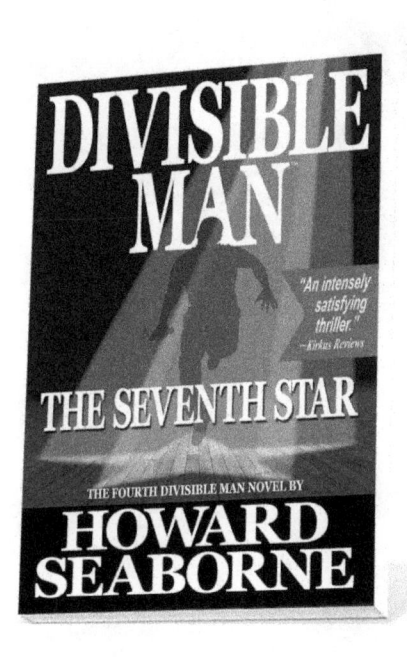

A horrifying message turns a holiday gathering tragic. An unsolved murder hangs a death threat over Detective Andy Stewart's head. And internet-fueled hatred targets Will and Andy's friend Lane. Will and Andy struggle to keep the ones they love safe, while hunting a dead murderer before he can kill again. As the tension tightens, Will confronts a troubling revelation about the extraordinary after-effect of his midair collision.

Available in print, digital and audio.

Learn more at **HowardSeaborne.com**

ALSO BY HOWARD SEABORNE

DIVISIBLE MAN: TEN MAN CREW

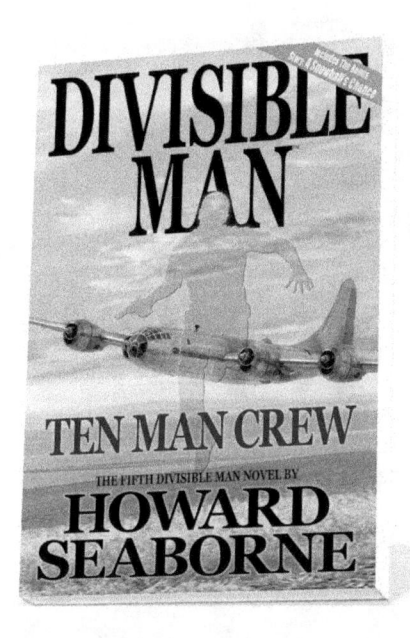

An unexpected visit from the FBI threatens Will Stewart's secret and sends Detective Andy Stewart on a collision course with her darkest impulses. A twisted road reveals how a long-buried Cold War secret has been weaponized. And Pidge shows a daring side of herself that could cost her dearly.

Available in print, digital and audio.

Learn more at **HowardSeaborne.com**

ALSO BY HOWARD SEABORNE

DIVISIBLE MAN: THE THIRD LIE

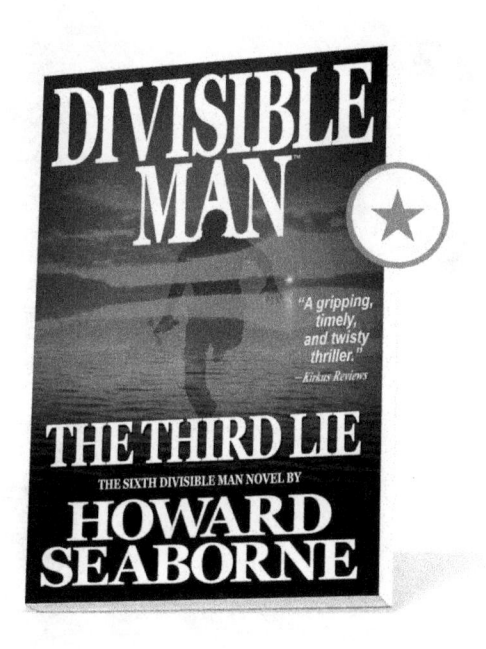

Caught up in a series of hideous crimes that generate national headlines, Will faces the critical question of whether to reveal himself or allow innocent lives to be lost. The stakes go higher than ever when Andy uncovers the real reason behind a celebrity athlete's assault on an underaged girl. And Will discovers that the limits of his ability can lead to disaster.

A Kirkus Starred Review.

A Kirkus Star is awarded to "books of exceptional merit."

Available in print, digital and audio.

Learn more at **HowardSeaborne.com**

ALSO BY HOWARD SEABORNE

DIVISIBLE MAN: THREE NINES FINE

A mysterious mission request from Earl Jackson sends Will into the sphere of a troubled celebrity. A meeting with the Deputy Director of the FBI that goes terribly wrong. Will and Andy find themselves on the run from Federal authorities, infiltrating a notorious cartel, and racing to prevent what might prove to be the crime of the century.

Available in print, digital and audio.

Learn more at **HowardSeaborne.com**

ALSO BY HOWARD SEABORNE

DIVISIBLE MAN: EIGHT BALL

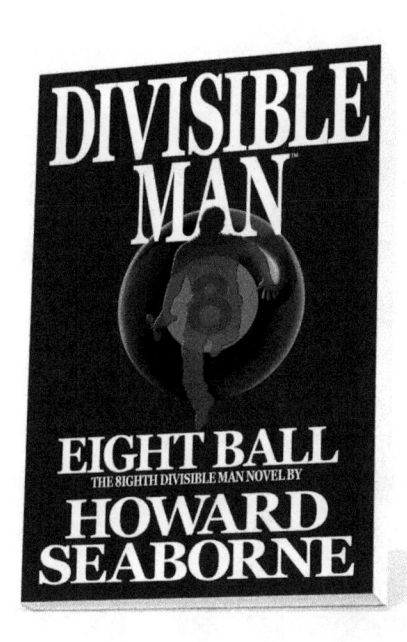

Will's encounter with a deadly sniper on a serial killing rampage sends him deeper into the FBI's hands with costly consequences for Andy. And when billionaire Spiro Lewko returns to the picture, Will and Andy's future takes a dark turn. The stakes could not be higher when the sniper's true target is revealed.

Available in print, digital and audio.

Learn more at **HowardSeaborne.com**

ALSO BY HOWARD SEABORNE

DIVISIBLE MAN:
ENGINE OUT AND OTHER SHORT FLIGHTS

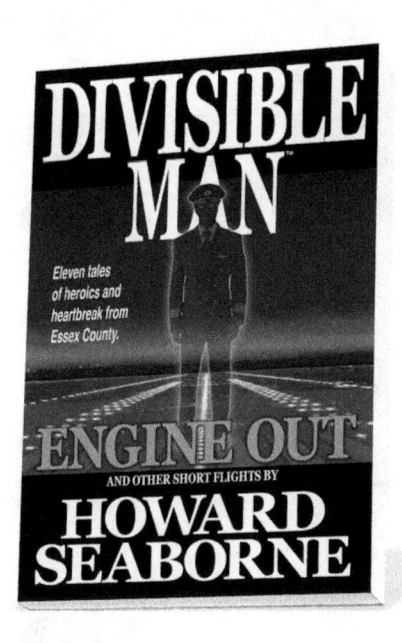

AVAILABLE: JUNE 2022

Things just have a way of happening around Will and Andy Stewart. In this collection of eleven tales from Essex County, boy meets girl, a mercy flight goes badly wrong, and Will crashes and burns when he tries dating again. Engines fail. Shots are fired. A rash of the unexpected breaks loose—from bank jobs to zombies.

Available in print, digital and audio.

Learn more at **HowardSeaborne.com**

ALSO BY HOWARD SEABORNE

DIVISIBLE MAN: NINE LIVES LOST

AVAILABLE: JUNE 2022

A simple request from Earl Jackson sends Will on a desperate cross-country chase ultimately looking for answers to a mystery that literally landed at Will and Andy's mailbox. At the same time, a threat to Andy's career takes a deadly turn. Before it all ends, Will confronts answers in a deep, dark place he never imagined.

Available in print, digital and audio.

Learn more at **HowardSeaborne.com**

Enjoy the growing DIVISIBLE MAN™ collection.

In Print, Digital and Audio

Printed in the USA
CPSIA information can be obtained
at www.ICGtesting.com
JSHW011710010823
45735JS00002B/58